18/1

Praise for **ve your**

ran

KT-419-269

'Some days, all you rea[d] you a wicked-good stor[y] reader's perpetual prayer' ... *the* *e Times*

'Barclay's speciality is to take o[rdina]ry people and to gradually dismantle all the meaningf[u]l elements in their lives ...This is Barclay firing on all cylinders' *Financial Times*

'No one can thrill you and chill you better than Linwood Barclay' Tess Gerritsen

'The spare, direct prose and cliff-hanger chapter endings drive a tension-fuelled tale that is underpinned by a bleakly fatalistic noir tone' *Irish Times*

'One of the best thriller writers in the world hands down' Mark Billingham

'Seamless, breathless and relentlessly paced, Barclay barely puts a foot wrong' *Mirror*

'A suspense master' Stephen King

'Twist-driven thrillers packed with explosive action are a hallmark of Linwood Barclay's career' *USA Today*

Linwood Barclay is the international bestselling author of many critically acclaimed novels, including *No Safe House*, A *Tap on the Window*, *Trust Your Eyes* and the Richard & Judy 2008 Summer Read winner and number one bestseller, *No Time For Goodbye*. He lives near Toronto with his wife. To find out more visit www.linwoodbarclay.com or follow Linwood on Twitter @linwood_barclay

Also by Linwood Barclay

Broken Promise
No Safe House
A Tap on the Window
Never Saw It Coming
Trust Your Eyes
The Accident
Never Look Away
Fear the Worst
Too Close to Home
No Time for Goodbye

Far From True

LINWOOD BARCLAY

An Orion paperback

First published in Great Britain in 2016
by Orion Books
This paperback edition published in 2016
by Orion Books,
an imprint of The Orion Publishing Group Ltd,
Carmelite House, 50 Victoria Embankment
London EC4Y 0DZ

An Hachette UK company

13

A CIP catalogue record for this book
is available from the British Library.

ISBN 978 1 4091 4651 3

Printed in Great Britain by Clays Ltd, Elcograf S.p.A.

www.orionbooks.co.uk

For Neetha

ONE

They ain't seen nothin' yet.

TWO

They decided Derek was the one who should get into the trunk.

Before heading off, the four of them, Derek Cutter included, thought it would be cool to smuggle someone in. Not because they couldn't afford a fourth ticket. That wasn't the issue. They just felt the situation demanded it of them. It was the sort of thing you were supposed to do.

After all, this was the last night they'd ever have the chance. Like so many other businesses in and around Promise Falls these days, the Constellation Drive-in Theater was packing it in. What with multiplexes, 3-D, DVDs, movies you could download at home and watch within seconds, why go to a drive-in, except maybe to make out? And given how much smaller cars had gotten since the drive-in was first conceived, even that wasn't much of a reason to watch a movie under the stars.

Still, even for people of Derek's generation, there was something nostalgic about a drive-in. He could remember his parents bringing him here for the first time when he was eight or nine, and how excited he'd been. It was a triple bill, the movies becoming successively more mature. The first was one of the *Toy Story* flicks—Derek had brought along his Buzz Lightyear and Woody action figures—which was followed by some rom-com Matthew

McConaughey thing, back when he was only doing crap, and then a Jason Bourne movie. Derek had barely managed to stay awake until the end of *Toy Story*. His parents had made a bed for him in the backseat so he could zonk out when they watched features two and three.

Derek longed for those times. When his parents were still together.

This night, the Constellation was showing one of those dumber-than-dumb Transformers movies, where alien robots inhabiting Earth had disguised themselves as cars—usually Chevrolets, thank you very much, product placement—and trucks. Morphing from car to robot involved a slew of special effects. Lots of things blew up; buildings were destroyed. It was the kind of movie none of the girls they knew were interested in seeing, and even though the guys tried to make them understand the movie itself didn't matter, that this was an *event*, that this night at the drive-in was *history*, they'd failed to win them over.

Even the guys knew this was a dumb movie. In fact, there had been agreement among them that the only way to see a movie like this—whether at a drive-in, at a regular theater, or at home—was drunk. Which led to a decision that they would try to sneak not only a person into the drive-in, but some beer, too.

Thing was, this was a milestone piled on top of a milestone. This was the last night for the Constellation, and it was the end of the academic year at Thackeray College, which Derek had been attending for four years, and was now leaving. For what, he had no clue. He had no job prospects, other than maybe working for his dad again, cutting lawns, planting shrubs, trimming hedges. Had he gone to college for four years to run a leaf blower? Even his dad didn't want that for him. And yet, there were worse things than working alongside his father.

For this one night, he wouldn't think about his job future, or a couple of other things that had been weighing heavily on him.

The first was the death of a friend, just about the most senseless thing ever. This guy, he comes to college, goes to class, writes essays, tries out for some school plays—he's just doing his thing like everybody else—and then one night campus security shoots him in the head while he's supposedly trying to rape somebody.

Derek still hadn't been able to get his head around it.

But then there was the other thing. Even bigger.

Derek was a *father*.

He had a goddamned kid.

A son named Matthew.

The news hadn't come as a shock just to him. Even the mother was surprised, which sounded kind of weird, but it was a pretty weird, fucked-up story, and Derek still didn't know all the details. He'd known that she was pregnant, but had believed the baby died at birth. Turned out not to be that way. He'd talked to her—Marla was her name—a few times since finding out the baby was alive, been over to visit her with his father in tow, and he was still kind of feeling his way through this, trying to sort out just what his responsibilities were.

"Hello?"

"Huh?" Derek said.

It was Canton Schultz, standing next to his four-door Nissan, the driver's door open. Flanking him were Derek's other friends from Thackeray, George Lydecker and Tyler Gross.

"We just took a vote," Tyler said.

4

"What?"

"While you were off in la-la land, daydreaming, we took a vote," said George. "You're it."

"I'm what?"

"You're the one going into the trunk."

"No way. I don't want to go into the trunk."

"Well, tough shit," said Canton. "We've been standing around here talking about it, and you had nothing to say, so we made a decision. Thing is, it's a very important job, being the guy in the trunk, because you're the one protecting the beer."

"Fuck it, fine," Derek said. "But I'm not getting in now. It's a ten-minute drive from here. We'll pull over when we're almost there—then I'll get in the back for a couple of minutes till we get inside."

The thing was, the trunk was very much a place he did not want to be. He didn't want to be cooped up in there for two minutes, let alone ten. Back when Derek was seventeen, while hiding in the basement crawl space of a friend's house, he'd had to listen while three people were murdered.

And hold his breath so the killer didn't find him, too.

It was a big story in Promise Falls at the time. Prominent lawyer, his wife and son, all executed. For a while there, the police even wondered if Derek had done it, but they got the killer in the end, and everything worked out, so long as you didn't count the fact that Derek was pretty much scarred for life.

Okay, maybe not for life. He'd managed to move on, pull his life together, go to school, make friends. His parents splitting up had actually hit him harder. But it didn't mean he was happy to jump into a car trunk.

Derek was not a fan of confined spaces.

But he wasn't a fan of looking like a wuss, either, which was why he'd proposed getting in just before their arrival at the drive-in. Everyone agreed that was reasonable. So, after putting a case of beer into the trunk, they piled into the car. Canton behind the wheel, George shotgun, and Derek and Tyler in the backseat.

It was already dark, and it would be after eleven by the time they got to the Constellation. The first feature would probably already be nearly over, but they weren't interested in it anyway, since it was always something for kids. Not that a Transformers movie wasn't for kids, but the opening flick would most likely be a cartoon that wasn't all that scary. And even if they ended up late for the Transformers flick, how hard would it be to catch up? And before long, they'd be too drunk to care.

While Derek had not volunteered to be the guy in the trunk, he had stepped up to be the designated driver on the way home, and everyone was fine with that. One or two beers for him, and that'd be it. He'd get everyone back safely.

And after that, Derek didn't know when he would see any of them again. Canton and Tyler would be heading home to Pittsburgh and Bangor, respectively. George Lydecker, like Derek, was a local, but Derek didn't see himself hanging out with him. Derek was reminded of a phrase his own grandfather used to say about people like George. *"He's not wrapped too tight."*

The words that came to mind for Derek were "loose cannon." George was always the one who acted first, thought later. Like turning over a professor's Smart car and leaving it on its roof. Slipping a baby alligator from a pet shop into Thackeray Pond. (That little guy still hadn't been found.) George had even boasted about breaking into people's garages late at night, not just to help himself to a set of tools or a bicycle, but for the pure thrill of it.

As if George could read Derek's thoughts at that moment in the car, he decided to do something monumentally stupid.

George dropped the passenger window, allowing cool night air to blow in as they sped down a country road that ran around the south end of Promise Falls. Next thing Derek knew, George had his arm extended out the window.

There was a loud bang. And an instantaneous *PING!*

"Jesus!" Derek said. "What the hell was that?"

George brought his arm back in, turned around in the seat, and grinned. He showed off the gun in his hand.

"Just shooting at some signs," he said. "I fucking nailed that speed limit one."

"Are you out of your mind?" Canton shouted, glancing over. "What the fuck!"

"Put that away!" Derek screamed. "Asshole!"

George grimaced. "Come on, lighten up. I know what I'm doing."

"Where did you get that?" Tyler asked. "You steal *that* out of someone's garage?"

"It's *mine*, okay?" he said. "It's no big deal. I figured I could take a couple of shots at the screen. I mean, they're going to be knocking it down in a week or two anyway. Who cares if it's got a couple of holes in it?"

"Are you really that stupid?" Canton asked. "You think you can fire that thing off with hundreds of people there, lots of them with little kids, and they won't call in a goddamn SWAT team and arrest your stupid fucking ass?"

"Promise Falls has a SWAT team?"

"That's not the point. The point is—"

"I figured when the Transformers are knocking over a bunch of skyscrapers, nobody'll even notice. It'll be so loud anyway."

"You're unbelievable," Tyler said.

"Okay, okay, okay," George said, lowering the weapon, resting it in his lap. "I wouldn't really have done that. I just wanted to shoot some signs, maybe a mailbox."

The other three shook their heads.

"Idiot," Derek said under his breath.

"I said *okay*," George said. "God, what a bunch of pussies. I'm glad to be getting the hell out of here." George had already told them he was off to Vancouver the day after tomorrow.

They traveled the next few minutes in silence. It was Canton who broke it. "How about here?"

"Huh?" Tyler said.

"This is a good spot. No one around. Derek, this is where you get in the back."

"Are we still doing this?" he asked. "It's stupid."

"It's *tradition*—that's what it is. When you go to the drive-in, you smuggle someone in. It's *expected*. If you don't do it, the management is actually disappointed."

Derek felt resigned to his fate. "Fine."

The car pulled over to the shoulder, gravel crunching beneath the tires. Derek got out on the passenger side, gave George a withering look, then went around to the back of the car. Canton had popped the truck from the inside, pulling on the tiny lever by the driver's seat, but had gotten out so he could close the lid once Derek was inside.

"It's not exactly huge in here," Derek said, standing there, staring into the gaping hole.

"You getting in or what?" Canton asked.

Derek nodded, turned around, dropped his butt in first.

"So it's not an Oldsmobile," Canton said. "Stop whining. Once we get inside, you can get out. It'll be, like, five minutes."

Derek said, "I hate this."

"What's the big—" Canton stopped himself in mid-sentence. "Oh shit, it's about that thing that happened, isn't it? When you were hiding in that house?"

"It's okay."

"No, I'll do it. I'll get in, and you get back in the car."

"I *said* I would *do* it."

Derek noticed, with some relief, the emergency lever inside the trunk that allowed it to be opened from the inside. He got his head in, then brought up his legs. He lay on his side, the case of beer tucked behind his knees.

"Okay, so don't start screaming or anything," Canton said, and slammed the lid shut.

It was nearly pitch-black in there, save for some red glow from the back side of the taillights. Derek felt the car veer back onto the pavement, then pick up speed.

Despite the rear seat between him and his friends, he could hear them talking.

"Just everyone be cool," Canton said.

"Yeah," said Tyler. "Like I'm going to say, 'We got nothin' in the trunk!' I'm not an idiot. Not like George."

"Fuck you," said George.

"Okay, here we go," Canton said. "Jeez, there's still a line."

"It's only like ten cars. It won't take long."

Derek struggled to get comfortable. He hoped it wouldn't take them long to buy tickets and get parked. He knew it was his imagination, but he felt

9

as though he were running out of air, that he was having trouble breathing. His heartbeat was moving into second gear.

He felt the Nissan turn. Canton would be pulling up to the gate, where there were two ticket booths. Right beyond them, towering over them, in fact, would be the back side of the four-story screen. Once the tickets were bought and the gate was cleared, the car would pass through an opening in a ten-foot wooden perimeter fence designed to keep people from sneaking in.

The car would follow the driveway to the far end of the property, where the concession stand was located, then do a one-eighty to face the screen head-on. Derek figured once they'd picked a good viewing spot, they'd let him out.

But first, they had to clear the gate.

The car stopped, inched forward. Stopped, inched forward.

Come on come on come on.

Finally, Derek heard Canton shout: "Three tickets."

Then, not quite as clearly, a man's voice. "Just the three?"

"Yep, just us."

"Ten bucks each."

"There ya go."

A brief pause, then the man's voice again. "You sure it's just the three of you?"

Canton: "Yep."

Tyler: "Just us."

George: "You can't count?"

Shit, Derek thought. What the hell was wrong with him tonight?

The man selling tickets said, "And you guys know

10

there's no booze allowed. You can't be bringing anything in like that."

"Of course," Canton said.

Another pause.

Then: "I'm gonna have to ask you to pop the trunk."

"Sorry?" Canton said.

"The trunk. Pop it."

Shit shit shit shit.

Well, what was the worst that could happen? Derek figured, once this guy found him in the trunk, with the beer, he could do one of three things. He could deny them entry. Or he could charge Derek ten bucks, confiscate the beer, and tell them they could pick it up on the way out. Or the son of a bitch could call the cops.

Derek figured bringing in the police was pretty unlikely. Did the Promise Falls cops really want to be bothered with someone sneaking into the drive-in for free?

At this point, Derek didn't much care. Right now, he'd happily endure a full body-cavity search if it meant getting the hell out of here.

Canton said, "Uh, I don't think you have the right to do that."

"Yeah?" the man said.

"Yeah. I don't think you have the authority. You're just some dick selling tickets."

"Really. Well, my name is Lionel Grayson, and I'm the owner and manager of this place, and if you don't pop that trunk, I'm calling the cops."

Maybe it was more likely than Derek thought. *Fine, so be it.*

"Okay, then," Canton said.

Derek heard the driver's door open. But then another door, on the other side of the car. Tyler had been sitting behind Canton. Which meant George was getting out.

Tyler said, "Jesus, George, what are you—"

Derek didn't hear the rest as both doors slammed shut.

Canton was saying, "You know, this being the last night you guys are open, we were just wanting to have a little fun and—"

The man, this Mr. Grayson, sounding closer now: "Just open it up."

"Okay, I hear ya, I hear ya."

Then, George. "You know, man, this is America. You think being a fucking ticket seller gives you the right to violate our constitutional rights?"

"George, just let it go."

All three voices at the back of the car now. Derek was still pretty sure Lionel Grayson wouldn't call the cops. He'd just tell them to piss off. Turn their car around and send them on their way. Derek already had a plan. They'd go back to his place, download a Transformers movie to the flat-screen, and get drunk on his couch.

No need for him to be the designated driver any—

Bang.

No, it was more than that. So much more than just a bang. In the trunk, it sounded to Derek like a sonic boom. The whole car seemed to shake.

It couldn't have been something on the screen. One of the Transformer robots blowing up, say. You had to be in the car, have the radio tuned to the right frequency, to hear the movie.

And even if this had been a regular movie, in a theater, the bang was too loud.

It sounded very close.

George.

Could he really have been that dumb? Had he gotten

out of the car with the gun? Had he started waving it at the manager? Had he pulled the trigger?

That stupid, stupid, stupid son of a bitch. Surely to God he didn't think getting caught over something like this was cause to shoot a guy.

There were screams. Lots of screams. But they sounded off in the distance.

"Jesus!" someone shouted. Derek was pretty sure that was Canton.

Then: "Oh my God!" That sounded a lot like George.

Derek frantically patted the back wall of the trunk, looking for the emergency release. His heart was pounding. He'd broken out in an instant sweat. He found the lever, grabbed hold, yanked.

The trunk lid swung open.

Canton was there, and George was there. So was a third man. A black man Derek figured was Lionel Grayson, the manager. Not one of them was looking into the trunk. In fact, all three had their backs to Derek, their collective attention focused elsewhere.

Derek sat up so quickly he banged his head on the edge of the opening. He instinctively put his hand on the injury, but he was too spellbound to feel any pain.

He could scarcely believe what he was seeing.

The Constellation Drive-in Theater's four-story screen was coming down.

Dark smoke billowed from the width of its base as it slowly pitched forward, in the direction of the parking lot, as though being blown over by a mighty wind.

Except there was no wind.

The immense wall came down with a great whomping crash that shook the ground beneath them. Clouds of smoke and dust billowed skyward from beyond the fence.

There was a moment of stunned silence. Barely a second. Then a strangled symphony of car alarms, whooping and screeching in a discordant chorus of panic.

And more screams. Many, many more screams.

THREE

"Hello? Georgina?"

"No, it's not Georgina. It's *me*. You heard what's happened?"

"I've just been waiting for Georgina to come home, to call, let me know where she is. What's going on?"

"The goddamn drive-in just fell down."

"What?"

"The screen toppled over. Like a huge fucking wall."

"That's crazy. But it's closed, right? So nobody was hurt or—"

"No, listen to me. This was the last night for the place. It's packed. It's just happened. First responders barely even there yet."

"Jesus."

"Look, we've got a problem."

"What do you mean?"

"I saw Adam."

"What? You saw Adam where?"

"Adam and Miriam. I was going by the drive-in as cars were going in, caught a glimpse of Adam's Jag, that old convertible of his? Had to be him and Miriam. Not another car like that in Promise Falls. I'd stopped for a coffee up the road, and when I heard the explosion—"

"It was an explosion?"

"Whatever it was. When I heard it, I drove back, got a quick look at what's happened. That Jag is toast. I could see the tail end of it sticking out of the rubble."

"Oh, God, that's terrible. I can't believe it. Adam and Miriam, maybe they got out before—"

"No, there's no way. You don't see the problem?"

"They're dead. Yeah, it's horrendous. My God."

"There's a bigger problem, for us. With them dead, someone'll have to clear out their house, go through their things. Next of kin. Adam's daughter, what's-her-name."

A pause at the other end of the line.

"You there?"

"Yeah."

"Now do you see the problem?"

"I do."

FOUR

Cal

"That was delicious, Celeste," I said. "Thanks again."

"You know you're welcome here anytime," my sister said across the kitchen table to me. "You want some of the tortellini to take home with you? There's tons of it. I can put it in a container."

"That's okay."

"I know you're tired of hearing it, but you know you're more than welcome to stay here. We've got two spare rooms." She glanced to her right at Dwayne. "Isn't that right?"

Dwayne Rogers turned to me and said, without emotion, "Of course. We'd love to have you."

I raised a hand in protest. I didn't want to live here any more than Dwayne wanted me to.

"No, hear me out, Cal," Celeste said. "I'm not saying you have to live here forever. Just until you find a place to live."

"I have a place to live," I reminded her. Celeste was two years older than me, and had always seen me as her baby brother, even though we were both now in our forties.

"Oh, please," she said. "A room over a used-book store. That's not a home."

"It's all I need."

"He says it's all he needs," Dwayne told his wife.

17

She ignored him. "It's a room—that's all it is. You need a proper house. You used to live in a proper house."

I smiled weakly. "I don't need a big empty house. I've got all the space I need."

"I just think," Celeste continued, "that living in that miserable space is holding you back."

"Jesus, let it go," Dwayne said, pushing back his chair and going back to the fridge for his fifth beer, not that I was counting. "If he's happy living where he is, then leave him be."

"This has nothing to do with you," Celeste told him.

"Cal's doing just fine," he said. "Aren't you fine?"

"I'm fine," I said. "Dwayne just nailed it."

He twisted the cap off the beer, drew hard on it. "I'm gonna get some air," he said.

"You do that," Celeste said, and looked relieved once her husband was gone. "He can be such an asshole." She smiled. "He's my husband, so I can say that."

I forced a grin. "He's okay."

"He doesn't get it. He thinks people should just suck it up, no matter what. Except, of course, when it's something that's happened to him."

"Maybe he's right. People have to move on."

"Oh, come on," she said. "If it had happened to someone else, if you knew someone whose wife and son had both been, you know . . ."

"Murdered," I said.

"Right. Is that what you'd tell them? Just get over it?"

"No," I said. "But I wouldn't hound them, either."

I knew it was a poor choice of words the moment I'd uttered them.

"Is that what I'm doing?" Celeste asked. "Hounding you?"

"No," I said quickly. I reached across the table and took her hand in mine, aware of the absurdity of the moment. Here I was, comforting her over my reluctance to let her comfort me. "That came out wrong."

"I'm sorry if that's what I'm doing," she said. "I just think that if you don't deal with these things, if you don't give a voice to your feelings, you'll make yourself sick."

I wondered when Celeste would get around to doing that with Dwayne. Dealing with him, giving a voice to her feelings.

"I appreciate your concern. I do. But I'm fine. I'm moving forward." I paused. "I don't see as I've got much choice. I've got work here. I'm getting referrals."

To prove the point, I'd given my sister one of my new business cards. The words *Cal Weaver: Private Investigations* in black, raised type. A cell phone number. Even a Web site and an e-mail address. Maybe one of these days, I'd even be on Twitter.

"I worry about you in that apartment," she said.

"I like it there. The guy who runs the bookshop, who owns the building, is a decent landlord, and he's got a good selection of stuff to read, too. I'm good." I figured if I said it enough, I might even believe it.

"It was smart, you moving back here from Griffon. After . . . you know."

Celeste wanted me to face what happened, but could never bring herself to say what that actually was. My son, Scott, had been tossed off the top of a building, and my wife, Donna, had been shot. The people responsible for their deaths were either dead or serving time.

"Couldn't stay there," I said. "Augie had the good sense to leave, too. They're down in Florida." Donna's brother,

Augustus, the chief of police in Griffon, had taken an early retirement and, along with his wife, headed for warmer climes.

"You keep in touch?"

"No," I said. After a few seconds, I nodded my head in the direction of the front door and asked, "How's he doing?"

Celeste forced a smile. "He's just out of sorts."

"You guys okay?"

"He's not getting so much work from the town." Dwayne had a paving business. "They're cutting back. Figure unless a pothole's big enough to swallow up a car whole, they don't have to fill it. Ninety percent of Dwayne's business is with Promise Falls. The town's always contracted out road repair. They're just letting things go to shit—at least that's the way it looks to me. I heard that Finley guy is gonna run for mayor again. He might be able to set things straight."

I didn't know much about him, except that his previous stint in the position had ended badly. We'd been living in Griffon when all that happened.

"Things'll pick up for Dwayne," I said, because it seemed like the thing to say. Maybe this was why Celeste wanted me to bunk in with them. She knew I'd insist on paying room and board. But I couldn't live here, not under this roof. Not with my controlling sister and her moody, beer-guzzling husband. It didn't mean I couldn't help, however.

"You short?" I asked. "If you need some money, just something to get you—"

"No," Celeste said. "I couldn't accept that." But she protested no further, and I wondered whether she was waiting for me to insist.

Next time.

I got up, gave Celeste a peck on the cheek and half a hug. On my way through the living room, I heard sirens.

As I came out the front door, the last in what looked like a convoy of half a dozen ambulances went screaming up the street. Dwayne was standing at the porch railing, beer in hand, watching the vehicles tear past, with a wry grin on his face.

"There's always work for those bastards," he said. "You don't see the town layin' them off, do ya?"

FIVE

Once he was out of the trunk, Derek ran. Not away, not back down the road, but past the gate and onto the grounds of the drive-in theater.

Toward the screams.

He couldn't run directly to where the screen had fallen. A fence too high to scale ran alongside the driveway for about fifty yards. Once he'd cleared it, he doubled back, sprinting to the disaster site.

There were at least a hundred cars in the lot, and it was Derek's experience, from the few times he'd been here, that hardly anyone parked in the first row, right in front of the screen. Just as most people didn't want to sit in the front row of a conventional theater, and have to crane their necks at an awkward angle for two hours, very few were interested in leaning forward, heads perched over the dashboard, to take in a flick.

Except maybe for owners of convertibles.

It was a cool evening, but not too cool to drop the top, if you had a blanket or two. You put down the roof, reclined the seat all the way, and watched the show.

Derek was betting that the two cars that had been crushed by the falling screen were ragtops.

Everyone was out of their cars. Some stood by their vehicles, too shocked to do anything but look toward the collapsed screen in horror. Cars that hadn't been buried in debris had still been hit by some of it. Many cars had busted windshields. Some of the people milling about in shock were unaware of the blood running from minor cuts on their faces. Others had their phones out, either making calls or taking video of the mayhem. Probably uploading it to Twitter and Facebook so they could brag that they were the first to do so.

There was random shouting.

"Call 911!"

"Oh my God!"

"Terrorists! It's a terror attack!"

"Get out of here! Run! *Run!*"

But the only ones running were several men who, like Derek, were heading toward the collapsed screen. By the time he reached it, he was part of a pack huddling around the tail ends of cars that had been crushed. Several people were waving their arms, trying to keep the clouds of dust out of their faces.

Lots of coughing.

"We need a crane!" someone shouted.

"Has anyone called 911?"

"Where the hell's the fire department?"

Derek was reminded of pictures he'd seen on the news. The aftermaths of earthquakes. Entire buildings crumbling into the streets. But Derek didn't think this was an earthquake. It wasn't as if the ground had opened up anywhere. The only thing that had come down was the screen.

And the noise he'd heard while he was still in the trunk, if he was guessing, sure had sounded like an explosion. Could there be gas lines or something under that screen? Propane tanks that linked to the concession stand, where they barbecued the hot dogs?

23

Or could that guy shouting about terrorists be onto something? Could this have been a bomb?

But how much sense did that make? If you were al-Qaeda or ISIS or whoever was the latest threat to world peace, was this part of your grand scheme to make America surrender? Blow up a drive-in in some half-assed town in upstate New York?

"Grab that!" a man standing near Derek said.

Together, he and three other men tried to shift a piece of the screen, about the size of two sheets of plywood but ten times as thick, off the top of a small red car that Derek could see, from the markings on the trunk, was the remains of some old sports car. Derek knew enough about cars to guess this was a midsixties Jaguar.

"One . . . two . . . three!"

The four of them, putting everything they had into it, shifted the piece about four feet to the left, enough to expose the passenger side of the two-seater.

"Oh Jesus," someone said, turned, and threw up.

It was a person. Or had been, once. It was hard to tell much more than that. The head, little more than pulp and bone now, had been mashed down into the rest of the body.

A woman, it looked like to Derek.

A man with a stronger stomach stepped carefully around to the side of the car and leaned over the body. At first Derek thought he was trying to get a better look at the dead woman, but now the man was peering beneath the debris that obscured the driver's side. He'd taken out his phone, opening a flashlight app, and was shining it under there.

"This one's a goner, too," he said. "Let's check the other car."

Sirens could be heard in the distance. The deep fog-hornlike moans of fire trucks.

The second car—Derek could tell from the taillights that it was a Mustang—was buried under much more debris than the first. The men stood there, shaking their heads.

"The fire department might have something to lift it off," Derek said. "I don't think we can budge it."

"Hello?" someone yelled into the pile of wood and plaster. "Can anyone hear me in there?"

Nothing.

Derek wondered, briefly, what had happened to his so-called friends. They sure weren't here trying to help. Probably took off in the car while they had the chance. Assholes, the lot of them.

"Those bastards!" a man shouted. "Those goddamn bastards! Idiots!"

Derek spun around, saw that it was the man who'd wanted to inspect the trunk. The drive-in owner, Lionel Grayson. At first, Derek wondered if he was talking about his friends, but quickly figured out his tirade was directed at someone else.

"Fucking idiots!" he screamed at the top of his lungs. He put his hands on his forehead and started to wail. "Oh God, oh dear God!"

Derek took a step toward him. "What are you talking about?" he asked. "What idiots?"

Grayson wasn't hearing him. His eyes were fixed on the catastrophe before him. "Not happening," he whispered. "Can't be happening."

"What idiots?" Derek asked again.

"The demolition people," he said, not looking at Derek. "It comes down next week . . . They weren't even supposed to . . . they're not supposed to put the charges in until . . . I don't know . . . I don't know how this could . . ."

Grayson dropped to his knees, the upper half of his body wavering. Derek and a woman standing nearby rushed to the man's side, knelt down, kept him from toppling over.

Three ambulances screamed into the parking area, lights swirling. People waved them toward the front. Paramedics leapt out, ran in their direction.

Derek was thinking about what the manager had said. How the screen was set to come down soon. How some demolition had been scheduled for a later date. But someone had screwed up, big-time, and allowed the dynamite—or whatever it was—to go off early.

And kill people.

Derek was pretty sure no one was going to give a shit about him trying to sneak in for free.

SIX

David Harwood was asleep when he realized his cell phone was buzzing on the bedside table.

He'd muted it, as he always did before turning out the light. He didn't want to wake his parents, who were on the other side of the wall. He wasn't worried about waking his nine-year-old son, Ethan, who was impervious to alarm clocks. It was a kind of childhood superpower. But Don and Arlene Harwood were light sleepers, and David's mother could become quite agitated by the sound of a phone ringing in the middle of the night.

That almost always meant bad news.

There had been more than enough of that lately. Just recently, Arlene's sister, Agnes—David's aunt—had died. Taken her own life, jumping off the bridge that spanned the waterfall from which Promise Falls took its name. Arlene had taken it pretty hard. Not just her sister's death, but everything surrounding it.

Recent events had taken a toll on everyone. The Harwood family, Agnes's husband, and, more than anyone else, their daughter, Marla.

As if all that hadn't been enough, there was the fire. You can have one of those when someone leaves something on the burner and forgets about it.

The kitchen in David's parents' home was being

rebuilt. There'd been a lot of water damage, too, particularly in the basement. If there'd been any good news, it was that the house hadn't burned to the ground. In another month or so, Don and Arlene would be able to move back in.

But for now, David's parents were living with Ethan and him, a complete reversal of the way things had recently been. After the fire, David, who now had a job and could afford to get a place of his own, found a house for rent a few blocks from his parents' place.

He'd fallen into bed an hour ago, at half past ten. It had been a long day. Working for Randall Finley, helping that jackass with his political comeback, was not David's idea of a dream job. But it was paying the bills, at least for now, and helping David earn back some of the self-respect he'd lost since his former employer, the *Promise Falls Standard*, went under.

He'd pretty much found himself—and as a former newspaper writer he hated the cliché—between a rock and a hard place. He could ditch his principles and work for a man like Finley, or he could fail to be a provider to his son.

He'd placed his phone on the table, no more than two feet from his head, but he had not turned off the vibrating feature. So when the phone went off, it sent a reverberation through the wood disruptive enough to wake David.

He opened his eyes, rolled over in the bed, grabbed the phone. The screen was so bright it took his eyes a moment to adjust, but even half-blind, he could identify the caller.

"Jesus Christ," he mumbled. Up on one elbow, he put the phone to his ear. "Yeah."

"You in bed?"

David looked at the clock radio. It was eleven thirty-five p.m.

"Of course I'm in bed, Randy. It's nearly midnight."

"Get up. Get dressed. We've got work to do."

"I'll talk to you in the morning."

"David! This is serious. Come on. Haven't you heard?"

"Heard what? Randy, I've been in bed for an hour. What the hell's going on?"

"You sure you actually worked in the newspaper business? The whole world's going to shit around you and you haven't got a fucking clue?"

"Just tell me."

"The drive-in. You know, the Constellation?"

David sat up, dropping his legs over the edge of the bed. He turned on the lamp, blinked some more.

"Of course I know it."

"The whole thing just blew up."

"What?"

"I have to get out there. Help out, be a comfort to people." The former mayor of Promise Falls paused. "Be seen. Get my picture taken."

"Tell me what happened, exactly."

"The fucking screen fell over. Onto cars. There's people dead, David. You got your pants on yet?"

There was still newspaper ink running through David's veins. He felt the adrenaline rush. He wanted to get out there, see what was going on, interview people. Record the event.

God, he hated that he didn't have a paper to write for anymore.

What he did not want to do was be part of turning a human tragedy into a public relations stunt for Randall Finley.

"It's wrong," David said.

"What?"

"It's wrong. Going out there to have your picture taken."

"Christ, David, it's not like I'm asking you to follow me around like a *60 Minutes* crew. You'll be discreet. I have to tell you how to do your job? You blend into the background. I'm just helping people—I don't even know you're there. Whaddya call 'em, candid shots? We'll be able to use them later. We're wasting time talkin' about this. And did it occur to you that I might actually give a shit and want to help?"

It had not.

Finley didn't wait for an answer. "Be out front of your place in three minutes." He ended the call.

David pulled a pair of jeans on over his boxers, threw on a pullover shirt so he wouldn't waste valuable time fiddling with buttons, jammed his feet, sockless, into a pair of sneakers. He could shoot pics and video with his phone, but thought he might need something better than that, so he grabbed a camera from the home office he was in the process of setting up across the hall from his bedroom.

Despite his best efforts to be quiet, the door to his parents' bedroom opened. His mother stood there in her pajamas.

"What's going on?"

"I'm heading out. Don't know how long I'll be. If I'm not here when you wake up, get Ethan off to school."

From inside the bedroom, his father shouted, "What's the ruckus?"

"Work," David said.

30

"Finley expects you to go out at this hour?" his mother asked.

"Does he know it's almost midnight?" Don asked, making no attempt to whisper.

"Don't wake Ethan," David said.

"Why's that man calling you out in the middle of the night?" Arlene Harwood persisted. "That's outrageous. Doesn't the man realize you have a young son to look after and—"

"Mom!" David snapped. "Jesus! I'll be back when I'm back."

When he was living under his parents' roof, he couldn't wait to get Ethan and himself out of there. Now he had his own place, and nothing had changed. They made him feel like he was thirteen.

He raced down the stairs, caught a brief glimpse of himself in the front hall mirror. Hair sticking up at odd angles.

Finley's Lincoln screeched to a stop out front of David's house. David stepped out, made sure the door was locked behind him, and ran to the curb.

Finley had powered down the window. "Chop-chop," he said.

David got in on the passenger side. The leather upholstery was cool, and the night air was cold on his bare ankles.

Finley glanced at David's hair. "You didn't have time to run a comb through that?"

"Go."

"Is that a decent camera you've got there?" the former mayor asked. "I hope so. I don't want some shitty phone shots. This is an opportunity too good to piss away."

David, staring straight ahead through the windshield,

could not bring himself to look at the man.

"Just go," David said.

"All I can say is, good thing I'm not counting on you to keep me posted on current events," Finley said. "Good thing I was up, heard the sirens."

David said, "You don't live anywhere near the Constellation." And, for the first time, glanced over at the man.

"I got more ears than just my own," Finley said. "I've had some fridge magnets made up. Got a box of them in the trunk. *Finley for Mayor*, they say. But I don't know, might be bad form to hand them out at an accident scene."

"You think?" David asked, wondering, not for the first time in recent months, how it had come to this.

SEVEN

It was the worst thing Detective Barry Duckworth had seen in twenty years of working for the Promise Falls police.

He'd arrived at the drive-in at 11:49 p.m., and by 12:31 a.m. he'd established a few basic facts.

The screen had come down about twenty minutes past eleven. It had fallen in the direction of the parking lot, and while scattered debris had hit several cars, two had been crushed. Although it was hard to look at it this way right now, later the thinking would be that it could have been a lot worse.

Given that the rear license plates were visible, Duckworth was able to determine quickly to whom the cars belonged. The first, an older-model Jaguar, had been registered to an Adam Chalmers, of Ridgewood Drive. The fire department had cleared off enough of the car to see that there were two casualties in the vehicle, a man and a woman.

Chalmers and his wife, Duckworth guessed.

The other car, a 2006 Mustang convertible, was registered jointly to a Floyd and Renata Gravelle, of Canterbury Street. One of the firefighters had told Duckworth that it looked like two kids in the car. A boy and a girl, probably late teens.

Both dead. Heads crushed.

There were some nonfatal injuries. Bud Hillier, forty-two—whose three children, aged eight, eleven, and thirteen, were in the car with him—was resting his hands atop the steering wheel of his Taurus station wagon when a chunk of screen came through the glass and lopped off two of his fingers. Dolores Whitney, thirty-seven—who'd brought her daughter, Chloe, eight, to a drive-in for the first and, undoubtedly, last time—suffered four broken ribs when a large piece of wood pierced her windshield.

Compared with the people in the two convertibles in the first row, these folks had gotten off easy.

Arriving shortly after Duckworth was Angus Carlson, who'd recently been moved up from uniformed officer to detective status because the department was short of investigators. Duckworth hadn't yet made his mind up about Carlson. The younger cop struck him as inexperienced and, at times, a bit of a jerk.

When Carlson spotted Duckworth, he went straight to him, took a quick glance at the scene, and asked, "So what movie was playing? *Crash*? *Flatliners*? *Good Luck Chuck*?"

Duckworth gave him the addresses he'd gotten from running the plates on the two cars. "Go to those houses, find out who the people in those cars likely are. See if you can do it without cracking any jokes."

Carlson frowned. "Just breaking the tension."

"Go."

Lionel Grayson, who'd been identified as the owner and manager, was being treated by one of the paramedics. He gave every indication of being in mild shock, and had nearly passed out before Duckworth's arrival.

"Mr. Grayson," Duckworth said, "I need to ask you some questions."

The man looked at Duckworth vacantly. "It was our last night."

"I understand that, yes."

"It was supposed to be a . . . celebration. Sad, too, but a night to remember all the wonderful times people had here . . ."

He looked away. Duckworth could see the dried trail of tears that had run down the man's cheeks.

"How many?" the man asked.

"How many what?"

"How many are dead?" Grayson asked.

"It appears to be four, sir, although until all the debris is removed, we won't know for sure. Someone might have been walking along there, but it's two cars that were crushed. Do you have any idea how this happened?"

"Marsden," he said. "He should be here soon. I called him."

"Who's Marsden?"

"Clifford Marsden. He owns Marsden Demolition."

"Are you saying he did this? He blew up the screen?"

"He must have," Grayson said. "But he mixed up the dates, or set the timer wrong, or something."

"You hired him to demolish the screen?"

Grayson nodded.

"When was that supposed to happen?"

"In another week," he said. "A week from today. I didn't even think he'd planted the explosives yet. That's crazy. Why would he put in the explosives a week early? Run the risk of something like this happening?"

"That's something we'll want to ask him."

"He's on his way. I tried to call him, but my hands

were shaking. I couldn't handle my phone. Someone did it for me. But he's coming. When I get my hands on him, I . . . I don't know what I'll do."

"Why was the screen supposed to come down so soon after closing?"

"It was part of the deal."

"What deal?"

"The sale," Grayson said. "To Mancini Homes."

"All this land has been sold?"

Grayson nodded. "The sale goes through in a month. Before then, I have to clear the property. The screen, the outbuildings, the fencing, it all has to come down. It was one of the conditions."

"What's happening with the land?"

Grayson shrugged. "Houses, I guess. I don't know. It never really mattered to me. I got just under three mil for the land. I was going to go to Florida. With my wife. Retire. But now . . . how do I . . . this is so horrible."

Duckworth put a hand on the man's shoulder. "We're going to find out what happened, okay? You just hang in."

He noticed a big car snaking its way between fire engines and ambulances, then pulling over near the fence. Duckworth wondered whether this was Clifford Marsden. But when the driver opened the door, and the interior light went on, he saw that it was someone else.

Randall Finley.

Getting out of the passenger side was another man the detective recognized. David Harwood. Former reporter, now assistant to the former mayor. Camera in hand.

Finley had already spotted something that interested him. A black SUV, covered in dust, some small chunks of the movie screen decorating the roof and the hood.

The tailgate was wide open, and a woman was tending to two small girls—neither more than ten years old—sitting with their legs dangling over the bumper. One of the girls was crying and the woman was trying to console her.

Duckworth said, "Excuse me, Mr. Grayson. I'll be right back."

Finley walked quickly to the SUV, then slowed his approach when he was nearly there.

"How are you folks doing?" he asked.

The woman glanced around. "Hello?"

"I just wanted to see if you were okay," he said kindly. "Are these your daughters?"

The woman indicated the girl who was crying. "This is Kaylie. She's my niece, and this is her friend Alicia. Are you with the police?"

"No, my name's Randall Finley. What's your name?"

The woman blinked. "Patricia. Patricia Henderson."

"Hello, Patricia. And hi, Kaylie, Alicia. I need to know, are any of you hurt? Do you need any medical attention?"

"We're . . . okay," Patricia said. "Just shook-up. Some of that . . . stuff . . . fell onto the car. The girls—not just the girls, me too—were pretty scared when it happened."

"I'll bet."

"Are you with the police?" Patricia asked again.

Finley shook his head. "No, like I said, my name is Randall Finley, and I'm just a concerned citizen, seeing if there's anything I can do."

"Didn't you used to be mayor?" Patricia asked.

"That was some time ago," he said, shrugging.

"Why is that man taking pictures?"

Finley glanced over his shoulder. "I don't know. Could

be the press, or someone who has to document the accident scene. Just someone doing his job. I wouldn't worry about him. Is there anything I can get for you? Do you need some water? I have some bottled water in the trunk of my car. From my own company. Or maybe there's someone you'd like me to call for you?"

"I'm not married," the woman said. "I'm waiting around, in case I have to talk to the police or anyone about insurance matters. But I really want to get the girls home. This is all so horrible."

Finley nodded sympathetically, moved in closer, bent over to smile at the girls, making sure he positioned himself so David could get a good shot. "Maybe Kaylie's or Alicia's parents could come get the girls, and then only you'd have to stay here. Would you like me to call them for—"

"Randy!"

Finley whirled around. "Why, Barry, hello. What a terrible thing that's happened here. What do you know so far?"

Duckworth approached. "What are you doing here?"

"Lending support," he said. "Pitching in where I can."

"And what about him?" Duckworth asked, pointing to David Harwood. "What support is he lending?"

"Him?"

"Why's he taking pictures?"

"Perhaps he's back working for the press. Out of Albany."

"He's working for you."

"Well, I suppose that's true, but I certainly wouldn't stand in Mr. Harwood's way if he wanted to sell some photos to the media."

"What's going on?" Patricia asked.

Finley turned around and flashed her his most sincere smile. "Just working out with the detective here how best to help you folks deal with this tragic situation. If you'll give me just a moment."

"I don't really need your help anyway," the woman said.

"Well, then, why are you wasting my valuable time?" Finley asked her, turning back to face Duckworth before he had a chance to see the woman's jaw drop.

"Let's go talk over here," Finley said, attempting to lead Duckworth away. But the detective wouldn't move.

"You're in the way," Duckworth said. "I've got dead people up there. Injured people. I want you out of here now."

"Barry, come on," Finley said. "I'm just doing my job, same as you."

"If I have to ask you again, you'll be leaving here in handcuffs."

Finley met the man's gaze. "I'm someone you'd rather have as a friend than an enemy."

"I'd rather have you on the side of a milk carton," Duckworth said, not breaking eye contact.

It was Finley who finally looked away. "David!" he called out, loud enough for anyone nearby to hear him. "The last thing we want to do is get underfoot. Detective Duckworth, thank you for your continued support. God bless you and all the wonderful emergency workers we have here in Promise Falls. I don't know where we would be without you!"

And with that, he headed back to the Lincoln, taking David with him. Duckworth watched until they were both in the car and heading out of the lot.

"You goddamn son of a bitch!"

39

Duckworth turned. Lionel Grayson had tackled a man, brought him down to the ground, and was now pummeling him in the face.

Evidently the demolitions guy had arrived while Duckworth was dealing with Finley. Duckworth ran, grabbed Grayson around the shoulders, and pulled him off the other man.

"Mr. Grayson!" he shouted. "Mr. Grayson, please!"

But Grayson continued to struggle, pointing at the man on the ground. "You son of a bitch! You stupid bastard! You fucking—"

"I didn't do it!" the man shouted back, struggling to his feet. "Listen to me! I'm telling you—"

"Over there!" Duckworth barked at Grayson. He made him stand alongside the ambulance and got himself between the two men. He asked the man who'd been taking the beating, "You Marsden?"

The man stood, brushed himself off. "I am."

"You're the one Mr. Grayson here hired to bring that screen down?"

Marsden nodded, caught his breath. "The screen, and everything else."

"You think maybe you got a little ahead of yourself here?"

"That's what I've been trying to tell him," he said, pointing a finger at Grayson.

"What?" Duckworth asked.

"We haven't done a damn thing here yet. Only thing we've done is signed the contract. My guys weren't coming out for another few days. We haven't planted so much as a firecracker out here."

EIGHT

Cal

I saw it first on CNN the next morning. Flipped over to the *Today* show, found they were covering it, too. All the morning shows were focused on Promise Falls. We were famous. I'd noticed the emergency vehicles the night before, as I stood on the porch next to my brother-in-law, but figured it was probably just a multicar accident.

Turned out to be much bigger.

I'd said my good-byes to Celeste and Dwayne and, having no interest in chasing ambulances, headed home.

I woke around six, but lay in bed for nearly two more hours. There was nothing to get up for, so it didn't make much sense to me to greet the day with any enthusiasm. But a logy head finally forced me to throw back the covers. I padded, barefoot, into the kitchen nook—the apartment wasn't big enough to have an actual kitchen, but a fridge, a stove, and a sink were tucked off into the corner of the living area. I put on some coffee, turned on the small TV beyond the couch—I like having some noise going on in the background—and intended to have a shower while the coffeemaker did its thing, but the first two words I heard were "Promise Falls."

So I stopped. Stood by the couch and watched. When the coffeemaker beeped, I poured myself a cup and continued to watch.

Jesus.

Four dead. A couple in their sixties tentatively identified as Adam and Miriam Chalmers, whose vintage Jag had been turned into a sandwich board by the plummeting screen. And a teenage girl and her boyfriend, seventeen, who'd borrowed his parents' Mustang convertible so he could take her out. Their names hadn't been officially released yet.

There was my old friend Barry Duckworth talking to TV crews that had swarmed in from Albany and beyond.

"Is this an act of terror?" someone shouted at him.

Barry looked at the reporter stone-faced. "We have a long investigation ahead of us. There's nothing at this time to suggest anything remotely connected to terrorism."

"But it was a bomb, wasn't it? The screen didn't just fall down. People say there was a huge explosion."

"Like I said, we're just at the beginning of our investigation."

A number of people who'd gone to enjoy the Constellation Drive-in's last night of business had shot video with their cells and sent it to various media outlets. At least one person was actually recording what was on the screen—something about trucks turning into robots—when all hell broke loose.

So now I knew where all those ambulances had been heading last night when I stood on the porch with Dwayne. I'd figured they were headed to a major car accident on the bypass. Never would have guessed it was something like this.

I gave it about half an hour, left the set on, and had my shower. When I got out, they were still covering it. Matt Lauer was talking to a mother who'd taken her daughter and her daughter's friend. When he was done with them, he brought someone else on camera.

"This is Randall Finley, the former mayor of Promise Falls. You were one of the first to the scene, Mr. Finley. Can you tell us what you saw?"

"Bedlam, Matt. Pure bedlam. It was like a war zone."

Finally someone said it. Every disaster was always "like a war zone." That's how these things were always described by people who'd never seen a war zone.

"I got there as fast as I could to lend help in any way possible. This is a terrible tragedy for the people of Promise Falls and I'm in the process of setting up a relief fund to help the families affected by this disaster. There'll be more later today at 'Randall Finley dot com' for those who want to contribute."

It was laundry day.

I returned to the bedroom and gathered up some stray socks and boxers and tucked them into my laundry bag. Shirts I kept separate in a second bag, which I'd drop off at the dry cleaner's on the way. There were no laundry facilities in my apartment, or anywhere in the building, so I trekked over to a Laundromat several blocks away once a week.

I shaved, got dressed. Made myself a piece of toast with strawberry jam, ate it standing in front of the sink. Washed off the plate and left it there. My mini-palace was also minus a dishwasher, except for me.

I slung the bag over my shoulder and headed out, pockets stuffed with quarters.

My place was right downtown, and being above a bookstore had its advantages. I could have done worse, like renting over a bar. I didn't have to suffer through late-night parties, drunken fights, fried-food smells, people throwing up and taking a piss out back.

Occasionally, when home through the day, which was often, I could hear opera music coming up through the vents. Naman Safar, who ran the place, was an opera buff. I was not, so I never knew whether I was being subjected to Offenbach or Bellini. I'd broken the music down into two categories. Some of it was annoying, and some of it was less annoying. But none of it was annoying enough that I ever complained to Naman. He was, after all, my landlord, and it was smart to stay on his good side in case the toilet plugged up or I started hearing mice in the walls.

The door to my place—it was the one with the very small plaque that read CAL WEAVER INVESTIGATIONS—opened from the sidewalk right onto a flight of stairs and was directly beside the entrance to Naman's Books. As I was coming out, he was going in. The sign in Naman's window said he opened at ten, but that was only an approximation. Some days he was there early, but most days he didn't open up until at least half past. Today was one of those days. It didn't matter to his customers, who knew better than to come before eleven. They also knew there was a good chance Naman might be there hours after closing time.

"There's nothing to do at home," he told me once. He'd never married, had no kids. "I get bored."

Born in Egypt, Naman and his family moved to America when he was nine. He'd majored in English literature and taught high school for a couple of decades, but trying to manage a classroom full of kids eventually became too much for him. He didn't know whether he'd become less tolerant or the students had gotten worse. Either way, he opted for running a shop that was devoted to his love of books.

"Did you hear?" he asked when he saw me.

"I heard," I said.

"A shock. A terrible shock. They are saying it could be terrorism."

"A bit early to say."

"Yes, yes, I agree. That's the first thing everybody thinks these days. This country is totally paranoid. Everyone is out to get America."

I wasn't up for a discussion of America's temperament.

"Laundry day?" Naman asked.

"Heading over now. Catch you later."

The Laundromat was five blocks from home, the dry cleaner en route. I dropped off the shirts, continued on. The place wasn't that busy. I'd found midmorning was a good time to be sure of getting a couple of machines.

The woman who ran the joint—Samantha Worthington was her name, but she went by Sam—was taking a rag to a washer, wiping away spilled soap.

"Hey, Sam," I said.

She gave me a nod. She didn't talk a lot.

I didn't know much about her, except that she had a nine-year-old kid named Carl. He hung out here after school many days. She was an attractive woman, but there was a hardness about her. She'd been through things. She looked thirty-five, but I was betting she was late twenties.

"Hey," I said.

She glanced my way. "Hey," she said back. "Hear about the drive-in?"

"Terrible," I said.

That seemed to cover it. She went into the office at the back, returned with a small leather bag. Using a key, she unlocked the coin boxes on each of the machines and dumped quarters into the bag. She drew the drawstring tight at the top and went back into the office, where I was betting she had a machine that would collect those quarters into neat stacks for taking to the bank.

I dumped my stuff into two machines, dug to the bottom of the bag for the box of soap powder and the plastic bottle of fabric softener I'd brought along, poured them into both washers, and closed the lids. I brought out all the quarters from my pocket, fed them into the appropriate slots, and drove them home.

As always, I'd brought a book, one I'd picked up at Naman's. A Philip Roth novel. I'd only gotten around to him recently, starting with *The Plot Against America*, but today I was into *Nemesis*, about a polio epidemic in 1940s Newark. I guess I'd been thinking that reading about people whose problems were as bad as my own or worse might have the effect of putting things into perspective.

No, don't think that way, I told myself. No self-pity. It was like I'd told Celeste. Had to look forward, not backward. No sense worrying about things that could not be undone.

I grabbed a spot on the bench from where I could keep an eye on my two washers, set the box of soap and the bottle of softener next to me, and opened the novel to where I'd last left my bookmark.

I'd read only a couple of pages when I heard, "What do you think?"

I looked up. It was Sam.

"It's good," I said.

"Some people say he's a misogynist, but I don't buy it," Sam said. "Have you read *The Human Stain*?"

I shook my head.

"It's about a college professor who has an affair with this woman who's a janitor. He gets accused of racism by

46

two black students, but what no one realizes is—whoa, I shouldn't tell you if you haven't read it."

"Okay," I said. "I might get to it at some point." I managed a smile. "I've only read a couple of books by him. You?"

"Most of them," she said. "The one on baseball did nothing for me. And there's a satire about Watergate or something, which I couldn't care less about." Sam leaned her head back, like she was sizing me up. "You're thinking, a woman who runs a Laundromat reads?"

"I wasn't thinking that," I said.

"Or if she does read, it's just *Fifty Shades* shit," she said.

"I really wasn't giving your reading habits much thought, one way or another," I said. "But thanks for the recommendation. *The Human Stain*, you said?"

"Yeah." Sam smiled. "Sorry, didn't mean to give you a hard time there."

"It's okay."

The opening of the Laundromat door caught her eye. It was a man, six feet, pushing two fifty, dark, greasy black hair, stubble on his neck and cheeks, jeans and jean jacket.

I noticed he didn't have any laundry with him. Just a swagger.

"Excuse me," Sam said, and walked toward the door. "Get out of here, Ed," she told the man.

Ed opened his arms wide in innocence. "Hey, just dropping by to say hello."

"I told you, get out."

"I thought I might do my laundry?"

"Where is it?" she asked.

"Huh?"

"Your fucking laundry. You forget that?"

47

Ed grinned. "Guessin' I did." The grin broadened. "Brandon's folks say hi."

"You can tell Brandon's psycho parents, and Brandon, too, that they can kiss my ass."

"Not me, too? Because I wouldn't mind."

I put the book down.

"I know the lawyers have been in touch," Ed said, "but I thought I'd drop by to reinforce what they had to say. Carl's going home."

"Carl *is* home. If he's with me, he's home."

"Well, from what I understand, that home is not suitable, Samantha. It's an unfit environment."

"You think Carl'd be better off being raised by his dad? Getting some time every day in the exercise yard? Making license plates in the machine shop? Sounds like real father–son bonding time."

"Now you're just being silly. Brandon's folks are ready to step up and do the right thing just as soon as you come to your senses. And right now, they're playing nice, just using the lawyers. You don't want it to go beyond that, do you?"

I said, "Is there a problem here?"

I was standing just behind and to the side of Sam, my hands positioned unthreateningly behind my back. She turned when she heard my voice, and Ed squinted at me.

"I think there is now," Ed said. "The lady and I are talkin', pal. I think it's time you moved your panties into the dryer."

I said to Sam, "Is this man bothering you?"

"It's okay," she said. "Ed's leaving."

"That right, Ed?" I asked.

He looked back at Sam and said, "You fucking this one, too?"

48

Sam opened her mouth to speak, but nothing came out.

"You don't speak to a lady that way," I said.

Ed fixed his eyes on me again. "Excuse me?"

"Apologize."

"Apologize?"

"About a block down, there's a clinic where you can get your ears tested, if there's something wrong with your hearing."

That was when he decided to have a go at me. Started to pull his right arm back, planted his left foot forward. When the punch was just starting to come my way, I brought my hands out from behind my back and tossed the powdered soap I'd been keeping in my right into his face.

"Shit!" he said, stopping the swing halfway, putting both hands to his eyes.

That was when I drove a fist into his considerable gut. It was like punching a massive Pillsbury Doughboy. Or maybe the Michelin Man.

Didn't really matter.

What mattered was that he dropped to the floor like a sack of cement, gasping for air, still unable to see.

I felt like giving him a good swift kick while he was down there, and might have, but the ding from my cell phone indicated I'd just received a text. I reached into my pocket, glanced at the screen, which read *Lucy Brighton*.

The message was: *Please call. URGENT.*

I said to Ed, "Don't move or I'll add fabric softener." He kept wiping his eyes.

I brought up Lucy Brighton's number from my contacts list, dialed.

"Oh, Cal, thank you," Lucy said, her voice shaky. "You remember me?"

49

"Of course," I said. A recent investigation involving a student and the school board had brought us together. A former teacher and guidance counselor, she now worked as an administrator at the board office. "What's wrong? Another school thing?"

"No, not this time. It's . . . more personal."

"You want to meet?" I asked, watching Ed brush soap powder from his eyes.

She didn't immediately answer. I had the sense she was trying to hold it together.

"I think something has happened. At my parents' house. Well, my father and his wife." She paused, collecting herself. "His third wife, actually. Something's not right there. At the house. Something might have been taken—I'm not sure. There might have been a break-in. It's . . . very hard to explain."

"And you're taking this on instead of your father, and his wife, why?"

"Because they're dead," Lucy Brighton said. "Last night. At the drive-in. My father's car was crushed."

NINE

"You're awfully quiet," Arlene Harwood remarked.

"It was a late night," her son, David, said.

They were in the kitchen of his house. David's nine-year-old son, Ethan, was already off to school, and David's father, Don, was back at the elder couple's house, checking in on the rebuilding of the kitchen since the fire. Arlene would probably head over and join him shortly.

"It must have been awful," she said.

"Which part?"

Of course, he knew the worst part was what had happened to those people in the cars that had been crushed by the toppling screen. But almost as horrible were the antics of his new boss. Finley had no sense of propriety. No idea of what constituted appropriate behavior.

In other words, he had no shame.

At least Finley'd had the good sense to get out of there before Duckworth slapped the cuffs on him. All the people with phones out—for sure someone would have gotten a picture. So the dumbass dodged a bullet there.

David had to talk to him, try to make him understand that his efforts to raise his profile ran the risk of backfiring spectacularly. The problem was, Finley wasn't very good about accepting advice. The man simply did not listen to anything but the big, stupid voice in his own head. David wondered whether it would be worth talking to his wife, Jane. Finley didn't talk about her much, and ignored David when he suggested bringing her into the discussion. Maybe Jane Finley could persuade her husband to dial it back a bit. Although, David guessed, she might well have been trying to do that through their entire marriage.

"What do you mean, which part?" Arlene asked.

"Nothing," David said, sitting at the kitchen table, scanning news stories on the drive-in disaster on his laptop. "It was all bad. I've never seen anything like it."

"There's just been so much sadness," she said, pouring a coffee for herself.

David knew she was really talking about her sister, Agnes, not what had happened at the drive-in. Agnes wasn't the first to jump to her death from Promise Falls, and probably wouldn't be the last, but her suicide had attracted more attention than any other in recent memory. First of all, as the boss of the local hospital, she'd been a prominent member of the community. But when it came out that she'd tricked her own daughter into believing her newborn baby had died, she was labeled a monster.

David believed the judgments being made about his aunt troubled Arlene nearly as much as her sister's death. Arlene herself had called Agnes a monster shortly before she'd killed herself.

David figured Agnes had known it to be true. Unlike the town's former mayor, Agnes had had a capacity for shame.

But in the days since Agnes's death, Arlene had been trying to come to understand her sister, trying to figure out her motivations. "She wasn't a completely terrible person," she'd said several times in recent days. Trying to

52

convince herself, as much as others, David suspected.

But while Agnes was very much on Arlene's mind, she wasn't occupying David's thoughts. He was thinking about last night's disaster, his job, and one other matter.

Sam Worthington.

He'd been reaching out to her, trying to explain he hadn't done anything—at least not intentionally—to betray her. Someone had evidently taken pictures through her kitchen window of the two of them having sex, and now the pics were being used as evidence that she was somehow an unfit mother.

He felt sick about it.

He'd tried calling her several times, left messages. He'd considered knocking on her door, but the first time he'd tried, before he'd ever actually met her, he'd found himself staring down the barrel of a shotgun. The last time Sam spoke to him, she'd promised him the next time he showed up, she'd pull the trigger.

He'd been considering dropping by her place of work. Sam wouldn't shoot him in the middle of the Laundromat, would she?

David wasn't sure he was cut out for this much drama. He'd had more than enough of it with his now late wife, Jan. The whole episode with Marla and her baby had left him shaken. And working with Finley was no bucket of joy, either. His reporting days hadn't prepared him for this kind of unrelenting stress. He'd never been a war correspondent. He hadn't been Woodward or Bernstein. He'd always been a small-town reporter.

"I don't know if I'm up to all this," he said.

"What's that?" his mother asked.

"Nothing."

"Have you talked to your father lately?" Arlene asked.

"Of course. I talk to him every day. We all live together, Mom."

He was sorry as soon as he said it.

"Don't you worry. We'll be gone soon," she said. "Another few weeks and we'll be out of your hair. Your father says they're coming along really well with the work. They're ahead of schedule." A pause. "Lucky for you."

"I'm sorry. I didn't mean it the way it sounded. And yes, I talk to Dad. Why?"

"I don't mean the simple day-to-day stuff. I mean really *talked* to him."

"Yeah, I have. Back when I was debating whether to accept the job with Finley, Dad and I had a heart-to-heart. He was the one who said I should take it."

"So now you blame your father that you're having to deal with that man?"

"I didn't say that," David said. "It was my decision. I needed a job. Why are you worried about Dad? What's going on?"

"He just has a lot on his mind. You should talk to him sometime about it."

"Is he okay? Is this about his heart?"

Arlene shook her head. "His heart's fine." She waved a hand at him. "Forget I even brought this up."

He was about to pursue this further when his cell phone, resting facedown on the table next to the laptop, vibrated. He turned it over, looked at the screen.

"Shit," he said.

There was a time when his mother might have reprimanded him for that, but not today.

"Him?" she asked.

David nodded. He picked up the phone and put it to his ear.

"Yeah," he said.

"Genius!" Randall Finley said. "Sheer genius!"

"I'm sorry, Randy. What are you talking about?"

"Your idea about setting up a fund! To help the drive-in disaster victims! They ate that right up. I was on the fucking *Today* show. Some of the Albany media are already running with it." He laughed. "Bringing you on wasn't such a bad idea after all."

"Randy, I—"

"I was just kidding about that. Hiring you, that's one of the smartest moves I've made lately. You got good instincts."

"I'll make sure the account's up and running first thing," David said. "I already talked to the bank, let them know we'd be doing this."

"Good, good. What you need to do now is—maybe some big company wants to cough up a few thousand or something. We need to get a picture of them giving me the check. Why don't you start calling around? You know what? Call Gloria Fenwick. She's wrapping up Five Mountains. Ask her if her bosses would like to make a generous contribution so we'd have something to remember them by other than abandoning our community."

I hate myself, David thought.

"I'll see what I can do," he said.

"We'll touch base a little later. But I'm going to be unavailable at lunch."

David didn't know about any lunch meeting the would-be mayor had. He was supposed to keep him up-to-date on any changes in the schedule. "What's going on?"

"I'm meeting with Francis. Frank."

"Frank who?"

"Frank Mancini."

David put the index finger of his free hand on the laptop track pad. He scrolled back up a story he'd been reading, looking for something he'd just come across.

He found this:

> *The drive-in property had recently been sold to Mancini Homes, presumably for a housing development, although that could not be confirmed. The company has not returned calls, or answered e-mails, regarding its plans.*

"You there?" Finley asked.

"This is the Mancini Homes guy? A developer?"

"That's right."

"The one who's bought the drive-in land."

"Yeah," said Finley, a hint of caution in his voice.

"If you're meeting with him to discuss the accident, I should be there. I need to know what your strategy is here, Randy. How are you planning to spin this?"

"This has nothing to do with what happened, David," Finley said.

"If it's got nothing to do with it, why are you in a rush to set up a meeting with this guy?"

"I'm not in a rush," Finley said. "This meeting was set up a long time ago."

"Wait. What?"

"Don't worry about it," Finley said. "It's got nothing to do with you. Like I said, we'll touch base this afternoon. And, David, again, thanks for the idea. Top-shelf, that one. You're gonna make me the poster boy for humanitarianism." The man laughed. "One day, they'll erect a statue in my honor that the pigeons can shit all over."

Before David could ask him another question, Finley had hung up.

TEN

"So how've you been, Vick?"

Victor Rooney struggled to sit up straight in the chair. He was tired, and a little hungover, but when he'd gotten up this morning, he'd done his best to make himself look presentable for a job interview, although he wasn't entirely sure that the man behind the desk, the man he hoped might hire him, was aware this was a job interview. So far as he knew, Victor had dropped by to say hello.

"Pretty decent, Stan," Victor said. "Not bad, all things considered."

Stan Mulgrew owned Mulgrew & Son Fittings, even though he was the son. His father, Edmund, had died the year before, and now Stan was running the business, which made industrial fittings. Stan didn't want to change the name to just "Mulgrew Fittings." Didn't sound as personal. So he left the "& Son" even though he had three daughters, none of whom showed the slightest interest in pursuing a career in the manufacture of quality brass fittings.

"Haven't seen you in a while," said Stan. "Not since high school?"

"I don't think so," Victor said. "You're looking good."

"Yeah," said Stan. "Thanks."

What else could he say? If he'd returned the compliment, Victor wouldn't have believed it. He knew he didn't look all that great. He'd lost enough weight that his clothes were starting to hang off him, there were dark circles under his eyes, and he'd missed a couple of spots when he'd shaved this morning.

"I just wanted to say," Stan said hesitantly, "that even though it's been—I don't know—a few years ..."

"Three," Victor said.

"Three, yeah, wow, I thought it was actually longer. But anyway, I'm awful sorry about Olivia. You guys were going to get married, right?"

Victor shook his head. "That's right."

Stan grimaced. "Hell of a thing. They still haven't caught the sick fuck who did it, have they?"

"No," Victor said.

"And, Jesus, this thing that happened last night at the Constellation? That's totally unfuckingbelievable. They're saying it was a bomb. Can you believe that? I hear it was the demolition people who were going to bring the screen down next week, that they totally screwed things up."

Victor studied the pens and stapler sitting on top of Stan's desk. "That sounds like what probably happened. Pretty awful thing."

"Part of me—this is crazy, I know—but part of me kind of wishes I'd been there. Just to see the screen come down. Must have been wild."

"Maybe you'll get lucky when something else bad happens," Victor said.

"What?"

"I'm saying, maybe someday you'll be around when something else terrible goes down. So you can say you were there. I read somewhere that there are people who say they were in New York on 9/11 but weren't anywhere near it. Because they think it makes them seem more important or something."

"Is that what you think I'm saying?" Stan asked.

"Shit, no. It was just a thought that popped into my head." Victor grinned. "That happens to me a lot. Some random idea just hits me."

"Well, believe me, I'm not praying for more tragedies or anything. But anyway, what's up? To what do I owe the honor?"

Victor Rooney shrugged. "I was thinking, we hadn't seen each other in a long while, and I was on the high school Facebook page, the one for people who've graduated and like to keep in touch, and I saw your picture, and wondered what you're up to, and thought I'd drop by."

"Nice," Stan said, nodding slowly. "You know, nice."

"And I had something I wanted to give to you." Victor reached into his jacket and pulled out an unsealed envelope. He took out an unevenly folded sheet of paper and handed it across the desk.

"What's this?"

"That's my résumé," Victor said.

"Oh," Stan said, setting the paper on his desk, taking note of a grease stain that had turned the paper translucent. "We're not hiring right now, Victor."

"Yeah, but I wanted to drop that off anyway. In case. You look on there, you'll see I have experience. I know all sorts of mechanical-type things. I know how to run machines. I know electrical work. Something doesn't work, I can get it going. And anything I'd need to know here at your place, I'm a fast learner. I can put just about anything together. I didn't actually get my engineering degree—I kind of dropped out after Olivia passed away—but I learned a lot. I'm thinking of going back, finishing it."

Stan glanced at the page for a full three seconds. "You worked one summer at the water plant, and I see here you were with the Promise Falls Fire Department." He took a closer look, frowned. "But not for long."

"But while I was there, I did good work. You know, reasonable."

"Why'd you leave? A job with the Promise Falls Fire Department, that's like a job for life."

"I was . . . having some problems at the time."

Stan studied him. "What kind of problems, Vick?"

"You know, I guess I was still dealing with Olivia."

Stan nodded sympathetically. "Sure, of course."

"So, I went through a period . . . when I didn't quite have it all together. So I had to leave. Go for, you know, treatment. Kind of put the pieces back together."

A moment of silence passed between them. "So how'd that go, Vick? Do you have it together now?"

"You think I don't?"

Stan swallowed. "You just—I mean, forgive me for saying this, but you look like you had kind of a rough night. Your eyes look a bit bloodshot."

Victor's eyes narrowed. "They always look like that. And I started running last night, so I'm kind of tired."

"Running?"

"You know, trying to get back in shape. Didn't get real far. About half a mile. But I'm building up slowly." It was true. The part he'd left out was that after half a mile he was throwing up. He'd walked home and had a drink.

"Sure, I guess that could be it," Stan said, trying to sound as though he actually believed it.

"You don't believe me," Victor said.

Stan shrugged. "Look, it's not up to me to judge, Vick." He raised the piece of paper in his hands. "Why don't I hang on to this? Keep it on file. And if something comes up, I can give you a call. But I'm sure I don't have to tell you, we've been going through a real slowdown lately. Who hasn't, right? Just about everybody I know isn't doing as good as they were a year ago." He raised his hands in a gesture of futility. "I had to let a couple guys go in the last six months, and if I did do any hiring, I'd have to bring them back first, if they haven't found something else. And odds are, they haven't. I hope you understand."

Victor rolled his tongue along the inside of his cheek. "Yeah, sure."

"You might want to consider looking elsewhere. Like Albany, Schenectady, Binghamton."

"I'm not leaving Promise Falls," Victor Rooney said. "I've got a history here. This is my town."

"Maybe, if you're interested in anything part-time, if something like that came up, I could give you a shout." He glanced back down at the page for a second. "Your number is on there—that's good." He smiled.

Victor stood up.

"You're no better than the rest of them," he said.

"I'm sorry. I don't know what you're—"

"The ones who did fuck all."

That took a moment to sink in. Finally, Stan stood up from his chair. "Come on, Vick, that's pretty low."

"No one in this town has the guts to do what's right."

"I don't know about that. Sometimes, people, they want to do the right thing, but they're scared. They're kind of, you know, frozen. By the time they know what the right thing to do is, it's too late."

"You sound like you speak from experience," Victor said. "Makes me wonder if you were one of them. The police, after all the interviews they did, figured there was twenty-two—whaddya call 'em—eyewitnesses, but they never released the names. The paper tried to get them but couldn't. For all I know, you were on the list."

"For Christ's sake, Vick, I wasn't."

"You give me a job, you try to do the right thing now, maybe I could find it in my heart to forgive you."

Stan pushed back his chair an inch. "Excuse me?"

"I'm saying, you could hire me. Do some good."

"I don't owe you anything, Vick. I got no reason to ask for your forgiveness. And even if I wanted to give you a job, which, frankly, I don't, I can't just pull one out of my ass." He shook his head sadly. "Look, I'll hang on to your résumé. Maybe, if something comes up sometime, I'll have forgotten how you just behaved here."

Victor stared at the man.

"Did you hear her screams?" he asked.

"What?"

"When Olivia was being killed. Did you hear the screams?"

"Vick, you should go."

"It's a simple question."

"I wasn't even *in* Promise Falls then," Stan said, sighing. "I was in England. I was staying with my aunt and uncle. Working over there for a few months. I was reading the *Standard*, online. That's how I found out about it. Couldn't believe it, it was so horrible."

"Sure."

"You should talk to somebody, Vick. Or whoever you

63

were talking to, you should go talk to them again."

Victor turned and headed for the door.

"Come on, man," Stan Mulgrew said. "Look, I'm sorry. I know you've been through hell. Maybe there's some other way I can help you out. Why don't we have lunch? How 'bout you come back later—we go get a beer?" He choked on the word. "Well, maybe not a beer, if, like you say, you're trying to stay off the stuff and—"

Victor kept on going.

Stan came around the desk and followed his onetime high school friend out to the parking lot.

"I didn't mean to offend you," he said. "If I offended you, I'm sorry."

Victor got behind the wheel of his old van, slammed the door, and, without looking Stan's way, gave him the finger as he drove off.

ELEVEN

Cal

I agreed to meet Lucy Brighton at her father's house within the hour.

Once Ed was back on his feet, and had blinked the soap powder out of his eyes, he stumbled out of the Laundromat. I'd moved my wet clothes into a dryer and had about thirty minutes to go, which I figured was enough time for him to send the police my way. But no officer from the Promise Falls department materialized by the time I'd folded my boxers, so I was guessing Ed—last name unknown—had decided not to press charges.

Just as well, because I really didn't know how many friends I still had on the force.

I'd given Sam Worthington one of my business cards and said, "If he gives you any more trouble, call me. Or call the cops."

She took the card but did not look at it. "Don't get involved in my troubles," she said, and went back to cleaning the machines.

Everyone expresses gratitude in his or her own way.

I walked back to my place, dropped off the laundry, and got into my Accord, which I kept parked around the back of the bookshop. Lucy Brighton had given me an address on Skelton Drive, which I remembered as a nice part of town. The house, a sprawling ranch with a two-car garage and a deep, well-tended front yard, enjoyed the shade of several stately oak trees that had probably gotten their start before Promise Falls had been incorporated.

Lucy Brighton had said she would wait for me in the driveway, and that was where I found her, alone, behind the wheel of a silver Buick. She got out of the car as I pulled in.

I stood an inch under six feet, and I recalled from when I'd met her before that she could look me straight in the eye through her wire-framed, oval glasses. Everything about her seemed vertical. She had straight brown hair that fell to her shoulders, a long, narrow nose, a light jacket that went down to midcalf, and perfectly creased black slacks.

Her brown eyes were largely red right now, and she took off her glasses briefly to dab them with the wadded tissue in her hand.

"Cal, thank you for coming."

"I'm very sorry," I said.

"This is the last thing I need to be dealing with. I've just come from the . . . the morgue, I guess they call it." She put her hand briefly over her mouth, composing herself. "I had to identify my . . . it was horrible. I wanted to think there'd been a mistake, but it was him. It was my father. Someone else will have to identify Miriam. I'm not really next of kin. Her brother's going to come up, from Providence. It was so . . . so . . . it doesn't make any sense, for something like this to happen."

"No," I said.

"They were going to demolish the screen in another week," she said. "Someone made a mistake. How could someone make a mistake like that?"

"I don't know," I said. "I'm sure they'll get to the bottom

of it." I started to wonder whether this was the real reason she'd wanted to speak with me. Did she want me looking into who was responsible for the drive-in disaster? If she did, she'd be wasting her money. The Promise Falls police would most likely be getting state and federal help. Homeland Security might even be sticking its nose in if they thought it was more than some screwup by a demolitions firm. Collectively, all those levels of investigation would do a better job than I could.

"I'm probably in some kind of shock," Lucy Brighton said. "Like I'm walking around in a fog. Like none of this is happening. It *can't* be happening."

"You seem to be holding it together."

"If this is holding it together, I'd hate to think what losing it'll feel like. Because I guarantee you, that's coming. I don't know when they're going to release him to the funeral home. There's so much to arrange. People to phone, relatives who may want to fly in."

I remembered that she was divorced. I wondered what kind of family support she had right now.

"Your ex-husband," I said. "Is he coming?"

She laughed. "Yeah, right, Gerald. Mr. There-for-You."

"I guess that's a no."

"He's in San Francisco. I've called and told him, but he hasn't got enough money to get a bus to L.A., let alone fly back here. And the truth is, I'm just as glad. It gets Crystal all agitated when he comes, and that's the last thing she needs."

Her daughter. Lucy had mentioned her before, but I'd never met her.

"Agitated how?"

"Crystal has this fantasy view of her father, that he's not with us because he's doing something even more

67

important. Fighting aliens, saving whales, building some colossal shield that will stop global warming. She doesn't want to consider that the reason he's not with us, doesn't come to visit his own daughter, is because he just doesn't care. Not that she actually talks about how she feels or anything. But it all comes through in her drawings."

"Drawings?"

Lucy waved a hand. "It doesn't matter. I didn't call you to bore you with my personal life."

And then, suddenly, she put both hands over her mouth and turned away from me, her shoulders hunched and shaking. "I'm sorry," she managed to say, not looking at me.

I rested a tentative hand on her shoulder, left it there for a good five seconds before taking it away. "It's okay. You're on overload. Anyone would be."

She sniffed a couple of times, used the wadded tissue to wipe her nose. She half turned back toward me. "Crystal's only eleven. It'd be hard enough to explain to any child that sometimes parents aren't there for you. But to explain it to Crystal . . ."

"I don't understand."

Another sniff. "She's just . . . not like other kids." Lucy tucked the tissue into her purse, attempted to stand straighter. "It's fine. Everything is fine. She's staying with a friend right now while I deal with this. I didn't want to bring her here, not after what's happened."

Lucy swallowed hard, lifted her chin. She was determined to get through this, whatever this was. I still had no real idea why we were here, in front of this house.

"Okay," I said. "Suppose you tell me why you called."

She focused on the house, looking at it with what almost seemed a sense of wonder. No, not wonder. More like trepidation. "Something's not right here," she said.

"You said you thought there was a break-in."

"I think so."

"You came out to the house this morning? After you heard your parents were killed at the drive-in?"

Lucy shot me a look. "Not my parents. My father, and his wife."

"Adam Chalmers was your father, but Miriam . . ."

"His third wife," Lucy said. "My mother died when I was in my teens. Then my father remarried, to Felicia, and that lasted six years before she left him, and then Miriam came along."

"Were you close with her?"

"No," Lucy said. "I suppose . . . I suppose I disapproved."

"Why?"

She hesitated. "I don't want to be that kind of person."

"What kind of person?"

"The neighborhood priss-ass," Lucy said.

Lucy Brighton had never struck me that way. From the first time I'd met her, she'd struck me as open-minded, nonjudgmental. She exuded a kind of athletic sexuality. I hadn't asked, but would have guessed she was a onetime track star, or gymnast. She had the build for it. When nonprofessional thoughts crossed my mind, it occurred to me that she had the build for a number of things.

"I doubt you're that kind of person."

"It bothered me that Miriam was younger than I am," she said.

"How old was she?"

"Thirty. I'm thirty-three, and my father is—*was* fifty-nine. Do you know how strange it is—how *weird* it is—to be three years older than a woman who goes

69

around claiming she's your stepmother?"

"I guess that'd be odd."

"The only woman who was age appropriate for my father was my mother. They married when they were both twenty. Thirteen years later, she died, and within a year my father remarried."

"To Felicia."

Lucy nodded. "At least she was older than me, but only by five years. Nineteen years old. Anyone could have guessed that wasn't going to work out, and six years later she left him. It took a while for the divorce to be finalized, and while that was going on, Dad went out with plenty of other women, and then he found Miriam three years ago. Twenty-nine years' difference in their ages."

I was doing some basic math in my head. Calculating the age difference between Lucy and myself. A decade, give or take.

"It happens," I said.

"I know. And I should have been able to roll with it, but it embarrassed me, that my father wasn't able to act his age. I think he made a fool of himself. That Miriam may have made a fool of him. That he . . ."

I waited.

"That he may have been drawn into things to try to prove to her, to prove to himself, that he was still a young man."

"A man on the verge of sixty may be trying to prove something to himself, and to others. That he isn't really old."

But it was time to get back to why she'd called me here.

"Why do you think someone broke in?"

She took a deep breath. "When I heard about what had

happened, when the police got in touch, I came over here. I didn't know quite what else to do, but I also knew that sooner or later I was going to have to pick out clothes, for the funeral home, and then there'd be the whole matter of what to do with the house and ..."

"And what?"

"When I stepped into the house, I heard the back door close. Someone was leaving as I was coming in."

TWELVE

Angus Carlson was managing on less than two hours' sleep.

He hadn't returned home until shortly after four in the morning. After leaving the drive-in, he'd gone first to the address registered to the crushed 2006 Mustang convertible. It belonged to Floyd and Renata Gravelle, of Canterbury Street, but it was highly unlikely it was Floyd or Renata in the car, given that the male and female victims appeared to be in their teens.

He had to ring the bell twice, leaning on it pretty hard the second time, to wake anyone. After a minute, he heard someone yell, "Coming!" Another minute after that, a man in his pajamas opened the front door, joined seconds later by a woman tying the sash of her robe.

Carlson apologized, identified himself, confirmed their identities, and asked whether they owned a Mustang convertible.

"Yes," Renata said. "But it's not here right now. Galen has it. That's our son. Has there been—oh my God."

"What's happened?" Floyd asked.

"Do you know if your son was taking someone on a date with him tonight? To the drive-in?"

Floyd looked to his wife. She said, "He was taking Lisa. Lisa Kroft."

"Would you have an address for Lisa, ma'am?"

"What's happened?" the father asked again.

It did not go well. Nor did it go any better at the Kroft household. He felt wrung out by the time he'd been to those two houses. But he wasn't done.

At the home of Adam Chalmers, he'd been unable to raise anyone. Which told him it was likely Chalmers and his wife lived here alone. Now the trick was going to be locating next of kin.

Carlson noticed a sticker in the window of the Chalmers home, indicating that it was protected by UNYSS. Upper New York State Security, a monitoring firm that covered a large area north and east of Albany. Carlson made a call to the twenty-four-hour line, identified himself, and explained that he was trying to find anyone related to Adam Chalmers. After conferring with a supervisor, the man on duty consulted their files and said there was a Lucy Brighton listed as a contact. If the alarm went off, and UNYSS could not reach Mr. Chalmers, the next call would be to Ms. Brighton. A phone number was provided, after some verbal arm-twisting, to Carlson.

You couldn't phone someone in the middle of the night with this kind of news. You had to go to the door. So he Googled the number from his phone and came up with an address on Promise Falls' south side. A split-level with a Buick sedan in the driveway.

Again, it took several rings of the doorbell to raise someone, but Lucy Brighton finally appeared, trailed by a sleepy-eyed young girl who just stood there but didn't say anything. The child obeyed when the woman told her to go back upstairs to bed, her arms hanging straight down at her sides as she walked.

Weird kid.

Lucy Brighton's cry of despair when he told her the news brought her daughter back, although Ms. Brighton didn't know she was standing there when she said, "Dad was telling me, just the other day, about the drive-in closing, about it having its last night, how he might go but hadn't made up his mind. He's a huge film buff, he's written for the movies, and . . . I can't believe this. I can't believe it. There must be some mistake. What was the car?"

"A Jaguar. An old classic one, red. An E-Type, I think." Carlson, who'd worked out of a cruiser for years, knew every kind of car out there, even the antiques.

Lucy Brighton put a hand on the wall to steady herself. "Was the license plate AFV-5218?" the girl asked. Her mother turned, saw that her daughter had returned.

"Oh, Crystal." She reached out an arm and pulled her daughter close.

"Uh," said Carlson, glancing at his notes, "yes. That is the plate." He looked at the girl. "You have a good memory."

"Has something happened to Grandpa's car?" To the police detective, Crystal said, "It's an antique."

"I'm afraid so," Carlson said.

"I like that car."

"I bet."

"Sweetheart," Lucy said, "I'm just trying to find out what—"

"Are they dead?"

Lucy hugged the child, patted her head. "It's okay. It's going to be okay."

"I hope they're not dead," she said flatly, trying to free herself. "I'm supposed to go over there on Saturday when you go to the conference. I like to go over." Crystal said

74

to Carlson, "My grandpa has pinball games in his basement."

"Is that so?" Carlson said.

"Miriam is nice to me. She isn't my grandmother, but she's nice to me."

"Sweetheart, please go up to bed. I'll come see you after the policeman leaves."

"Okay." Crystal made the trip back up the stairs.

"I just have a few more questions," Carlson said. But he also had information to pass along, including where the bodies would be taken. In another ten minutes, he was out of there.

He headed home to get some sleep before reporting back to the station at eight. He entered the house as quietly as possible, but those damned hardwood floors gave him away every time. The boards creaked under his feet as he came inside.

"Angus?" The voice came from upstairs.

"Just me. Go back to sleep, Gale."

A woman in her thirties appeared at the second-floor landing. She flipped on a light. She had short, streaked hair and wore a frayed housecoat. "This is way past the end of your shift." Not an accusation, just a statement of fact.

"I would have called, but then I'd have just woken you up."

"What's going on?"

"There was a crazy thing. The screen at the drive-in fell over, killed some people."

"Oh my God, how could that happen?"

He waved his hand tiredly, too weary to explain. "Who knows? Just go back to sleep."

"I was awake anyway."

75

"Still, you should—"

"I was thinking."

"I gotta eat something," he said, and went into the kitchen.

Gale descended the stairs, followed him, asked what he wanted. There was some leftover beef stew she could reheat in the microwave. Or, given that the clock was closer to breakfast than dinner, she could scramble him some eggs.

He opened the refrigerator, took out a beer. "This'll do for now."

"I was thinking that—"

"I'm really tired. Do we have to do this now?"

"You don't even know what I'm going to say."

"I don't?" he said before drawing on the bottle, wiping his mouth with the back of his hand. "Let me see if I can guess." He opened a hamper in the fridge, took out some wrapped deli meat, put the package on the counter, and ripped it open. He grabbed a handful of thinly shaved Italian salami and shoved it into his mouth.

"You think we're ready," he said. "Your biological clock is ticking. If we're ever going to do it, now is the time. Why should we wait? A child will make us a family." He cocked his head at her. "How'm I doing?"

Her eyes were starting to swim.

"Thought so," Carlson said.

"You'd be a wonderful father," Gale said. "I know you would."

"That's not what I'm worried about," he said, shoving another handful of meat into his mouth.

"You're worried about me? That's it? You're saying I won't be a good mother?"

"That's not what I mean," he said, although it came

out much less clear than that with his mouth full of salami.

"That's what you think."

"No one has a kid thinking they're going to be anything less than a great mother. A great parent. It's after they have the kid they find out they're no good at it."

"I know we'd be good."

Angus Carlson studied her. "No one knows anything for sure."

"It doesn't have to be the way it was for you," she said, reaching out, touching his arm. "Just because your mother—"

He pulled away. "I've got to get some sleep. I have to be in early."

He set his phone to wake him in two hours. Thirty minutes after that, he was at the station, expecting to head back out to the drive-in, but Duckworth had other ideas.

"Some bomb experts from the state are helping us at the site today. We've got plenty of uniformed officers interviewing witnesses, people who were there, who'd gone to see the movie. I want you out at Thackeray."

Thackeray College?

"What do you want me out there for?" Carlson asked.

"The Mason Helt business," Duckworth said.

Mason Helt, the Thackeray student who'd been shot dead by the college's head of security. Helt had been killed after attacking Thackeray security guard Joyce Pilgrim, who'd been acting as a decoy, hoping to get the attention of whoever had grabbed and molested three female Thackeray students.

"What's left to do?" Carlson said. "They got the guy."

77

Duckworth said, "According to Ms. Pilgrim, before Helt died, he said something about being put up to this, like it was a gig, a hired performance. I want to know what the others have to say. If there was someone else involved, we need to know."

"You think I'm not good enough to work the drive-in," Carlson said.

Duckworth shot him a look, but sidestepped the accusation. "If that screen hadn't fallen over last night, I'd be at Thackeray myself this morning asking questions."

Carlson said, "Fine."

Duckworth started to walk away, paused, turned back. "About Duncomb."

"Duncomb?"

"Clive Duncomb. Their chief of security, who put the bullet into Helt. Former Boston PD. Thinks he's John Wayne. Should have brought us in on this from the very beginning but chose to handle it himself. So far, he seems to have admin behind him, even though Helt's parents have filed a multimillion-dollar suit against the college. He wrote the book on how to be an asshole."

"Okay," Carlson said. A pause, then, "Thanks for the heads-up."

The three students who'd been attacked—presumably all by Helt—were Denise Lambton, Erin Stotter, and Lorraine Plummer. None of them had seen the man's face, but their descriptions of what he'd been wearing—a hoodie with the number 23 on the front—matched.

He had contact information for all three, but only one of them, Lorraine Plummer, was available for a face-to-face. This, it turned out, was the end of the semester, and most students had returned home. Erin Stotter had gone back to Danbury, Connecticut, and

Denise Lambton had gone to Hawaii—a graduation present from her parents.

Lorraine, however, was staying, having signed up to take courses from May to August so she could obtain her degree more quickly. She agreed to meet with Carlson in the college's main dining hall, an arena-sized room with a vaulted ceiling. There were only half a dozen students there when Carlson arrived. Lorraine was sitting near one corner, working on a small laptop, a paper cup of coffee next to it.

"Ms. Plummer?" he said.

"You're the policeman?" said the student, who Carlson guessed wasn't more than five feet tall, maybe 110 pounds wet. She wore her black hair to her shoulders and was dressed in a gray sweatshirt and jeans.

He offered a hand, which she took. "Carlson," he said, taking a seat across from her. "Pretty empty in here today."

"Most everyone's gone, but they're still keeping the cafeteria open with a skeleton staff," she said. "Thank God, or I'd starve to death."

"So you're hanging in for the summer?"

She shrugged, made a face. "Yeah. I'm trying to fast-track my degree. Don't want to be here for four solid years. Want to get on with my life, do something, you know? Try to get started on a career before having kids and stuff."

"You have a boyfriend?"

She blushed. "No. I just think way ahead."

"Nothing wrong with that."

"So, you have questions? About the guy who grabbed me?"

He nodded. "I'm sure you've had to go over all this before, but it would help us if you could do it again."

"But they got the guy, right? I mean, isn't it over?"

"What we're wondering is what Mason Helt—and we've no reason to think it wasn't Helt who attacked you—might have said."

"Okay, well, I was walking by the pond. You know, Thackeray Pond?"

"Yeah." It was a small body of water at the college. Most pictures of Thackeray featured the pond with the stately buildings in the background reflected within in it. Students hung out by it, strolled and jogged around it.

"It's real pretty there, although I'm totally freaked about even putting my toe into it. Some kid here put a baby alligator in there as a joke. I mean, it might be dead, but you never know. So I was walking around it at about ten. At night. No one else was out, which was kind of dumb of me—I realize that now. When I got close to some trees, all of a sudden this guy runs out and grabs me. I'm not very heavy, you know, and he puts his arms around me and lifts me right off my feet and takes me into the bushes. And I'm totally scared and ready to scream, and he puts his hand over my mouth and puts me down on the ground, and then he's all, hey, don't worry, it's okay."

"What'd he say, exactly?"

She paused, took a sip of her coffee. "I was kind of scared, you know? So it's hard to remember exactly. But it was like, 'I'm not going to hurt you. I'm not going to do anything to you. But tell them what happened. Tell them to be afraid.' Yeah, like that."

"'Tell them to be afraid'?"

Lorraine nodded.

"Tell who to be afraid?"

"Well, he didn't exactly say. I guess he meant, tell everyone?"

"There were two other students," Carlson said. "Erin Stotter and Denise Lambton."

"Yeah," she said. "I know them, but not really well. But they told me he said kind of the same thing to them, too. But you probably know all of this, right? Mr. Duncomb—he's the head campus-cop guy—would have told you right after it happened?"

Carlson knew, from what Duckworth had passed along, that all this information had come late to the Promise Falls police.

"What makes you think he would have done that?" he asked.

"Well, I told him I was going to call the police myself, but he said that wouldn't be necessary, that he'd be calling them. And that he'd be passing along my statement, and if you needed more from me, you'd interview me."

Carlson smiled. "He did, did he?"

Lorraine nodded.

"I figured he'd do it. Because I sort of already know him, and figured he'd be straight with me."

"How do you know the security chief?"

"He knows this writer guy. And he invited me out to his place once so I could meet him." Her face flushed again.

"A writer?" Carlson asked.

"I made a total fool of myself. Had too much to drink and kind of passed out, and felt—I don't know—kind of weird the next day." She hesitated a moment, then said, "But they were all real nice about it."

"But you're saying he said he'd fill in the local police on what happened?"

Her head went up and down.

As he walked out of the dining hall, Carlson put in a

call to Duckworth's cell. "I just talked to the Plummer woman."

"Okay."

"She wanted to go to the police right after she was assaulted, and Duncomb said he'd do it on her behalf."

"Which he never did."

"Yeah. Thought you'd want to know."

Silence. Then, "I'll be having a word with him about that."

"I'm going to pay him a visit."

"No," Duckworth said. "Leave that for me. In fact, Rhonda may want to have a word with him." Rhonda Finderman, the Promise Falls police chief.

"I'm here now," Angus Carlson said.

"No, wait—"

But it was too late. Carlson had ended the call.

"I'm looking for Duncomb," Carlson told the young man guarding the desk outside the offices of campus security.

"He's in a meeting right now. But if you'd like to have a seat, I can—"

Carlson headed for the closed door that bore Clive Duncomb's name and position. He turned the handle and entered.

Duncomb was behind his desk, talking to a man seated across from him. He looked up and said, "Excuse me."

"Angus Carlson," he said. "Promise Falls police." He flashed his credentials.

"That's pretty," Duncomb said. "But I'm talking to somebody right now."

"It's important."

Duncomb sighed and looked at the man, who Carlson

guessed was in his forties, 140 pounds tops, unkempt hair hanging over his collar, tweed jacket that was worn at the cuffs. The guy had everything needed to peg him short of a name tag that said "Professor."

"Sorry, Peter," Duncomb said to the man. "Why don't you wait outside while I deal with this?"

The man named Peter turned in his chair to look at Carlson and said, "You're with the police?"

"That's right."

Peter glanced nervously back at Duncomb and said, "Clive, maybe it wouldn't hurt to—"

Duncomb shook his head abruptly. "Peter, I'm sure it's nothing. We'll talk shortly. I've no doubt everything will be fine."

"And the other matter—"

Duncomb gave the man a sharp look. "I told you, that's in hand. You don't have to worry about that."

Hesitantly, Peter got to his feet and squeezed past Carlson on his way out of the office. Carlson took the man's seat, which was still warm.

"Where's Detective Duckworth today?" Duncomb asked. "Out having a doughnut?"

"Who was that?" Carlson asked, tipping his head in the direction of the man who'd departed.

"One of the professors."

"Why did he want to talk to me?"

"He didn't want to talk to you. He doesn't want to talk to you. It's nothing. A personal matter. What do you want?"

Carlson settled into the chair, opened up his notebook. "I've just been talking to Lorraine Plummer."

"Lorraine Plummer, Lorraine Plummer . . ." His eyes rolled up toward the ceiling.

"One of the three women who was attacked here at Thackeray."

Duncomb grinned. "I know. Erin Stotter, Denise Lambton, and, last but not least, Lorraine Plummer. The three students Mason Helt went after before I took care of the problem."

"By shooting him in the head."

Duncomb's shoulders rose, fell. A shrug. "Which, it would seem, has failed to ruffle any feathers, given that I haven't been charged with anything. It was a righteous shoot. I saved one of my people. Joyce Pilgrim. Helt would have killed her if I hadn't shown up."

"That's not my understanding."

"Not *your* understanding? What *is* your understanding?"

"That he'd told her he wasn't going to hurt her."

Duncomb nodded in mock agreement. "Yes, that's always a good strategy when you're dealing with someone who's just dragged you into the bushes to rip your pants off. To believe him when he says he means you no harm."

"It's the same thing he told the Plummer woman."

Another shrug. "Let me ask you this—what'd you say your name was again?"

"Carlson. Angus Carlson."

"Angus? What kind of name is that? Isn't that a kind of cow?"

Carlson felt his neck getting hot.

"How long have you been a detective, Angus Carlson?" Putting emphasis on the first name.

He hesitated. "It's a recent appointment. But I've been with the Promise Falls police for a few years. Came here from Ohio. Lorraine Plummer told me she was going to call the police, but you talked her out of it. That it wouldn't be necessary, because you were going to do that yourself."

Duncomb said nothing.

"Which you never did," Carlson added. "Lorraine Plummer was assured, by you, her concerns would be relayed to the proper authorities. They weren't. I wonder if Mason Helt's family, which I hear is suing the college for one shitload of money, is aware of that. If the police had been brought in from the beginning, they might have arrested Helt peacefully before you found it necessary to shoot him."

Duncomb's cheek twitched.

"One other thing," Carlson said. "When I mentioned Lorraine Plummer's name, you seemed to have a hard time calling it up."

"I can't remember the name of every single student who attends Thackeray. Not even the ones who come to my attention."

"Sure. Except she said she kind of knew you. That you introduced her to some writer friend, that you all had dinner together." Carlson smiled. "I'm sure we'll be talking again."

He let himself out.

Duncomb stayed at his desk, turned to his computer, typed in a name. A student's profile filled the screen. A head shot of Lorraine Plummer, phone number, e-mail address, a list of the courses she'd just completed, and those she'd signed up to take during the summer.

"Stupid little bitch," he said.

THIRTEEN

Detective Duckworth wished major crimes could be more conveniently scheduled.

He really did not need a drive-in bombing right now. If someone wanted to blow up the Constellation, he thought to himself, why couldn't they have done it back in March? Or put it off until the fall? Why didn't the bad guys of upstate New York check in with him first before they did these things?

He sat wearily at his desk after Angus Carlson struck off for Thackeray College. And why, Duckworth asked himself, did he have to be saddled with a new guy to look after? Who did Carlson think he was, acting like he was too good to go out to Thackeray to ask about Mason Helt's mini reign of terror?

Up until the moment the night before when Duckworth got the call about the screen coming down, his head had been someplace else.

He'd been preoccupied with the murders of Olivia Fisher and Rosemary Gaynor. The former three years ago, the latter this month.

He'd been thinking he had the Gaynor case figured out. Maybe not nailed down completely, but he had a suspect. Dr. Jack Sturgess, who had engineered stealing Marla Pickens's infant child and placing it with Bill and Rosemary

Gaynor, and who was also responsible for the murders of a blackmailer and an elderly woman, sure looked good for it. There was motive. Rosemary Gaynor had figured out the adoption was far from legal. It wasn't a stretch to think Sturgess killed her to keep her quiet. If she'd spoken out, he'd have been ruined.

Bill Gaynor, currently in jail awaiting trial for assisting in the murder of that blackmailer, had acknowledged it was possible the doctor had killed his wife.

What had troubled Duckworth was that Rosemary's death was so savage compared with the killings he knew, with certainty, Sturgess had committed. That blackmailer, Marshall Kemper, had been killed with a lethal injection. Kemper's elderly neighbor, Doris Stemple, had been suffocated with a pillow. But Rosemary Gaynor had been sliced wide open.

That horrific, jagged smile from hip to hip.

It didn't seem like the doc's style.

Duckworth wanted to believe Sturgess had varied his routine, just so he could wrap this one up. It wasn't as though Duckworth had to prove Sturgess guilty beyond a reasonable doubt.

Sturgess was dead.

Then came that meeting with Wanda Therrieult, where she displayed autopsy photos of Rosemary Gaynor alongside those of Olivia Fisher. The manner in which they'd been killed was identical. That downward curving slice across the abdomen. Similar marks on the neck from where their assailant had grabbed them from behind.

If Sturgess had killed Gaynor, then he must have killed Fisher. But, so far, Duckworth had found no connection between the doctor and Olivia.

Maybe Sturgess hadn't killed either of them.

And if that was the case, then whoever had was still out there.

It had been all Barry had been able to think about until the Constellation came crashing down.

Okay, that wasn't quite true.

There was the number twenty-three.

There had been twenty-three dead squirrels hanging from that fence. It was the number on Mason Helt's hoodie. Those three mannequins painted with the words "YOU'LL BE SORRY" were in carriage twenty-three of that decommissioned Ferris wheel at Five Mountains.

Maybe—*maybe* it was coincidence.

But figuring out the significance of that number took a backseat to finding the killer of those two women.

Duckworth still wondered about Bill Gaynor. Not so much where Olivia Fisher's death was concerned, but with regard to his wife. Husbands and boyfriends always topped the suspect list when a woman was murdered.

There was a motive. There was a million-dollar life insurance policy on Rosemary.

The problem was opportunity. Bill Gaynor had been at a weekend conference in Boston when his wife was killed. His car hadn't left the hotel until he drove back home Monday morning.

Duckworth was going to take another look at that alibi. He was also going to take a much closer look at Bill Gaynor. What kind of man was he? While it was true he'd helped Sturgess murder Marshall Kemper, he wasn't the one who'd shoved that syringe into his neck. Up until then, Gaynor'd never been in trouble with the law.

Then again, neither had Jack Sturgess.

There was a lot more legwork to do on this one.

His cell phone rang.

"Yes?"

"This Barry Duckworth?"

"Yes."

"This is Michelle Watkins. They call me the Bomb Lady. I'm here at the drive-in. Where the hell are you?"

He'd get to that legwork whenever he could.

FOURTEEN

Cal

I saw no obvious signs of a break-in at the home of Adam and Miriam Chalmers, but clearly, if Lucy heard someone running out the back door as she was coming in, someone had been here.

I did a walk around the house, Lucy Brighton trailing behind me. The place was built onto the side of a gentle hill, with just enough of a slope at the back to allow for a basement walkout to a thirty-foot-long kidney-shaped pool. The sliding glass doors were locked, but only, Lucy explained, because she had secured the place after the incident.

A wooded area came to within about fifty feet of the house. It was a narrow strip of forest. On the other side were the backyards of houses from the next street over. Whoever'd been in Adam Chalmers's house had probably parked over there.

There were no scratches on the front door lock. Lucy, using her own set of keys, let me in. There was the immediate beeping of an alarm system. Lucy entered a four-digit code into a keypad and the noise ceased.

"Did you get a call from the alarm company?" I asked. If someone had broken in and the security company was alerted, they'd probably have called Lucy when the Chalmerses could not be reached. People usually listed close relatives as backup contacts—or at least someone who lived nearby—in case there was trouble at home while they were away.

"No," she said. "I got a visit from the police. They figured out how to find me through the alarm company. They saw the stickers in the window."

"Stickers?"

"With the security company's name on it."

"Was the alarm engaged when they went to the movie last night?"

"I would imagine so," she said.

"But you don't know for certain."

"No, but it wasn't like my father to ever leave the house without setting the alarm. He was . . . he was aware of what people with bad intentions can do."

"So if someone got in, they'd have to know the code, or the cops would be along shortly."

"That's right."

"And they'd need a key, too."

"Yes."

"Do you know anyone else your father, or his wife, entrusted with a key and the code?"

"No," Lucy said. "But that doesn't mean there wasn't someone."

Once we were in the front hall, she closed the door behind us.

I don't know a lot about decorating. A visit to my apartment would confirm that. When I had a family, and a house, Donna was in charge of how it looked, and she did a nice job of it. But she never gave up trying to educate me when it came time to get a new couch or dining room table. I could distinguish between the arts and crafts style and eclectic, which is a bit like bragging that you could tell a cat from a mongoose. The Chalmers house looked to me like "contemporary." The living room furniture, with sleek, clean lines, was in various shades of gray and taupe. Metal legs on the chairs, a coffee table set low to the floor, recent issues of *Vanity Fair* and *The New Yorker* fanned perfectly on top of it. The paintings on the wall were not so abstract that I couldn't tell what they were supposed to be. One was a woman sitting before a mirror, fixing her hair. Another, a riderless horse running off the side of a cliff.

"What's missing?" I asked.

Lucy hesitated. "Nothing that jumps out at me," she said. "But it might be something I don't even know about. That's why I have to find out who got in here. Maybe when I know who it was, I'll have an idea what they were after."

"Were you here often enough to notice if there were a missing painting, or something else of value?"

She gave me a look. Maybe she took the question another way. Maybe she thought I was asking whether she was close with her father and his wife.

"I think so," she said slowly.

"Did your father keep money in the house? Is there a safe?"

"Not that I know of. But there is an office."

"Let's start there."

To get there, we traveled through the kitchen, which was straight out of one of those shows on the home-and-garden channel, and bigger than my entire apartment. A long kitchen with seven leather stools running down one side. High-end German appliances in brushed aluminum. A fridge that could have had a cow in it.

We went down a hall, passed a master bedroom. I

poked my head in. A bed the size of Massachusetts, and still room to walk around it. At a glance, there was nothing out of place. No drawers yanked out, the bedcovers untouched. I saw a door to an en suite bathroom. I didn't notice anything odd there, either.

The next room was clearly the office. Big desk, a large monitor and a keyboard, plus a laptop off to one side. Books, two mugs full of pens. A printer with no paper in the tray, an empty Staples wrapper that had once held 8½ x 11 sheets.

"My father was a writer," Lucy said.

There were several enlarged reproductions of book covers framed on the wall. There was one for *Scum of America*, another called *Hate on Wheels*. Both featured biker imagery. And blood.

Then my eyes landed on a large, framed black-and-white photo. Five bearded bikers, arms over one another's shoulders, Harleys in the background.

"Dad's the one in the middle," Lucy said.

I leaned in for a closer look. Hard to make out what he really looked like with all the facial hair and the kerchief tied around his forehead.

I looked at Lucy. "This house doesn't look like a biker pad."

"What's a biker pad look like?"

I thought. "A bunker. Cinder blocks with bars at the window would be how I'd decorate."

"My father's biker days were over. It was years ago. He got out of that, started a new life."

I glanced at the book covers. "But he wrote about it."

She nodded. "And sold enough books to buy this place, and live a pretty decent life. Although there hasn't been a book in a few years."

"What was he into?" I asked, nodding at the photo. "Illegally, that is."

"A lot," Lucy said. "But it was a long time ago." She shook her head, like she wanted to change the subject. "Anything look out of place here?"

"Not that I can see."

I dropped myself into the chair behind the desk, surveyed the domain before me. Not a lot to see aside from the computer, cups of Sharpies, a few books. I moved the mouse to bring the screen to life. Nothing there but a view of Earth from space, a standard Apple background. The usual row of programs along the bottom.

There were drawers on each side. When I went to open one, Lucy said, "Should you do that?"

"Why? You think they're booby-trapped?"

"No. I was thinking, if someone broke in to search this office, maybe there are fingerprints. Should you be—what do you call it?—dusting for prints first?"

"I'm not really equipped for that, Lucy. And even if I did look for prints, I don't have access to a national database. You need the police for that, and—"

"The police are too busy. They're not going to come out here and do anything, not when they're trying to find out what happened at the drive-in."

"That's what I was about to say. The cops have limited resources, particularly in Promise Falls. And when all you have to tell them is you think someone was in the house, but can't even tell them what's missing, they're not going to put much effort into this. So . . ." I opened the top drawer. Checkbooks, more pens, paper clips.

I went through all of them. Receipts, old tax returns, a few book review clippings. Nothing of interest. Of course, if there'd been something of interest that someone took, it wasn't here to be seen. But nothing looked disrupted.

"Let's keep looking around," I said. "Check that basement walkout from the inside."

Lucy led me to a curving staircase with a wrought-iron railing. It did a quarter circle on the way to the lower floor. Along the way I asked, "What about Miriam? Your father was a writer. What about her?"

"She tended to my father's needs." There was something in the way she said it that suggested more than the running of a household.

"And before that?"

"A photographer. Portraits. She met Dad when she was asked by his publisher for an updated author photo. They were reissuing a couple of his early books, and she came to the house to do the shoot and didn't leave for a week."

That hint of disapproval in her voice.

There was a five-foot-wide, floor-to-ceiling bookcase at the bottom of the stairs. A lot of the books were oversized coffee-table-type volumes. I glanced at some of the spines, saw that many of them were about cinema. Books on Orson Welles, Steven Spielberg, François Truffaut, Alfred Hitchcock. Several tomes on the history of sex in the cinema. One called, quite simply, *Filth in Film*.

Lucy noticed me reading the spines of the books and said, "I don't know how many times I asked Dad to put those where Crystal wouldn't come across them, but he kept insisting she was still too young to care."

"Crystal spent time here?"

"She loved her grandfather very much. I mean, she's not a demonstrative child, but I could tell. Crystal loved him and he loved her. He was patient with her, with all her idiosyncrasies, which was kind of something, for him."

"What do you mean?"

"My father, and Miriam even more so ... they tended to view the world from their own perspective. If something didn't bother Miriam, she couldn't understand why it would bother anyone else. She'd be the person who played her music loud and couldn't figure out why her neighbors wanted her to turn it down. Maybe, in some ways, they were perfect for each other. Classic hedonists."

"Your father only cared about himself?"

"Mostly, although I think, in the case of his daughter and granddaughter, he was willing to make an exception."

Ranch-style homes allow for bigger basements, and this place was no exception. I wandered off a few steps into a large room that contained a pool table, half a dozen pinball games lined up against one wall, a foosball game. Perhaps most impressive, at least to the kid in me, a slot car racetrack on a table about five by ten feet. It was completely scenicked, with hills and trees and buildings, even viewing stands filled with miniature people.

"Your dad liked to play," I said.

"Yes," Lucy Brighton said, still standing by the bookshelves. "He was a boy at heart."

I examined the sliding glass doors that led out to the pool. Once the alarm had been deactivated, the intruder would have felt no hesitation about fleeing this way. But there was no security pad near the door, which told me whoever'd entered the house had done so through the front door.

"Cameras?" I asked.

"No," she said. "Dad didn't have surveillance cameras."

Too bad. I rejoined her by the bookcase near the base of the stairs. "I don't know what to say, Lucy. Okay, someone was in the house. But we don't know that anything was taken, and it's not likely we're going to find out, given that the only ones who'd be able to tell us are your father and his wife."

"There must be something you can do," she said.

I leaned, wearily, up against the bookcase. "About all I can do is—"

The bookcase moved.

"What the—"

It was only a fraction of an inch, but I felt the entire bookcase slide. At first, I thought maybe it was going to pitch forward, but then realized it had moved sideways. Which didn't make much sense, given how weighted down it was with books.

"What happened?" Lucy asked.

"This bookcase . . ." I said, examining it.

The right end of the case butted up against the wall. There was a vertical bulkhead there, hiding, presumably, some ductwork, or drains or pipes that connected to the first floor, above us.

I noticed a gap between the edge of the bookcase and the bulkhead. I worked the fingers of both hands in and gave a slight push to the left. The fake wall shifted an inch.

"How are you doing that?" Lucy asked.

"It's on a track," I said. "It doesn't take much to move it. Is there a room back here or something?"

"Not that I know of," she said. "Is it some kind of panic room?"

It didn't strike me that anyone in Promise Falls would need a secret room to flee from home invaders. New

York, maybe. Like in that Jodie Foster movie from years ago. But here? Then again, maybe someone with a biker past would have concerns and enemies the rest of us didn't.

I pushed harder, moving the bookcase a good two and a half feet, at which point it came to a stop, revealing a floor-to-ceiling opening, and a room in darkness.

I felt around inside for a light switch, hit it.

The room was about fifteen feet square, dominated by a king-sized bed covered with a thick off-white satiny comforter and at least a dozen oversized pillows arranged by the headboard. The floor was carpeted in thick shag, also white, which provided quite a contrast to the red velvetlike wallpaper. A large flat-screen TV was mounted to the wall about four feet beyond the foot of the bed, a small black cabinet below. Undoubtedly the most arresting decorating touch was the six large, framed black-and-white photographs along three walls, all depicting naked men and women entwined with one another like they were auditioning for a remake of *Caligula*.

Scattered across the floor were half a dozen plastic DVD jewel cases. All open, all empty.

"I don't think it's a panic room," I said.

FIFTEEN

Barry Duckworth booted it back up to the drive-in site, where he met Michelle Watkins, the bomb expert the state police had sent in to assist.

"So what happened here?" he asked her as they stood amid the rubble. "The demolition guy screwed up, or are we looking at something else?"

Michelle Watkins said, "I'm saying that guy Marsden, the one who was hired to drop this sucker a week from now? He told you he hadn't even started on this job? He's not lying. This is not his work. At least, it's not the work of any professional demolition expert."

"What do you mean?"

"There's a big difference between how a pro would bring down a structure like this and how it was actually done. This is amateur hour. From what I can tell, we're looking at IEDs."

"Improvised . . ."

"Yeah. Improvised explosive devices."

"So more than one," he said.

"Walk with me," she said, then glanced down at his feet. "You got some proper shoes like I'm wearing?" She pointed to her own feet, which were protected with thick-soled steel-toed boots. "You go walking through this in those loafers and you'll end up with half a dozen spikes through your feet."

"In the car," Duckworth said.

"Go get 'em." She took out her phone. "I'll check my messages."

He was back in five minutes, the legs of his suit pants tucked into the tops of his boots.

"You still have to watch your step," Michelle said, moving gingerly over the wreckage. Duckworth noticed this woman—all five and a half feet of her—seemed to be entirely muscle. "First thing we had to do, of course, was be sure there weren't any other bombs planted in here that hadn't gone off. Hate to be poking about, then *kaboom*, there goes your left tit."

"Sure."

"We sent in some sniffer dogs this morning, poked around with a camera, and as far as we can tell, there's nothing else."

"As far as you can tell."

Michelle grinned. "Hey, nothing in life is a hundred percent. Except that, at some point, it will end. Oh, and that everything that tastes good is bad for you."

"What's your background?" Duckworth asked, stepping carefully over broken boards.

"I was a bomb disposal officer with the army. Iraq, Afghanistan. When my tours ended, and I'd had enough, I put my skills to work over here, got a job with the staties."

"Like that movie," Duckworth said. "What was it called?"

"The Hurt Locker."

"That's the one. Was it like that over there?"

"Meh," she said, shrugging. "Movies. If it hasn't got George Clooney in it, I don't much care. Okay, so our Marsden friend would have rigged this thing to drop nice and neat, rigging charges there, there, and there." She pointed. "But the guy who did this wasn't quite so tidy. Not that he did a completely terrible job. He did bring the damn thing down, after all."

"IEDs, you said."

"Yeah, homemade bombs."

"You're saying the same kinds of explosives you encountered in Iraq are what was used here? Some folks, they started wondering if this was terrorism or something, and my first thought was, Promise Falls can't be high on the list of targets for Islamic extremists."

"I wouldn't disagree with you there," Michelle said. "IED is just a fancy acronym for a bomb you build yourself. Doesn't mean it's a bomb made by some Middle Eastern terrorist group, but then again, it doesn't mean it's not. But there's plenty of places online where you can find out how to make one. Plenty of yahoos over here can figure out this stuff. Remember Timothy McVeigh and Oklahoma City? He was a fan of fertilizer. You get someone reasonably smart, pretty handy—they can put one of these together, do a lot of damage. Whoever did this did have some engineering smarts. He knew where to plant the devices to make the screen fall the way it did. Assuming he did, in fact, want it to fall on the audience."

She did some more pointing as they continued their slow trek over the remains of the screen. "The screen had four main supports, and my guess is there were four bombs, each attached to one of those supports, on the parking lot side, so the screen would drop in that direction."

"Would the bomber have had to be here? Close by? Maybe in one of the cars?"

She shook her head. "No. I'm guessing what we'll find

is there was a common timer for all four, so they went off simultaneously for maximum impact."

"So he could be anywhere. He could have been a thousand miles away when the bombs went off."

"Yup."

"And they could have been planted anytime."

"Double yup."

Duckworth felt a wave of hopelessness wash over him. Interviewing all the people present at the time of the explosion wasn't likely to produce anything helpful.

"No advance warnings, no threats, no one claiming responsibility?" Michelle Watkins asked.

"No," he said.

"Well, we're going to start pulling together bomb fragments. Once we get a handle on what it was made of, how it might have been put together, we'll cross-check that with other bombings, look for similarities. That may end up pointing us in the right direction."

"Appreciate it," Duckworth said. He was panting.

"You okay?"

"Yeah," he said. "I don't usually spend my day climbing over a mess like this."

"You might want to think about taking up jogging or something," she said. "Get yourself in shape."

"Thanks for that," Duckworth said.

"Maybe cut back on the Big Macs."

"I said thanks."

Michelle continued. "It's clear to me our bomber was hoping to hurt some people, having this thing come down at twenty-three twenty-three, when it was known there would be people here for the drive-in's last night. You ask me, it was lucky only four people got killed. If more people'd parked in that first row, there'd—"

"Sorry. What was that?"

"What was what?"

"When it came down?"

Michelle grinned. "Once you've been on military time, you're on it forever. More precise, at least to me, than saying a.m. or p.m. I'm always thinking of a twenty-four-hour clock. The screen came down at eleven twenty-three p.m. Twenty-three minutes past twenty-three hundred hours."

Duckworth had stopped.

"You out of breath again?" Michelle asked.

"No, I'm okay."

"What is it? You look like you've got something on your mind."

"Something just stopped being a bunch of coincidences," he said.

SIXTEEN

Cal

I stepped into the red-walled room.

"You're saying you've never been in here?" I asked Lucy.

Her eyes were wide. "Cal, I swear, I've never known anything about this."

"Did you grow up in this house?"

"Not really. Dad got this place just as I was finishing high school. Once I went to college I never moved back. I've been over here hundreds of times, of course, but I've sure as hell never been given a tour of this. What *is* this?"

Given the sexually graphic photos on the wall, and the bed, and the satin pillows, it seemed pretty obvious to me.

"It's not exactly a woodworking shop," I said.

"This is . . . unimaginable," she said.

The room wasn't added onto the house. It was within the perimeter of the foundation. Maybe, at one time, this really had been a woodworking shop, or a wine cellar, or an exercise room. All Chalmers would have had to do was cover over the access with that sliding bookcase to keep anyone from knowing the room was here.

Then the question was why.

There was no shame in the fact that couples living together shared bedrooms, with actual beds in them, where they had sex. No one would go to that kind of trouble to hide that fact. I was betting Adam and Miriam Chalmers had spent most of their nights in that bedroom upstairs. In that huge bed. Where they often had sex.

But this room, this was for something more than garden-variety sex. This was for when sex was an event. This was a room dedicated solely to sex. No sleeping went on in here. This was not a room where you put your aunt when she came to visit.

I took in the erotic photographs framed on the walls. "Would that be Miriam's work?" I asked.

Lucy nodded. "I think so. I've seen her stuff online. When she wasn't doing run-of-the-mill portraits and weddings, she fancied herself a female Mapplethorpe."

I stepped carefully over the discarded empty DVD cases, then knelt down on one knee in front of the small cabinet that was tucked up against the wall below the flat-screen TV. One of the doors was half-open, and I was guessing this was where the cases had come from. I pulled it open all the way. Lucy had come into the room and was standing behind me, looking down over my shoulder.

There were two shelves. On the top, to one side, was a DVD player. Next to it were an assortment of creams and lotions and condoms and an open jewel case. The bottom shelf was littered with what would be categorized as sex toys. Vibrators, rubber phalluses, various and assorted straps, handcuffs. Even a box filled with batteries, although not the kind you put in the smoke detectors.

I heard an intake of breath behind me. I turned my head to look at Lucy. "You okay?"

"Yes," she said slowly. "I mean, it's a lot to take in. I don't think I'm a prude. People have sex, sometimes with all the extras, and I've got nothing against that. Even when it's your own father." She paused. "But this . . .

I don't know what to think about this."

I glanced back at the bed, spotted some items on the table next to it. Remotes, for the TV and the DVD player.

"Lucy, can you grab me those?"

"What?"

"Those remotes."

She walked around the bed, appeared hesitant to grab them at first, but of the items I'd found in this room, the remotes were the ones I'd be the most comfortable touching. She handed them to me. I figured out which one was for the DVD player, powered it up, then hit the eject button. The tray slid out.

Empty.

Either Adam Chalmers was in the habit of taking the disc out of the machine when he was finished watching it, or whoever ransacked this place was thorough.

Even though my right knee was planted in shag carpeting, it was getting sore, so I switched to the other and, in the process, shifted in such a way that I caught a glimpse of something under the bed.

A black case. Plastic, it looked like.

I reached under, grabbed it by the handle, and slid it out.

"What's that?" Lucy asked.

I didn't answer. Instead, I flipped up the tabs on the front of the case and raised the lid. It was filled with soft gray foam, with cutouts to hold a camera and a couple of lenses that were packed neatly inside.

I pried out the camera. It was a nice, expensive model designed to take still photos or video.

"Oh my," Lucy said.

I glanced back at the empty DVD cases. "Yeah. Looks like your father's home movies are missing." I thought a moment. "My guess is, someone was looking for the DVD they wanted, heard you come in, slipped out of this room with the discs, slid the shelf back into position, and took off out the back door."

She nodded slowly.

"He probably figured he had time to go through the discs. Maybe they were labeled. Then he heard the door open, and he left these cases scattered all over the place."

I studied her.

"Are you sure you didn't know about this?" I asked. "You haven't received a phone call since what happened at the drive-in? Someone offering to sell these back to you."

Lucy shook her head. "Nothing like that. I swear."

Maybe the call had yet to come. But did blackmail really make sense? The ones you'd want to blackmail, if you had these discs, would be Adam Chalmers and his wife, Miriam.

But they were dead.

"At least now we know what they were after," I said. "We know what was taken. Do you want to bring the police into it now?"

Her mouth opened in horror. "God, no."

"What do you want me to do?"

"Find these DVDs. Find out who has them. I don't have any idea what's on them and I really don't want to know. But we need to get them back, and they need to be destroyed. There can't be anything on them that I'd want anyone to see."

"Your father's reputation is important to you."

"It's not that," she said. "I mean, it's partly that, but . . ."

"Your daughter," I said.

Lucy nodded. "If these get out somehow, I can survive

the embarrassment. But what about Crystal? You know how things are these days. Everything goes viral almost instantly. And even kids know what's happening. I can't bear the taunting she might endure, the humiliation. Or that she might go online one day and see this stuff herself, if that's what the person who took those discs plans to do. To put them up on YouTube."

"Sure," I said.

I wondered where to start. Who might know about this secret room? The guy who built it, perhaps, although Adam Chalmers might have done the work himself. A cleaning lady, maybe, or a person authorized to come into the house to do some kind of repair work? But how would they know the room even existed? And if they did, why would they want the discs?

Who'd care about acquiring videos of Adam Chalmers and his wife getting it on? Especially after they were dead.

And then it hit me.

Adam and Miriam weren't the only performers.

There were supporting players.

SEVENTEEN

Angus Carlson had exited the Thackeray College admin building and was almost to his car when he heard someone yelling in his direction.

"Excuse me! You!"

Carlson was the only one crossing the parking lot, so there was a pretty good chance that whoever was shouting was shouting at him. He stopped and turned. The man he knew only as Peter, the one he'd pegged as a Thackeray professor who'd been talking to Duncomb, was trying to get his attention.

"Me?" Carlson said, pointing to himself.

Peter nodded, closed the distance between them. He was panting.

"Sorry. I was waiting for you to come out of Clive's office, but I guess I missed you, didn't realize you'd already left. Had to run when I spotted you. You're with the police? You're a detective?"

"That's right," he said. *Acting* detective, but he didn't see any need to point that out. "Who are you?"

"Oh, I'm Peter Blackmore. *Professor* Blackmore." He extended a hand and Carlson took it. "English literature and psychology."

"Okay."

"I wondered if I could ask you a couple of questions. Kind of hypothetically."

"Sure. Go ahead."

"If someone is missing, how long do they have to be missing to be, you know, official?"

"Official?"

"Officially missing," Blackmore said.

"Who are we talking about here?" Angus Carlson asked.

"It's just a hypothetical."

"Hypothetically speaking, is this missing person a four-year-old girl who didn't show up at nursery school, a ninety-year-old man who wandered away from a nursing home, or a husband who ran off with his secretary?"

Blackmore blinked. "It's none of those."

"The point I'm trying to make is, it depends. A kid fails to show up for school, the police jump on it right away. You have to move quickly on something like that. An old guy who wanders off is pretty urgent, too, but at least with him you're less worried that he's the victim of an abduction. And the husband who runs off with his secretary, well, that's not really a concern of ours at all. Depending."

"I see," Blackmore said, thinking.

"Maybe if you could be more specific."

"It's a bit like the third one you mentioned, but not exactly. Do I have to wait twenty-four hours before reporting someone missing? That's what I've heard. That you have to wait twenty-four hours. Or is it forty-eight?"

Carlson shook his head. "That's a TV myth. You can report someone anytime you want. If there's reason to believe a crime was committed, that this missing person is in danger, the police will act right away. Was a crime committed in connection with this hypothetical disappearance?"

Blackmore paused, looked away. "Not that I know of, I guess. She just hasn't come home."

"Is it your wife, Professor? Is that who's missing?"

He swallowed, hesitated, then said, "Maybe. I mean, yes, it's my wife, but I can't say for sure that she's actually missing."

"What's her name?"

"Georgina Blackmore."

"When did you last see her?" Carlson was reaching into his pocket for his notebook.

"Uh, yesterday morning, when I left home to come out to the college."

"Does Mrs. Blackmore have a job?"

"Yes, yes, she does. She's a legal secretary. At Paine, Kay and Dunn."

"Did she show up for work yesterday?"

"She did."

"You talked to her through the day?"

"No, but I was talking to them—to her employers—today, and they say she was there yesterday."

"But she didn't come home last night?"

"I don't exactly know that."

Carlson cocked his head to one side. "How would you not know that?"

"I didn't go home last night. I stayed overnight here at the college. In my office."

"You slept in your office?"

"I wasn't *sleeping*," he said. "I was working. It's a habit of mine. I was preparing a lecture that I'm to give this afternoon on Melville and psychological determinism."

"Uh-huh."

"When I'm preparing a lecture, I work through the night. So I didn't go home. I had a short nap around five this morning." He started to raise his right arm and bend his head down, like he was going to give himself a sniff, then stopped himself. "I'll head home and freshen up after I give my lecture."

"Did you speak to Georgina at any time? On the phone? Did you text back and forth?"

He shook his head. "I don't text. I don't know how."

"You don't have a cell phone?"

Blackmore dug into his pocket, brought out an old flip phone. Carlson guessed it was at least ten years old. "I do, but I don't even know if you can text with it. I think maybe it takes pictures, but all I ever use it for is to make and receive calls."

"So you haven't spoken to your wife since yesterday morning, and you haven't tried to call her since then, either?"

Blackmore shook his head. "I tried this morning. After her office phoned me. They have my number. They wanted to know if I knew why Georgina hadn't come into work."

"She didn't come in today."

"No. They tried her at home, and on her cell. No answer. So I tried her cell, too, and I haven't been able to get her." His chin quivered. "I'm starting to get a little worried."

"Has Georgina ever gone missing before?"

Blackmore glanced away. "Not exactly."

"That's a yes-or-no question, Professor."

"No. She hasn't gone missing before. She's gone off by herself for a while, to collect her thoughts."

Carlson said, "Why don't you come with me down

to the station and I can take down all your wife's information? A full description, what kind of car she drives, people she might be in touch with, and if you have a picture of her, that would be—"

"No," the professor said abruptly. "It's okay. I'm sure everything's okay. It's probably what I just said. She just needs some alone time. That's all."

"You were discussing this with Clive Duncomb? When I walked in?"

Blackmore nodded. "Yes. Clive's a good friend. And a good adviser."

"But he didn't suggest you call the police."

"Not . . . just yet," Blackmore admitted.

"That seems to be his style."

Blackmore took a step back, his eyes filled with apprehension since the mention of Duncomb.

"You know what? Forget I even talked to you. I'm sure Georgina's fine—she might even be home now. I'm just overreacting. And please, don't mention to Clive that I approached you. He can get quite territorial about these things."

"And how about the other thing?" Carlson asked.

"I'm sorry?"

"When you were leaving Duncomb's office. You asked if you were okay on the other thing, and he said it was in hand, not to worry. Did that have to do with your wife, Professor Blackmore? Or was that something else altogether?"

The man paled. "I still have some tweaks to do on my lecture, and I deliver it in an hour, so I better go."

Blackmore turned and ran off, like a dog that had been yanked away with an invisible leash.

EIGHTEEN

Detective Duckworth found Lionel Grayson in the Constellation Drive-in office, pacing the floor, cell phone to his ear, talking with someone from his insurance company.

"What do you mean, I might not be covered?" Grayson shouted. "What are you talking about? Yes, yes, I was going to bring down the screen anyway, but I'm not talking about that. I don't care about that! I'm talking about the people who died! On my property! Four people! And all the other people who were injured, and the cars that were damaged! Those people, there's already talk that I'm going to be sued, that they're going to take me for everything I've got! Yes, yes, I'm going after the demolition company, but they hadn't even—"

"Mr. Grayson," Duckworth said.

Grayson raised a finger. "Listen to me. They hadn't even done anything yet. They didn't have anything to do with this. Somebody planted some bombs and—what do you mean I may not be covered for terrorism? Who said anything about terrorism? What the hell are you talking about? You think a bunch of al-Qaeda crazies snuck into America to blow up a drive-in in fucking Promise Falls? You think—"

"Mr. Grayson, I need to speak with you," Duckworth said.

"Hang on, hang on. Listen to me. I'm retiring. I sold this property so I could retire. I can't lose all that money if all these people sue me! You insurance people are all the same! You're just out to screw people over and—hello? Hello?"

He stopped pacing and looked at the detective. "The son of a bitch hung up on me."

"I want to ask you a couple of questions," the detective said.

"What?"

"Why don't we sit down?"

"I can't. I can't stop moving."

"Please. Have a seat."

Reluctantly, Grayson sat down on one of two cheap folding aluminum lawn chairs. Duckworth sat opposite him, planted his elbows on his thighs, and leaned forward.

"You okay?"

"I'm going out of my mind." He was bobbing one knee up and down like a human sewing machine.

Duckworth nodded. "I get that. It's a horrible thing. I want to ask you a couple of things, but I need you to calm down first, so you can really think about what I'm asking."

"Okay," he said, taking a breath. Then another. "I can't do it. I'm too wound up. Just ask me what you have to ask me."

"Okay. Can you think of anyone who'd want to do you harm? To you, or to your business here?"

"Nobody. No. And who'd care about hurting our business? I'm going *out* of business."

"Okay, but have you had any problems with suppliers, or maybe an angry customer, someone you had a disagreement with?"

Grayson thought. "I can't think of anyone. Just the usual things. Nothing very serious. I mean, sometimes you have people unhappy with the movie who want their money back."

"Do you give it to them?"

The question stunned him. "Of course not! I make no guarantees about the quality of the movie. Let them read the reviews. If they don't like the movie, let them write a letter to Tom Hanks or Nicole Kidman and ask them for their money back."

"Have you had an incident like that lately?"

Grayson shrugged. "A couple of weeks ago, a man, he was very upset because the movie had nudity and bad language in it, and his five-year-old daughter was in the car. But it was the last feature. They're always for a more mature audience. If the people bring their kids, they're usually asleep by that time. That's why we show the kid movies first."

"Did he want his money back?"

"He didn't even care about that. He said he was going to report me to the authorities."

"What authorities?"

Grayson laughed. "Who knows? I never heard from anybody. So many people, they're just assholes. There's nothing you can do."

"Did the man give you his name?"

Grayson shook his head. "No." His eyes widened. "But . . . hang on. I just remembered, I wrote his license plate number down. I do that sometimes. People who cause trouble, like kids who party or are drinking. I've got it somewhere." He got out of the chair and began looking through papers on his desk.

"Here it is." He handed over a scrap of paper, with a

plate number and the word "Odyssey" scribbled on it.

Duckworth glanced at it, looked up. "Odyssey?"

"The van. A Honda."

Duckworth pocketed the piece of paper. "How about outside of work, Mr. Grayson? Anyone else got a beef with you? Any kind of personal issues?"

"What? No. Nothing. You have to find out who did this. And don't go blaming terrorists for it, or my insurance company might not help me out."

"One last thing," Duckworth said. "Does the number twenty-three mean anything special to you?"

Grayson screwed up his face. "What?"

"The screen came down twenty-three minutes after the twenty-third hour. Does that seem significant in any way?"

The man shook his head. "You're kidding me, right?"

He hadn't been.

Duckworth no longer believed that the frequency with which "23" was popping up was just happenstance. Not since learning when the drive-in screen came down.

Something was going on.

He'd already done some online searching with regard to that number. It was in the Matrix movies. It was on Michael Jordan's shirt when he played for the Bulls. It was the atomic number for vanadium. (Wanda Therrieult had actually known what that was.) It was the ninth prime number. There was the Twenty-third Psalm.

The number might be related to any of those things, or none of those things. But Duckworth was sure it meant something very specific to someone.

It meant something to the person who'd hung up

those squirrels, and fired up that Ferris wheel. If Mason Helt, who'd been wearing a hoodie with that number, were alive, Duckworth would be taking a serious look at him. The drive-in bombing had come after his death. But Duckworth believed there was a connection.

The question now was whether to release this information, speculative as it was. Maybe it was time to enlist the public's help. Someone out there might know something. A troubled family member, perhaps, with an inexplicable fixation on that number. If it had something to do with the Twenty-third Psalm—"Yea, though I walk through the valley of the shadow of death, I shall fear no evil"—maybe some kind of religious zealot was at work here.

He needed to talk to his boss, Chief Rhonda Finderman, about this. Soon.

But "23" was not the only thing on his mind. There was Olivia Fisher.

He wanted to determine if there might, in fact, be a link between Jack Sturgess and Olivia Fisher. One person he thought might be able to tell him was Olivia's father, Walden.

If there was a connection—if Sturgess, for example, turned out to be the Fishers' family physician—Duckworth might be less reluctant to write him off as the killer of both women.

He was always looking for connections.

It would certainly make Rhonda happy if he found a way to hang everything on Sturgess. She saw an opportunity to close two cases. And why wouldn't she, considering that the Olivia Fisher murder had been her case, back when she was a detective? Finderman, who hadn't kept herself up to speed on the Gaynor case in its early days, would have seen the similarities to the Fisher murder. Duckworth wished the chief had been a little more on the ball, but he kept that opinion to himself.

Duckworth parked his car out front of Walden Fisher's house, a white two-story wood-frame structure with a separate two-car garage at the back of the lot. He walked up to the front door and rang the bell.

"Yes?" said Fisher as he opened the door six inches and eyed Duckworth.

The detective showed him his ID. "Barry Duckworth, with the Promise Falls police."

Fisher squinted at the ID. "Duckworth?"

"That's right."

"What's this about, Detective?"

"I had a couple of questions, sir, about your daughter. About Olivia. I wonder if I could speak to you and Mrs. Fisher."

"She passed away," he said, finally opening the door.

Duckworth winced inwardly. "I'm sorry. I didn't know. I appreciate that it must be painful to answer questions about Olivia, but if you wouldn't mind, I'll try not to take up too much of your time."

"Of course, yes, come in."

He led the detective to the kitchen and invited him to sit. There was a copy of the Albany paper on the table and a metal nail file with a plastic handle. Maybe Walden had been giving himself a manicure.

"I just made some coffee. Would you like some?"

"That'd be great."

"Have you been up at the drive-in?" Walden asked. "It's all over the news."

Duckworth nodded. "Yes. I'm on my way back from there. But I've been wanting to talk to you."

"What a terrible thing," Walden said, taking two mugs down from the cupboard. "Just unimaginable. To be going to a movie, and have the screen come down and kill you."

He filled the two mugs, brought them over to the table. He moved the paper out of the way, and tucked the nail file into his shirt pocket. He rubbed his index finger over the tip of his thumb. "I bite my nails," he said. "Bad habit. Never used to do it before Olivia passed. And then after I lost my wife, I got even worse. It's the stress."

Duckworth took a mug, felt its warmth in his hands, and took a sip. It was strong, and he did his best not to make a face.

"What did you want to ask me?" Walden Fisher said. "Have you found out something? Have you found out who killed Olivia?"

Duckworth sidestepped the question. "Have you ever heard of a doctor by the name of Jack Sturgess?"

Fisher took a sip of his own coffee. "Sturgess? Didn't I see something on the news about him?"

"You probably did."

"About that woman and her baby? He stole a baby and gave it to somebody else?"

"Yes. That's the one."

"He's dead, right? That woman who ran the hospital. She killed him, and then she killed herself."

"You're pretty up to speed on this," Duckworth said.

"It's not as easy as it used to be, with the *Standard* gone. But I listen to radio and watch the TV news out of Albany." He tipped his head toward the paper. "Once the *Standard* went under, I started getting the Albany one, but there's not much news from around here in it."

"I guess you know, then, that Dr. Sturgess is being looked at in Rosemary Gaynor's death."

Walden nodded.

"Do you know if Olivia ever went to Dr. Sturgess? Whether she was ever a patient of his? Or whether she even knew him at all?"

The murdered woman's father shook his head slowly. "Not that I know of. We had a family doctor, Dr. Silverman. Ruth Silverman. She was my wife's doctor, and I think Olivia saw her. I *still* see her. I got all kinds of things going wrong with me. Sciatic pain, indigestion, you name it—every day you wake up with something different bothering you. And yet, in my head, I'm still sixteen years old. You know what I mean?"

"I do."

"I'm pretty sure I'd never heard of this Sturgess character until he was splashed all over the news." He leaned in over the table. "Are you saying you think he had something to do with what happened to Olivia?"

"I'm not saying that. But I was looking for any possible connection."

"What kind of connection could there be?"

Duckworth smiled weakly. "There might not be any at all. I'm just looking at everything."

"So you're not going to tell me."

"I don't want to raise things that might turn out to be nothing."

Walden Fisher nodded slowly. "What if it is this doctor? What if he's the one who killed our Olivia?"

"I'm not saying it was him."

"But if it was, he'll never pay for it, will he? He won't be punished."

"I don't know how to answer that, Mr. Fisher. I know you would have gone over this a million times with Detective Finderman three years ago."

"She's the chief now," he said.

"That's right."

"Too busy, I guess, to keep investigating my daughter's murder."

"I wouldn't say that. Just because she's moved up doesn't mean the department isn't actively investigating. But what I wanted to ask is, was there anyone you could think of who might have wanted to hurt Olivia? Any kind of personal problems she might have been having with anyone?"

"No, nothing."

"How about with the law? Had she ever been in any kind of trouble?"

Walden frowned, offended by the question. "Olivia never got in any kind of trouble. I mean, she'd got a ticket for speeding a while before she died, and you'd have thought she'd robbed a bank—she felt so bad about it. She was worried about her insurance going up, too."

Walden Fisher's eyes moistened. He moved his coffee cup to one side and made two fists. "It's with me every day, you know."

"Yes."

"I think, ultimately, it's what killed Beth."

"Your wife."

Walden nodded. "I mean, officially, it was the cancer, but it was the grief that was eating her up inside. That, and no justice."

Duckworth didn't say anything.

"Every day, for three years, I've been hoping someone would answer for Olivia being taken from us. To find out it was someone already dead, I don't know how I'd handle that. What do you do? Go piss on a man's grave? Is that any way to get revenge?"

Duckworth took one last sip of the coffee. "If you come across anything, or remember anything, that might connect your daughter to Dr. Sturgess, would you let me know?"

He placed a business card on the table. Walden drew it toward him, glanced at it.

"Yeah, sure."

"And I'll keep you posted of any developments."

"I'm worried about Victor," Walden blurted.

"Victor?"

"Victor Rooney. He was going out with Olivia back then. When it happened. He's never really got over it."

"How do you mean?" Duckworth said as he was pushing back his chair.

"It's been three years and he's never really moved on. He drinks too much. Has a hard time holding down a job. Blames everyone in Promise Falls for what happened." He looked into Duckworth's face. "He's harboring a lot of guilt."

"What kind of guilt? Do you think he had something to do with Olivia's death?"

That caught him up short. "Jesus, not directly. I mean, I don't think so. He was with a friend when it happened. A drinking buddy. He had an alibi. He was supposed to be meeting Olivia but got held up. Unless . . ."

Walden's voice trailed off.

"Unless what?"

"Unless he got someone to lie for him." Walden Fisher gazed through the window into his backyard. "And all this stuff he's going through lately, this show of grief, this not being able to move on, is some kind of act." He shook his head dismissively. "No, there's no way. Victor's not perfect, but he'd never be capable of that."

Duckworth stood and was walking down the hall toward the front of the house when, as he was passing an open door to a small bathroom, something occurred to him.

"Let me ask you about someone else," he said. "Did you or Olivia ever know a Bill Gaynor?"

"Bill Gaynor?" Walden Fisher said. "Same name as that woman that was murdered?"

"Rosemary was his wife."

"Son of a bitch," he said. "They were married? Bill was our insurance guy."

NINETEEN

Randall Finley and Frank Mancini had arranged to meet for lunch at the Clover, an upscale—at least by Promise Falls standards—restaurant on the town's outskirts. Finley was more at home at a place like Casey's, a bar over on Charlton, but when he had an important business meeting, the Clover, with its white linen tablecloths, fine china, and waitstaff who were less inclined to tell you to fuck off, was always his first choice.

Finley had reserved his favorite booth, with high-backed seats and a divider that offered some privacy from the next table over. There was always the possibility he'd say something he didn't want anyone but his luncheon guest to hear.

He was already seated when Mancini came into the room. He was short and stocky but not fat, a walking fire hydrant. A well-dressed one, too. While the man had spent his life in construction, he didn't go around wearing a hard hat. He was in a dark blue suit—Armani, Finley guessed—with a crisp white shirt and a red tie.

"Don't get up," Mancini said as Finley started struggling to get out of the booth.

Finley stayed seated, shook hands, waited for Mancini to get settled in across from him.

"What can I get you?" Finley asked.

"Scotch."

Finley waved over the waitress, whose name tag read KIMMY.

"Are you new, Kimmy?" the former mayor asked as she handed them menus.

The young woman smiled. "This is my first week."

Finley smiled and shook his head admiringly. "Just when you think the Clover can't hire waitresses any prettier, they bring in someone like you. Isn't she a peach, Frank?"

Mancini smiled.

Kimmy accepted the praise with an awkward smile. "What can I get you gentlemen?"

Finley ordered two scotches. Once the waitress had slipped away, Mancini said, "Shouldn't a guy who once got caught with an underage hooker cool it when it comes to the young ones?"

"I was paying her a compliment. And that other business was years ago."

"It cost you your job."

"A job I'm going to get back. Voters have a great capacity for forgiveness, especially the kind of bumpkins we have in this town. Nobody cares about that kind of stuff these days. Look at Clinton. Fools around with an intern, he's the most popular former president these days."

Mancini sighed. "See yourself as Clintonesque, do you?"

Finley chuckled. "Okay, so maybe I'm not quite as popular as good ol' Bill. But the people in this town can't remember what they had for breakfast, let alone something I did years ago."

"Keep insulting them like that. Jesus, Randy, you'll never get reelected if the voters know you think they're a bunch of idiots."

"I never said that. They're good people." Finley smiled. "And I have to be who I am. You want me to be somebody I'm not?"

"Randy, I'd like you to be almost anybody else. I'd rather be sitting here with fucking Al Capone. I'd feel safer."

Finley laughed. Mancini, not so much.

"You love fuckin' with me," Finley said. He lowered his voice. "So tell me, what the hell was that at the drive-in?"

"What are you talking about?"

"What am I talking about? You kidding me? The fucking explosion? The screen coming down? Four people dead?"

"It was a tragedy—that's what it was," Mancini said.

"Yeah, yeah, I know. We're all broken up about it. But just between us, was that you?"

"Are you fucking kidding me?" Mancini said, loud enough to be heard by nearby diners.

"Jesus, keep your voice down," Finley said. "So you're saying you had nothing to do with it?"

"Why the hell would I do that? It had to be the demolition people. They screwed up."

"Not what I'm hearing," Finley said. "I'm hearing they hadn't even started yet."

"What else are they going to say? They're in cover-your-ass mode."

"I don't know. Thing is, guy like you, you'd have all the expertise to do that."

"Randy, have you completely lost your mind? We've bought the land, and the deal requires that Grayson drop the structures before we acquire it. What've I got to gain by blowing things up and killing people? What sense does that make?"

Finley was quiet for a moment. "I have to admit, I can't figure out an angle. Unless this gives you an out on the deal—then Grayson comes back, slashes his price so he can unload the place."

"There's no goddamn angle. I had nothing to do with it. It was the demolition company. You can take that to the bank. Let's move on. Let's talk about you and what you're going to do for me."

"I have to get elected first."

"You haven't even officially declared."

"Imminent."

"You need to get moving. You need to win this thing. I got no chance with that Amanda Croydon sitting in the mayor's chair. I gotta get her out of there. She's an eco-bitch. You'd think she'd be behind me, but anytime anyone else has ever proposed anything similar, there's noise concerns—everyone's worried about soil pollution, contamination of the water table, all kinds of shit that never really happens, at least not as bad as they say it does. I've made a major investment here, Randy, buying that land. You need to get that woman out of there and start running things again."

"All in good time," Finley said. "And come on, you never bought property before without knowing if you'd get all the proper approvals? It's all part of doing business. And what's the worst-case scenario? If somehow I don't get in, if Amanda hangs on, you can always just build houses there. You're not going to get a fight on that."

"Houses don't bring in a daily revenue stream," Mancini said. "You build a house, you sell it, you make your profit, and you move on. But a metal recycling plant, that's money coming in twenty-four/seven, years into the future. Jobs, too."

"Jobs, sure. But like you said, there's money to be made. Once I'm in, I can use my connections. I know people—I can grease palms—I can get this thing approved. I'm not promising there won't be a few bumps along the way, but it'll happen."

The drinks arrived.

"That's terrific, sweetheart," Finley said to Kimmy.

"You ready to order lunch?" she asked.

"Steak frites, rare," Finley said. "Frank?"

"I haven't even looked at the menu."

"Just get the steak."

"I don't know if I feel like steak."

"What are you, a homo?" Finley grinned, glanced at Kimmy. "Just joking. I'm totally okay with homos."

"Fine, the steak," Mancini said. "Well-done."

Kimmy slipped away.

"I wonder if she's seeing anybody," Finley said.

"You ever think you may have overestimated your attractiveness?" the builder asked.

"Women are drawn to power."

Mancini laughed. "You used to be the mayor of Promise Falls, not the goddamn secretary of defense."

"Still, people know me. They know who I am."

"They know what you are," Mancini said. "That's what worries me about whether you can actually get yourself elected again."

"I feel pretty good about it," he said. "All I have to do is convince everyone I'm the town's savior."

"What, like Jesus?"

"But with Florsheims instead of sandals," Finley said. He leaned in closer. "This town owes me, Frank. This town owes me another chance. I got fucked over here. These people let me down, and I'm going to give them a chance to make it up to me. I was the victim of a smear campaign, plain and simple."

"Did the left-wing media force that hooker to blow you?"

Finley did a backhand flip, waving away Mancini's concern. "People act like they care about that stuff—they love to read about it—but in their hearts they really don't give a shit. They know I'm one of them. I'm just a regular guy. I get their concerns. I'm not some elitist asshole talking down to them."

"You're rich, Randy. You got a thriving water-bottling business. You're one of the one percent."

"Yeah, well, I don't come across that way, and that's what matters. It's all about perception."

Finley told Mancini about how he'd brought someone on to help manage his image, plan a campaign. The guy, Finley said, wasn't exactly James Carville, but for Promise Falls, he wasn't bad. Former newspaper guy, worked for the *Standard* before they pulled the plug on it. Which led to a ten-minute discussion of how it was a lot easier to do what you wanted to do when there was no local paper breathing down your neck.

"No headlines about kickbacks," Mancini said.

Finley frowned. "That's a very cynical point of view, Frank. What I am is a facilitator. I make things happen. You want to set up a business that will not only profit you, but serve your community. I can help facilitate that. It's not unreasonable that I should expect some compensation for my efforts. Be they material or political. It's the system working the way it was designed to work."

Kimmy returned with their two orders of steak frites.

Mancini said, "Could I get another scotch, and a glass of water?"

"Tap, or bottled?"

Before he could answer, Finley said, "I wouldn't go with tap. Never, *ever* tap. Unless you're brushing your teeth. Sweetheart, you've got Finley Springs, right?"

"I'm not sure," she said. "I think we have San Pellegrino in sparkling, and probably Evian in flat."

Finley cocked his head. "Are you sure about that?"

"Uh, I think so."

"Maybe you better go check." Finley's voice had turned subtly menacing.

Kimmy withdrew.

"You're making a scene," Mancini said. "So what if they don't carry your water? There's lots of brands of bottled water."

"I'm thinking, once I get in, this place definitely is getting a visit from the health inspector. Fire, too."

"This is what I mean," Mancini said. "You can't let yourself get tripped up by the small shit."

"Look, she's talking to the manager," Finley said.

Seconds later, a balding, portly man in a black suit approached the table. "Mr. Finley, how nice to see you today."

"Carmine. How are you?"

"Excellent. You'll have to excuse Kimmy. She's new, and she was unaware that she was looking after one of our most special customers. She's getting some Finley Springs Water for your friend here as we speak."

"Oh, Carmine, I don't care, one way or the other. I'm not about to tell you how to run your restaurant."

Carmine smiled. "If there's anything you need, don't hesitate to see me directly."

Once he was gone, Finley said, "What do you want to bet someone's running to 7-Eleven right now?"

"What's this going to cost me?" Mancini said.

"We've already sorted out my compensation on this, Frank."

"I'm talking incidentals. The greasing of palms."

Finley shrugged. "Hard to say. Some people come cheaper than others. Some, if you've got the goods on them, it doesn't cost you a dime. Start-up costs are always unpredictable."

Mancini cut a piece off the end of his steak and put it into his mouth. "Did you ever do anything as a politician, back when you were mayor, that you did strictly for the people, because you thought it was the right thing to do?"

"The welfare of my constituents was and is always my first consideration, Frank, my guiding principle, as it were."

"I like how you did that without even smiling."

"It's a gift," Finley said.

At the next table, which was separated from Finley and Mancini by a crosshatched wood divider, David Harwood had ordered only a house salad. Steak was beyond his budget.

He knew the spot Randall Finley always asked for at the Clover, and had phoned ahead in a bid for a nearby table. The one they initially showed him to was across the aisle, in full view of where Finley and Mancini would be sitting. So David asked for the table on the other side of the divider.

He didn't hear everything the two men said, but he heard enough. He wasn't shocked. He wasn't even sure he was horrified. You signed on to work with someone like Finley, well, what did you expect?

The question was whether he could stomach it.

Carmine placed the leather folder with the check inside at his elbow.

"Thank you, sir," he said.

David flipped it open, glanced at the total, felt his heart skip a beat. If this was what a salad cost, what would the steak frites have run him?

He wanted to invite Sam Worthington to dinner, but maybe not at a place as expensive as this.

If she'd even answer his call.

TWENTY

Cal

Before stumbling upon the secret room, I'd been about ready to give up thinking I could help Lucy Brighton find out who'd been in her father's house. Up to then, I had no idea why anyone would have broken in, or what they might have been looking for.

Now I had a pretty good idea what someone wanted.

Someone knew about that hidden room, knew what was in it. Namely, those discs, which, I was guessing, were homemade porno. It struck me that someone who'd go to all that trouble to get them was probably on them. And if so, knew Adam and Miriam Chalmers.

Knew them pretty well.

I asked Lucy to find, for starters, an address book and phone bills, while I went back to Adam's office, dropped into the chair behind the desk, and started looking at e-mails on his desktop computer.

I clicked on the stamp icon, and immediately I was asked to enter a password. I decided to try "Lucy." When that didn't let me in, I called out: "Lucy!"

She was in the kitchen. Her father always paid the bills sitting at the kitchen table—he didn't trust the Internet to pay for things online—and he kept old phone bills in the drawer there.

"Yes?" she said.

"It wants a password. And I tried your name."

There was a moment's silence. Then Lucy said, "Try 'Crystal.'"

I tried it. No luck.

"Nope!" I cried out.

Another short silence. Then, more quietly: "'Miriam.'"

I typed in the letters. Again, no joy.

"Got any other ideas?" I said.

"I'm thinking." I was guessing she was at least pleased that Miriam hadn't been picked over her or her daughter. "Try 'Devils' Chosen.'"

"What?"

She repeated it. "That was the name of the motorcycle gang he was with years ago."

I gave it a try. The first time, with an *s* apostrophe, didn't work. I tried it again without, and still no luck. The third time, I used an uppercase *D* and *C*.

Bingo.

"I'm in," I said.

I scanned the mail program. There were dozens of e-mails in the in-box, the sent file, and the trash. It would take hours to go through all of these, but the answer might be here.

The most recent—it had come in early this morning and had not been opened—was from a Gilbert Frobisher. He wrote:

Heard about that crazy drive-in explosion on CNN
this morning. Wow. Hope no one you knew was up
there. Hell of a way to put Promise Falls on the map.
Talked to your old editor at Putnam, who says if you
have anything kicking around, any ideas, they'd be
willing to talk, but she was not overly optimistic.

You haven't done a book in five years, your name recognition has slipped some, but still, if you had something good, she'd look at it. But she can't guarantee the kind of advance you had in the past. Not so much money up front, but with the right book you could cash in on the back end. So, start thinking. Talk later.

That e-mail had been a reply to one from Adam, which had read:

Gilbert, my man, I could use some good news. If we don't get some nibbles soon, I'm going to have to start burning the furniture. I need to live in the manner that not only I have become accustomed to, but Miriam, too. Can't you start circulating some of the early books around again to the studios, see if there's any interest? God knows they don't actually have to be made into movies. A bit of option money would hold me over nicely. And go back to Debra at Putnam. Sound her out. Tell her I have a great pitch, a knockout idea, but I want to see some money on the table before I tell her what it is. I know it's a bit of a pig in a poke, but she owes me.

The next one, which had been opened, had come in late yesterday afternoon. It was from Felicia Chalmers. I called out: "What did you say your father's ex-wife's name was?"

"Felicia." Excitedly, "I've found the phone bills."

"Look for numbers that come up a lot."

I clicked on the e-mail from Felicia. It was short.

Nice to talk to you. I'd like to say you'll work it out,
and maybe you will, but you do have kind of a track
record, you know. Maybe she just needs some time
to think things through. But I wish you all the best.
Call me if you want, like you need my permission.
Love, Felicia.

What I really wanted to find was an e-mail that said,
"Hey, Adam, I've got a key. I'll come by and get the discs."
But things were never that simple. But it was interesting
that Adam Chalmers still kept in touch with his ex.

The next e-mail was a fan letter from someone who'd
read one of his books, and wanted to know, if he mailed
Chalmers a copy of it, could he autograph it and send it
back? Adam had not responded. And there was an e-mail
from Lucy herself, which read:

Hi Dad: Is it okay if Crystal comes over Saturday?
I've got a conference workshop thing I really need to
go to, and if she could spend the afternoon with you,
that'd be terrific. So long as you and Miriam don't
have anything planned. I'd really appreciate it. I'd
drop her off around eleven and pick her up by four.

The message had been replied to. I looked in the sent
file, found a quick note from Adam to his daughter saying, *No prob.*

I glanced through some of the more recent sent messages. A couple of replies to other fans who'd read and
enjoyed one of his books. There was a request from an
aspiring author, asking Chalmers to read his book. His
reply read:

I can't think of anything I would rather do than set aside eight or more hours for no compensation whatsoever to read a book about which I know nothing from a complete and total stranger. Do you have friends who have written books, too, that you could send along with yours? Please gather them all up and send them to me, but I want actual paper manuscripts because it has been my experience that the e-mailed ones are much harder to keep lit when you put them in the fireplace to get the logs going.

I continued scanning the e-mails, including those in the trash file. There wasn't much there. Adam had purged most of the deleted e-mails from the computer. There were only about twenty in there, the oldest from six days ago.

This wasn't proving to be productive.

Lucy came into the office. "There are three numbers that show up quite a few times on my father's cell phone bill. Well, four, actually. But the fourth is Miriam's cell, and that just makes sense."

"What are the others?"

She read the first one out to me. I opened a browser on the computer and Googled it. If it was a landline, and not unlisted, there was a good chance whoever it belonged to would turn up.

Felicia Chalmers.

"Tell me about Felicia," I said.

"Is it her number?"

I nodded.

Lucy Brighton stopped to think. "She still lives in Promise Falls, far as I know. I mean, I have nothing to do with her. We weren't enemies or anything, but once she and Dad broke up, there was no reason to keep in touch. I think she's got a condo somewhere around here. I think if she'd remarried, Dad would have mentioned it."

"The two of them clearly have kept in touch. Did your father have financial obligations to her?"

"He gave her a lump sum when they divorced, but not all that much. I wouldn't be surprised if he slipped her some money now and then. But there were no kids to worry about. And she was the one who'd pushed to get out of the marriage."

"But she kept the name," I said.

"Her own last name is Dimpfelmyer. What would you do?"

The Google search had brought up an address on Braymore Drive. I wrote it down in my notebook. Maybe Felicia was still trusted to have a key. And to know the code. Maybe Adam and Miriam's sex life included his ex. A threesome. I could imagine Felicia might want those DVDs back. If she'd heard about Adam and Miriam getting killed at the drive-in, she wouldn't want whoever had to empty the house—Lucy, presumably—finding those home movies. So she busted in, grabbed them, and ran out the back when Lucy got here.

It wasn't a bad theory. And it was a good place to start.

"What's the next number?" I asked.

She read it off. I did another Google search and came up with nothing. Probably a cell.

"Let's have a look at the address book," I said. Lucy handed it to me. I started flipping through the pages, looking for a number that matched the one she'd just given me.

I went through the entire book without getting a hit. I made a note of it, would check it later.

"What's the last one?" I asked, scribbling it down as Lucy read it off to me. I went to the Google search field again and entered it. Again, no luck. Probably another cell. So I went back to the address book.

This time, I had better luck. And I only had to go to the *D*s.

"You ever heard of someone named Clive Duncomb?" I asked Lucy.

She shook her head.

I turned again to my friend Mr. Google.

"Whoa," I said, seeing a number of stories come up.

"What?"

"He's the head of security at Thackeray. And a few days ago he blew some kid's head off."

"My God. Why?"

"If it was plagiarism, things have gotten a lot tougher than when I was at school."

I decided to start with Felicia Chalmers.

She lived in the Waterside Towers condo development, about half a mile downstream from the falls in the center of town. To call it a tower was a stretch. It was a five-story building, which, with the exception of the water tower, was as tall as structures got in Promise Falls.

I parked in a guest spot and entered the outer lobby. No one was on duty, but that didn't mean I was able to walk in. There was a directory and a panel of buttons by the second door. I found Felicia Chalmers in 502, which meant she was on the top floor.

I hated buzzers. If the woman didn't want to talk to me, she wouldn't have to let me in. It was a lot easier to say no to people when you didn't have to see them face-to-face.

And I didn't want to have to explain, through a speaker, why I was here.

Someone was coming along the sidewalk, heading to the main door of the building. A middle-aged woman with a set of keys in her hand.

I leaned in close to the panel of buttons, appeared to be taking my hand away from one of them, and as the woman came into the building, I said, loudly, "Okay, then, I'll be up in a second."

I turned, smiled at the woman with the key. She unlocked the door, glanced my way.

"I'm just waiting to be buzzed in," I said, making no move to try to sneak in as she pulled open the glass door.

"Oh, just go ahead," she said, holding the door for me.

"Oh, thanks."

I scooted in, then politely stepped aside to let her walk ahead of me as we headed for the elevator. The woman got off at three, and I stayed on until the doors opened at five. I got my bearings, figured that 502 was to the left, and walked down the carpeted hallway until I was at Felicia Chalmers's apartment.

I could hear music inside as I rapped on the door.

Five seconds later, I heard a chain sliding back, and then the door opened. I had to adjust my gaze downward. In high heels, she might have been five-three, but she was barefoot and the top of her head was barely level with my chin. Her blond hair was pulled back into a ponytail, and she was dressed in some turquoise workout clothes. Trickles of sweat ran down her temple.

"Yes?" she asked over the sound of Chicago performing "Does Anybody Really Know What Time It Is?"

"Ms. Chalmers? Felicia Chalmers?"

"How did you get into the building?"

I got out my ID. "I'm Cal Weaver. I'm a private investigator. I'd like to ask you a few questions."

She put a hand on her hip. "About what?"

"About your former husband, Adam Chalmers."

Her eyebrows shot up. "God, what's he done? Wait, let me guess. There's a woman involved. There's always a woman involved one way or another."

Shit.

"Ms. Chalmers, you haven't heard?"

"Haven't heard what?"

"May I come in?"

Worry washed over her face. She opened the door wide, let me in, and closed it. She went over to an iPod resting on a Bose stereo unit, muted it, then crossed the room to what I was guessing was the bedroom, and pulled the door shut.

Having completed those errands, she asked, "What's going on?"

"The accident last night? At the Constellation Drive-in?"

"What accident at what drive-in?"

"Have you watched TV this morning, been online? Facebook, Twitter? Seen the news?"

She shook her head slowly. "I don't watch the news. It's all bad. And I'm not on those other things. About the only thing I use is e-mail. Please tell me what's going on."

"There was an explosion last night, at the drive-in. The screen came down on a couple of the cars. One of them belonged to Adam Chalmers. He was in the car with his wife, Miriam."

"What?"

"Mr. Chalmers and his wife were killed. I'm sorry to be the one to break this to you."

"Adam's dead?"

"I thought someone would have been in touch. Or that you would have heard somehow."

"That's impossible. Oh my God, this is awful. This is unbelievable. I was talking to him yesterday. I mean, not on the phone, but e-mail." She shook her head. "God, I need a drink. Get me a drink."

She pointed toward the kitchen.

"What would you like?"

"There's a bottle of red in the rack there. Glasses on the right. Fill one of them to the fucking brim."

She dropped herself onto an oversized couch, brought her feet up, and tucked them under her thighs. "Help yourself, too."

I went into the kitchen, where I noticed three empty beer bottles standing in the sink. Given what she'd sent me in here for, beer didn't strike me as her beverage of choice, but you never knew. Maybe she liked wine in the morning, and beer at night. But my beer theory was buttressed by the opened bag of spicy Doritos, rolled up and kept fresh with a rubber band. Didn't seem to match the workout regimen.

I came back with a full glass of red wine. She downed half of it, handed it back, and said, "Top it up."

I'd brought the bottle, and obliged. I sat down on a chair opposite her.

"You're not having anything?"

"I'm good," I said.

"I'd tell you I hate to drink alone, but you're a detective, so you'd figure out I was lying pretty fast." She shot a quick look at the closed bedroom door, then gave me a critical look. "Jesus, this is unbelievable. Tell me again what happened."

I told her what I knew.

"Oh my God. The two of them crushed? And they'd have been in his old Jag. Oh, Jesus, he loved that car. If he were here now, that's what he'd say was the most tragic part of this. Sure, Miriam getting killed, that's bad, but he really loved that car."

I didn't know what to say. But I didn't have to come up with anything. "Why are you here?" she asked.

"Issues related to Mr. Chalmers's death. As his ex-wife they may have some impact on you."

She pursed her lips. That seemed to be good enough for her. "You know, I could see Adam dying any number of ways, but a movie screen falling on him?"

"What other ways could you imagine?"

Felicia shrugged. "Some old biker from his past killing him for ripping him off, maybe. A jealous husband who didn't like Adam fucking his wife. Or maybe a former wife like me who was tired of listening to his bullshit. I don't know. Take your pick."

"Was there some old biker buddy from his past who got ripped off?"

"Shit, there were probably a bunch. Except Adam would have been smart enough to cover his tracks, or cover up the guy he ripped off with enough dirt that he'd never be coming after him, if you get my drift."

"I think I do."

She leaned forward. "I don't want to give you the wrong impression. Adam was a good guy. He just had one hell of a past, is all."

"Why'd the two of you divorce? I gather you were the one who wanted out."

She took another big swallow of wine. "And why, exactly, would I even answer that question? I don't know

144

who the hell you are or why you're really here. Some bullshit about *issues* related to his death?"

I smiled. "Someone broke into your ex-husband's home. After it became known that he'd been killed in the accident."

Her eyes widened. "What kind of sick bastard does that? I've heard about something like that. Creeps who break into people's houses when they're at funerals. They know they won't be home. People get home, all broken up over the death of a loved one, and their flat-screen TV and jewelry's gone."

"It wasn't quite like that. This thief was looking for something very specific, in a very specific place."

Felicia Chalmers blinked.

"Oh," she said.

"I think whoever came into the house had a key, and knew how to deactivate the security system. Someone Adam or Miriam, or both, trusted."

Felicia nodded slowly. "I see. And you're wondering if I'm that person?"

"I'm wondering if you have any idea who it could be."

"Well, it's not me. I can tell you that much. Adam would surely have changed the locks after our divorce. I mean, probably. Although I don't think he ever distrusted me. But once he married Miriam, I'll bet she'd have wanted to be sure I could never get into that house."

"You never tried?"

"Of course not. I had no reason. I probably still do have a key somewhere, but I can't say whether it would work or not."

"Could you find it?"

"Now?"

I nodded.

145

A sigh. She got off the couch and went into the kitchen. I could hear her rummaging around in a drawer. "Maybe I got rid of it," she said, loud enough for me to hear. "Oh, wait. I think this is it. Oh, looks like I've actually still got two of them."

She returned to the living room with a key held between thumb and forefinger.

"May I have that?" I asked. "I'd like to see if it actually works."

Felicia hesitated.

"If you'd like to call his daughter, Lucy Brighton, to confirm I'm legit, that's fine with me," I said.

She hesitated another second, then decided it was less trouble to trust me than to take the time to learn the truth from Lucy. "Here, take this one. I don't need it."

I did. I slipped it into the pocket of my sport jacket.

"Let me try asking again. Why did you and Adam get a divorce?"

She studied me for a few seconds, then gave a what-the-hell shrug. "I couldn't take it anymore. I just couldn't."

"Couldn't take what?"

"The lifestyle."

"I'm sorry. What lifestyle?"

"*The* lifestyle," she said.

Now I was the one shaking my head. "I don't understand. Are you saying Adam Chalmers was gay?"

"No, no, no. Although I suppose he was bisexual to some point. I mean, you'd kind of have to be."

"Wait, are you talking about wife-swapping?"

She frowned. "That's what they used to call it in the dark ages. But that's not a very politically correct term anymore. Made women sound like baseball cards. It's not wife-swapping, but spouse-sharing."

"Like group sex?"

Felicia looked at me like I was five. "Where are you from? Mayberry?"

"Enlighten me."

"The lifestyle is when one couple meets up with another couple for sex. Okay, it could be three couples. Anything more than that and I guess it would be an orgy. Adam always liked to keep it to two other couples. You have six people, and there are quite a number of permutations, even more if the men are into men and the women are into women. Or at least give it a try. Everything consensual, more or less—at least that's what they pretend. Everyone fooling around with each other, right in the open, no one going behind anyone's back to have an affair. Supposedly. The openness, the freedom, actually makes relationships stronger. Gets the urge to stray out of your system. You indulge your fantasies with your partner's blessing."

"Supposedly."

"Some spouses go along because it's what their partner wants. They tell themselves they're into it, too. But . . . not so much."

"Like you."

Felicia shrugged, knocked back some more wine. "You think it's all out in the open, that that would eliminate the need for an actual affair. Why sneak around behind your spouse's back when you can fuck someone else right in front of her? But with Adam, it was the secrecy he liked. That was the thrill. So even if he was banging his best friend's wife right in front of him, the real thrill was to do it someplace else when he wasn't there."

"Is that what Adam did?"

She smiled sadly. "Oh, yeah. He had to see women

147

outside the playroom. When I learned he was doing that, I'd had enough. I wanted out."

"The playroom," I said.

Felicia took a moment to size me up, wondering how much I knew. "You found it," she said.

"Yes."

She closed her eyes, as though trying to picture it. "It all seems so silly, when you think about it. And a little bit tacky, I guess. But Adam felt those activities deserved to be relegated to a special room. Like it shouldn't taint the rest of the house. But it had to be hidden. He didn't want anyone wandering in there by mistake."

"I saw the DVD player. And the camera equipment under the bed."

"Adam liked to record sessions," she said, opening her eyes. "We'd play them back sometimes, with guests. Kind of like reviewing a football game play by play."

"So everyone knew they were being videoed. The camera wasn't hidden."

Felicia shook her head.

"The DVDs are gone," I said.

Her eyes widened. "What?"

"I think that's what someone was after. Those DVDs."

"Christ on a taco," she said.

"That worries you?"

"Not me. Not personally. When we split up, Adam gave me any video he had of me, of us, either alone or with others."

"How do you know he didn't hold something back? Didn't make copies?"

"Because I just know. Adam, for all his faults, was a more or less honest guy. At least with me. If he said he gave me everything, he did. And he never put anything online, never did computer files. He knew that kind of stuff always got hacked or sent by mistake. He liked hard copies, no pun intended."

"And you destroyed them? The discs he gave you?"

"I did."

"You're sure?"

She scowled. "I told you."

"Because I'm trying to recover those DVDs, or be assured that they're no longer in existence."

"Who for? No, wait, you already mentioned Lucy."

I nodded.

"*She* wants them?"

"She'd be happy knowing that they've been destroyed. She doesn't have to get them back. But we need to know who took them to get that kind of assurance."

Felicia softened. "Sure. Look, I'm telling you the truth. Adam gave me any discs from our time together and I smashed them into a million pieces. They went out in the trash years ago."

"Who else was on them?"

I was thinking that if the couples participating in the *lifestyle* with Adam and Felicia were still taking part with Adam and Miriam, I'd have some likely suspects where the missing DVDs were concerned.

Felicia shook her head. "I know what you must be thinking, and I don't think it's going to help. There were two other couples we saw back then. One moved to Paris around that time—she got transferred—and I don't think they ever came back. And the other couple, there was kind of a big falling-out because she was the one Adam saw on the side."

"On the side."

"Yeah. Any discs from back then that featured those

people also featured me, so they'd have been the ones Adam gave me."

"When you were married to Adam, did he ever trust another couple enough that he'd give them a key to the house?"

She nodded. "The ones who moved to France. Adam gave him a key. In case we were away, it was someone who could check the house, if he didn't want to trouble Lucy."

"Do you know who Adam and Miriam were involved with more recently?"

"How would I know that?"

"Because you and Adam still talked. At least through e-mails."

Her eyes widened for half a second. "It's true, but I don't think Miriam knew. She'd have been pissed."

"I saw your exchange from yesterday. You said someone needed time to think something through. What was that about?"

"Jesus, you really are a detective. I was talking about Miriam. They were having some ups and downs."

"The same kind you were having? Another woman?"

"He didn't get too specific, but probably. Maybe that's why he took her to the movies. Trying to smooth things over. Christ, maybe he took her to the drive-in to rekindle some of what they used to have, and they ended up dead."

"You think Adam was interested in starting up a relationship with you again?"

She nearly choked on the wine. "Hardly. Been there, done that."

I looked at the closed bedroom door, held it for two beats. "And you've moved on, anyway."

Felicia followed my gaze, smiled. "I've moved on more times than I can count." She put the glass to her lips and tipped it back.

"Had you and Adam always kept in touch since the divorce?"

She shrugged. "We stayed friends."

"Did he give you money?"

The look she gave me suggested I'd just asked how much she weighed. "Money?"

"Beyond whatever settlement you had when you divorced."

"It was a lump sum. But—" She paused for more wine. "But occasionally, when I needed a little help, he'd be there for me. He just didn't want Miriam to know."

"Did the two of you continue to be intimate?"

She grinned. "That is so charming. *Intimate*. You mean, were we still fucking?"

"Yes."

She pursed her lips provocatively, then retracted them, perhaps realizing that whatever hookups she and her ex had had, there would be no more. "There was the occasional itch," she conceded. "But mostly, he just liked to talk."

Her expression turned sorrowful. "He felt I was one of the few people who understood him. Who knew that even if he behaved badly, he wasn't a bad person." She sniffed. "He was just a big boy, is what he was. I mean, he had problems. Some people would probably want to label him, say he had some sort of sexual addiction problem. You ask me, he just always wanted to be nineteen. I think he missed his bad-boy biker days."

"What'd he do back then?"

"You don't know?"

"No," I said.

"He ran girls. Prostitution. Made a lot of money out of it, too. He's always liked the ladies, one way or another."

"I didn't know."

Despite whatever sorrow she was feeling, she managed a smile.

"It was how me met," she said. "Adam wasn't the only one who reinvented himself."

TWENTY-ONE

The lecture hall, which could accommodate more than a hundred students, currently held no more than thirty. This was a summer class, so attendance was a fraction of what it would have been through the school year. When Professor Peter Blackmore entered, the students were getting settled into their seats, opening their laptops on the teardrop-shaped fold-down tables, or putting out their smartphones and setting them to record. Blackmore didn't see one student getting out a pen and paper.

There was a time, ten years ago, when he would have walked in with a briefcase jammed with student essays, half a dozen books, and a copy of his speech. But today he'd arrived with nothing but a digital tablet in his pocket. He'd e-mailed his lecture on Melville and psychological determinism to himself, and once he reached the lectern, he'd open the file and, using his index finger, glide his way through the talk. He might not have the most up-to-date phone, or know how to text, but when it came to delivering a lecture, he was totally twenty-first century.

"If everyone could take a seat . . ." he said.

A handful of students continued chatting. The odds were none of them was talking about Melville, or psychological determinism, or anything else academic for that matter. It was more likely they were making plans for later. Where they'd meet for a drink. Who wanted to go in on a pizza order. Sharing gossip. Who was sleeping with whom.

He was thinking he shouldn't have told the detective about Georgina.

"Okay, I trust everyone's well into *Moby-Dick*," Blackmore said. "Or at the very least, the CliffsNotes version."

Some nervous laughter rippled through the hall.

He reached into the deep pocket of his jacket, brought out the tablet. Hit the button at the bottom, slid his finger across the screen to unlock it.

"Just one second here," Blackmore said.

He knew Clive Duncomb would be pissed if he knew he'd talked to Angus Carlson. Duncomb liked to handle problems on his own. Not just his problems, but the problems of those close to him.

Duncomb didn't like dealing with the local police. He considered them a bunch of hicks. A Promise Falls detective, Duncomb liked to say, couldn't find his own ass in a snowstorm.

Blackmore wasn't sure he took as dim a view of the local force. Not that he'd had many dealings with them, but he wasn't aware of any examples of gross incompetence. It wasn't as though a professor of English literature had much reason to interact with the police.

There'd certainly been plenty of them on campus after Duncomb shot and killed that student who was going around attacking young women.

Didn't seem to bother Duncomb at all to blow that kid's brains out.

Sure, Blackmore thought, you could argue Duncomb did the right thing, but you'd think he'd feel something afterward. Taking another person's life? But the guy carried on as though ending a young man's life was just another day at the office.

Maybe, Blackmore thought, he shouldn't be all that surprised, considering Duncomb's background. Or his wife, Liz's, for that matter. The details had trickled out over the last few years. How Duncomb had been working vice for the Boston PD when he met Elizabeth Palmer. He'd been gathering evidence on the escort business she ran, hoping to round her up in a sting, but he was the one who ended up being drawn into her net.

But the Boston cops hadn't been the only ones looking at Liz. There was the IRS, for one. Duncomb, sabotaging his own department's investigation, helped Liz destroy evidence. Records were shredded and burned. People were paid off. Duncomb quit, married Liz—motivated not just by love but by the two of them never having to testify against each other—and moved to Promise Falls when he got his security chief gig.

Was it a stretch to think a man like that might take extreme measures?

"Professor?"

"Hmm?"

It was a girl in the front row. Trish, or Tricia, something like that.

"Is something wrong?"

He realized he'd been standing there, saying nothing, off in his own world for the better part of fifteen seconds. Maybe longer. He wasn't sure.

"Sorry," he said. "I really am the absentminded professor, aren't I?"

A few chuckles. Most of them, he realized, had probably never heard of the movie. A reference lost to the generations.

"Okay," he said, resting the tablet on the lectern. The speech magically appeared. He'd bumped up the font size so he could read without having to wear his glasses.

Seconds before coming into the lecture hall, he had tried again to reach Georgina. He'd called home and her cell. No answers. He'd put in a call to the law office where she worked, just in case she'd shown up. No luck there, either.

He had a feeling maybe she was home. She was angry with him, he was guessing, and when his name came up on the caller ID of her cell or the landline, she was refusing to answer.

Making him suffer.

Well, it was working.

"Uh, when we talk about psychological determinism, what is it exactly we're talking about? It's quite a mouthful, I grant you. But it goes to the heart of . . . the heart of . . ."

He'd swiped upward a little too hard with his finger, placing him ten paragraphs into his lecture. He tried to move the text back into position.

"Uh, hang on here, hang on . . ."

She's fallen. Good God, she's been hurt.

It seemed so obvious. Frighteningly obvious. Up to now, he'd assumed she was trying to teach him some sort of lesson. That she'd run off somewhere. Gone to stay with a friend. Or, if she was home, was giving him the silent treatment. She'd done it before when she'd been angry with him for something he'd done.

And he had done something. Or rather, he'd said something. Something he shouldn't have said. Made some terrible accusations.

She hadn't taken it well.

So there'd been every reason to believe she'd gone off somewhere to cool off. But it wasn't like her to be gone this long. He'd seen her storm off and get in her car and come back in an hour or two.

Not overnight.

And she'd never been so pissed with him that she failed to show up for work.

God, what an idiot I've been, he thought. He should have gone home when her office had called. She could have tripped on the stairs. Slipped getting out of the tub. Electrocuted herself somehow.

He had to get home. Right now.

Blackmore looked at his class, at the thirty expectant and confused faces. "I'm sorry," he said. "I can't do this today."

He picked up the tablet, shoved it into his pocket, and headed for the exit.

He walked hurriedly to his rusting, twenty-year-old Volvo, sped out of the faculty parking lot in a cloud of exhaust.

The Blackmores lived in a two-story redbrick Victorian in the old part of Promise Falls. Over the last decade— as long as he and Georgina had been married—they'd worked to restore the home to its original glory. They'd replaced the gingerbread trim and railings on the small front porch. Reshingled the roof. Replaced the furnace.

Georgina's car, a four-year-old Prius, was parked at the side of the house. At first, the sight of the car gave him reason for hope. He brought the Volvo to a halt behind it, killed the engine, and got out of the car so quickly he didn't bother to close the door.

He was fumbling with his keys as he approached the side entrance. But before he inserted the key, he tried opening it. Half the time, Georgina left the house unlocked when she was home.

The knob turned in his hand.

As he pushed it open, he shouted, "Georgie! Georgie?"

No answer.

The side door opened onto a landing between two short flights of stairs. Four steps up would take him to the kitchen, four steps down to the basement.

He decided to go up to the kitchen first. What he saw stopped him dead.

Drawers pulled out, cupboards opened. Dishes and cups and utensils out of position, dumped onto the countertop.

"Jesus," he whispered. Then, shouting, he said, "Georgina!"

He made his way to the stairs and scaled them two steps at a time to reach the second floor. He headed straight for their bedroom. It was like the kitchen. Dresser drawers pulled out, clothes tossed, suitcases pulled out from under the bed. The closet door was open, and empty shoe boxes had been opened and tossed.

"Oh my God," he said.

The guest bedroom had been similarly tossed. Someone had been searching the house from top to bottom.

"Oh my God oh my God oh my God," Blackmore kept repeating.

"Calm down," said a voice behind him.

Blackmore spun around. Standing in the doorway was Clive Duncomb.

"Jesus Christ!" Blackmore cried. "What the hell is going on?"

"I came by to look for Georgina," he said calmly.

"Where is she? Where's Georgina?"

"I don't know."

"Her car's here," Blackmore said. "If her car's here, where the hell is she?"

"I didn't find a purse."

"Her purse?"

"I didn't find it."

"Georgina probably has half a dozen purses."

Duncomb nodded. "Yes, that's true. But the one she'd currently be using would have her car keys and her wallet and her driver's license. I didn't find a purse with those things."

Blackmore waved his arms at the disarray. "Look at this. Something happened here. Someone tore this place apart. Maybe Georgina caught someone doing this. Oh God. Maybe someone kidnapped her, or even—"

"I did this," Duncomb said.

Blackmore said, "What?"

"I've been tearing the place apart. I just finished looking through the basement. If she took it, and if it's here, it's well hidden."

"Clive, what the hell are you talking about?"

"It occurred to me that it might be Georgina. She was always uncomfortable about that one disc. And she wasn't wrong to be. Maybe she got into the house before I did. Or maybe she took it a long time ago."

"Goddamn it, Clive, all you had to do was ask me. If Georgina'd taken it, she'd have told me."

"Would she? Maybe she'd have been afraid to. Maybe she did it on her own."

"Even if—even if you're right, she wouldn't have hidden it. She'd have *destroyed* it."

Duncomb nodded, thinking. "Probably. It'd be good if she did. But I need to know. I need to know it doesn't exist anymore."

Blackmore ran his fingers through his hair, then kept his hand there and pushed down, as though keeping his head from exploding.

"But if she took it or didn't take it, it doesn't explain where she is," he said. "Where the hell did she go?"

"That's the part that worries me," Clive Duncomb said. "Maybe she has it, and now she's deciding what to do with it."

It took Blackmore a moment to take in what Clive was getting at. "She wouldn't go to the police. She wouldn't. That makes no sense at all. She's my *wife*. She'd be ruining all of us, herself included. It's absolutely impossible. It's unthinkable."

"I hope you're right. Because the last thing any of us need is a video of us fucking the brains out of some girl who ended up dead."

"We didn't have anything to do with what happened to Olivia Fisher," Blackmore said, searching Duncomb's face. "Right?"

"Of course not," he said. "But it's not the sort of thing I'd want to have to prove."

TWENTY-TWO

The door to Felicia Chalmers's bedroom opened. A lean, six-foot-tall man, arms adorned with dragon tattoos and dressed in nothing but a pair of airplane-themed boxers, stood there, scratching his right buttock. He blinked his eyes repeatedly, bringing Felicia, and the apartment, into focus.

"The Corbin rises," Felicia said, having just shown out the detective, the nearly empty glass of red wine still in her hand.

"I heard talking," Corbin said.

"You didn't hear the music, but you could hear the talking?"

"The music I'm used to," he said. "I can sleep through Metallica. But I heard you yakking with somebody and it woke me up. Something going on?"

"Adam's dead."

"Uh," Corbin said, "who's Adam again?"

Felicia frowned. "My ex."

That brought him fully awake. "Shit! What happened?" Felicia filled him in. "Sorry, babe. You need a hug?" He opened his arms.

"No, I do not need a hug," she said, and went into the kitchen. She set down her wineglass and rooted around in a drawer until she found an address book.

"Whatcha looking for?"

"The number for the guy who handled my divorce. Arthur Clement, his name was. In Albany."

Corbin's face scrunched up. "What do you need him for? You already divorced the dude. And now he's dead."

"Exactly," she said. "And he's not the only one."

"I'm not following."

She found the number, used her index finger as a bookmark, turned to look at the nearly naked man standing at the entrance to the kitchen. "I'm sure you aren't."

"Come on, help me out here."

"His wife died, too," Felicia explained. "And his first wife died years ago. So maybe I'm entitled to something."

"Didn't you say he's got a daughter? Like, all grown-up?"

"Lucy," Felicia said. "Yeah. But everything shouldn't all go to her."

"Was the guy that loaded?"

Felicia shrugged. "Maybe not. But there'll be something. There's the house. He probably had investments and stuff like that. As his only surviving ex-wife, I must be entitled to *something*. Who knows? Maybe he mentioned me in his will."

"Did he tell you he had?"

Felicia bit her lip. "Not exactly."

"I think you're pissing up a rope here, Felish," Corbin said. "Whatever he's got will probably go to his kid. I'm not a lawyer, but—"

"No, you're a bartender."

"I'm just saying, I'm not a lawyer, but that's how it looks to me."

"It won't bother you if I get a more professional opinion?"

162

Corbin leaned into the doorframe, ran his tongue over his teeth. "You know, Felish, I'm not sure this is working out."

She had the address book open again and was reaching for the phone.

"Uh-huh," she said.

"I don't think you respect me for who I am."

She had the receiver in her hand, was entering a number. "Respect you? Of course I do. I respect you for exactly what you are. You're—hello?" Felicia turned her back to Corbin. "I need to talk to Arthur. No, I need to speak to him right this second. This is an emergency. That's right. This is Felicia Chalmers. You tell him there's been a death—tell him that. Yes, I'll hold."

Felicia spun around, wanting to say something to Corbin, but he'd disappeared. She heard a toilet flush.

Then, "Yes? Is this Mr. Clement? You handled my divorce from Adam Chalmers? That's right, that's right. Well, there was a big accident here in Promise Falls last night and—yes, the drive-in. My ex and his new wife, Miriam? They were killed. Which means I'm his only surviving ex-wife. Yes, yes, there's a daughter, but shouldn't there be something for me? What if I could prove that I've been a source of moral support all this time? I have e-mails. Lots of e-mails and texts that would prove that. And there was more than that going on. We still maintained a physical relationship, wifely duties basically. That would have to mean something and—"

She listened. "Uh-huh." Listened some more. "Uh-huh."

Then, "Well, I don't care if that's your opinion off the top of your head. The opinion I'm getting from my gut is that I might be entitled to something, especially with

Miriam dead. When can I come in to see you? Next week? I can pull together all my paperwork by then, yes. And I can find out what the house might be worth. Okay. Good, thank you. I'll see you then."

Felicia hung up the phone. When she turned around, Corbin was back, a towel wrapped around his waist.

Felicia said, "Good thing I didn't listen to the bartender."

TWENTY-THREE

Samantha Worthington, in the middle of restocking the vending machines with small packages of detergent, jumped when the cell phone tucked into the front pocket of her jeans went off. She'd been on edge ever since Ed had come to visit her at the Laundromat that morning, and it didn't take much to give her a heart attack.

She dug out the phone, looked at the caller ID.

David Harwood.

Jesus, the guy just didn't give up. She supposed one had to give him points for trying. She let it ring. She had her voice mail set to cut in after six rings. So she didn't have to wait long for the phone to shut up. But she held on to it for another minute, wondering if he would leave her a message.

A red dot with a 1 inside it appeared on her phone. Did she want to listen to anything else this guy had to say?

She tapped the dot, put the phone to her ear.

"Sam, it's David. Look, I get why you don't want to take my calls. You think I set you up for something, and I swear I didn't. Maybe, shit, I don't know, but if we could talk about it . . . Maybe dinner? Something simple. We could even—if you're okay with this—Carl could come over to my place and hang out with Ethan. My parents would be there. Or—I don't know. Look, I won't call again. I don't want to be some stalker asshole. It's just, the thing is . . . I like you. We've both got a shitload of problems, and maybe you don't need any more, but I just . . . I gotta go. If you're up for dinner, or anything, call me. Bye."

Sam was offered the choice of pressing seven to delete the message, or nine to save it. She had her thumb over the nine, then hit the seven.

David Harwood was right. She had enough problems right now.

Starting with Ed. The war with her in-laws over her son, Carl, was heating up.

Of course, it was already well under way. They'd been trying to get Carl away from her ever since their son, Brandon—Sam's ex-husband—was sentenced to six years for holding up a branch of the Revere Federal Bank. The court had tacked on an extra two years because Brandon had waved a gun around.

The stupid bastard. At least he hadn't shot anyone.

His parents—especially Yolanda—had always hated Sam, particularly when she filed for divorce before Brandon turned to bank robbery. But that hatred multiplied exponentially after she and Carl left Boston. That meant Brandon's parents didn't get to see their grandson nearly as often—it had been difficult to cut them off completely when they all lived in the same town—and they were the kind of people who were used to getting what they wanted. Garnet was the manager of one of Revere's other branches—the ironies abounded—and Yolanda behaved as though she were married to the secretary of finance.

Sam hadn't even told them she planned to move. She liked to imagine the surprise on their faces the first time they dropped by unannounced and found someone else living in her apartment. How that must have pissed them off.

It was such an embarrassment, particularly for Garnet, that Brandon had robbed not just a bank but a Revere bank, that he and his wife were desperate to pin the blame on Sam.

Their theory, and the one they shared with everyone they talked to, including a reporter for the *Boston Globe*, was that Brandon had turned to robbing banks as a way to win Sam back. Garnet and Yolanda Worthington said their son believed he could buy back Sam's affections if he had the money to get her anything she wanted.

It was a version of temporary insanity, they argued. Brandon's lawyer argued it, too, in court, but failed to win over a jury. Despite that, her ex-husband's parents stuck to the story.

It wasn't their fault. It wasn't Brandon's.

It was hers.

One hundred percent total bullshit.

Sam wanted to put a few hundred miles between Brandon's parents, and Carl and her. If she'd had the means, she'd have moved to Australia, but Promise Falls was as far as she could afford to go. An aunt used to live here, and she'd spent three summers in the town as a teenager. Even though her aunt had passed away, she believed she could make a new home here for Carl and herself.

She had underestimated her former in-laws' resolve.

They'd had lawyers send her threatening letters demanding custody. Sam had ignored them—torn them up and thrown them in the trash. There was no way, she convinced herself, that they had any legal right to take her own child away from her.

But then they upped their game.

They'd sent someone to spy on her, try to catch her in any kind of compromising position.

They'd gone so far as to put a camera up to her window when she had a quick hookup with David Harwood, whose son, Ethan, was in her son's class at Clinton Public School. It was an impulsive, reckless thing to do, having sex with the man. And not even in the bedroom, but right there in the kitchen, like they were acting out some tawdry scene in *The Postman Always Rings Twice*, for God's sake.

She wondered if it had been Ed who took the picture. If he'd been the one peering through her window. Probably just one hand on the camera, his other one busy.

She still harbored suspicions that Harwood was in on it. That he'd set her up somehow.

And yet . . .

Hadn't she been the one who'd initiated it? When she asked him, "How long has it been?" A reference to the last time he'd been with anyone.

A long time, for both of them, as it turned out.

Whoever had been peering through the window with a camera had clearly been in touch with Garnet and Yolanda soon after. Within a day, an e-mail arrived from Yolanda, with an attached photo.

Sam couldn't believe it when she saw it.

And there was Yolanda's message: "So this is how Carl's mother spends her time at home. What kind of mother behaves this way?"

Then, this morning, her ex-husband's longtime buddy Ed strolled into her work to intimidate her. This was how they planned to do it, she told herself. Scare her into turning Carl over.

No fucking way.

Carl was only nine, but he understood what was going on. She'd warned him to be on the lookout for his grandparents or any of his father's old friends. Sam worried that one day they'd go too far, that they'd cross the line, and just try to grab Carl and take him back to Boston.

Many days, she drove him to school and picked him up at the end of the day.

You couldn't be too careful.

She held the card that nice, but sad-looking, man had given her after he'd thrown soap powder in Ed's face. She was used to seeing him once a week when he came in with his laundry, and had smiled at him the odd time, even talked to him about the book he was reading when he'd come earlier today, but she hadn't known his name, and she certainly hadn't known what he did for a living.

But there it was, on the card: *Cal Weaver: Private Investigations.* And a phone number. At first, she was inclined to throw it into the trash. She didn't want to drag strangers into her personal business. But a private detective might be someone worth knowing. Not because she was planning to hire him or anything. But a man in that line of work might know people who could be helpful to her. A lawyer specializing in custody issues, for example.

So she'd hung on to the card, left it tucked in the front pocket of her jeans, next to her phone.

The place had been busy around the noon hour, but things had slowed down by midafternoon. No one was there, none of the machines running. Which was why Sam had taken this time to restock the dispenser with small boxes of soap. She glanced at the clock and realized it was almost the end of Carl's school day. This was a good time to slip away and pick him up.

And then they walked in.

Garnet and Yolanda.

Sam froze. She was stunned that they would actually confront her. Travel all the way from Boston for a face-to-face.

Garnet looking distinguished in a suit, like he was dressed for a day at the bank, even though he'd have had to take the entire day off to come here. Yolanda all in black, save for the strand of pearls at her neck. Fancy silk blouse, slacks, three-inch heels, silver hair all poufed out.

Sam stared but said nothing. It was Garnet who spoke first.

"Samantha, how are you?" Speaking in a soft, non-threatening tone. His bank voice.

Yolanda flashed a smile that looked remarkably lifelike. "It's good to see you, Samantha. You're looking well."

Sam knew, after seven hours of working in this overheated hellhole, she looked like a drowning victim pulled from the river, and probably smelled like one, too.

"This . . . is a surprise," Sam said.

"Yolanda and I've been talking, and we, well, we thought it was time to try to make peace," Garnet said. "Stop with all this bickering and backstabbing. It's not good for any of us, and it's certainly not good for Carl, and he's the one that really matters here." He pointed to three plastic chairs. "Would it be okay if we sat down?"

Sam, dumbstruck, nodded. Garnet turned the chairs around into a Y so they could all face one another. Before sitting, Yolanda took a long look at the chair and swept it with the back of her hand. If there'd been anything on it, Sam couldn't see it.

"We know we've kind of been playing hardball lately,"

Garnet said. "We've employed tactics which, in retrospect, have gone too far."

"You mean taking pictures of me through a window?" Sam asked, starting to feel her way. "When I was with someone?"

"*With,*" Yolanda said under her breath.

Garnet reached out a hand and touched his wife on the knee. "Now, dear, we promised to be good."

"I'm sorry," Brandon's mother said. "And I'm sorry for sending that photo to you. That was . . . uncalled for."

"You think?" Sam said. "Would it be okay with you if I hired someone to spy on you? I'm sure you and Garnet still get it on once in a while. Does that make you bad people?"

Yolanda flinched. She looked ready to bite back, but then composed herself. "You make an excellent point, Samantha."

"And what about today? Sending that thug Ed in here? What the hell was that about?"

Garnet's face contorted. "What are you talking about? Ed was here?"

"Are you saying you don't know?"

He shook his head sorrowfully. "He goes off half-cocked sometimes. Thinks he knows what we want, but really, he shouldn't have bothered you. We're very sorry about that, aren't we, Yolanda?"

"We sure are," she said.

"We just want everyone to be happy or, if that's too much to ask, to understand one another," Garnet said. "And before I forget, Brandon asked me to say hello and pass along his best wishes to you and Carl."

"You've seen him?"

"We go every week," Garnet said.

"He forgives you," Yolanda said.

"I'm sorry, what?"

"He forgives you for leading him down a reckless path."

Sam swallowed hard, made a fist that she managed to keep pointed at the floor. "What that man did was his choice and his choice alone and I had absolutely nothing to do with it. He could have stolen the crown jewels for me and I still wouldn't have gone back to him. Do you know what he did to me? He kept me living in a constant state of fear. He was capable of violence, and sooner or later I knew I'd be on the receiving end."

"I seriously doubt that," Yolanda said. "Not my son. He was always a very gentle child and—"

Garnet grabbed her knee and pinched it hard enough to make her shut up. "We're getting a little off topic here, love. Let's not lose sight of why we came here to see Samantha."

Sam glanced at the clock. It was time for her to leave to get Carl.

"I don't know why you've driven all this way, but I really have to go," she told them.

"Just another minute," Garnet said. "I know you don't trust us. I know that if I were to extend an invitation to our grandson to come stay with us for a week or two in the summer, at our beach house on the Cape, you'd be suspicious. I get that. So what we wondered was, would you be our guest, too? You and Carl could both come down. You could stay in the guest room. Would you feel comfortable with that? You'd love it there. I know we invited you and Brandon, and you were never able to find the time, but it's quite beautiful and relaxing. We could take the ferry to Martha's Vineyard. Go to Edgartown."

Sam took another look at the clock.

"I don't think all of us being under the same roof would work very well," Sam said, her eyes fixed on Yolanda. "And I don't know if the owner could find someone else to run this place if I went away."

Yolanda made a derisive scan of the premises. "How hard could it be to find someone to do this?"

Garnet shot his wife a look, then smiled understandingly at Sam. "Well, then, what if we were to come up here? Book a hotel, or maybe a resort around Saratoga. Someplace close to Promise Falls. We could give Carl a little vacation close to home. And we could book a room for you, too. We could make it close enough that you could drive in here every day, make sure everything's running like clockwork."

Sam didn't get it. Why the change of heart? Were Garnet and Yolanda really on the level?

"What about all this talk of trying to take Carl away from me?" Sam said. "Would that end?"

Garnet smiled. "That hasn't been productive, has it? We think there has to be a better way."

"And Brandon would like to see his son," Yolanda said.

Garnet gave her a look that suggested that was not on the agenda.

"Prison is no place for a nine-year-old boy," Sam said. "One day, when Brandon is released, I'm willing to sit down and work out some kind of visitation arrangement. Despite what you may think of me, I don't want to turn my son against his father." Again, she looked at the clock. "I can't be here another minute. I have to go pick up Carl."

Garnet held up a hand. "Just wait. I think what you're saying is very mature, very honorable," he said. "I'm pleased to hear you say that. What we're wondering is—"

"You're not hearing me," Sam said. "Carl will be looking for my car. When—"

Sam cut herself off. She suddenly understood what they were doing.

They were stalling her.

She stood, ran to the office at the back end of the Laundromat to grab her purse.

"Samantha!" Garnet said, standing. "Please! There's more we want to say!"

She grabbed her purse, and as she headed for the alleyway out back where she kept her car, she searched it for her car keys. Once she'd found them, she pointed the remote at her car and hit the button to unlock it. The car was listing to one side. Both tires on the driver's side were completely flat.

"No, no," she said. "This isn't happening."

Behind her, standing framed in the back door of the Laundromat, Garnet and Yolanda Worthington smiled. "Got you good, you bitch," Yolanda said.

They're sending Ed. They're sending Ed to the school to grab Carl and take him back to Boston.

TWENTY-FOUR

Cal

I got back into my car, which I'd parked in a visitors' spot at Felicia Chalmers's building, and took out my notebook. I turned to the page where I'd written down the numbers Lucy had read out to me from Adam Chalmers's phone bill.

There was one we hadn't been able to connect to anyone. I figured, what the hell, and dialed it.

The number rang four times, then went to voice mail.

"Hi! This is Georgina. I'd love to talk to you, but I can't take your call right now, so leave me a message!"

Cheerful. I chose not to leave a message. I called Lucy.

"Hi," she said when she picked up. "Did you talk to Felicia?"

"Yeah. But I wanted to ask, does the name Georgina mean anything to you?"

"Georgina?"

"Yeah."

"No, nothing."

"Okay, just thought I would ask. I'll check in with you later, okay?"

I pointed the car in the direction of Thackeray, on the outer edges of Promise Falls. Took the better part of twenty minutes.

It was the first time I'd been on the Thackeray grounds

since returning to Promise Falls. I'd spent time out here when I was in my late teens and early twenties, although never as a student. I'd done two years at the state university in Albany before dropping out. If I could have gotten a degree in partying, I'd have done well, but things didn't work that way. So I switched institutions, taking a six-month course at the New York State Police Academy, still in Albany. After graduation, I managed to get on with the Promise Falls cops.

Where I stayed until I screwed up, moved my wife, Donna, and son, Scott, to Griffon, a small town north of Buffalo, and went private. We had a few good years there, maybe the best I ever had or ever will, before darkness took them both away from me.

When I was a kid, we always thought of the Thackeray students as "them." We were "us." They were a bunch of stuck-up, elitist know-it-alls, but we were the street-smart locals. Until, of course, many of us locals attended the school. And even before that, we weren't above heading out to campus pubs to try to pick up Thackeray girls.

I found one by the name of Donna who was willing to share her life with me. Until that life ended.

So I had mixed feelings driving out to the campus. I was in no mood for reminiscing. I wondered if my sister, Celeste, was right, that I wasn't dealing with what had happened to Donna and Scott. I'd felt that I was. By burying it.

You couldn't change the past.

I paid to park in the lot close to the admin building and found my way to the security offices. A young man on the desk took one of my business cards with him as he went into the office of Clive Duncomb.

I'd done more background reading on Duncomb

before coming out here. His killing of a student predator, and the fact that he had not, at least so far, been charged with anything.

Seconds later, a man whose picture I recognized from the Internet came out of the office, hand extended.

"Mr. Weaver?" he said, holding my card by the edges between thumb and forefinger.

"Mr. Duncomb?"

"What can I do for you?"

"Mind if we talk in your office?"

He hesitated. "You want to tell me what this is about?"

"Could we talk in your office?" I said again.

With some reluctance, he led me in and pointed to a chair. "I don't think we've met before," Duncomb said.

"No," I said. "I only recently came back to Promise Falls."

"But you're from here originally."

"Yes. I grew up here."

"Where've you been?"

"Griffon. North of Buffalo."

"No more jealous wives in Griffon wanting their husbands spied on?"

I forced a smile. "How about yourself? I'm picking up a bit of an accent."

"When you're from Boston, there's no hiding it," he said. "Let me guess why you're here. It's about the shooting."

"Mason Helt?"

"Yeah. You working for the kid's family? Insurance company? Which is it? Doesn't matter—my answer's the same. It was justified. That son of a bitch had one of my people on the ground, with a gun, and if I hadn't done what I did, God knows what would have happened to Joyce."

"Joyce?"

"Pilgrim. Joyce Pilgrim. I'll tell you this. I've taken some heat for putting her out there in the first place to lure this guy out, but if I hadn't done it, he'd still be out there, and who the hell knows what he might have done by now? Killed some poor girl, maybe."

"That's not why I'm here," I said.

"Oh," Duncomb said, almost looking disappointed. "What's this about, then?"

"Adam Chalmers," I said.

"Chalmers? The writer?"

"That's right."

"What do you want to know about him?"

"I don't know if you're aware, but Mr. Chalmers and his wife were killed last night when that screen came down at the drive-in."

His mouth dropped. "Jesus Christ, you're kidding."

"No."

Duncomb's head went side to side. "I can't believe that. Son of a bitch. When I heard about that, first thing I wondered was whether any Thackeray students were hurt or killed. Far as I know, none were. I heard a couple of kids were, but they weren't students here. Not that that makes it any less tragic. But Christ Almighty, I never realized Adam . . . and Miriam . . . Good people. *Nice* people." Another incredulous head shake. "Do you know anything about a service? Which funeral home they went to, anything like that?"

"I don't. His daughter's looking after that today. At least where Mr. Chalmers is concerned. I think Miriam Chalmers has a brother driving in from Rhode Island."

"Goddamn," Duncomb said. Then, recovering from the shock, he asked, "What's your involvement? Why are you here talking to me?"

"I gather you and Adam—Mr. Chalmers—were friends."

Duncomb didn't speak right away. I sensed that he was sizing me up.

"On occasion," he said.

"You *were* friends, then?"

"We knew each other a little, yeah."

"Well enough that you know his wife's name," I said.

Another hesitation. "I knew the two of them. That's right. Like I said, they were good people."

"Did you and your wife socialize with Adam and Miriam?" I asked.

"Did I say I was married?"

"I just assumed," I said. "Saw the band on your finger there."

Duncomb glanced down at his own left hand. "Yeah, Liz and I were friends with them. Let me ask you something, Mr. Weaver."

"Go ahead."

"You a cop once?"

"Yeah."

"I used to be with the Boston PD."

"Well."

"So I've been around long enough to know you're working up to something, so why not just get the fuck to it?"

"I'm looking into circumstances possibly related to the deaths of Mr. and Mrs. Chalmers."

"Oh, well, *circumstances*. That's clear enough. Why didn't you say that in the first place?"

I moved my tongue around my teeth for a second or two. I'd allowed this to get away from me. "I thought you might be able to help because Mr. Chalmers was in contact with you quite often." I paused. "That's what his cell phone records show."

Duncomb leaned back in his chair, his head up, like he was sniffing the air.

"Like I said, we were friends." Another shake of the head. "God, I still can't believe what's happened."

"How'd you know him?"

Duncomb cleared his throat. "He came out here to talk to some creative writing students. We got talking, and when he found out I had a law enforcement background, he asked if he could call me when he had questions about police work. And we got to be friends. Simple as that."

"What was it he wanted help with lately?"

"Hmm?"

"When he last called you. What was he writing that he needed your expertise for?"

"Fingerprints," Duncomb said without hesitation. "Whether you can get fingerprints off fabric. Different surfaces. That's what we were talking about."

"So he was working on a book."

"Sure."

"Because he had an e-mail from his—I guess it was his literary agent—saying that if he could get a publisher interested, he'd try to write another book, but it didn't sound like he was currently working on anything."

Duncomb moved his lips in and out. "Maybe he hadn't told his agent he was running something around in his head."

"Doesn't that seem odd? That he'd be telling you before he'd tell his own agent?"

He forced a laugh. "How the hell would I know? The thing is, the fingerprints call might have been a while ago.

Sometimes Adam just called to shoot the shit. We were *friends*. Did I mention that part?"

"When's the last time you were out to see Adam and Miriam?"

A big shrug. "I don't know. There was a dinner a while ago."

"It's quite a house," I said.

"I guess," he said.

"Did you ever look after the place when the Chalmerses were away? You being in security and all, if I were going away, I'd be glad to know someone like you. Who could check the house, make sure everything was okay."

Duncomb eyed me curiously.

"What are you asking?"

"It's a simple question."

"There's nothing simple about it. Just put it out there, Weaver. What do you want to know?"

I stood. "I have a message. From Adam's daughter. She wants to know she doesn't have anything to worry about. She wants to know that what was taken from the house isn't going to be used to tarnish her father's memory. She either wants it back or some assurance that it has been destroyed."

Duncomb's face didn't move.

"Is that it?" he asked.

I nodded.

"Well, thanks for dropping by," he said.

I was about to make the observation that since he didn't want to know what was taken from the house, he already knew, but I was interrupted with a phone call.

I took out my cell, glanced at the number. It wasn't one I recognized.

"Hello?"

"He's going after Carl! I know it! This whole thing, acting nice, it was a trick! They're going to get him!"

It was a woman, and she was beyond frantic. I couldn't place the voice, and I had no idea who Carl was.

"Who's this?" I said.

"Jesus, it's *Sam*! You gave me your card! They slashed my tires! The one you got in the eyes? With soap? Ed? He's going to grab Carl! I *know* it."

TWENTY-FIVE

"How was your lunch?" David Harwood asked Randall Finley when he found him walking through his water-bottling plant.

"Good, good lunch," Finley said.

"Who were you meeting again? Frank Mancini?"

"Yup. Good guy. Good businessman. So did you get the thing set up at the bank?"

"I did. You can now make a donation to the Constellation Drive-in disaster fund to help people and their families affected by the tragedy."

"And you called it the Randall Finley Relief Fund?"

Harwood thought that he'd like nothing more than to be relieved of Randall Finley. "No, I did not call it that. I called it the May 17 Fund. Pegged it to the day it happened. People around here will remember that date for a long time. It'll resonate."

Finley couldn't hide the disappointment on his face. "I suppose that's okay."

"It would have looked self-serving to put your name on it. But people will know. You can remind them when you give talks. Tell people to throw a few bucks at the account you set up."

"Sure, I hear what you're saying."

"You look like I took away your favorite toy."

"No, you're right." He smiled and clapped a hand on Harwood's shoulder. "That's why I picked you, David. You've got smarts. You know how to rein me in. You know how to keep me from making an even bigger asshole of myself."

"That's why you pay me the big bucks," David said.

Finley laughed. "We need to talk about when I should officially announce. I have to tell you, I feel ready. The election's still more than five months off, but you need time to build momentum. You know what I'm saying?"

"Sure."

"I'm thinking, maybe there's no point in holding off. We just do it. You know what I mean? We call a news conference, today or tomorrow, and we tie it in to the disaster fund. Shows my heart's in the right place. That I care about this town. At first, I was thinking, we go slow. Do an announcement to announce that I'm going to announce." He laughed. "Kind of like foreplay."

"I get it."

"But now I'm thinking more of taking a slam-bam-thank-you-ma'am approach. Let's just get it the fuck out there."

"You're the boss," David said. "I'm just not sure who'll come out to a news conference. We're kind of dependent on the Albany media now, more than ever, with the *Standard* gone."

"You'll figure something out," he said. He frowned, kept that hand on David's shoulder. "Everything okay?"

"Yup."

"I feel like I'm picking up a vibe that you're less than enthusiastic about working for me." He grinned. "Am I on to something there?"

"I do my job. That's what you pay me for. You don't pay me to like you."

"I certainly don't. I'm sure there's not enough money in the world to make that happen. You don't have to like me, David. You just have to get me elected."

David moved a step back, forcing Finley to release his grip on his shoulder. "Then we need to talk about your platform. If you're going to announce, the people have to know what you stand for."

"Hmm."

"Like a five-point plan for the town. Five reasons why the people of Promise Falls should give you another chance."

Finley nodded. "I like that." He laughed. "You think we can come up with five?"

"Why don't we turn it around? Instead of five reasons why people should vote for you, give me five reasons why you want to be mayor again."

"Okay, okay. Why don't we go outside?"

They exited the building through the loading docks, when Finley spotted a young man loading flats of bottled water into the back of a van.

"Trevor!" Finley said. "How's it going?"

Trevor Duckworth turned, saw Finley, offered up half a wave.

"Have you met Trevor?" Finley asked David. When David shook his head, Finley did introductions. "David, this is Trevor Duckworth. Trevor, this is David Harwood."

"Hey," Trevor said.

"Duckworth?" David said. "Any relation to Barry, with the Promise Falls police?"

"My dad," he said with little enthusiasm.

"We've met," David said. "Not always under the best circumstances, but we've met. He's a good guy."

Trevor said nothing.

"David's going to be handling my campaign strategy," Finley said. To David, he added, "It's a pretty open secret around here that I'm going back into politics."

"I've got to do a run," Trevor said, closing the back doors of the van. "Nice to meet you."

"Same," David said.

"Bit of a sad sack," Finley said as Trevor Duckworth got behind the wheel of the van. "But I like to help people when they're down and out."

"What do you mean, down and out?"

"Kid had been looking for work for some time, and I gave him a job. That should be one of the five things. Why I want to be mayor. Because I like to help people out."

"Noted," David said.

They went down a short flight of concrete steps to the parking area, walked over to a picnic table set under the shade of a large oak. Finley dropped onto the bench and, with some effort, swung his thick legs over it and under the table. David sat opposite.

"How about a second one?"

"I want to see Promise Falls move into the future."

"What's that mean?"

"It doesn't have to mean anything, David. It's a campaign platform. How long did you work in newspapers, anyway?"

"A third."

Finley pondered. "How about this? For me, it's a way to seek redemption. I'm a flawed man—I made mistakes—but all I ever wanted was an opportunity to serve my fellow citizens. I want another chance at that."

David was caught off guard. "That's actually kind of good."

"You know why?"

"Why?"

"Because it's from the heart, that's why."

At that moment David understood the central appeal of the man sitting across from him. He had the ability to connect. David had his doubts about Finley's sincerity, but he came across as the real deal. A regular voter would believe him. A regular voter would look at Finley and think, *Yeah, he's an asshole, but who isn't, really? So what the hell, I'd rather have him than some other guy who thinks he's better than me.*

"You should be writing these down," Finley said.

"I'll remember. That leaves two more."

"Okay. Uh, how about jobs? I want to bring jobs to Promise Falls."

"That's kind of like the first one. Wanting to help people out."

"Oh yeah. It is kind of the same. How about Five Mountains?"

David flinched on the inside. He had bad memories of the amusement park. It was where his wife had gone missing five years ago. Ultimately, she was found, but there was no happy ending.

"What about Five Mountains?"

"I want it reopened," Finley said. "I want to shame the corporate owners into canceling their plans to close it. And failing that, I want someone else to come in and take it over. That drew plenty of dollars to the town. It should stay open."

"What do you think the odds are they'll change their mind?"

"Oh, zero," Finley said. "Not a chance. Already tried talking to Gloria Fenwick." David remembered her. Finley grinned. "Even offered her a small inducement, but she declined."

"Jesus, a bribe?"

Finley sighed. "David, please. Anyway, that should be in my platform."

"But if there's nothing you can do about it, then . . ."

"Just because it can't be done doesn't mean I can't tell the people I want it to be done," he said. "You hear Amanda even raising a peep about this?"

Amanda Croydon, the current mayor, who, based on anything David had heard, was planning to run again.

"I can nail her for not even trying," he said.

"When you're making a speech, I'd avoid phrases like 'nail her.'"

Another grin. "So what's that leave us? What are we down to? One reason left for why I want to be mayor." He pursed his lips. He seemed to be struggling with this one.

"Maybe the real reason is harder to acknowledge publicly," David said.

His eyes went to slits. "I'm sorry. What?"

"I'm just saying that maybe some of your motivations for running have less to do with the public good and more to do with personal gain."

"What are you getting at, David?"

David put his palms a few feet apart on the picnic table, as though bracing himself. "What was your meeting with Frank Mancini about?"

"Why you asking?"

"Because you wouldn't tell me. I'm supposed to be working for you, but you keep things from me."

"You don't have to know everything. You only need to know what I want you to know."

"Suppose I'm asked? You've put me in the role of your spokesperson. If someone wants to know why you've been meeting with Mancini, what should I say?"

"Who's going to ask?"

"I am. Right now."

"He's a developer. He's the kind of guy who brings jobs and money to the table. Of course I'm going to talk to a guy like that."

"Whose money and whose table?" David asked.

Finley's eyes narrowed. "Is there something you want to get off your chest?"

"I'm just saying, Mancini's bought the land where four people died last night. That property, for a whole slew of reasons, is going to be under the microscope for some time. That's something you need to think about."

"You seem to be suggesting a policy of openness and transparency. That be right, David?"

"Always better to get ahead of bad news," David said. "That way you're able to handle it when it breaks. So, yeah, openness might be one of your five. How you want to run an open and aboveboard city hall."

Finley nodded slowly. "So, is that the policy you've adopted with your boy? Ethan, right?"

"What?"

"So you've told him, then?"

David wondered what the hell his nine-year-old son had to do with any of this. "I'm sorry?"

"You've told Ethan about his mother. About Jan."

"What about Jan?"

"That she wasn't all she claimed to be. A lot of her story never became public. But you hear things. It was a tragic story, no doubt about it. But some might say Jan brought that on herself. Killed by the man whose hand she cut off.

189

Came here to live a normal life, married a regular guy like you. But she was hiding out, wasn't she? Thing is, the past has a way of catching up with you. Oh, yes, the story got around. I heard bits and pieces. I have to say, her exploits make me look like an amateur."

"You're a piece of work."

"I'm just trying to make a point that we all keep some facts back. Maybe it was all for the good that Ethan's mother met a sudden end. That way there were never charges, no trial. A couple of stories, and then it all went away."

"My son was four years old when his mother died," David said. "*Of course* I didn't tell him the whole story then."

"And since? What is he now? Nine, ten years old?"

"Eventually, I'll fill him in."

Finley leaned toward David. "If it would help in any way, I could tell him."

"Don't go there, Randy."

"It'd be my way of lessening the burden for you." He opened his arms in a welcoming gesture. "It's what I do."

David felt his face warming with rage.

"You know, I like this," Finley said. "We have a good back-and-forth, a nice rapport. We can get things out in the open. You can say what's on your mind, and I can say what's on my mind. I think that bodes well for moving forward. Anyway, here's number five: Cut the bullshit. That's what I'm about. I want to cut the bullshit. I think the voters will like that."

Finley got up and headed back into the office, leaving David to dig his fingernails into the top of the picnic table.

TWENTY-SIX

After his meeting with Olivia Fisher's father, Barry Duckworth stopped at a Burger King to grab some lunch.

He went in telling himself he would order one of their salads. They had a straight garden salad, then a couple with chicken in them. Plus some wraps with lots of lettuce, and more chicken, stuffed into them. Any of those would be better than his usual order: a Whopper with a side order of fries.

He needed to curb that kind of eating. Change his habits. Get some of that fat off his belly. Didn't the doctors say that was the worst kind of fat? That stuff that gathered at your waist? But then, what the hell other kind of fat was there? Did you see people walking around with big fat thighs and thick arms and washboard stomachs?

Duckworth could have done the drive-through, but he didn't want to eat in the car. He'd end up with ketchup and mustard on his shirt. So he parked the unmarked cruiser, went inside, approached the counter, and said, "I'll have a Whopper and a small order of fries." Paused. "With a Diet Coke."

"Cheese on the Whopper?" the girl behind the counter asked.

"Sure," he said.

Once he had his tray, sat down, and unwrapped his burger, he got out his phone and entered a number.

Six rings, then: "You've reached Chief Rhonda Finderman. Please leave a message at the beep."

"It's Barry. There's something I think we need to go public about, but I gotta bounce it off you first. Call me when you get a chance."

He set the phone down and shoved four french fries into his mouth before attacking the burger. He felt a small measure of guilt with every bite. When he was done, he felt something more than that.

A slight pain in his side. He stood up, kept one hand on the table to steady himself. He figured it was indigestion, or maybe it was something muscular. Sitting all the time, either in the car or at his desk, even here at Burger King.

Duckworth took a few deep breaths.

"You okay?"

A young woman clearing off tables was looking at him with concern.

"I'm fine," he said. "I'm good. Thank you."

And he was pretty sure he was. The pain was receding. He saw that he had missed one last fry, snatched it up, and tossed it into his mouth before heading out to his car.

At the station, he ran down the plate Lionel Grayson had written on a scrap of paper. It was from the Honda van belonging to the man who'd complained angrily about a drive-in movie he'd deemed inappropriate for his children.

Did it make sense that someone unhappy about a film's content would blow up a drive-in? Not really, Duckworth thought. And yet, *someone* had a reason. Duckworth knew that whatever the bomber's motive was, it wasn't going to be rational. So Angry Dad was as good a place to start as any.

The van was registered to Harvey Coughlin, of 32 Riverside Drive. When Duckworth Googled the name, a LinkedIn business listing popped up. Harvey Coughlin, assuming it was the same man who owned the Honda, was the manager of PF Lumber and Building Supplies. Duckworth knew the place. A few years ago, when he'd attempted to build a deck onto the back of his house, he'd bought all his wood and hardware at PF Lumber. And the contractor who'd come in to dismantle and redo everything Duckworth had done had also gotten what he'd needed at PF.

Duckworth figured there was a better chance of finding Coughlin at work than at home.

Once he'd talked to him, he had one more person he wanted to drop in on.

"I think Harvey's out in the yard somewhere," said the woman at the checkout.

Duckworth noticed a microphone on the counter in front of her that he guessed she could use to page the store manager. "Can you get him on this?" he asked.

The woman glanced at the microphone. "I could."

"Would you, please?"

The woman sighed. She picked up the mike, and through the store her voice rang out. "Harv. Front counter. Harv to the front." She looked at Duckworth and said, "He should be around in a minute or so."

It took three. A short, heavyset man in a plaid shirt and

jeans with a HARVEY name tag strode up. Duckworth was watching for him and said, "Mr. Coughlin?"

"Yeah?" he said, with more cheer in his voice than the woman who'd paged him.

"I'm Barry Duckworth," he said, adding quietly, "Promise Falls police."

Harvey's eyes widened. "Oh, hi. Good to meet you." He offered a hand and Duckworth took it. "This about the thefts?"

Duckworth suggested they move away from the cashier so they could talk more privately.

"You've had trouble here?"

"Yeah. Twice in the last three months. Guys coming in sometime between Saturday night and Sunday morning. Making off with stacks of plywood. Not easy to do that without attracting some attention. You caught somebody?"

"Sorry. That's not why I'm here."

"What is it?"

"A few weeks ago, you took the family to the Constellation."

"The drive-in?"

"That's right. You heard about what happened last night."

"Heard? It's all anybody's talking about. Like you say, I was there a few weeks ago, but not last night. I can ask around, see if anybody here went last night, if it's witnesses you're looking for."

"Do you know who Lionel Grayson is?"

Harvey Coughlin looked blank. "No idea."

"He's the manager—or he was the manager—of the Constellation. He says you and he spoke a few weeks ago. When you were unhappy about a film you thought was inappropriate for your kids."

His face drained of color. "Jesus, you're here because of *that*?"

"I wanted to ask you about that conversation. Mr. Grayson says you were very upset."

"I—I mean, yeah, I was angry. But it wasn't a big deal or anything. I mean—"

"Mr. Grayson thought it was a big enough deal to make a note of your license plate."

"No way."

"Why don't you tell me your version of what happened?"

"I—you don't seriously think I had something to do with what happened up there, do you?"

"Just tell me what happened."

He thought back. "It was nothing. I just—Jesus, I just thought it was wrong to be showing a movie with a whole lot of the f-word after they'd run a kids' movie. You know? Tiffany, my daughter? We have a hard time getting her to settle down. You think she's going to fall asleep after the first movie, but she doesn't, so she's wide-awake, and everyone is saying 'fuck' this and 'fuck' that, so we had to leave and I wanted my money back and I looked for the manager on the way out and, you know, let him know I wasn't happy."

"What did you say?"

"I don't remember exactly."

"Did you tell him you were going to take your complaint elsewhere? To the town?"

Harvey shrugged. "I might have."

"Were you shouting at him?"

"I might have raised my voice a little. But shouting? I don't know that I was shouting."

"Did you follow it up? Did you make a complaint with anyone?"

195

He shrugged. "No. I was just blowing off steam. By the next morning I'd kinda forgotten all about it."

"Do you lose your temper like that a lot?"

"I don't think I lost my temper. No, I don't do that."

"You sell explosives here?" Duckworth asked.

"What?"

"Dynamite? Anything like that?"

"No, we don't sell anything like that at all," Harvey said. "What are you trying to say?"

"But you'd know how to procure it, I imagine. People always having to bring something down to put up something new."

"Listen to me. I would never, ever, *ever* do anything like that," Coughlin protested. Duckworth could see fear in the man's eyes. "People were *killed* up there. You think I would kill people because I was upset about a *movie*?"

"Somebody did it," Duckworth said. "Maybe it was because their popcorn wasn't buttered enough."

He shouldn't have said that. All he could think of now was buttered popcorn.

Next stop: the widow of Dr. Jack Sturgess.

Duckworth wasn't looking forward to the interview. The woman had been through a lot. Not only had she lost her husband, but she'd had to endure the destruction of her husband's reputation.

There was no doubt he'd murdered two people. There was the nursing home employee turned blackmailer, and the old lady who lived next door to him.

But had he killed Rosemary Gaynor, too? If it turned out he had, then he was Duckworth's number one suspect in the Fisher murder, too. He'd already been turning this over in his head, however. Killers tended to repeat their methods. Sturgess had used lethal injection in one murder, a pillow in another.

Gaynor and Fisher had not died so easily.

There was a For Sale sign on the front lawn when he parked out front of the handsome two-story house. Ten seconds after he rang the bell, Tanya Sturgess opened the door. She was dressed in a pair of gray sweats, graying hair pulled back, several damp strands hanging over her eyes.

"Oh," she said. "You."

They had met, of course, during the investigation that had followed her husband's death.

"Mrs. Sturgess," he said. "I'm sorry to disturb you."

"I'm sure you are. Well, you better get it out of your system because I'm getting out of here as soon as I can."

"May I come in?"

"Why the hell not?"

She left the door open as she turned and went back into the house. Duckworth noticed the moving boxes everywhere. Framed pictures leaned up against boxes, square shadows on the walls where they'd once hung. Three rolled-up area rugs were in the living room.

"I'm not waiting for the house to be sold," she said without his having to ask. "It can sit on the market empty. Let them stage it if they have to."

"Where are you going?" he asked.

"Texas," she said. "Outside Houston. I have family there. I'm putting all this on a truck, sending it that way, putting it into storage until I find a place to live. I can't get out of this goddamn town fast enough."

Duckworth said nothing.

"They've crucified him," Tanya Sturgess said. "They've fucking crucified him. Accused my husband of monstrous things when he's not here to defend himself. Agnes Pickens was the one behind it all. Why else would she throw herself off the falls? The woman was consumed with guilt."

Duckworth listened.

"You know what happened last Thursday? Believe me, if I didn't ever have to leave this house, I wouldn't, but I had to go to the store the other day. I'm going up and down the aisle and a woman sees me—I don't even know who she was—and she looks me right in the eye and she says, 'What was it like to be married to a man who steals a baby?' What gives her the right to speak to me that way? What gives her the right?"

"People judge," Duckworth said.

"Don't they, though?"

He followed the woman into a ground-floor study, where she'd evidently been packing books. She took a handful off the shelf and dropped them into a box.

"Is that why you're here?" she asked. "To destroy whatever small shred of reputation Jack might have left?"

"I'm here following up on one thing," he said.

"What's that?"

"It's from three years ago."

"Three years?"

"Three years ago, this month. The third anniversary is actually later this month. I wondered if your husband kept his old appointment books. Something that would tell me what he was doing at that time. That day, if possible."

"Why on earth would you need to know that?"

"It's part of the overall investigation," he said.

She dropped some more books into the box. "Well, you're two days too late."

198

"What do you mean?"

She opened her arms wide to indicate the scope of the task before her. "I'm going through all this stuff and I'm not taking it all with me. I'm pitching as I pack. I didn't see any reason to keep Jack's old appointment books. They went out with the trash."

Even if the doctor's own calendar was gone, the hospital might have what he was looking for, Duckworth thought. If Sturgess had been the ER doctor on call, for example, on the night Olivia Fisher was murdered, it would have been hard for him to slip out to the park to kill someone.

"The only one who keeps stuff like that is me," Tanya Sturgess said.

"I'm sorry?"

"I keep my own old date books."

Duckworth nodded slowly. "Would you have one from three years ago?"

She studied him. "Why should I look? Why should I bother? Why should I help you?"

Duckworth could think of several reasons why helping him was in his interest, but not one that was in hers.

He shook his head slowly. "I don't know. If I were you, I wouldn't help me at all. But it could be important."

Tanya Sturgess dumped some books on a desk and said, "Follow me."

She went to a drawer in the kitchen, pulled out several old date books with wire spines. "Three years ago?"

Duckworth nodded.

She found the right one, opened it, fanned the pages until she got to May. "Here we go," she said, and handed the book to him.

It wasn't like he was looking for a notation for the day

Olivia Fisher died that read: "Jack kills girl, home late for dinner." But knowing what the doctor was up to that week might help.

He scanned the week's entries. On Tuesday evening, she'd written down "dinner Mannings." Friday at eleven, "mani-pedi." Wednesday: "Dry cleaning."

He saw an entry for Monday at ten thirty a.m. that caught his eye. "What's this, Dr. Gleber?"

"Dentist," she said. "That would have been my semi-annual cleaning."

"Okay."

"Really, what's this about?" she asked.

He ignored the question and continued to study the days leading up to the day Olivia had been murdered: May 25. Duckworth noticed an appointment for the twenty-second that appeared to be something medical: "1 p.m. Seward clinic."

Duckworth showed it to Jack Sturgess's wife. "What would this be? Is Dr. Seward your doctor?"

"Seward's not a doctor. He's a physiotherapist."

"You were seeing a physio?"

"Let me see that," she said, taking back the book. She went back a couple of weeks. "I remember this."

"What?"

"This was when Jack got hurt."

"Hurt?"

"Two weeks before. Yes, here it is. We went to see friends in Maine, and Jack was hiking in the woods and twisted his ankle. His right ankle. Hurt so much he couldn't drive home. Had to use a cane for a few weeks, and went to the Seward clinic for physio. It was a couple of months before he could walk normally again."

"So all through this period, this week here," Duckworth said, taking the book back and pointing to the two pages, "your husband was basically disabled? He had trouble getting around?"

The dead doctor's wife nodded.

Did a guy with a bum ankle attack a woman in a park? And run away after he'd killed her?

"Thank you," Duckworth said, and handed the book back to Tanya Sturgess.

He'd want to confirm the doctor's injury with the Seward clinic, but he felt, with some confidence, that he could rule out Jack Sturgess in the murder of Olivia Fisher, and because the modus operandi was identical, the death of Rosemary Gaynor, too.

"Tell me about the Gaynors," Duckworth said.

"I know what you're trying to do."

"What am I trying to do, Mrs. Sturgess?"

"You're trying to find a way to blame Jack for that, too. For what happened to her. That'd really help you out, wouldn't it? Find a way to prove Jack killed Rosemary. Well, he didn't do that, and I won't help you frame him for it. You want to pin everything you can on him. He's not here to defend himself. Have you found a way to connect him to the Lindbergh kidnapping? The Kennedy assassination?"

"That's not what I'm doing," Duckworth said. "I don't think he killed Rosemary Gaynor any more than you do. But I want to find out who did."

She eyed him dubiously. "You're trying to trick me."

Duckworth shook his head. "No. Let me ask you again about the Gaynors. How well did you know them?"

"Bill and Jack were friends. I didn't really know Rosemary. We went out for dinner once or twice a year."

"Did Bill and Rosemary get along?"

"I suppose. They did when we were all together. The four of us never socialized after the baby came, or even in the months before that. When Bill and Rosemary were in Boston."

"But you saw Bill occasionally in the period before his wife died?"

"I did. The odd time."

"What was he like?"

"I guess, looking back, I'd say he was on edge." Bitterly, she said, "I didn't like him then and I hate him even more now. He's as much to blame as Agnes Pickens. He was a horrible person, dragging Jack into a scheme to get that baby for him and his wife. Jack devoted his life to helping others and look what he got for it."

That didn't quite line up with the facts as Duckworth knew them. Jack Sturgess needed money to pay off gambling debts. He saw Bill and Rosemary's quest for a child as an opportunity to get it. And as far as Duckworth could tell, no one had forced Sturgess to murder Marshall Kemper or Doris Stemple. Or threaten to plunge a syringe into the neck of David Harwood's father.

But Duckworth thought it best to keep those thoughts to himself for the moment.

"What do you mean by 'on edge'?"

"Nervous. Anytime I'd walk into the room where the two were huddled together, he'd suddenly clam up."

"When was the last time you found them doing that?"

She thought. "Just before Bill went to Boston on that last conference. When Rosemary was killed. He seemed very worried."

Around that time, Duckworth had learned from his interviews with the Gaynors' nanny, Sarita Gomez, Bill had come to realize that his wife knew the adoption of Matthew was not legal.

She remembered something. "One time I walked in on him when he was in Jack's study, waiting for him to get back from a hospital call. Bill was looking at one of Jack's old medical books about surgical technique. When he realized I was there, he closed it and put it back on the shelf, his face red as a beet. You'd have thought I'd caught him looking at porn."

Duckworth was still thinking about Tanya Sturgess's comments as he got back behind the wheel of his car, and his phone started to ring.

"Duckworth."

"It's me," Rhonda Finderman said. "You called."

Duckworth had to think for a moment about why he'd been trying to get in touch with her.

"Right," he said. "I've got a story I want to tell you, and you're going to think I'm crazy, but you need to hear it right to the end."

TWENTY-SEVEN

Cal

I bolted from Clive Duncomb's office, down a flight of stairs, out of the Thackeray College admin building, and straight to my car. I had the phone to my ear the entire time, trying to get Samantha Worthington to explain to me what had happened.

"His parents came to visit . . . They stalled me . . . trying to make me late to pick up Carl," she said. The pauses were her catching her breath. It sounded like she was running, too.

"But you don't know for sure," I said, reaching into my pocket for my keys with my other hand, "that Ed's going to get Carl."

"He's here! You saw him this morning! They're working together."

"Hang on," I said. "Putting you on speaker."

I got the car open, tossed my phone onto the passenger seat, keyed the ignition. Backing out of the spot, I nearly broadsided a FedEx truck.

"Asshole!" someone yelled.

I got the car aimed for downtown. I didn't even know where I was going.

"Sam?" I shouted. "You still there?"

"Yes!"

"Where are you?"

"I'm running to the school! They slashed my tires! Those bastards!"

"Where's the school?"

"It's Clinton Public!"

I thought back to my days as a Promise Falls cop, when I could walk this town blindfolded and always know where I was. I knew Clinton. After accessing the GPS in my brain for a second, I could picture the location of the school.

But the school was quite a hike from Thackeray. Even breaking every speed limit and running every light, I was a good fifteen minutes away.

"Where are you?" I shouted. I was wondering if I should swing by and grab her along the way, but if we were both going to get there at the same time, I'd just head straight for the school.

"It's a few blocks," she said, sounding very winded. "Not . . . too . . . long."

"When does school officially let out?"

"Now, right now!"

"Hang up, call the school, see if they can call Carl to the office!"

"I tried that! I can't"—a pause to catch her breath—"get through!"

"Then call the police!"

"They won't care!"

"What?"

"They never care about this shit!"

If she meant custody disputes, she was half-right. There were some things a cop in a patrol car couldn't solve. But what she was talking about now seemed to suggest an outright kidnapping that was about to take place.

My heart was pounding, my hands slippery with sweat

on the steering wheel. Ahead of me, cars were stopped at a light.

"I'm a long way away!" I shouted. "I don't know if I can get there in time!"

I didn't know whether Samantha had heard me. I grabbed the phone, put it to my ear. Said, "You there?"

Nothing.

The light turned green up ahead, but the cars were moving slowly. I laid on the horn, swerved around two cars, narrowly missing a pickup truck coming in the opposite lane. Floored it.

As I sped into town, I realized I didn't know the whole story. For all I knew, Sam had abducted her own kid and what was going on now was payback. Maybe she'd been in the midst of a custody dispute and run off with Carl without the court's permission.

But if that was the case, the courts didn't usually send thugs around to your place of work and threaten you. Ed did not come across as an officer of the court.

So I gambled that the angels were with Sam and her boy. My gut told me that Ed taking Carl away was very, very wrong. Even if it turned out Sam didn't have the law on her side, kidnapping a kid from school was no way to resolve custody disputes.

"Come on, come on," I said, seeing another set of cars bunching up ahead of me at the next intersection. I was looking for an opening. Too many cars coming the other way for me to pass. I wondered whether, if I took the next right, I could make up some time on less-traveled residential streets.

"Let's go, let's go," I shouted at the drivers ahead of me.

I made the decision. When I got to the intersection, I'd hang a right. Find another way to get to Clinton Public.

An old Volkswagen inched far enough ahead that I could make the turn. I cranked the wheel, put my foot down on the gas.

Just as a jogger crossed my path.

"Shit!" I said, slamming my foot on the brake pedal so hard I was surprised it didn't snap off.

The jogger, a shirtless man in shorts and running shoes who was probably in his midthirties, stopped as abruptly as I had, turned, and looked at me. He slapped both hands onto the hood of the Accord.

"The fuck!" he screamed, spraying spit.

Had I hit him? I was pretty sure I hadn't. But if I was going to be any help to Sam and Carl, I was going to have to run him down anyway.

I powered down the window. "You ran right in front of me!"

He pointed to the WALK sign. "You see that! Are you blind?"

He wasn't moving. If I could get him to move from the front of the car, if I could get him to approach my window, I could boot it.

"Yeah!" I said. "It says walk, not run!"

The man shook his head, started coming around the fender. Good, good. *Come give me shit face-to-face, so my way is clear and I can floor it.*

He came up alongside the car. But as he did, several other people started walking through the intersection, blocking my way.

"You fucking think you own the road?" he asked, at my window now, hands on the sill, close enough that I could smell his sweat. "Is what you got to do so important it justifies running people over? That what you think?"

207

I didn't think I was going to make it.

I didn't think I was going to make it in time to help Carl.

TWENTY-EIGHT

Ed idled his pickup truck down the street from Clinton Public Elementary School. He figured that Carl Worthington's route to his mother's work, or their home, would take him this way, right past where he was parked. It was a good thing the little guy had never seen him. It'd be easier to pull off what he had planned that way.

Of course, there was a chance he wouldn't be walking this way, if he decided to go to a friend's house, say, before going home. But Ed's information was that his mother picked him up most days. He'd probably be looking for her, standing around, wondering why she was late.

That worked for Ed. He had his story ready.

Ed sat behind the wheel of the truck, waiting for the bell to ring, which was when he'd go on high alert. While Carl had never seen him, he'd seen plenty of pictures of the kid—Yolanda had given them to him—so he didn't anticipate having any trouble picking out the little bastard.

While he waited, he ate a Mars bar. Unwrapped it, bit off half, chewed it up in a few seconds, then shoved the other half into his mouth. Licked his lips, glanced into the rearview mirror to make sure he didn't have chocolate in the corners of his mouth. His mother had taught him that. Always check the corners of your mouth.

He looked okay.

The bell rang.

Seconds later, the school doors flew open and hordes of kids made their escape. Jesus, there were way more of them coming out at once than he'd imagined. Ed had to keep a close watch on everyone.

But then he saw him. And just as he'd hoped, he was coming this way. He'd gotten about twenty yards from the school when he stopped, looked around.

"Looking for your mommy?" Ed said.

He got out of the truck, stood by the open driver's door.

"Hey!" he called. "Carl? You Carl?"

The boy looked his way. He was about sixty feet from the truck. *Don't scare him,* Ed thought. If the kid took off running, he'd never be able to catch him.

"Me?" Carl said, pointing to himself.

Ed nodded furiously, forced a smile. "There was a fire!"

Carl's jaw dropped and he started running toward the man. "A fire?"

"Your mom asked me to come get you," he said. "I was doing a couple of loads of laundry, and your mom was in the office, and one of the dryers just kind of blew up. All kinds of flame coming out of it and stuff."

"Is she okay?" the boy asked.

"She's good—she's fine—but she had to call the fire department, and she asked me if I could come pick you up. She described you pretty good! I picked you right out of the crowd!"

Carl's feet stayed rooted to the ground about ten feet away from the man. "I don't know," he said.

Ed put both hands out in front of him, palms out. "Look, I get it. I told your mom—I said, 'Your son's going to think I'm some sort of creepy stranger.' I mean, you don't know me. And if you're not comfortable letting me give you a ride to the Laundromat, I understand. Go back into the office and maybe in a couple of hours or so, when the fire department is finished up, your mom can come get you. I can go back and tell her you decided to stay. I mean, she could probably use your help right now, with all the trouble that's going on, but I think she'll understand."

Ed could see that the kid was right on the edge.

He started to get back into the truck. "Don't worry about it, Carl. I'll tell her you're fine and that you'll be waiting—"

"It's okay!" he said, and closed the distance between them.

"You can get in on my side," Ed said, moving back to allow the boy to jump in and scoot across the seat to the passenger side.

"You sure my mom's okay?" he asked as he settled in up against the passenger door and buckled his seat belt.

"I think she might have burned her hand a bit, but not real bad. When the fire started, she tried to smother it with some wet clothes from a washer, but it was kind of coming from the back side of the dryer. So then she went for a fire extinguisher, but by then it was really going. But you should have seen her! She was amazing! I called 911 for her, and once the fire trucks got there, she was all worked up because she couldn't come get you."

"Are they going to have to close the laundry?" Carl asked, his face full of worry. "Because if it closes, my mom doesn't make any money."

Ed, putting the truck in drive, shook his head. "Hard to say. She got insurance?"

"What's that?" Carl asked.

"Huh? They not teach you anything these days?" Ed checked his mirrors, prepared to move out into the street. But suddenly it was like trying to get out of the airport parking lot at Christmas. All these other cars blocking his way, mothers picking up their kids.

"Jesus, would it kill these little bastards to walk home from school?" Ed said. "Nobody got picked up when I was a kid."

He glanced over at the boy. Carl had begun to look uneasy.

"Sorry, I just get stressed-out in traffic," he said. "I'll get you to your mom right away."

"It's back that way," Carl said.

"Yeah, I know, but I gotta get out of this traffic jam first—then I'll double back. Your mom or dad never tell you not to be a backseat driver?"

"A what?"

Ed laughed. "You're not much brighter than your old man—you know that?"

"You know my dad?" Carl asked.

"Come on!" Ed yelled, putting down his window. There were three minivans and an SUV ahead of him, waiting to get past a crossing guard in an orange vest who was guiding kids across the street. "Honest to Christ!"

"How do you know my dad?" Carl persisted.

Ed glanced over as he powered up his window. "We're old buddies."

Carl's hand went for the door handle. Ed hit the lock button on his own door. "Don't even think about it, little man. We're about to get moving. You jump out of a moving truck, you'll turn into street pizza."

"There was no fire," Carl said.

Ed grinned. "That's good news, huh?"

The crossing guard stepped back onto the sidewalk and started waving the other cars through. "Here we go," Ed said. "Hope you like Boston because—Jesus!"

There was a banging on his window. There was a man running alongside the truck, slapping the palm of his hand on the glass and shouting.

"Stop the truck!" he yelled, his voice half-muffled by the glass. "Stop the damn truck!"

The man grabbed for the door handle, tried to open it without success.

It took half a second for Ed to realize who the man was, but he sure recognized him. He looked ahead, wanting to hit the gas, but the other cars were still holding him up. "Back off!" he shouted, but when he turned his head to the window, the man was gone.

"Carl!"

The guy was on the other side of the truck now, banging on Carl's glass. "Open the door!"

Ed reached across, grabbed the kid by his shirt collar, and yanked him toward the center of the seat. "Don't touch that fucking door."

The guy was holding up a phone, looking at Ed. "Hey, asshole! Next call is 911! Every cop in New York State's gonna be looking for this pickup!"

Ed's cheek twitched.

"Think about it!" the man yelled.

On the sidewalk, kids had stopped to watch what was happening. A few mothers, still waiting at the curb, had gotten out of their cars. At least one of them was getting out a phone, maybe to take pictures.

The cars ahead were finally moving.

Ed looked forward, hit the gas.

213

Felt the truck lurch for a second as it accelerated. Heard a *thunk*.

When Ed glanced right, the man was gone. He grinned, released his grip on the kid. "Showed him," he said.

"Not exactly," Carl said, and nodded rearward.

Ed looked in his mirror. The guy was in back. He was in the pickup bed. On his knees, amid a litter of dirt and decaying leaves. He was keeping low, in case Ed decided to start veering back and forth in a bid to throw him off-balance.

The engine sputtered and roared as the truck gained speed. A second crossing guard at the next cross street had to shoo kids out of the truck's path. Ed took the corner fast enough that the man was tossed into the wall of the pickup bed. But as long as he kept his center of gravity low, there was no way Ed could ditch him unless he found a way to drive upside down.

The man glanced through the window at Carl, gave him a thumbs-up gesture. Then he rolled onto his back and started fiddling with his phone.

"What's he doing?" Ed asked. "I can't see him."

"I think he's calling the police," Carl said.

Ed cranked the wheel hard left, hard right, and back again. See if the guy could enter any numbers while bouncing around like a pinball. He caught glimpses in his mirror of the guy being jostled back and forth. Didn't look like he had the phone in his hand anymore. Which could mean he'd already called the cops, or maybe he'd just given up. Maybe the phone had been knocked out of his hand.

"Gotta lose this guy," he said. But even Ed, who had failed physics in high school—and just about everything else for that matter—realized that no matter how quickly he drove, he wasn't going to put any more distance between himself and this asshole in the back of his truck.

The only way he was going to get rid of him was to get him out of his truck.

"Hang on, kid," Ed said, and slammed his foot on the brake with everything he had.

The truck squealed to a stop. The man in the back was thrown up against the back of the cab. Ed jammed the truck into park, threw open his door, and jumped out. He was going to reach in, grab the son of a bitch by his jacket, and throw him out onto the road.

What he hadn't counted on was how quickly the man would get to his feet.

Or that he would kick him in the face.

"Fuck!" Ed shouted, staggering back, putting both hands over a nose that was already spurting blood.

"Carl!" the man yelled. "Get out of the truck! Run!"

Carl hesitated for half a second, then scrambled across the front seat of the vehicle and bailed out of the open driver's door. The man placed both hands on the edge of the pickup bed and swung himself over, like he was dismounting a pommel horse.

While Ed still had his hands over his face, trying to stop the blood, the man drove a fist hard into his bloated stomach. Ed tumbled backward onto the street.

Carl, safely positioned behind a tree on a nearby front lawn, watched things play out.

In the distance, sirens could be heard. One of the many mothers at the school who'd witnessed all this must have called the police.

"You better get moving," the man said. "Cavalry's coming."

Ed slowly got to his feet, blood dripping down his chin.

"You're fucking dead," Ed muttered, making his way back to the truck. He got behind the wheel, slammed the door, and sped off.

Carl came out from behind the tree and ran over to the man, who was now bent over, hands on his knees, throwing up.

"Jeez, Mr. Harwood, are you okay?" he asked.

David Harwood went from bending over to collapsing onto the grass. He wiped his mouth with the back of a hand that was shaking.

"I don't know," he said. "I was really glad when your mom finally returned my call, but now, I'm not so sure."

TWENTY-NINE

Barry Duckworth was getting off the phone after speaking with the department's media relations officer about the imminent news conference he'd cleared with Chief Finderman when Angus Carlson came in and dropped into a chair at the next desk over.

"I've had it," Angus said.

Duckworth slowly looked over. Carlson was at least fifteen years younger than him. To Duckworth's way of thinking, that meant Carlson had nothing to complain about whatsoever.

"Hardly had any sleep," he added, without being prompted.

"Yeah," Barry said. "You're the only one."

Carlson flushed with embarrassment. "Yeah, okay. I get it."

"Tell me what happened at Thackeray," Duckworth said.

"I saw their security chief. Clive Dickhead."

Duckworth had no argument there. "What'd you say to him?"

"This big lawsuit that's been filed against the college by Mason Helt's family? I told him they were going to love it when they found out *Clive* never kept his promise to those women who'd been attacked to report what happened to them to us. I talked to one of the girls, Lorraine Plummer. She told me."

"You shouldn't have gotten into it with him."

"He pissed me off."

Duckworth worked his jaw around, hoping to reduce the tension. Day one working in the detective bureau and already Carlson thought he knew everything.

"There was something else that happened," Carlson said.

Duckworth waited.

"When I was leaving, one of the profs, a guy named Blackmore? Peter Blackmore? He chased me out to the parking lot to tell me his wife was missing."

Duckworth perked up. "Since when?" His first thought was of Helt, that maybe he was involved, but Helt had been dead nearly two weeks.

"Since yesterday, it looks like," Carlson said.

"We putting out an official report?"

"I would have, but Blackmore backed off. Soft-pedaled it, said his wife would probably turn up before long. Anyway, for what it's worth, I thought I'd mention it. He was in Duncomb's office when I got there. I think he was asking for his help on it."

Duckworth wondered whether Thackeray's security chief was following the same course with a professor's missing spouse as he had with the attacked girls. Trying to deal with it without bringing in the local police.

Duckworth glanced at his watch, rolled back his chair. "Gotta face the cameras."

"What?"

"About the drive-in, other stuff," he said.

"Something's happened?" Carlson asked. "You got some—"

His desk phone rang. "Hang on," he said to Duck-worth. "I want to hear about this." He snatched up the receiver, twirled it around his fingers like a baton, and put it to his ear.

"Hello? Oh, Gale."

Duckworth wanted to get going, but Carlson was holding up a finger.

Talking into the phone, Carlson said, "Don't worry about it. There's nothing to be sorry about . . . We were both tired . . . Yeah, well, maybe it *wasn't* the best time to talk about it . . . I think we *are* a family, even if it's just the two of us . . . Look, if I want to talk to my mother about it, I will . . . No, it's helpful to me . . . I have to go. I'll see you later."

He hung up, looked at Duckworth apologetically. "Sorry about that."

"It's okay," he said. "Trouble at home?"

Angus Carlson shrugged. "No big deal. I came in at like four in the morning and we kind of got into it."

"This kind of job can play hell with your home life," Duckworth said with some sympathy. "Long hours, ter-rible shifts, you see stuff you can't really explain to other people. My son, Trevor? He and I, we don't see eye to eye. I'm suspicious of the whole world, questioning every-one's motives. Not his, but the people around him."

Like Randall Finley.

Angus eyed Duckworth warily, as though debating whether to confide in him. "Gale wants a child. And . . . I don't."

Duckworth nodded. "I get that. You think, is this any kind of world to bring a kid into? But it's not all bad out there. We just see more of it than anyone else."

"It's not the rest of the world I worry about."

Duckworth didn't nod this time. "What do you mean?"

"It's what families do to their own. Mothers—parents, I mean—are supposed to love their kids. Lots of times, they don't."

"Yeah, but that doesn't have to be you," Duckworth said.

"Do you love your son?" Carlson asked.

"Absolutely."

"Does he love you?"

Duckworth waited a beat before replying. "Of course."

The corner of Carlson's mouth went up. "Truth is in the pauses," he said, got up, and walked out of the room.

"Thanks for coming," Duckworth said to the various media representatives who had turned out on short notice. Normally, there might have been people here from only Albany, but the drive-in bombing had brought journalists from as far away as Boston and New York, and they were still in town. The small meeting room in the police building was crowded, and with that many bodies, and lights, it was quickly getting warm in there.

Duckworth introduced himself and spelled out his name.

"I wanted to bring everyone up to speed on what happened at the drive-in, and a possible link between that and some other recent incidents in Promise Falls."

"Has there been an arrest?" someone shouted.

Duckworth raised a hand. "Hold your questions till the end. We're hoping to enlist the public's help today. Someone out there, someone watching, may have information that would prove valuable to our investigation.

Something they may not even know is important. Let me start by saying that every effort is being made to find out how the Constellation Drive-in came down, whether it was an accident or a deliberate act. The screen came down at twenty-three minutes past eleven, which in military time or the twenty-four-hour clock is twenty-three twenty-three. That in and of itself is not particularly noteworthy. But it may be when we look at some other occurrences which, up to now, have not attracted much attention."

With Finderman's approval, he'd had some photos blown up and mounted onto foam core board. He set the first one up on an easel next to his podium. It showed the twenty-three dead squirrels strung up on the fence in Clampett Park.

"Oh, yuck," said someone in the room.

"This act of animal cruelty went largely unnoticed earlier this month. Not that we don't take something like this seriously. But we hadn't issued any release on it, and no arrests have been made."

"Is that even illegal?" asked a reporter. "I mean, I kill squirrels all the time with my car and I haven't been charged with murder."

A wave of laughter.

"I said I'd take questions at the end," Duckworth said. "If you count them, you'll notice there are twenty-three animals here. Now, let me put this second photo up . . . Okay, this is the Ferris wheel at Five Mountains. That ride was in the process of being mothballed because the park, as you know, has gone out of business. But the other night, someone fired it up, got it running."

The picture showed the three naked mannequins in a carriage, the "YOU'LL BE SORRY" message painted across them in red. A buzz went through the room.

"What the hell?"

"Jesus."

"What kind of sicko does that?"

Duckworth raised a hand, put up a third picture, taken from the side of the carriage, showing the "23" on the side.

"Whoa," someone said.

"This was our second incident," Duckworth said. "No particular harm done, but there is this ominous message painted onto the mannequins. At the time, no special importance was attached to the number of the car they were sitting in."

He put his last picture in place. It was the hoodie Mason Helt had been wearing the night he attacked Joyce Pilgrim. The local media knew the Helt story, but this aspect of it was new to them.

"Now," Duckworth said, "it may be just one huge coincidence that this same number keeps popping up. But maybe it isn't. That's why I'm asking for the public's help. If you know of someone with a fixation on this number, if you have any idea how these various incidents might be connected, we want you to get in touch with us. All tips will be treated as confidential."

A reporter's hand shot up. "Can I ask a question now?"

Duckworth nodded. "Yeah, sure."

"So you think you're looking for a guy who likes to torture squirrels *and* blow up drive-ins?"

Soft chuckles went around the room again.

"I'm saying we see a possible link here," Duckworth said, "and we're asking the public for their help. Four people died when that screen came down, so you'll forgive me if I don't laugh along with the rest of you."

Another hand. "So let's say the same person or persons are responsible for all these things. Why? What's the deal? Those words painted onto the dummies, 'you'll be sorry.' Who'll be sorry, and for what? If someone's trying to send a message, what is it?"

"There's nothing I'd like to know more," Duckworth said.

THIRTY

Clive Duncomb brought home dinner, although that hardly made this evening special.

Duncomb picked up something on the way home most days. And those that he didn't, Liz generally ordered something in. Or threw some Stouffer's frozen thing into the microwave. Tonight, he had stopped at Angelino's, an Italian place that did mostly takeout. Pizza was Angelino's biggest seller, but they did pasta, too, so Clive got two orders of linguine with clams, and a single Caesar salad that he and Liz could split.

Cooking had never been Liz's calling. Even back when she ran her own business, in Boston, where she had a devoted clientele, when a customer asked for something spicy off the menu, a dildo was a more likely ingredient than dill. Nor was Liz's "Round the World" option a sampling of global cuisine.

But then again, Duncomb did not choose to make a life with Liz for her terrific soufflés. They had not met at the Cambridge School of Culinary Arts. Liz's mentor was not Julia Child. They met during an investigation into a Boston escort business. Duncomb, working vice at the time, had been gathering evidence to shut the place down, but had something of a change of heart when he met Elizabeth Palmer. She was willing to bring to life just about any fantasy he could imagine—especially those that involved extra players—if it meant turning a blind eye to her business operations.

Liz didn't even have to provide the handcuffs. Although, when it came to threesomes, or younger girls, she used her connections.

Not quite enough connections, however, to feel she could keep her business going without eventually getting busted, or keep Clive from getting brought up on police charges. When they sensed their luck was running out, they each bailed on their lines of work, but not before tracks were covered. Files were shredded or deleted, pay-offs made, threats to potential squealers delivered.

So they put their Boston lives behind them and came to Promise Falls. But it didn't mean they had to abandon their interests. Just because you move to the North Pole doesn't mean you don't still like water-skiing.

"Hey," he said when he came through the side door, directly into the kitchen. Liz was leaning up against the counter, watching *Dr. Oz* on a small television that hung from under one of the cabinets. Her long brown hair was twirled into a knot at the back of her head, and her feet were bare. Her red tank top was cut off, exposing several inches of skin above her jeans.

"Shh," she said, holding up a finger. "Dr. Oz says we should be having sex two hundred times a year. I'm not sure I could handle that."

"If you got down to two hundred," Duncomb said, setting the takeout on the counter, "you could take up another hobby. Scrapbooking, maybe."

"What constitutes a single sexual act, anyway?" Liz said, picking up a remote and turning down the volume. "I've got my doubts Dr. Oz will address this, but if I'm sucking your cock while Miriam's eating me out, is that one act or two?"

She suddenly frowned like a child expecting to be reprimanded. "I shouldn't speak that way of the dead, I suppose." She looked in the bag. "What do we have here?"

"Linguine, salad."

"Good," Liz said without enthusiasm.

"You're not happy?"

"I don't know. I was feeling a little bit like Thai. But this is fine. I can eat this."

"Are you really gonna bust my balls about dinner *today*?"

Liz rubbed his shoulder and forced a pout. "Big man have bad day?"

"Yeah, I had a bad day. And it's not over. Blackmore's freaking out because Georgina hasn't come home, and the most important disc is the one I can't find."

Liz got down plates, opened up the take-out containers, and divvied up the pasta and salad. "I'll get some Parm," she said, and brought out a container of cheese from the refrigerator door.

"Are you hearing me?" he said.

"No matter how bad things are," she said, "we still have to eat."

They did so, standing at the counter. The kitchen table was littered with newspapers, bills, boxes of paperwork that appeared to have taken up permanent residence there. They twirled pasta onto their forks, speared salad leaves.

"So, what do you mean, you can't find it?" Liz asked.

"Like I said. You know how Georgina's been lately. Like she wants out. I started to wonder whether it was her that took it from Adam's place. Tore her—well, her

226

and Peter's—place apart, but it wasn't there."

"Shit," she said. "I wish you'd find it." She smiled. "I'd like to watch it."

"Jesus, Liz, the second I find it, I'm breaking it into a hundred pieces."

"She was a foxy little thing, that Olivia."

Clive shook his head, not wanting to talk about it.

"What?" Liz said. "That was a fun session. It was too bad what happened to her. She might have liked to come back for more. We didn't even have to spike her wine like any of the others. She was coming on to Adam in the kitchen. She didn't even know what we were all into. She just wanted to fuck a washed-up writer."

"We should have," he said.

"Should have what?"

"Spiked her wine like the others. It was a huge risk, bringing her into the mix and letting her remember what actually happened."

"She never told a soul," Liz said. "I mean, the girl was engaged, for God's sake. Who was she going to tell? Her fiancé? I think she wanted one last wild experience before she tied the knot." A grin. "You know, in the marriage sense. I seem to recall a bit of knot-tying that night."

"Honestly, Liz, dial it down for Christ's sake. This is no joke."

"Okay, okay. You're just so serious all the time."

"I'm going to go through all the discs again tonight, at Peter's. Maybe I missed her. I fast-forwarded through all of them once I got them out of Adam's house. I didn't see her. But maybe she was there, and I just went too fast."

"It must have looked funny."

"What looked funny?"

"All that fast-motion fucking. All those asses going up

and down at a hundred miles an hour."

Duncomb opened the fridge, took out a beer, uncapped it. "A cop came out to the campus today," he said.

"Why?"

"About the Mason Helt thing. They're still asking questions about that. I didn't do anything wrong there."

"Of course you didn't," she said, almost purring.

"I saw Peter run after him when he left. I think he was asking about Georgina, whether to file a missing persons report. I told him I'd look after this, but he doesn't listen."

Liz touched a finger to Duncomb's chest, worked it between the buttons of his shirt, and made tiny circles on his chest. "I like Peter."

"You like his tongue—that's what you like."

She withdrew the finger. "Maybe. But I feel terrible about Adam. There was a man who had it all."

Duncomb didn't respond.

"Don't take that the wrong way. I don't even mean sexually, necessarily. You know I love *you*, Clive. More than anyone else. I'm just saying he was an interesting man. And I can't get over the irony of it. Here was a guy who loved the movies, and he dies when a movie screen falls on him. It's like some sort of cosmic joke, you know? Like that jogger guy, years ago? You know, who wrote the book about it? And how does he die? He has a heart attack while out for a run. It's like that."

"I guess," Duncomb said.

"You sound hurt. You can't be jealous of a dead man."

"I'm not."

"And you have to be missing Miriam." She smiled. "Be honest. She was very creative. I'd never seen anyone with that kind of imagination who wasn't in the business."

228

"I love *you*," he said.

"Of course you do. That's the way it's always been. We love each other, and *make* love with others. But Miriam was very special. And totally bi. The rest of us basically swapped partners, but Miriam had as much fun with me or Georgina as she did with you or Peter."

"It feels kind of strange, talking about Adam and Miriam like this. Now."

"But, you see, what'll help us through this is, we've always been good at separating the physical from the emotional. Otherwise, right now, we'd be devastated. Losing Adam and Miriam would, under different circumstances, be very hard for us. But I'm okay. Aren't you?"

Duncomb hesitated. "Sure."

"And you never had any reason to be jealous of Adam. The fact is, you were much alike. You've done things you don't like to talk about, and so had he. Back to his days when he was in that gang. Those weren't weekend bikers he hung out with. Those were bad, bad people. Some of them were never heard from again after Adam left that life behind."

"I know."

"I've always had this theory that he must have ripped them off before he left. I don't think he ever made enough writing books to have a nice house like that, or that antique Jag. I think he did okay for himself. He talked about it some with me. He managed girls—I managed girls. We had that in common. But there were drugs, too. I think that's where he got his money."

"Maybe," Duncomb said. "I've been thinking, with what's happened, it's time to put a stop to this kind of stuff."

"Just because Adam's playroom's no longer available

doesn't mean things have to be over."

"I don't want to do this anymore with Peter and Georgina. He's getting too skittish about things, and her, I don't know how to read her anymore. I don't trust her."

"I get that. You get tired of people. We'll find new friends."

She stopped eating and slipped her finger into his shirt again, started to unbutton it. She pushed Duncomb up against the counter and pressed herself into him, felt his hardness grow against her. She wrapped her arms around herself, gripped the bottom of the tank top, and slipped it off over her head. She was wearing nothing underneath.

"Touch me," she said.

Clive Duncomb did as he was instructed.

Liz, moving herself slowly against him, said, "Tell me again . . . starting from the beginning . . . and tell me very, very slowly . . . about when you shot that kid in the head."

THIRTY-ONE

When it got to be dusk, George Lydecker was itching to do it again. Actually, he'd been itching to do it all day, but daylight break-ins were not the smartest thing in the world.

He wanted to break into another garage. In a weird way, he needed to do it to calm his nerves. George hadn't been to sleep in a day and a half.

He'd been pretty freaked-out the night before when he and his friends Derek and Canton and Tyler had tried to sneak into the Constellation, only to see the whole goddamn thing come crashing down. They were about to get busted by the manager for trying to smuggle Derek in by hiding him in the trunk of the car. George had even gotten out to try to argue that the guy didn't have the constitutional right to search the vehicle.

But then none of that mattered. Not when a bunch of bombs went off and the people started screaming.

Derek, the dumb bastard, had actually run toward the disaster, but George and his buddies figured the smartest thing to do was get the hell out of there. Especially since George had brought a gun along—and yes, he had actually found it in somebody's garage and stolen it, just as Tyler had suggested—and the police would be showing up any minute.

They'd raced back into town. George got dropped off at his parents' place, but he was too wound up to go in and go to bed. He'd wandered around his neighborhood, even then, checking for garages that had been left unlocked. A lot of people actually went to bed with their garage doors wide open. They'd be doing something out there, go inside for dinner, decide to watch some TV, and go to bed without ever remembering to close the damn thing.

You went strolling in, used your phone as a flashlight, and helped yourself to whatever you wanted.

He'd looked around two garages in the hours after the drive-in bombing, hadn't seen much that he liked. So he was out again tonight, scratching that itch, wondering what he might find before he went to Canada the following morning.

The whole damn family, or *fam damily*, as he liked to think of it, was off to Vancouver to spend time with his father's stupid relatives. And the taxi was coming at— get this!—five in the fucking morning. That was when George was usually crawling under the covers. So he'd promised his mother he'd be home in good time, which would allow him at least a couple of hours' sleep before he had to get up.

George was easily bored. The doctors said it was more than just simple attention deficit disorder. George's brain just wasn't wired right. He'd always shown signs of being a smart little bugger. All he had to do was apply himself, his teachers—from every single grade—repeatedly told his parents.

That always made George think of that line, from a comic book or something: "If only he'd used his powers for good instead of evil."

Not that George was evil. He definitely did not see himself as evil. He just couldn't sit still.

And he liked to steal shit.

His parents, determined that he make something of himself, had insisted he go to Thackeray, and what a disaster that had turned out to be. He'd just finished two years there, and had successfully completed only four classes in all that time. He was not going back in the fall. There was absolutely no point. That professor whose Smart car he'd turned upside down had been pushing for him to be permanently expelled anyway. Plus, admin was still holding a grudge for his putting a baby alligator in the pond.

If you couldn't have a bit of fun when you were in college, when could you?

Oh well, fuck 'em. Time to concentrate on the task at hand.

There was a garage he'd spotted one night the week before that had looked promising.

The first thing it had going for it was that it was separate from the house. So anyone at home was a lot less likely to hear anything. The other thing was, it had a side door, as well as two big car-sized doors at the front. So someone was going to have to remember to lock not one door but three.

On top of that, it was a nice enough house. So there might be good stuff that had been tucked in the garage that was worth taking.

The thing was, most of the crap he took, he threw away. Tossed into a Dumpster. Threw into the river. He'd kept some tools one time, and that gun (which he had dropped into a storm drain after getting back from the drive-in) was a nice score. Found it, and a box of bullets, in the drawer of a workbench. But it was the act of taking it that gave him the thrill. Getting in, getting out.

It was a *high*.

He decided to come at his latest target from the back. Just as streetlights were coming on, he walked down a narrow alley between two houses, reached their back property line, then hopped a fence that was shrouded with trees and bushes, and landed by the back wall of the garage.

Bonus. There was a window on that wall. That meant four possible ways inside. He peered through the heavily grimed glass, but it was almost totally dark in there.

He came along the side of the garage, right up to the corner, where he could get a look at the house. No one in the backyard, and only one light on in the house that he could see, in the kitchen.

The light didn't worry him. He could get into this garage without being seen. Standing at the side door, he turned the knob. It was locked.

But hang on.

The door had not been pulled tight into the frame. So while the knob couldn't be turned, when George gave the door a nudge, it moved.

Bingo.

Quickly, he opened the door, stepped in, and eased it shut behind him, nearly knocking over an old croquet set off to the side.

There was no car in here, and there wouldn't have been room for one. Most of the garage was being used for storage. Using his phone for light, he could see the opposite wall was lined with metal shelving. There was a lot of the usual junk you'd expect to find. Gardening supplies, partially filled paint cans, small rolls of scrap carpet. On the floor, white plastic lawn furniture weathered with leaf stains. A case of beer bottles. Garbage cans.

On one shelf, half a dozen small wire-cage traps. A funneled entry at one end that would allow an animal to crawl inside, but which would be nearly impossible to crawl back out of without getting jabbed by the wire. The kind of thing, George thought, you might catch rats in.

Or squirrels.

And what the hell was that on the top shelf? Looked like an arm and a leg. A closer look revealed that they were a couple of limbs from mannequins.

But the most curious thing was the blue tarp spread over a large mound of something, in the middle of the garage floor. The surface of the tarp was bumpy and irregular.

Topsoil, maybe?

The pile was about five feet across, about two feet high. Four bricks held down the corners of the tarp. George kicked one away, reached down and threw the tarp back, and took a look.

The fuck?

At first, he thought it was drugs. Oversized bags—dozens, if not hundreds—of the stuff. More than he could count, that was for sure. Could it be a pile of cocaine or heroin or some shit like that? Weren't they both white? When you saw bags of it on TV, it was usually white.

But when you saw drugs like that on *The Wire* or *The Shield* or any of those other cop shows, weren't they packaged up the size of bricks? And wouldn't one briefcase full be enough to buy a small country?

These bags were much larger, like sacks. Industrial grade, semi-opaque plastic. They reminded George of the large bags pool chemicals came in. He'd once spent a summer working for a pool maintenance company. But the stuff in this pile here did not give off any whiff of chlorine.

So what was it? It looked a lot like salt.

That was some huge load of salt for someone to keep in the garage. Even in the winter, you wouldn't need that much to melt the ice on your driveway. This was enough to keep the entire New York Thruway from freezing over.

He knelt down, unwound the twist tie on the top of the bag, and opened it. Didn't smell a thing. He reached into the bag, touched his finger to the stuff, thinking it would stick like powder, but it was more like crystal. A couple of tiny granules stuck to his finger, and he put it to his tongue.

George didn't taste a thing, but whatever this stuff was, it burned a little.

Was this shit worth something? Was even one bag of it worth stealing?

And if he did steal it, what would he do with—

The lights came on.

George whirled around so quickly he stumbled, his ass landing on the cold concrete floor.

"Holy Jesus!" he said when he saw what was standing in the doorway staring at him.

It was a huge walking bug.

It had huge round eyes, maybe two inches across, and an all-black, shiny face. Plus, there was some strange thing sticking out of one side of its face the size and shape of a hockey puck, but black and rubbery, like the face.

It was some kind of monster.

Fuck, no, it wasn't a monster. It was a man, in a gas mask. Like one of those things you'd see someone wearing in a war movie, or on the news when they were looking after people with the Ebola virus.

George came this close to wetting his pants.

The man in the gas mask said, "What the hell are you doing in here?" But it came out funny because of the mask. Like a bad phone connection.

"Hey!" said George. "God, you just about scared the piss out of me there! What's with the getup, pal?"

"I asked you what you're doing in here."

"Nothing, just, you know, just looking around. God, you sound like Darth Vader."

The masked man looked at the pile of bags George had uncovered.

"Why did you do that? Why are you looking at that?"

"Just wondered what it was. That's all. I'm guessing it must be some kind of bad shit if you're wearing a fucking gas mask. You got another one of those?"

"Who are you? You're not with the police. You don't look like you're from the police."

"No way, no, I'm no cop."

"Did someone send you?" The voice sounded creepy through the rubber.

"Nobody sent me, man. I just wandered in. The door, it wasn't shut. I haven't taken anything. Don't call the cops on me. I'm not stealing anything. Just let me out of here. I don't know what this shit is, but I just put some of it on my tongue. My nuts going to fall off or something?"

The man stared at him.

"Listen, what is this shit? It's not coke or heroin, right? I mean, if you're some big-time drug dealer, I am so sorry I wandered in here, and you can be sure I'm not going to say—"

"It's not drugs," the man said.

"It's sure not chlorine. I used to work for a pool company, you know? And I can tell it's not chlorine." George was smiling, trying to be as sociable as possible. Like he wanted to be Mask Man's new best friend. "I mean, if it was chlorine, we could hardly even breathe, right? Sometimes, if I was over a bucket of those pool pucks, when I pulled the lid off, I'd nearly pass out."

The man said nothing. He just stared at him through the bug eyes.

George started getting to his feet. "I'm just going to take off, if that's okay with you. You're not going to call the cops, right? We're cool there, okay?"

"I'm not going to call the cops," the man said.

George took two tentative steps toward the door, but the man wasn't stepping out of the way.

"Just let me go."

The man reached for a mallet from the croquet set by the door.

"Aw, come on, man. I'm just going to go."

As he took another step, the man brought the mallet up and swung.

George threw up a defensive arm, but the man managed to connect the end of the mallet with George's temple. Hard enough that the head broke off the shaft and landed on the garage floor.

George threw his hand to his head. "Fuck!" he shouted.

The man looked at the croquet mallet shaft in his hand, now nothing more than a striped stick with a jagged end.

He hesitated a moment, then drove it into George, just below the rib cage, through his T-shirt and into flesh. The force pushed George up against the wall, where the man kept pushing until he felt the end of the stick hit a hard surface, his breathing hard and raspy through the rubber mask.

Blood gurgled from George's mouth. He stirred briefly, then slid down the wall to the floor.

The man let the stick slip from his fingers, looked down at the dead man. Stood there. Breathing in, breathing out.

Good thing, he thought, that he had more than half a roll of plastic tarp left.

THIRTY-TWO

"Everybody's talking about Dad!" Ethan said at the dinner table, too excited to eat. He hadn't touched the lasagna his grandmother had made. "He, like, jumped into the back of a truck and everything! I wish I'd seen it. I came out a couple of minutes too late, but lots of other kids saw it. I wish you'd waited. I wish you'd waited till I came out before you jumped in the truck."

"Sorry," David said to his son.

"This boy that you rescued, is he the son of that woman who came over here the other night?" asked his mother, Arlene. "What's her name? I can't think of her name."

David nodded. "Sam," he said.

His mother looked puzzled. "Sam?"

"Short for Samantha."

"Oh, right. Well, I thought she seemed nice at the time, but now, I don't know. You don't need to get mixed up with a woman who's got those kinds of problems."

"You didn't even talk to her when she was here the first time, Mom."

"I saw her out the window and thought she was pretty. But looks aren't everything, you know. Sounds like you did a very stupid thing. You could have gotten yourself killed."

Don, who'd been overseeing kitchen reconstruction at their house and had arrived for dinner a few minutes late, had been brought up to speed quickly, and saw things somewhat differently.

"I'm proud of you," he said, reaching across the table, clamping a hand on his son's arm and squeezing. "You didn't just stand by. You did . . . something." David's father seemed to choke on his words, took his hand away, and looked down at his dinner.

"You okay?" Arlene asked him.

"I'm fine."

"I really didn't think about it," David said. "I just did it."

He'd quickly filled them in on what had happened. Sam Worthington's former in-laws had distracted her long enough to delay her trip to pick up her son, Carl. She figured they were going to send this Ed guy—whose name turned out to be Ed Noble, if you could believe it—to grab Carl, and she was right. She'd tried calling someone else first, some private detective she knew, but he was too far away. So then she tried David, who, it turned out, was only a mile away from the school when the call came in on his cell.

David drove to within a block of Clinton Public, unable to get any closer because of all the other parents who'd come to pick up their kids, bailed on the car, and ran flat out the rest of the way. He didn't know what Ed Noble looked like, but he caught a glimpse of Carl getting into a pickup truck, and took off after it.

The police were called, and statements given. The private eye, whose name was Cal Weaver, eventually showed up, too, and told the cops about Ed Noble coming around to the Laundromat in the morning to give Sam a hard time. The cops were still talking to Weaver, and Carl and Sam, who'd run all the way to the school, when David headed home.

He was pretty rattled.

And he hurt, too.

He had bruises on his shoulders from being tossed around in the pickup, and he'd done something to his back. And when he'd kicked that asshole in the face, he'd twisted his knee. He could still walk okay, but damn, did it hurt.

David figured he wasn't cut out for this sort of thing.

Shortly after coming in the door, he downed as many Tylenols as the label permitted. Ethan was already home, jumping up and down with excitement, demanding details. He'd already told his grandmother that David had foiled a hit man.

When Sam had called him, he'd been busy thinking about Randall Finley's veiled threat to tell Ethan the truth about the circumstances of his mother's death, the son of a bitch. That had been after David had pushed Finley about whatever under-the-table deal he had going on with developer Frank Mancini.

Then his phone had rung, and he'd seen who the caller was, and he'd answered in a second.

Cheerily. "Hey!" he'd said. A call from Sam would be the best news he'd had so far that day. But it turned out not to be that kind of call.

"Where are you?" Sam had screamed. "They're going after Carl!"

At which point his afternoon plans—he had been thinking of paying a visit to Randall Finley's wife, Jane, to get a better handle on the man—changed abruptly.

Adrenaline kept him going through the chase and the police interview afterward, but by the time he came through the door, he was shaking. He fell into his mother's arms and started breathing so quickly she wondered whether he was having some kind of panic attack.

David admitted he was, at that moment, overwhelmed.

"I could have been killed," he said, realizing it for the first time. "I don't know what the hell I was thinking. It could have gone wrong a hundred ways. He could have crashed that truck. He could have rolled it over. I could have fallen out when he was moving."

"It was a stupid thing to do," Arlene agreed.

He pulled himself together and got his mother to promise not to tell his father, or Ethan, that he'd temporarily lost it.

But now that dinner was over, and he was sitting, alone, on the front step of his house, he was starting to feel back to normal. A couple of beers had helped.

Now he was back to thinking about Randall Finley. David decided that whatever Finley had going on with Mancini, he couldn't worry about it. At least, not yet. If David wanted to work with only ethical politicians, then he might as well collect welfare.

But the thing with Ethan? There was no way David was going to put up with that. He couldn't allow Finley to have that kind of control over him.

David got up, opened the front door, and called inside: "Ethan!"

His son bounded down the stairs, came outside. "Yup?"

"Let's you and me take a walk."

"Where?"

"Nowhere in particular. I just want to talk."

"Is this about Carl? Because I know I'm not supposed to get in cars with strangers. Or pickup trucks. So you don't have to give me that lecture."

"That's not what I wanted to talk to you about, but yeah, you should never get into a car with someone you don't know."

"I just told you I know that."

"Okay." He placed his palm, briefly, on his son's back as they walked down the sidewalk. "Did what happened to Carl scare you?"

Ethan shrugged. "Not really. I don't know. I didn't really think about it that way. Is that what you wanted to talk about?"

"No. I wanted to talk to you about your mom."

"What about her?"

"She died when you were only four—"

"I know."

"What I was going to say is, because you were only four, it was hard to explain a lot of what happened."

"You mean like what happens to someone when they die? Like, if they really go to heaven, or they're just dead?"

David glanced down at the boy. "That's another discussion. No, I mean, there are a lot of things about your mom I didn't tell you at the time, that I kept from you, because it would have been hard to understand at that age. But you're older now, and there's things you probably should know. Things you should hear from me, instead of hearing them from somebody else. It kind of helped that we moved away for a while after she died, and no one knew us in Boston. And by the time we moved back here, people were kind of done talking about her."

"Okay," Ethan said.

"The first thing you need to know is, regardless of anything your mom did, or what anyone might say about her, she loved you very much."

"Okay."

"The last thing your mother did, before she died, was to make sure nothing bad happened to you. There was a very bad man, and he was threatening to hurt you, and she stopped him." David hesitated. "She killed him."

"Yeah," Ethan said. "I kind of knew that."

"I know there's bits and pieces of this that you know— you've probably heard your grandparents talking about it when they didn't think you were listening. The thing is, even though she loved you more than just about anything else in the world, your mother wasn't a very good person."

Ethan glanced up at his father. "I know."

"You know?"

He nodded. "I've read all about her."

"You have?"

Ethan nodded. "There's lots of stuff about her online. That she had a different name when she was born, that years ago she cut off the hand of that guy she killed, that she stole some diamonds that turned out to be—"

"You know all this?"

Ethan stopped. His lip quivered. "Am I in trouble? I just wanted to know. Anytime I've ever asked you about Mom, you just said there wasn't much to tell, and so then I would ask Nana and Poppa about her and they said I should talk to you, so I Googled her instead. There's a whole bunch of stories. Most of them are from around the time everything happened, like, after she died."

David felt an enormous weight coming off him, but at the same time, he felt saddened.

"I should have guessed that you'd do that. It's pretty impossible to keep anything a secret these days. Especially from kids."

"Yeah."

"So, how'd you feel about what you found out?"

Ethan shrugged. "I don't know. A bit weird. But it was also kind of cool."

"Cool?" David said sharply.

Ethan recoiled from his father's tone. "I don't mean cool, like, as in cool, neat. More like, you know, cool, interesting."

"I'm sorry. I didn't mean to jump down your throat. I think I understand."

"Like, I'm glad that you're sort of normal and ordinary, but it was kind of, you know, neat that my mom was someone people were talking about. I mean, if she was still alive, it would be awful, but because it happened a long, long time ago, it's not so bad."

To him, five years is an eternity, David thought. *For me, it was yesterday.*

"Is that it?" Ethan asked.

"Is what it?"

"That's why you wanted to talk to me?"

"Yeah."

"So can we go back?"

"Yeah, sure. Come here."

David pulled the boy into him, put his arms around him. But Ethan pushed back.

"Dad, we're on the street," he complained, twisting his head, looking up and down the sidewalk.

"Sorry," David said, releasing his grip. "Don't want to embarrass you."

"You can hug me when we get home if you still want to."

"I might. I just might."

When they got back to the house, they found two people waiting for them. Sam Worthington and her son,

246

Carl. Her car, slashed tires replaced, was at the curb.

"Hi," David said.

"Carl," Sam said, prodding her son.

"Mr. Harwood, thank you for what you did today," the boy said.

David smiled. "No problem."

Turning his attention to Ethan, the boy said, "Do you have trains here, too?"

Ethan shook his head. "Just at my grandpa's house. But Nana—that's my grandma—made some blueberry pie, although you have to be careful not to get it on your shirt because it won't come off."

"That sounds okay," Carl said, and the boys ran into the house, David and Sam watching them go.

David said, "How are you doing?"

"Okay," Sam said. "Got my tires replaced, although I don't know how I'll pay the Visa bill when it comes in. The cops are looking for Ed and my ex-in-laws. They figure they'll try to sneak back to Boston."

"You worried they'll try again?"

She shook her head slowly. "Not right now. Not after what happened. I mean, they have to know everyone's trying to find them. They're going to want to disappear for a while. Anyway, I came by to answer your question."

"My question?"

"The one you left on my voice mail. The answer's yes."

"What did I ask you?" he asked.

"You asked if I wanted to go to dinner. The answer is yes."

David nodded slowly. "Okay."

"We're going to do it right this time," Sam said. "Dinner *first*."

THIRTY-THREE

Cal

Once I was done talking to the police about Ed Noble's visit to the Laundromat that morning, I called Lucy Brighton and said I wanted to update her. She invited me to come to her house at eight.

On the way, I had the radio tuned to a local phone-in show.

"Who says we couldn't be a target of terrorists?" asked the bombastic host. "Are we too insignificant up here? A couple of hours away from New York? Is that what we're foolish enough to think? Let me tell you something, my friend. You want to strike fear into the hearts of Americans? Then *go* to the heart of America. The big cities are the obvious targets. But why not Promise Falls? Why not—I don't know—Lee, Massachusetts? Saratoga Springs? Middlebury, Vermont? Duluth? Make Americans feel unsafe wherever they happen to be. That's what those Islamist fanatics are thinking, and you can be damn sure blowing up a drive-in theater is totally their kind of style. Let's go to the phones. Go ahead, Dudley."

Dudley?

"Yeah, I think we need to be looking very closely at our neighbors, because these people, what they do is, they hide amongst us."

"No kidding, my friend, no kidding. And now we've

got Mr. Twenty-three out there trying to scare us half to death, according to the brilliant cops in Promise Falls. Well, I'm telling you right now, I don't scare easy. Your shtick with twenty-three might work on some people, but it won't work on me."

Mr. Twenty-three? What the hell was that about?

I decided it was something I didn't need to know right now, and turned off the radio. When I rang the bell at the Brighton house, a young girl answered the door. I remembered Lucy telling me her daughter was eleven.

She was holding a clipboard in one hand, several sheets of paper held down by the metal arm. In the fingers of her other hand, an uncapped, fine-point Sharpie pen. She had straight brown hair that fell below her ears, and bangs across her forehead. She reminded me of the *Peanuts* character Marcie, minus the glasses.

If she'd been Peppermint Patty, she probably would have offered some kind of greeting.

Crystal offered none. She stared at me.

"Hi," I said. "You must be Crystal."

Crystal said nothing.

"My name is Mr. Weaver. I think your mom's expecting me."

She turned and shouted: "Mom!"

So, she could speak. She fixed her gaze on me again. I pointed to the clipboard.

"What are you working on?"

Crystal turned the clipboard so I could see it. She had divided the page into six squares, and filled each of them with crudely drawn characters and word bubbles.

"A comic book," I said.

"No."

"Sorry, I thought, with the panels, that it looked like a—"

"It's a graphic novel," she said. She flipped ahead through the pages. Dozens of them, all drawn in a similar style to the top one. Some of the pages were just scraps; a few were construction paper in red and green. On every one, more squares, more drawings. While the people were simply drawn, I understood what they were about. She'd managed to capture hand gestures and expressions, which seemed odd, given that, so far, Crystal seemed to have very few of her own.

I pointed to one of the panels. "Is that a car?"

"Yes."

"Looks like a sports car."

"It's a Jaguar. My grandfather has one. But it's flat now. Something big fell on it."

Suddenly, Lucy was there.

"Sorry!" she said to me, pushing her daughter to one side. "Go on in, sweetheart." The child withdrew. "I was downstairs putting something into the dryer and didn't even hear the bell."

"It's okay. It gave me a chance to meet Crystal."

Lucy made a smile that was more a grimace. "If she seemed rude—"

"She wasn't."

"If she seemed rude," Lucy pressed on, "she doesn't mean to be."

"She was showing me her graphic novel. I made the mistake of calling it a comic book."

"Oh, you shouldn't have done that," Lucy said. She led me into the living room, where she'd already put out cups, a plate of cheese and crackers, and a carafe of coffee.

"Whoa," I said.

"It's no bother."

"I like Crystal's drawing style. Kind of minimalist, but you can tell what's going on, what people are thinking."

Lucy smiled, shook her head. "That child. She's drawing all the time, on any shred of paper she can get her hands on. The other day I'd run out of checks and found out she'd been turning the backs of them into four-panel strips. The perfect size, she said. I try not to get mad, but—"

"She's a talented kid."

"Yeah, well, sometimes talent and trouble go hand in hand."

"What do you mean?"

"You've just met her, but you can see she lacks certain social graces. She's challenged that way. Doesn't quite know how to act. Sometimes"—and almost instantly Lucy began to tear up—"other kids . . . they can be so cruel to her. She's the oddball, you know?"

"Sure," I said. "My son, Scott, was kind of like that."

"Was he diagnosed?"

"Diagnosed?"

"Did they figure out what was wrong with him?"

"It wasn't quite like that. He just had different interests than other kids. He didn't fit into the mainstream."

"So it wasn't anything like Asperger's?"

"Is that what Crystal has?"

"I don't even know. Her GP thinks maybe. She has some of the checkmarks. Poor social communication, repetitive behavior. And this obsession with drawing, doing her doodles on everything. I couldn't find one of my reports the other day, found Crystal had done 'The Adventures of Lizardman' on the backs of the pages."

"Years from now, she'll be making a million a year drawing for Marvel," I offered.

"Yeah, well, I could use some of that cash now. There's a place I'd like to take her, where they'd test her, and then there's a school that would be better suited to her needs, where they'd find a way to draw her out, even let her do more of this stuff she's so good at. But I don't exactly get paid a fortune. I'd talked to my father about it, whether he could, you know, help out. He said he would think about it . . ."

"And now . . ."

"Yeah, and now. Crystal has always been kind of like this, but I think it got worse when her father left us. She needed a male figure in her life. I think that's why she liked spending time around my dad. She was good with him."

I didn't know what to say.

"Well, enough about all this," Lucy said, and then lowered her voice to a whisper. "I take it you called because you've found out something? Do you have the discs?"

I reached for a cracker, put a slice of cheese on it. It occurred to me I hadn't eaten anything for hours.

"I don't have the discs."

"But do you know who took them?"

"You know a Clive Duncomb?"

She shook her head. "You mentioned him before, when you were looking up contacts at my father's house."

"Yeah. He works at Thackeray. Heads up security there. He and your father—he and his wife were friends with your dad and Miriam."

Lucy repeated the name. "I know a few people out at Thackeray, given what I do. But the people I know are more in the academic end of things and—"

Lucy stopped herself.

"What is it?"

"I don't know what the name was, but my father mentioned, I'm pretty sure, that he knew someone at the college who'd given him tips for when he was writing about the police. But this man wasn't a security guard or anything. He was a policeman, or used to be."

"That could be Duncomb," I said. "He's an ex-cop. Did he say much else about him?"

"I was over there once, and he happened to say something about having this ex-cop, and his wife, and another couple over for dinner. And maybe even a student from Thackeray who wanted to know what it was like to be a writer. I'd dropped by in the afternoon and Miriam already had the table set and everything."

"Did he say who the other couple was?"

Lucy shook her head.

"What are you thinking?" she asked me.

"I don't know. I mean, I think we have a pretty good idea what's on those DVDs. I had it confirmed for me by your father's ex-wife, Felicia." I grimaced. "She hadn't heard about what happened at the drive-in. I ended up being the one to break it to her."

"Oh, God, that must have been awful. For her, and for you. You don't think she was faking, do you? That she already knew but was pretending not to?"

I thought about that. "It seemed legit." I smiled. "But I've been fooled by women before."

That brought a smile to Lucy's face, too. "So, if she really didn't know, there wouldn't be any urgency on her part to break into my father's house."

I nodded. "Anyway, she says that when she and your father split, he gave her any discs that featured her. She destroyed them herself."

"Unless there were copies."

"There's that," I said. "Sometimes I have nothing to go on but my gut, and my gut says she didn't do it. But I feel differently about Clive Duncomb."

"Tell me about him."

"He acts like he's head of the FBI instead of security chief at a small college. But when I brought up that something was taken from the house, he didn't even ask me what it was."

She let that sink in. "He already knew."

"That's what I was thinking. Also, he's the kind of guy your father might have trusted with a key and the code. Being an ex-cop and all."

"You're saying my father, and Miriam, maybe they were having sex with this Duncomb man and his wife? And recording it?"

This had to be uncomfortable for her. It wasn't exactly comfortable for me, discussing her father's colorful sex life.

"Maybe," I said. "One thing I've learned over the years is you simply don't know what goes on behind closed doors. And I'm not just talking about sex. Husbands and wives, parents and their children, they treat each other differently in the privacy of their homes than they do when they're in public."

"I got a taste of that when I was in the classroom. The things small children would say to you. Things like, 'My mom can't volunteer for the school trip because my daddy pushed her down the stairs.' And they'd say it so innocently."

"That's awful," I said.

"It's all so ridiculously sordid. Maybe that's not the word. I don't care if people want to fool around or wife-swap or whatever. It's a free country. I'm not like the Taliban—or somebody's church for that matter—wanting to tell everybody how to live. But when it's your own father . . . it's embarrassing."

"Sure."

She went to take a bite of a cracker, then put it back on the plate. No appetite.

"I just need to know who it was. If it's this Duncomb man, maybe I can make a personal appeal to him. Not even accuse him of anything, but just say, 'Look, if you have those discs, please don't ever make them public. Please destroy them.'"

I didn't know whether that was a good idea, but said, "If he took them, and he took them to protect his own reputation, it strikes me as unlikely that he's going to post them online, if you know what I mean." I glanced up the stairs. "I'd say the chances of Crystal stumbling onto videos starring her grandfather are pretty unlikely."

"Oh, God, the very thought."

I ate another cracker with cheese, poured myself some coffee from the carafe.

"Oh, I should have done that," Lucy said apologetically.

I took a sip, told her it was good. "You have to decide whether you want me to pursue this any further. I want to have one more look around your father's house—you've hired my services for the whole day—and see if I come across anything else of interest, maybe take a closer look at his e-mails, but I don't know how much further I can take this."

Lucy considered. "Maybe another day or two?" She made it sound like she was asking for another sliver of cake. I sensed that she wanted a reason for me to come back here tomorrow, and the day after that.

"Why don't I see what I learn tonight, and then we can make a decision?" I said.

"That sounds good. I can't leave Crystal, so you'll have to go to the house by yourself. I can give you one of my spare keys for the house, and the code is two-six-six-nine. Do you want me to write it down?"

"I can remember."

We both stood, almost uncomfortably close. A kind of electricity seemed to be passing between us.

The phone rang.

"Just a second," she said, detouring back into the kitchen.

"Hello?" I heard her say. "Oh, Martin. Martin, I'm so sorry."

I poked my head into the kitchen.

"Hang on just one second," she said. She put her hand over the mouthpiece and looked my way. "It's Miriam's brother. Martin Kilmer. He's driving up from Providence."

I raised my hand, a mini-wave. "I'll be in touch," I said softly, let myself out.

As I got into the car, I noticed something on the passenger seat. Several pieces of paper, stapled together.

I kept the door open to keep the dome light on and picked up the document. The cover page featured a drawing of a little girl walking through a forest at night. It was titled "Noises in the Night by Crystal Brighton."

There was a yellow sticker attached that read: "NOT a comic book."

I looked back at the house, to a second-floor window, presumably Crystal's bedroom. She was silhouetted against the light, watching me.

THIRTY-FOUR

Randall Finley pulled his Lincoln into his home driveway, up next to a red Kia, killed the engine. He sat behind the wheel for a moment, listened to the ticking of the engine as it began its cooldown, then got out. He walked wearily to the front door, but did not get out his key. He expected the door would be unlocked, which it was.

He heard stirring in the kitchen.

"Mr. Finley?" a woman called out.

"Hey, Lindsay," he said, walking down the hall, loosening his tie on the way to the kitchen.

"You look tired," said Lindsay. She was in her late sixties, her thinning hair pinned tightly to her head. Her thin, ropy arms were busy wiping down one of the countertops. "Long day?"

"I should have called," he told her. "Sorry to keep you here so long."

"It's okay," she said. "Did you eat? There's something in the fridge. Some ham, and some potato salad."

"That'd be nice, actually," he said. "I could use a drink first."

He went to the cupboard, brought down a bottle of scotch and a glass. Then he turned on the small television that was mounted below a cupboard, turned it to the news channel.

There was Duckworth, saying something about squirrels.

Squirrels? So maybe Duckworth was finally taking seriously those dead rodents he'd alerted him to. Finley turned up the volume.

"—*you count them, you'll notice there are twenty-three animals here. Now, let me put this second photo up . . . Okay, this is the Ferris wheel at Five Mountains. That ride—*"

The detective was talking about several incidents linked by the number twenty-three.

"Well," said Finley. "You hear about this, Lindsay?"

"Hear about what?"

"This guy doing all these things around town, he's got this sort of signature? A number?"

"I don't know anything about that," she said. "You know me. I never put on the TV news. I don't listen to the radio. All the news is depressing. I don't need that. I just listen to my music." She pointed to the iPod and earbuds on the kitchen table. Finley had asked her not to wear them when she was in the house, looking after Jane, but Lindsay swore she kept the volume low.

As if anticipating his next question, Lindsay said, "She had a good day. She slept a lot, but she had a good day."

She took the ham and potato salad from the fridge. One entire shelf was lined with bottles of Finley Springs Water.

"She drank a whole pitcher of lemonade!" Lindsay said as she made up a plate for Finley. "She just loves the frozen concentrate. Sometimes, before I mix in the water, she likes to have a little of the frozen stuff on a spoon." Lindsay chuckled. "She's such a character. She makes me laugh. All that lemonade, I had to help her to the bathroom a few times."

Finley downed his scotch, his eyes still on the Duckworth news conference. When it ended, he turned off the TV. "What was that?"

"The lemonade. She loves it."

"She needs the fluids," Finley said. "I'll bring home some more cases of water."

"I just use tap water when I mix up the lemonade. I let it run until it gets cold."

Finley shook his head. "Use my water. It's so much better."

"It just takes longer. I have to uncap so many bottles and—"

"I'll bring home one of those big jugs, make it easier."

"Sure, okay," Lindsay said.

"I don't know what we would do without you."

Lindsay put the plate on the kitchen table. "There you go," she said.

"I'm going to go up and see Jane first," the former mayor said. "You go home. I'll take it from here."

"Okay."

"Got a busy day tomorrow, though."

"I'll be here by seven," Lindsay said.

"You're worth a million dollars."

Lindsay smiled. "You can give me a raise if you want."

Finley walked over and gave the woman a kiss on the forehead. "Has she had her pills?" he asked her.

"She's good to go. All you have to do is tuck her in for the night and she should be good till the morning. Unless she has to go to the bathroom or something, you'll—"

"I can help her with that," Finley said. "Go, go on, get out of here. You've done enough."

Lindsay gave the man a hug, grabbed a jacket and purse that were hanging off the back of a kitchen chair,

259

and headed for the door. "See you tomorrow," she said.

"Bye, love," he said. He poured himself a second scotch and knocked it back.

He went upstairs.

Were there more stairs today than yesterday? he wondered. Climbing up the flight seemed to take more energy every day. But he needed his strength. He hadn't even declared officially yet. There was so much hard work ahead.

Interesting development on the news. He could use that.

Finley passed by the guest bedroom, stepped in, took off his watch, and rested it on the bedside table. Removed his tie and threw it on the bed. He sat on the end and took off his shoes, scrunched his toes into the carpet.

"That feels better," he said to himself.

He stood, went a few more feet down the hall. The door to Jane Finley's room was open an inch, and he slowly pushed it open.

"Hey, sweetheart," he said softly.

His wife was in bed, on her back, the covers pulled up to her neck. Her skin was pale, her hair sparse. A soft bedside lamp cast light on a pair of reading glasses, a hardcover Ken Follett novel, and several jars of pills.

Jane's eyes fluttered open.

"You're home," she said. "Does Lindsay know?"

"I just sent her home."

"Have you eaten?"

"She made something up for me. I'll have it in a sec. Lindsay said you had a good day."

"I guess," Jane said, her eyelids heavy. "What did you do today?"

"This and that," he said. "I'm thinking I'll declare tomorrow."

260

Jane took a long, deep breath. "You don't have to do this."

Finley sat on the edge of the bed, reached through the covers until he found his wife's hand, and gave it a squeeze. "I can be the man you always wanted me to be."

"You don't have to prove anything."

"I shamed you. I—"

"Stop," she said, her head moving from side to side on the pillow.

"But I did. I want people to see I'm not that man anymore. That I'm a better man. Someone worthy of you."

He put a hand to her forehead. "You feel warm. Would you like a cool cloth?"

"I don't want to trouble you," Jane said. "Go eat."

He got up, went into the bathroom, and ran the water from the tap until it was cold. He held a washcloth under the stream, turned off the water, wrung as much water as he could from the cloth, and returned to his wife's side.

"Here," he said, and rested the cloth on her forehead.

"That feels good," she said. "That feels really nice."

Finley picked up the Follett book. "How is this?"

"It's good," she said. "But it's so long, and heavy. It's hard to hold up."

Finley opened it to where she'd left her bookmark. "Would you like me to read some of it to you?"

"What about your dinner?" Jane asked.

"It's not hot. Just ham and potato salad."

"Okay, then."

He only got through half a page before Jane was asleep. He placed the book back on the bedside table, took the cloth from her forehead, turned off the light, and slipped quietly from the room.

THIRTY-FIVE

When Duckworth saw the Finley Springs Water truck parked in his driveway, he figured it meant one of two things. The former mayor had dropped by to visit, or his son, Trevor, was here.

Duckworth wasn't sure whose visit he dreaded more.

Without question, Randall was not welcome. Duckworth had had to chase him off the parking lot of the drive-in the night before when the opportunistic gasbag had tried to get his picture taken helping people out. The detective almost wished the man had refused to leave. He'd have loved to slap the cuffs on him and throw him into the back of his car.

So that made Trevor a more welcome visitor. But it had been almost two weeks since Duckworth had seen his son, and that visit had not gone well. Trevor had spent the night at his parents' house, showing up in a Finley truck just like the one that was in the driveway now. When Duckworth found out Randy had given his son a job, his radar kicked in.

Randy had been leaning on Duckworth to pass along anything that might help him in his upcoming campaign—in particular, problems within the police department. He'd even suggested to Barry that if he helped him out, once elected, he'd see about firing

Rhonda Finderman and making him the new chief.

Duckworth wanted none of it.

So when he found out his son was working for the ex-mayor's water company, Duckworth couldn't help but suspect Finley of wanting payback. *I gave your boy a job. Now give me something I can use.*

But when he told Trevor his suspicions, it all came out wrong. Trevor, proud to have found work after months of unemployment, felt demeaned, as though his father were suggesting he couldn't find a job on his own terms. Trevor got in his water company van and took off.

The two hadn't spoken since.

Duckworth got out of his car and walked to the front door, stood there a moment, steeling himself to whatever was coming.

He opened the door and stepped inside.

"Barry?" His wife's voice, coming from upstairs. Seconds later, he saw her legs first, then the rest of her, as she descended the stairs.

"Hey," he said.

"Trevor's here."

"I saw the truck."

"He's upstairs. He was doing a run somewhere—I can't remember where—and decided to stop by before dropping off the van at the end of his shift."

"Great," Duckworth said.

Maureen said, "He was helping himself to a beer in the fridge, but I said because he was still technically working, and responsible for one of Finley's water delivery trucks, he should just have a Coke, and he got annoyed, said he was hardly going to get drunk on one beer, and I said, 'Let's say you have an accident, and it isn't even your fault, but they do a breath test and find out you'd been

263

drinking. That could make you and your employer liable. It could lose you your job.' Do you think I told him the right thing? Or am I just picking on him? Do you want dinner now? It's all ready. I asked him if he wanted anything, but he said no. He's upstairs going through some of his old CDs that he wants to put onto his computer so he can put them on his iThingie or whatever. How'd it go today?"

The two of them went into the kitchen. Duckworth reached into the fridge and grabbed one of the beers his son had lusted after.

"Lousy day," he said, dropping his butt onto a chair at the table.

"Well, since you asked, mine wasn't much better," Maureen said.

"Sorry," Duckworth said. "You go first."

"Well, we lost Mrs. Grover's bifocals." Maureen managed a store that sold eyeglasses. "Things went downhill from there."

"Oh, shit. Did you find them?"

"When the new pair we ordered come in, that's when we'll find them. But I'm guessing that's small change to what you've had to deal with. The drive-in and all."

"Yeah. And all."

Maureen soon had a plate in front of him. Baked chicken without the skin, asparagus, a few carrots. Duckworth studied it, wondering what had happened to the butter-smothered baked potato.

"The drive-in," Maureen reminded him.

He twisted the cap off the beer and took a drink. "They had a bomb expert out there today. It was no accident. And they've got this guy working with me, who I sent out to Thackeray today. I don't know what to make of him. And the Fisher-Gaynor stuff is still driving me crazy."

"That's a full plate," she said.

Duckworth looked down. "Speaking of which, why is there no potato?"

"You've got two vegetables."

"But neither one of them's a potato."

"If I cooked you a potato, you'd bury it in butter and sour cream. What's the latest with Rosemary Gaynor? I thought the doctor killed her."

"I don't think so. It had to be somebody else. I think it's Olivia Fisher's killer."

"That was horrible. All those people in the park who heard her screaming and didn't do a thing. And such a black mark against the town. All that media attention, the stories about the town that didn't care, the twenty-two people who heard what happened and did nothing. Remember they compared it to the Kitty Genovese story? You know? The woman in Queens, in 1964? Stabbed to death in Kew Gardens with a whole bunch of witnesses and nobody did anything."

"How many people did you say heard her?"

"Kitty Genovese?"

"No. Olivia Fisher."

"Oh. The stories back then said twenty-two."

Duckworth frowned. "Off by one."

"Sorry?"

He filled her in on the incidents that were linked by that one number. He'd thought, briefly, maybe it had something to do with the Fisher case, but the number twenty-two hadn't popped up anywhere.

"What about some buttered noodles?" he asked his wife. "How long would it take to cook some noodles?"

"What about the Twenty-third Psalm?" she asked.

"That's the first thing everyone thinks of. I wish I'd been here when the Olivia thing happened. I'd have a better handle on it. I was away around that time three years ago. You remember? I was in Canada. Opening of pickerel season."

"Oh yeah. You didn't catch a thing."

"Rhonda Finderman was the primary on that. Before she was promoted to chief," Barry said, picking at the asparagus. "What happened to the chicken skin?"

"Please stop."

"Anyway, the thing that's really been bugging me, and there's not really anything I can do about it, is that I kind of feel like Rhonda dropped the ball here. She couldn't have been paying very much attention to the Gaynor murder, or she'd have made a connection right away at how similar it was to the Fisher case. If we'd known that from the beginning, we might have gone at this another way. We've lost time on this thing."

"What should she have done?"

"She can't be reading the reports. She's too caught up in the bureaucratic stuff, I guess. Maybe I'm being too hard on her. Maybe it's not a big deal."

"It seems to be to you."

"You already eaten?" he asked his wife.

"I'm sorry. This is my book club night. I'm supposed to be at Shirley's in twenty minutes. I ate a while ago."

"I forgot it was tonight. What's the book?"

"You'd hate it. It's about *feelings*."

"Say no more."

Trevor walked into the kitchen.

"I didn't even hear you come down the stairs," Maureen said. "Say hello to your father."

266

"Hey," he said.

Duckworth got up. "Trev. How's it going?"

"Okay." He waved a handful of CDs at his mother. "I found what I was looking for."

"You have to go?" Barry asked.

"I gotta get the truck back."

"Job going good?"

"It's a job," Trevor said.

"You want to come by after? Your mother's got her book club thing. I'm just hanging out here. Probably watching a game or something."

The young man hesitated. "I don't know. Probably not. Kind of beat."

"It'd be fun," Barry said.

Trevor shrugged. "I gotta go." He gave his mother a hug, half a wave to his father, and then he was gone.

"Shit," Barry said.

"You tried," his wife said. "I think he was right on the edge there. Maybe if you'd asked once more."

"I'm not going to beg my son to hang out with me," he said, moving the vegetables around with his fork.

"You hate your dinner."

He looked at his wife. "I don't have the energy anymore."

"What?"

"I don't have the energy I once did. This drive-in thing, I figure by tomorrow the feds will be all over it—maybe Homeland Security will want it to justify their existence. Part of me wants to tell the feds to go jump in the lake if they try to take this away, and part of me would be relieved if they did take it. I may be in over my head."

"That's not true," Maureen said.

Then, out of the blue, Duckworth said, "Victor Rooney."

"What?"

"I dropped by Walden Fisher's house today, asked him a few things about his daughter's death. He brought up Victor Rooney."

"Who's that?"

"I just thought of him again because he and Trevor, they'd be about the same age. Rooney and Olivia were going to get married. Walden said Victor's never gotten over it, that he's been acting weird lately, what with the third anniversary of Olivia's murder coming up."

"Have you talked to him? To this Rooney person?"

Duckworth shook his head. "That's what I've been thinking I should do." He pushed the beer away. He'd had about a third of the bottle. "If I'm gonna go back out, I can't have that."

Maureen smiled. "I'm going to hate myself for this."

"What?"

"There's a cupcake in the fridge. One. Chocolate, with chocolate icing."

He wondered whether he should tell her about the pain he'd had when he was at the Burger King. But not only would it get Maureen to worrying; it would mean admitting that he'd had lunch at Burger King.

"I love you," he said.

Before Duckworth left the house, he put in a call to Clark Andover, the lawyer Bill Gaynor'd hired to defend him against a slew of charges, including the murder of Marshall Kemper.

"I'm going to drop by and see your client tonight,"

Duckworth said, "and I figured you'd want to be there."

"Tonight?" Andover said. "You can't be serious."

"In about an hour," Duckworth said.

"I can't just drop everything and—"

"I'll bring the coffee."

It was dark by the time the detective tracked Victor Rooney to a house in an older part of downtown. These were mostly postwar—World War II—homes. Modest, but built to last. Rooney rented a room from a retired schoolteacher named Emily Townsend, whose husband had died several years ago. Hers was a small white two-story house with black shutters. There was a rusty old van in the driveway, parked next to a shiny blue Toyota.

"I'm pretty sure Victor's in," she said after Duckworth showed up at the door and told her who he was. "Is he in some kind of trouble?"

"No," he said. "I'm just hoping he can help me with something."

"He's a good boy," she said. "Well, he's not a boy, of course. He's a man. He's a great help to me. Most days."

"What do you mean, most days?"

"Oh—" She waved a hand. "Nothing, really. He just has his ups and downs. He's looking for a job. Do you have any openings at the police department?"

"I don't think so."

"It wouldn't have to be as a policeman. I know you have to get special training for that. But maybe something looking after the police cars? Victor's very handy with machinery. He's got a real knack for it. That's one of the reasons I like to have him around, as a boarder. Ever since my husband, Virgil, died, he's looked after things around here. Cuts the grass, replaces the furnace filter, changes the batteries in the smoke detectors. Even knows how to fix electrical stuff. All the things Virgil looked after. I give him a real break on the rent because of that, and just as well, because some months he can't pay it at all."

"Sounds as though you're very good to him."

"And vice versa. Let me get him for you." She called up the stairs. "Vick! Vick! There's someone here to see you!"

A door could be heard opening, and Victor Rooney appeared at the top of the stairs. He was wearing a T-shirt, running shorts, and sneakers. He was glassy-eyed, and Duckworth wasn't sure if he was heading out for a run or had just come back.

"What's that?" he said.

"This man wants to talk to you," Emily Townsend said. "He's from the police!"

Slowly, Victor descended the stairs, not taking his eyes off Duckworth. "Do I know you?"

"I don't think so," the detective said.

"What do you want?" he asked, reaching the step one from the bottom, so he could look down at Duckworth.

"Why don't we step outside and talk for a minute. Mrs. Townsend, thank you for everything."

"Oh, that's okay," she said.

Duckworth led Rooney outside, ambled over toward the driveway, near the rusted van. A nearby streetlight and a light on Emily Townsend's front porch were more than enough for the two men to see each other.

"A bit chilly tonight," Duckworth said. "But it'll be summer soon enough."

"I don't mind if it's cool. Once I start running, I warm up."

"You do marathons?"

"God, no. I'm just getting back into it. A mile, maybe."
He rolled his head around on his shoulders, stretching his
neck muscles. "I'm trying to improve myself."

"Good for you."

"People seem to think I need to do that."

Duckworth let that one go. "I'm still looking into
Olivia's murder," he told Rooney. "I was talking to her
father earlier today."

"That guy," Rooney said, blinking slowly.

"Yeah. That guy."

"Why were you talking to him? You got some news?
You and your buddies finally get off your collective asses
and arrest someone?"

"No," Duckworth said. "We haven't. Mr. Fisher told
me that what happened still weighs pretty heavily on
you."

"I'm fine," he said. "No one has to worry about me."

"I was wondering if, even after all this time, maybe
something new has occurred to you. Something that
might help us make an arrest. Someone who might have
had a fight with Olivia. Were there any men who were
interested in her, maybe an ex-boyfriend who was upset
she was going to marry you?"

"No other boyfriend," he said.

"So she wasn't involved in any other relationship?"

Victor hesitated, then said, "No."

"You don't sound sure."

"I . . . I don't know. I don't think it's anything."

"That's often what people say later. They say they
didn't think it was anything. But it turned out to be
something."

"She was kind of—it's hard to describe—but sort of
distant for a while," he said.

"When was this?"

"Like, a month before it happened? Maybe three weeks. Just . . . she acted like she had something on her mind. I thought maybe it was the idea of getting engaged to me, but she swore up and down it wasn't that. She said one time she wondered if she was a good person. Like she'd done something she felt bad about."

"What did you think it was?"

Victor shrugged. "I thought maybe she'd spent the night with another guy. A one-night-stand thing. I might have pressed harder, but I guess I just didn't want to know. But what happened to Olivia? In the park? That was some fucking maniac—that's what that was. So I don't even know what the point of your questions is. They've got nothing to do with what happened to her."

"You might be right."

"This, what you're doing? You just want me to think you're getting somewhere, but you're never going to catch the guy. Why don't you go after the others? The people who did fuck all? The ones who listened while she screamed."

"It must be hard to get over," Duckworth said, his eyes scanning the house and the property, the detached garage in the backyard. "How long was it before you started seeing anyone else?"

"Are you for real? You honestly came by to ask me when I started dating again?" Rooney turned away, spit onto the driveway.

The front door of the house opened. It was Mrs. Townsend.

"Oh, Victor?"

He turned around, said, "Yeah?"

"Sorry to interrupt. Before you go on your run, could

272

you get me a garbage bag? I thought I had some in the kitchen, but they're all gone, but I think there's a package of them in the garage."

"Sure," he said, and the woman withdrew. He looked at Duckworth and said, "I help Mrs. Townsend around the place."

"She was telling me. You do all the chores."

"Most of them. Are we done here?"

"I guess," Duckworth said.

"Okay, well, fine. See ya." He started walking toward the garage, then stopped when he realized Duckworth hadn't moved, that he was watching him.

"Is there a problem?"

"No problem," Duckworth said.

Victor Rooney said, "Screw it. I'll do my run first."

He jogged past Duckworth and disappeared up the street.

THIRTY-SIX

Cal

I had the radio back on and this time I found out more about Mr. Twenty-three. That was the instant nickname the media had given some nut who had killed forest creatures, fired up abandoned amusement park rides, and very likely blown up the drive-in. A reporter had stopped people on the street to get their reaction.

"I'm pretty freaked-out, to tell you the truth."

"They better get this guy fast before he does something even bigger."

"I knew it was terrorism. Isn't that a verse or something in the Koran? Thou must kill everybody?"

I wondered sometimes why I even turned on the radio. I switched it off, choosing instead to occupy myself with my own thoughts.

I couldn't, in good conscience, drag this case out much longer. Lucy Brighton had hired me for a day's work, and I was prepared to run out the clock on this, but come tomorrow, we'd have to talk about how much more she wanted to spend. What I'd told her, that whoever took these discs probably wanted to bury them, was what I believed. This might be one of those problems that just went away.

I turned a corner and was about a block away from the Chalmers house when I noticed a car parked at the curb, taillights on, exhaust coming out of the tailpipe. A small black BMW coupe. I drove past slowly, and noticed there was enough light from the dash to make out Felicia Chalmers behind the wheel.

She was alone.

I stopped just ahead of her, put the car in reverse, and backed up until I was directly beside her. She glanced over, probably couldn't make me out at first.

I powered down the passenger window, raised my hand, and did a downward motion with my index finger. She got the idea and did the same.

"Ms. Chalmers," I said.

"Yes?"

I hit the interior light in my car for three seconds, long enough for her to get a look at me. "Cal Weaver. I came by your place."

Her mouth made an O. "Right, yes, of course," she said. And nothing else.

I didn't take my eyes off her and allowed the silence to go on.

"You're probably wondering what I'm doing here," she said.

"Maybe."

"But then again, I could ask what you're doing here," Felicia said. "Looks like you're going to the house."

"That's right," I said. "I'm still working for Adam Chalmers's daughter."

"Of course."

"Your turn," I said.

"I'm sorry?" she said. "I can't hear you that well over the engine."

"I said, your turn."

"Oh. I was just . . . I guess I was sitting here thinking about Adam."

"Sure," I said, nodding understandingly.

"It's still a shock."

"I can imagine."

"And . . . I was sort of driving around the neighborhood, looking at the houses. I'm . . . I probably shouldn't tell you this."

I waited.

"I've been talking to a lawyer. He says I might have . . . that as Adam's only surviving former spouse, I might have some claim . . . you know what I'm saying. On the estate. Whatever there is of it."

"I understand," I said, tempted to add that everyone handles grief in their own way, but holding my tongue.

"So I was taking another look at the house, considering where it stands in the market. Nothing in this town's worth as much as it was five or ten years ago."

"I can imagine," I said, the car still in drive, my foot on the brake.

"Anyway, nice to see you," she said, and powered her window back up.

I took my foot off the brake and continued on up the street. In my rearview, I saw Felicia do a three-point turn and take her Beemer around the corner.

I parked out front of the Chalmers house. The light over the front door was on. Probably on a timer. But the rest of the house was dark. If Adam and Miriam had been leaving for a holiday, they might have left some lights to go on and off in the house, but that's not the sort of thing you bother doing when you're just going to the movies.

When I got to the front door, I reached into my pocket for the key Lucy had given me, and found two.

Right. Felicia had given me her old key to the house where she once lived. She said she was pretty sure Adam had changed the locks since their divorce.

Instead of using Lucy's, I inserted the key I'd taken from Felicia, expecting some resistance. But it slid right in. I turned it, and opened the door. Immediately, the alarm system began to beep, warning me that if I didn't enter the code in the next few seconds, it would start whooping loud enough to wake the neighborhood and connect to the monitoring service. I entered the four digits Lucy had told me, and the beeping stopped.

Flicked on some lights.

I was betting that if Chalmers never bothered to change the locks, he'd never gotten around to changing that code, either. Which meant Felicia could have gotten into this house anytime she wanted. Or sent someone here on an errand, with that key.

I didn't think she'd looked very pleased that I'd caught her parked down the street from here.

There's always a strange feeling, walking into a place where the owners are no longer alive. You half expect one of them to pop out of a closet and ask what the hell you're doing in their house.

I wandered first through the living room and into the kitchen, noticed that the red light was flashing on the phone that rested on the countertop. A message. There hadn't been one when I was here before with Lucy. Someone had called who, evidently, did not know the homeowners were no longer available.

It could easily be a nuisance call. It was one of the pleasures, for me, of no longer having a landline that I wasn't pestered all night by duct cleaners, driveway resealers, window installers, and people wanting me to go on a cruise.

I looked through the recent calls, those that had come

in since Lucy and I had been here. There was only one, but it was an unidentified number.

I wanted to hear the message. But a four-digit code had to be entered to retrieve it. Given that most people don't want to have to remember half a dozen passwords, I figured there was a good chance it was the same code I'd used for the security panel.

I tried it.

"You have one new message," the voice said. "To hear your message, press one-one." I did so.

There was a pause, then, "Adam, it's me."

A woman. Speaking very softly.

"I tried your cell. Where are you? We . . . I've been thinking . . . I don't think I can carry on this way . . . I just don't . . . never mind. I have to go."

End of message.

I wondered whether it could be Felicia. I just couldn't tell. I checked the time of the call, saw that it had come in between the time Lucy and I had left the house this morning and my arrival at Felicia's apartment. I looked at the list of incoming calls, and made note of the number of the caller when that message had been left. I didn't recognize it.

She'd admitted the two of them kept in touch. I was betting that when they did talk, Adam usually used his cell, as the phone bill had suggested. Even if Miriam knew he kept in touch with his ex, she probably didn't like it.

Odd, though, that she would leave a message like that one. Felicia would have to know there was a good chance Miriam would end up hearing it.

The same would be true of any other woman calling here for Adam.

Maybe, when you were in the "lifestyle," you didn't worry about that sort of thing.

A thought that led me to pay another visit to the downstairs playroom. I could search through Adam's e-mails later.

Hitting light switches along the way, I descended the stairs to the bookcase. Lucy had slid it shut, concealing the room, before we left the house earlier in the day. No sense leaving it exposed in case someone else decided to break in.

It really was a marvel of engineering. Despite being loaded with books, the shelves practically floated on hidden casters. You had to put your back into it at first, pushing the case to the left, but once it was moving, it moved quite freely. The three-foot-wide doorway was revealed. I reached around inside, found the switch, and exposed the room to the light.

At a glance, nothing appeared to have changed since my first visit, suggesting that whoever had paid a visit here after the death of Adam and Miriam Chalmers hadn't returned.

It really was some room. Erotic photos on the wall, sex toys in the cabinet, expensive camera equipment under the bed. There were two small tables on either side of the bed, each with a drawer. I found the same thing in each of them. Condoms. A wide assortment. Different textures, different colors, lubricated and nonlubricated.

If there was something to be found here, I wasn't seeing it.

Then I thought: *Bathroom*.

Visits to bathrooms followed sex the way heartburn followed pizza. I figured there had to be a downstairs bathroom where folks could clean up, take a shower.

I came out of the playroom, crossed the large rec room area full of games, entered a short hallway leading to a storage room, a furnace room, and a bathroom. Not some rinky-dink basement powder room, either. There was a large marble-tiled shower big enough for two to soap up comfortably. And beyond that, a handsome wood door to a small cedar-lined sauna.

Everything was sparklingly clean and tidy. There was a stack of perfectly folded towels on chrome racks bolted to the wall over the toilet. The contents of the medicine cabinet indicated this was strictly a bathroom for visitors. New toothbrushes still in the packaging. Unopened tubes of toothpaste. Scented soaps wrapped in tissue paper. Mouthwash and small throwaway paper cups.

There was nothing in the garbage can.

Nothing particularly helpful at all in—

"Hello? Adam?"

A woman's voice coming from upstairs. At the front door. I hadn't heard anyone knock or ring the bell.

I exited the downstairs bathroom, made my way to the stairs at a steady pace. I could hear footsteps, what sounded like high heels, coming into the house.

"Adam?" she shouted again, sounding uncertain, but also slightly annoyed.

I reached the top of the stairs. I didn't see the woman, but I did see a leather overnight bag on the floor in the front hall. I was guessing the visitor had gone into the kitchen.

"Ma'am?" I said. "Hello?"

The heels turned, started marching furiously in my direction. When she materialized, she looked at me with a mix of fury and fear.

"Who the hell are you?" she demanded. "Is that your car out front?"

She was late twenties, early thirties, and, not to put too fine a point on it, a stunner. Five-six, long brown hair, wearing a knee-length black dress that clung to her like a second skin. She looked familiar. I was pretty sure I'd seen her picture around the house.

I was reaching for my ID. "My name is Cal Weaver. I'm a private investigator and I'm here with the permission of Lucy Brighton, who's the daughter of Adam Chalmers, and—"

"I know who the hell my stepdaughter is," the woman said.

I said, "Excuse me?"

"I said I know who my stepdaughter is."

I said, "Miriam Chalmers?"

"Who the hell else would I be? This is my house. And you better get the fuck out of it, but not before you tell me where my husband is."

THIRTY-SEVEN

After interviewing Victor Rooney, Detective Duckworth picked up three coffees at the Dunkin' Donuts drive-through on the way to the Promise Falls courthouse. He parked around back. The courts were not in session this time of night, but the wing where the jail cells were located was a 24-7 operation. Duckworth had called ahead to let them know he wanted to talk to Bill Gaynor, and that his lawyer, Clark Andover, would be in attendance.

Andover had tried, without success, to get Gaynor out on bail while he awaited trial. He'd argued that Gaynor had never been in trouble with the law before and was an upstanding member of the community. The judge didn't buy it.

Gaynor was due to be transferred to another facility, given that the local jail was not intended to keep those awaiting trial for extended periods.

"What's this about?" Andover, dressed casually in jeans and a button-down collared white shirt, asked Duckworth.

"Like I said, a few questions," the detective told him.

Bill Gaynor, a good five or more pounds thinner since Duckworth had last seen him, was brought to an interrogation room. He was wearing lightweight hunter green pants and a T-shirt. He and Andover sat side by side across the table from Duckworth.

"What's this about?" Gaynor asked. "What's going on?"

"Mr. Gaynor," Duckworth said, setting down a cardboard tray with three coffees. "There's some creams and sugars here if you need them."

Gaynor looked at his lawyer, then back at Duckworth.

"How are you this evening?" the detective asked, setting a coffee in front of him.

"How am I? Seriously? They wouldn't even let me attend my own wife's funeral. That's how I am."

Duckworth nodded sympathetically. "That's a terrible shame. You'd have thought they could have found a way to accommodate you." He pried off the plastic lid of his coffee, blew on it. "Mr. Gaynor, how long have you lived in Promise Falls?"

"What?"

"You didn't grow up here—isn't that right?"

"I grew up in Albany," he said, ignoring the coffee in front of him. Andover, however, had reached for the third one and was tearing off the ends of two sugar packets. "When Rosemary and I were looking for our first house, we came here. Houses were more affordable here, and it was an okay commute to my work in Albany."

"When was that?"

"That was around—it was in 2002."

"And you've been in that house ever since?"

"No. We were there eight years. Then we moved to Breckonwood."

"Your current residence."

"*This*," he said, looking around, "is my current residence."

"Not for long," Andover said, his eyes on Duckworth.

"And you were still commuting to Albany all that time? Every day?"

"Not every day. I usually worked from home one or two days a week. I have—had a lot of local clients."

"That's going to get cold."

"I don't want it," Gaynor said.

"So, three, four years ago, you'd have been working from home, as you say, a couple of days a week."

"That's right. Usually Thursday and Friday."

"Did you have a lot of people you did insurance work for right here in Promise Falls?"

Gaynor shrugged. "Maybe two, three dozen."

"Those clients included the Fisher family. Isn't that right?"

"Fisher?"

"Walden and Elizabeth Fisher."

"Uh, yes, I think, maybe—"

Andover stepped in. "What's going on, Barry?"

"I just wanted to know if Mr. Gaynor was the insurance agent for Walden and Elizabeth—she passed away recently, by the way—Fisher. Were you?"

"Yes," he said. "There was a hundred-thousand-dollar policy on Beth—on Elizabeth—that was paid a while ago."

"So you know the Fishers."

"I do," he said.

"So then you would also have known their daughter, Olivia."

Bill Gaynor's head slowly went up and down, once. "I did. But she didn't have life insurance. Of course, she was on the family's automotive policy. Their car insurance."

"Right," Duckworth said, taking a sip. "But even

though Olivia didn't have a life insurance policy, as someone who worked with the family on their insurance needs, I'm sure you must have reached out to them at the time of her death. To offer your sympathies, see how they were managing."

Gaynor looked at his lawyer, as though seeking guidance. He said to Duckworth, "Well, sure, of course. I felt terrible for them."

"And you kept in touch with the Fishers after."

"Like I said, we still handled the life insurance policies for Beth and Walden. After Beth passed away, Walden canceled his policy. He said there wasn't much need for it. He didn't have anyone left to provide for."

"Did you know Olivia well?" Duckworth asked.

Andover raised a palm. "Just what kind of fishing expedition is this, Barry?"

"Olivia's murder remains unsolved. We haven't given up on it. Mr. Gaynor, I thought it would be worth talking to you to see if you might remember anything that might help us in the investigation. Maybe Olivia confided in you. Told you something that didn't seem important then, but does now."

"I barely remember her," he said.

"Maybe this will help." Duckworth took from his jacket a reproduction of a three-by-five high school yearbook photo of the dead woman, placed it flat on the table. "This was from her senior year, before she went to Thackeray."

He glanced at it. "Sure. I mean, I remember what she looked like, but I don't even know if I ever had a single conversation with her. Does this have—you're not thinking that what happened to Rose was in any way connected to her, are you?"

Duckworth tossed it back to him. "Do *you* think there might be a connection?"

"You think whoever killed Rose also killed the Fisher girl?"

Duckworth tapped the picture with his finger. "You notice anything interesting about her?" he asked Gaynor.

"Interesting?"

"Maybe it's just me," the detective said, "but you look at her hair, the shape of her face, she reminds me a bit of your wife."

Gaynor studied the picture, then looked Duckworth in the eye. "What the hell are you talking about? What's going on?"

"We're done," Andover said.

"Did Jack kill both of them?" Gaynor asked. "Is that what's going on?"

"No," Duckworth said. "I've pretty much ruled him out."

"Then—" He stopped himself. "Jesus, you think *I* killed Rosemary? You think I killed my wife? And this girl? What the hell is wrong with you? I barely knew Olivia, and you know I was in Boston when Rose died. You *know* that!"

"Bill, enough," Andover said, putting his hand on the man's arm. "Enough!" He looked at Duckworth and said, "For God's sake, leave the poor man alone. You got someone out there killing animals and blowing up drive-ins, but you're in here harassing a man who lost his wife. You must be proud."

Duckworth retrieved the picture, put it in his jacket, pushed back his chair, and stood. "I want to thank you both for meeting on such short notice. You mind tossing those coffees in the trash on your way out?"

By the time he reached his desk, the phone was ringing.

"Duckworth."

It was the front desk. "There's a guy here wants to see you. Martin Kilmer. Says he's Miriam Chalmers's brother."

One of the four people killed at the drive-in. Her body had yet to be positively identified. Duckworth said he would be right out.

Martin Kilmer was about forty, trim, six feet tall, and decked out in an expensive suit, a white shirt, a silk tie, gleaming black dress shoes.

"Mr. Kilmer, I'm Detective Duckworth."

"I got a call from Lucy Brighton, my sister's step-daughter," he said abruptly. "She told me about the accident. She identified her father, but didn't identify Miriam. So I'm here. How the hell did something like this happen? A goddamn screen falling over?"

"We're still trying to find that out."

"I want to see her," he said.

Duckworth said, "I'll take you." He put in a call to the morgue so that they knew they were on their way.

On the drive over, Duckworth felt the need to warn Miriam Chalmers's brother that identification might prove difficult.

"Why?"

"Your sister sustained . . . the screen came down right on top of the car. A Jaguar convertible, with the top down. She wasn't afforded much in the way of protection."

"You telling me her face is all smashed in?" Kilmer asked bluntly.

"Yes." Sometimes, trying to be sensitive was a wasted

effort.

"Then how the hell do I identify her?" the man asked.

"Maybe other distinguishing features. A birthmark? A scar?"

"Christ, it's not like I saw my sister naked a lot. None of this would have happened if she hadn't married that son of a bitch."

"You didn't like Adam Chalmers?"

"No. He was too old for her, first of all. And there was his past."

"His biker days."

"I know they were long ago, but they go to character."

"What do you do, Mr. Kilmer?"

"Stocks," he said, as if that explained everything.

Duckworth's cell rang. "Yeah," he said.

"Yeah, hey, Barry, it's Garth."

Garth worked in the police garage. Actually, a wing attached to the police garage, where vehicles damaged in accidents were towed and inspected.

"Hey, Garth."

"You know that old Jag from the drive-in?"

Duckworth glanced at his passenger, who had used this opportunity to take out his own phone. He was looking down at the screen, sweeping his finger in an upward direction. It didn't look like e-mails. More likely an app for stocks.

The detective pressed the phone more tightly to his ear. "Yeah."

"Okay, so, it was crushed pretty bad. They managed to get the bodies out, but we've been going through the car, and it took some doing, but we finally got the trunk open, which wasn't easy since the whole back end of the car kind of got all smooshed together. We were kind of anxious to get in there so we could stop the ringing."

"Ringing?"

"Like a cell phone. We could hear it in the trunk. Figured one of the two deceased—well, most likely the woman—must have left her purse back there since the interior of one of those cars is so damn tiny. There was another phone, up by the driver, but it was all smashed to pieces."

"Uh-huh."

"So why I was calling is, we pried open the trunk, and it was a purse, and we figured you'd want to return it to the family or something like that."

Duckworth said, "Okay, I'll get back to you."

He ended the call, put the phone into his pocket, and said to Kilmer, "Sorry."

"Hmm?" Kilmer said, glancing over.

"I'm done."

Kilmer put his own phone away. "How far away is this place?"

"We're here," Duckworth said.

Duckworth's favorite coroner, Wanda Therrieult, wasn't on duty. They were met by a young, pasty-looking woman Duckworth thought was a student picking up some part-time hours. She wasn't qualified to perform an autopsy, but she could run the office alone until one needed to be done, at which point Wanda would be called.

She consulted her computer, then said, "Okay, um, Miriam Chalmers . . . okay, I know where she is. Hang on. If the two of you could wait here."

The body, Duckworth explained to Kilmer, had to be moved to a viewing area. While they waited, Kilmer went back to studying his phone.

"Were you and your sister close?" Duckworth asked.

"Not particularly," he said, not looking up.

"Were you in touch?"

Kilmer glanced up. "Christmas, sometimes. Weddings. Things like that."

"Did you come for her wedding to Adam?"

"No. I wasn't invited. No one was. They got married in Hawaii."

"Oh," Duckworth said.

A door opened. "We're ready," the young woman said. "She's just in here."

The two men moved toward the door, Duckworth in the lead. He caught a glimpse of a pair of naked feet on the table when his phone rang yet again.

"Damn," he muttered. "I'm really sorry about this." He took out his phone, wanting to check the caller's name, figuring that whatever it was, it could wait.

It was Garth agaih.

"Hang on," Duckworth said to Kilmer, turning and blocking him from going into the viewing room. Into the phone, he said, "What is it, Garth?"

"Okay, don't be pissed. Maybe I shouldn't have done this, but I did it, so sue me."

"What are you talking about?"

"The phone started ringing again, so I figured, shit, maybe I should just answer it, so I opened up the purse, found the phone, and answered it. I said hi, and it was some guy, and he said, 'Who's this?' And I said, 'Garth Duhl.' Which, I guess if he'd never heard of me, would seem kind of odd."

"What did he say, Garth?"

"He says, 'Where's Georgina?' And I say, 'What?' And

he says, 'Where's Georgina? Where's my wife?' And I say, 'Who is this?' And he says, 'This is Peter Blackmore. Why are you answering my wife's phone?' So I tell him that somebody would get back to him, and I hang up, and I look through the purse, and I find a driver's license, and you're not going to believe this."

"I'll get back to you," Duckworth said, ending the call. He looked at Kilmer and said, "We're not going to do this now."

THIRTY-EIGHT

Cal

Miriam Chalmers looked at me fiercely and said, "I'm calling the police." She was reaching into her purse, presumably, for a cell phone.

"Okay," I said evenly.

I was happy for her to call the Promise Falls cops, or Lucy Brighton. Then I could be spared the task of giving her the news about her husband.

Assuming, of course, that the police had *that* right. Lucy had identified his body, after all. I realized now everyone had just assumed the body next to him had been his wife's.

It was possible, I supposed, that Miriam already knew her husband was dead, that coming into the house and shouting his name was an act. But it didn't strike me that way. If she really did not know about what had happened at the drive-in, I had to marvel at the fact that Adam Chalmers had found two women—Miriam and Felicia—with an apparent disinterest in current events. In Felicia's defense, I'd found her much earlier in the day. But it was well into the evening now, nearly twenty-four hours since the drive-in bombing.

My lack of concern about Miriam calling the police seemed to have lessened the urgency on her part to do it. She still had the phone in her hand, poised to make the call, but she had stopped.

"Is Adam here?" she asked.

"No."

"Where is he? I called here earlier today and left a message, and he hasn't answered his cell."

The voice mail I'd heard. It had been from her. *I don't think I can carry on this way.* I was betting that number I'd made note of was her cell.

"You should talk to the police," I said. "Make the call. But not 911. Call one of their nonemergency lines. Or better yet, I could drive you down to the station."

She let the phone fall into her bag, then dropped the purse onto the nearest chair. She reached a tentative hand out to the wall. "What's happened?" she asked. "Who did you say you are?"

"Cal Weaver." I took out one of my business cards and handed it to her. She barely glanced at it before dropping it onto the chair. "When did you go away?"

"What?"

I nodded in the direction of the overnight bag on the floor. "Have you been out of town?"

"Two days," Miriam said.

"Where?"

"Lenox." A small town, just into Massachusetts, where they held the annual Tanglewood music festival. "There's an inn there I go to when I need some time."

"Time for what?"

"I don't know who you are, or why you're here, but I'm not answering another question until you tell me where Adam is. Is he okay? Has he had a heart attack?"

You did what you had to do.

"Have a seat," I told her.

"No."

293

"Please. Let's go into the kitchen."

She knew it was going to be bad. I could see it in her face. I pulled out a chair at the table for her, sat down close to her on the corner. My eyes were glancing around, wondering where the alcohol was kept.

"There was an accident last night," I said. "At the Constellation Drive-in. You know it?"

Miriam nodded.

"The screen toppled. It looks like it was a bomb. The screen fell on some cars, crushed them, including a Jag registered to your husband. He was in the car. The police got in touch with Lucy, told her that her father was dead."

"No," she whispered. "There must be a mistake. Why wasn't I called? Why's no one been in touch with me?"

"That might be because everyone thought you had died with your husband."

She let that sink in for a moment.

"There was someone else in the car," she said. It wasn't a question. "Of course. Who goes to the drive-in alone?" She fixed her eyes on me. "Who was it?"

"I don't know. I don't know if anyone knows at this point. I don't know if anyone realizes the mistake that's been made. Because you've been out of town, because you haven't been here."

"All Lucy had to do was look in the garage and see my car wasn't here and ... the stupid twat. Where is Adam? Where is he ... where are they keeping him?"

"You should talk to Lucy. Or the coroner's office. He may have been moved to a funeral home. Paisley and Wraith, for example. They're the biggest in town."

Miriam sniffed.

"There are probably people you should call," I said. "Your brother, for one. Lucy was in touch with him. I think he's coming here, with the intention of identifying your remains."

"Good God."

"Why were you in Lenox?" I asked.

"I needed some time to think. Adam and I have been . . . having a rough patch. I wanted to be alone with my thoughts. Even if someone had tried to reach me, I had my phone off most of the time. I didn't watch the news, didn't know anything about any of this. Today, I was ready to talk, but I couldn't get hold of him."

"You left a message. That you didn't think you could keep on going this way."

The tears were coming now. She tried to wipe them away from her cheeks with her fingers. "Purse," she whispered.

I retrieved it from the front hall, set it on the table, and sat back down. She reached in for some tissue, dabbed her eyes, then went back in and brought out a pack of Winstons and a lighter. She got a cigarette between her fingers, but her hand was shaking too much to light it. I gently took the lighter from her, held it to the end of the cigarette.

She pulled hard on it, held the smoke in her lungs, let it come out her nostrils.

"I think I know who it was," she said quietly.

"In the car? The woman?"

Miriam's head went up and down a quarter inch. "Felicia." Maybe thinking I was going to ask, she added, "His slut of an ex-wife. They kept in touch."

"No," I said. "I saw her this morning."

Miriam's damp eyes darted about, as though the answer were hidden here in the kitchen. "Then Georgina."

"Georgina?"

"Blackmore. Georgina Blackmore. Her husband's a

professor at Thackeray. English something or other."

Another connection between her husband and the college. First Clive Duncomb, now a Professor Blackmore.

"That little bitch," she said.

"Is the professor a friend of the head of security out there?" I asked. "Clive Duncomb."

Her eyes flashed for a second, then appraised me in a way they hadn't up until now.

"Why would you ask about him?"

"You and your husband have entertained him and his wife, here, for dinner. You're friends."

Miriam Chalmers eyed me with the same level of suspicion she'd displayed when first finding me in the house.

"Why, exactly, are you here, in my house? You're not with the police."

"No, I'm not. I'm private."

"You're here at Lucy's direction?"

"Someone was in the house," I said, nodding. "Since news broke of the disaster, and it became known your husband was among the victims, someone got in. To get something." I paused. "From the room downstairs."

It was as though she'd been Tasered.

"What?"

She pushed back her chair so quickly ashes fell from the end of the Winston and landed on her dress. She got up, taking the cigarette from her mouth and clutching it in her fingers, and headed straight for the stairs.

I followed.

She'd only descended three steps when she caught sight of the bookcase out of its usual position, the secret room exposed.

"Oh my God," she said. "No, no, no."

She entered the room, saw the scattered DVD cases on the floor.

"This isn't happening," she said.

Miriam spun around, pointed at me. "Where are they? What did you do with those? What is it you want? Is it money? Is that what you want?"

"I don't have them. But I'm guessing you might know who would."

Miriam was trying to take it all in.

"Get out," she said. "Get the fuck out of my house and tell Lucy I can solve my own goddamn problems."

THIRTY-NINE

When Trevor Duckworth dropped off the Finley Springs Water truck at the end of his shift, he went around to the office to see if the boss was in.

He wasn't.

"Do you have a number for him?" he asked one of the women in the office. A cell phone number was provided. He entered it straight into his own phone's contacts list.

But he didn't call Randall Finley right away. He had to think about whether this was the right thing to do.

It galled him that his father had been right. His dad had said the only reason Finley had hired him was that his father was a detective with the Promise Falls police. Finley wanted Barry Duckworth to feed him things, things about the department, that might help Finley when he went after the mayor's job.

Trevor's dad had said no when Finley asked him directly. But now Finley was coming at it another way. He'd had a chat with Trevor a couple of weeks ago, let him know that he was friends with the family of Trevor's former girlfriend, Trish Vandenburg.

Finley described himself as Trish's unofficial uncle. She'd told him things. She'd told him about the time Trevor had hit her in the face.

It was an accident.

Didn't seem like it to Trish, Finley told him. She'd spent three days in her apartment waiting for the bruise to fade before she went outside. Trevor tried to explain that he'd thought Trish was going to slap him, so he'd brought up his hand to stop her, but ended up backhanding her.

However it might have happened, Finley said, it happened. But the onetime mayor made clear to Trevor that he had done him a favor. Trish had been wondering about whether to report the assault to the police, but Finley had persuaded her it was a bad idea.

But who knew? Finley said. She might change her mind one day. Trevor's boss wanted the young man to know he'd keep his mistake under wraps as best he could, so long as Trevor was open to the idea of proving his gratitude.

Now Trevor sat in his apartment, phone in hand, thinking that maybe this was his chance to even things up with Finley. A way to show how grateful he was.

He made the call.

"Hello?" Randall Finley said.

"Mr. Finley, it's Trevor."

"Hmm?"

"Trevor Duckworth."

"Hey there, Trevor. How's it going?"

"Okay, I guess. Have you got a second?"

"For you, of course. What can I do ya for?"

Even though he was alone in his apartment, Trevor brought his voice down. "You remember that talk we had the other day?"

"Which talk would that be?" Finley said. Taunting him, Trevor felt. He knew exactly what he was talking about.

"You know. About Trish."

299

"Oh, yeah, that talk. Of course."

"I wanted . . . you said you did me a favor, and in return, you said if I ever heard anything that might be helpful to you, that if I passed it along, then we'd be square. You remember that?"

"I do."

"Well, I kind of heard something tonight, when I was home. Something that my dad was telling my mom."

Trevor's hand was becoming slippery with sweat. He switched the phone to his other hand, put it to his left ear.

"What did you hear?" Finley asked.

"Okay, so you know the chief? Rhonda something?"

"Finderman. Rhonda Finderman."

"Yeah, that's it. So, three years ago, she wasn't the chief. She was a detective, and she was in charge of finding out who killed Olivia Fisher."

"Awful thing," Finley said. "Just awful."

"Yeah. So, I guess no one's ever been arrested for that. And a couple of weeks ago, there was this other woman who got killed. Rosemary."

"Rosemary Gaynor."

"Yeah. My dad was telling my mom that it was the same person who killed both of them."

"Is that so?" Finley said.

"Yeah. But my dad only just realized that, because he didn't work the first murder, the Fisher one. But he was telling my mom that if the chief—Finderman?"

"That's right."

"He was saying that if Chief Finderman had been paying attention, she would have noticed the similarities between the two cases right away, but she wasn't, or didn't, and that kind of slowed my dad down."

"Well, that's something," Finley said.

"But then he said, maybe he was expecting too much. Like, maybe it was just one of those things that fell through the cracks. I guess the chief wants some doctor to be blamed for both murders, and since this doctor is dead, it kind of closes the book on everything. You get what I'm saying?"

"I do. Trevor, that's really remarkable. I do appreciate this."

"You can't ever say where you heard about this. You didn't hear it from me."

"Absolutely."

"And this squares things up, right? You're not going to hold that other thing over my head anymore."

A pause at the other end of the line.

"Mr. Finley."

"This is a good start, Trevor. A very good start. You keep your ears open and let me know what else you find out."

"Come on," Trevor said. "That's not fair."

"Anything else your dad has to say about the Fisher and Gaynor murders being done by the same person, you pass that along. If he starts making some progress there, you keep me in the loop. How about that?"

"Jeez, I feel shitty enough about what I told you already. And I'm not home all that much anyway."

"Maybe it's time you dropped by to see your parents more often," Finley said. "Remember, there's nothing more important than family."

FORTY

Barry Duckworth knew the name Peter Blackmore. Angus Carlson had mentioned it. He was the man who'd talked to Carlson after the meeting with Clive Duncomb at Thackeray.

Blackmore had said his wife was missing.

Seemed as though she might have been found.

As Duckworth reached out to stop Martin Kilmer from entering the examination room to identify the body of the woman they had all, up to now, believed was his sister, Miriam Chalmers, the man's cell rang.

Duckworth was putting his own phone away as Martin reached into his jacket for his. As he glanced at the number, his eyes went wide. He put the phone to his ear and said, "Miriam? Jesus! Miriam!"

Duckworth held his breath.

Kilmer said, "Where are you? They told me—Jesus, what's happened?" He shot a contemptuous look at Duckworth. "So you're not dead? You realize how far I had to drive to find that out? I had a critical meeting today that I had to blow off. Yes, yes, of course, terrible thing about Adam. I'm going to have to turn around and head straight back. I swear, these idiot police were about to have me identify you. Let me know when the funeral is and I'll see if I can move some things around. Yes, yes, okay. Good-bye."

He put the phone away.

"Is the entire department incompetent, or just you?" he said.

"That was your sister," Duckworth said. "You're sure."

"Of course I'm sure. Goddamn it, I drove all the way up here for nothing."

"Your brother-in-law's still dead," Duckworth said. "Just so the trip wasn't a total waste."

"Are you sure? Maybe it's Jimmy Hoffa. You might want to get your facts straight next time before you start sending people into a panic. How the hell do I get back to my car?"

"I'll take you."

"You sure you know the way?" Kilmer asked.

"Just give me one second."

Duckworth entered the room, on his own, to take a look at the body. "Let me see her," he said to the attendant.

She pulled back the sheet.

If this was, in fact, Peter Blackmore's wife, he was going to have a difficult time identifying her from her face. There was little left of it. The trauma hadn't ended there. The woman's left shoulder and upper arm were crushed. There were several gashes across her upper torso.

Her lower abdomen, right side, was spared any damage from the accident. Duckworth noticed three small moles, clustered within an inch of one another, that formed a rough triangle.

He took out his phone, leaned in close, and took a photo.

"That's all," he said to the woman. "Thank you."

*

303

He endured more complaining from Martin Kilmer before driving him back to the Promise Falls police station, where the man had left his car. Then Duckworth went searching for Garth, in the police garage, to retrieve the purse and phone that ostensibly belonged to Georgina Blackmore. He looked at the woman's license for a home address.

On the way, he put in a call to Angus Carlson's cell. The phone rang several times before it went to message. "It's Duckworth. Call me when you get this. It's about that professor who said his wife was missing."

He was putting the phone back into his jacket, still had it in his hand, when it rang. He brought it back out, put it to his ear.

"Duckworth."

"It's Carlson. Sorry. I just saw you called. Haven't listened to the message. I was kind of in the middle of something."

"Blackmore. He talked about his wife."

"Yeah. Did he come in, make an official report?"

"No, but I wanted to ask you if there was anything more to that. Anything else he might have said you didn't tell me."

"Not really. Like I said, at first he was concerned— then he said it was probably nothing, she'd show up sooner or later. Why, what's going on?"

"I'll get back to you if I need anything else," Duckworth said, and ended the call.

Before leaving the office, he made one other call, to the manager of the hotel in Boston where Bill Gaynor had been attending a conference when his wife was murdered. From his previous discussion with the manager, Duckworth had learned Gaynor's car had not left the hotel parking garage at all during his stay. Also, he'd been seen in the hotel throughout the weekend. The detective was wondering whether there were any holes that could be punched into Gaynor's alibi.

"Front desk."

"Sandra Bottsford, please."

"I'm afraid she's not here right now. Can I have her call you?"

Duckworth left his name and cell phone number. "She'll know what it's about."

Then he set off for Peter Blackmore's house.

It was a two-story redbrick Victorian in the old part of town. There were lights on behind the curtained windows, and what looked like the bluish light from a television.

Duckworth parked at the curb, got out of the car, taking the purse Garth had retrieved from the trunk of Adam Chalmers's crushed Jaguar, which he had tucked into a plastic grocery bag, and headed for the front door.

FORTY-ONE

Cal

Once Miriam Chalmers had kicked me out of her house, I phoned Lucy Brighton.

"Yes?" she said.

"You sitting down?"

"What is it?"

"Miriam's alive."

"What?" She said it so loud, I pulled the phone away from my ear.

"She just returned home, walked in while I was looking around. She'd gone to Lenox for a couple of days to think about her marriage, apparently, and didn't know anything about the drive-in."

"Oh my God," Lucy said. "That's . . . wonderful. I'm glad she's okay. I just wish my father had also . . ."

"I know."

A pause at the other end, and then, "If it wasn't Miriam in the car with my dad, then who was it?"

"Miriam thinks a woman named Georgina Blackmore. Ring a bell?"

"No. There's a professor at Thackeray with that last name, I think. But I'm not really sure. Cal, should I call the police? Tell them they've got it wrong? That it's somebody else?"

"I imagine they'll be hearing from Miriam herself

pretty soon. I told her she should call her brother. Lucy, I don't know that there's anything else I can do for you at this point. The missing discs, they're really Miriam's problem now."

"Yes, I guess so. I'm going to have to call her."

"A heads-up. She's pissed you hired me. She wasn't pleased to find me in the house. And she was beyond horrified when she realized someone had been into that room, and that the discs were taken."

"I have to—what am I going to say when I call her? I mean, I've started making the arrangements for my father. He's been moved to the funeral home. There are things to do, to plan, and—"

"Tell the funeral home. Have them call her," I suggested.

"This is all so hard to believe. Cal, thank you for everything you've done."

"It hasn't been much," I said, getting into my car. "Let me know if there's anything else I can do. In the meantime, I'm heading home." "Okay, thanks. Good-bye, Cal."

I keyed the engine and pulled away from the Chalmers house, thinking about Miriam. She'd looked more upset about the discovery of the playroom, and those missing discs, than she had about her husband's death.

But it wasn't my headache anymore.

There was a parking space set aside for me in the lot behind my building, but there was no access to my apartment from there. That meant I had to walk down a narrow alley that delivered me to the main street, where I'd find the ground-level door to my second-floor apartment right next to Naman's Books.

It was after ten, and the light was on in the store.

The jangling bell over the door announced my arrival.

Naman Safar was perched on a stool behind the cash register, his nose in an old Bantam paperback edition of *The Blue Hammer*, by Ross Macdonald, while some opera I'd never heard of played in the background. He glanced up at me.

"Hey, Cal." He tucked a strip of red ribbon between the pages, closed the book, and set it next to the cash register. "You're up late."

"Me? What are you doing open this late?"

Naman looked at his watch. "I guess it is kind of dumb. No one's out shopping for books at this hour. But what am I going to do at home? Sit around?"

"Naman, turn off the lights. Go home."

He nodded obediently. "Okay, okay."

He slid off the stool, planting his feet on the floor. He turned off the CD player and then popped open the cash register. "Big day," he said. "Twenty-nine dollars."

"Well," I said.

"E-books aren't just killing new-book stores. They're killing me, too. I hate those things, those little things with the screens. I hate them."

A book resting atop the pile closest to me caught my eye. Another Roth, in paperback. *The Human Stain*. I picked it up. "Am I too late? Have you closed the till?"

"Take it."

"No." I glanced at the price Naman had lightly penciled on the inside cover. Five bucks. "Here," I said, digging into my wallet. I had a five. "Take this."

He looked at the bill. "Okay."

As he was taking it from my fingers, we both heard tires squealing up the street somewhere. The gunning of an engine.

"I haven't read that one, so I can't tell you if it's one of his good ones," Naman said.

"Someone recommended it to me this morning," I said. "The woman who runs the Laundromat up the street."

The sound of that racing engine was getting closer. Then the sudden screeching of brakes.

We both looked out the store's front window at the same moment. A black pickup truck had appeared, passenger side facing us. The window was down, and a young white man, probably in his early twenties, was shouting.

He yelled, loud enough for us to hear through the glass, "Fucking terrorist!"

I saw an arm come up. There was something in the man's hand. A bottle, maybe, and what looked like flame.

"Get down!" I said to Naman.

As he threw himself to the floor, the Molotov cocktail sailed through the air, hit the window of the bookshop. The glass and the bottle shattered simultaneously, and the burning rag soaked in, presumably, gasoline landed on a pile of books.

Flames erupted instantly.

The truck's back tires squealed. The man who'd tossed the bottle let out a large whoop of victory as the vehicle sped off.

"Naman!" I shouted. "We have to get out!"

"My books!" he cried, stumbling to his feet. "My books!"

"Have you got an extinguisher?"

He looked at me with horror and panic. "No!"

"Get out!" I said again.

I dropped my copy of *The Human Stain* and pushed Naman toward the door, followed him out onto the sidewalk. I dug into my pocket for my phone to get the fire department.

I hated talk radio.

FORTY-TWO

"I keep hoping somehow I skipped over her," Clive Duncomb said to Peter Blackmore. Duncomb had the remote in his hand, his thumb on the fast-forward button, bodies gyrating and tangling and untangling at high speed on the TV screen.

"You're going so fast, it's starting to make me sick to my stomach," Peter said. "I can't look at it anymore."

"She's not on that one," Duncomb said, ejecting the disc. He picked up another one, glanced at what had been scribbled on it in marker. *Georgina-Miriam-Liz flying high.* "I don't think it could be this one. This is one where the girls had the stewardess costumes. That was *after* the Fisher girl died."

"You better check it just the same," Peter said. "I can't think about this. Why did that man answer Georgina's phone?"

"One crisis at a time," Duncomb said. But then his own phone rang. He looked at it, said to Peter, "It's Liz."

He put the phone to his ear. "Yeah."

"You find her yet?"

"Not yet."

"We may have another problem," Liz said.

"What?"

"Lucy called here."

311

"Lucy?"

"Lucy Brighton, Adam's—"

"I know who she is. What'd she want?"

"She said she knows you have it. That she wants it back."

"It?"

"She says she doesn't want any trouble if you return it."

"That private detective," Duncomb said. "He must have told her he suspects I've got the discs. What did you tell her?"

"I told her you weren't here. What do you want me to do?"

"Nothing. I'll try to sort her out later. Set up a private meeting, show her the discs, destroy them in front of her, maybe. I don't know. I can't deal with this now."

He ended the call.

The doorbell rang.

"Turn that off," Duncomb said to Blackmore. "Put those discs away." Once there were no longer naked bodies on the television, the Thackeray security chief opened the door.

"Well, whaddya know, it's Detective Duckworth. Won't you come on in?"

As Duckworth stepped into the living room, Blackmore was gathering together the discs and putting them into a cabinet under the television. He approached and extended a hand. "Hello. I—I don't think we've met. I'm Peter Blackmore."

Blackmore looked nervously at Duncomb, as though seeking permission to say anything more. Duncomb stepped in. "The detective here's been out to the campus a couple of times." He grinned. "Thinks we don't know how to do our job."

Blackmore said, "I don't work with Clive. I'm a professor." A pause, then, "English literature."

"So it's Professor Blackmore?" Duckworth asked.

"Yes." He looked at the security chief. "We should tell him."

"Peter, please."

"About Georgina's phone. About that man who answered. He—"

"Peter," Clive Duncomb said, struggling to remain patient, "let's see why the detective has decided to drop by."

Duckworth said, "Professor, I understand you were talking to someone else from the Promise Falls police today."

"I'm sorry?"

"Detective Carlson had interviewed Mr. Duncomb here, and you followed him out afterwards. About your wife. That she was missing."

"I didn't file an official report," the professor said, glancing at Duncomb. "I just had some basic questions for him."

"Did your wife finally turn up?"

Blackmore swallowed. "No, not yet. But . . . the last time I tried to call her—"

Duckworth reached into the plastic shopping bag and took out the purse. "Do you recognize this, Professor?"

"That . . . that looks like Georgina's."

"It has her wallet and ID in it as well," Duckworth said. "And her cell phone."

"Dear God, where did you find that?"

"It was in Adam Chalmers's Jaguar. The one that was crushed at the drive-in last night."

"Why would my wife leave her purse in Adam's car?" he asked.

Duncomb said, "Oh shit."

"I don't understand," Blackmore persisted.

"It wasn't Miriam in the car," Duncomb said to his friend. "It was Georgina."

Blackmore started to go weak in the knees. The detective put his hand on the professor's elbow and led him over to one side of the room. "I'm very sorry, Professor, but I think Mr. Duncomb is right."

Duckworth guided him to the couch, where the man collapsed. "Oh, Jesus, no. Oh dear God. I thought—I thought she was just mad at me. That she'd gone off for a few days. Georgina was very high-strung. Clive thought she was angry with me."

"Angry why?" Duckworth said.

"Just some disagreements, that's all."

"Professor, I'll need you to make an official identification of the body. We already know it's not Miriam. She contacted her brother a short while ago. She was out of town. She's alive."

"Jesus," Duncomb said.

"I have a picture," Duckworth said gently. "On my phone. It shows three tiny moles on the lower abdomen, making a kind of triangle."

Blackmore began to moan.

"May I show it to you?"

Blackmore nodded. Duckworth got out his phone, opened the photos app, held it in front of the professor.

"Oh, God, yes, that's her."

Duncomb's phone rang. As he looked to see who it was, both men turned their heads.

Duncomb was staring at the word *Miriam* on the screen. "It's my wife," he told them. "I'll be right back."

He slipped out the front door, put the phone to his ear,

and said, "Where the hell have you been?"

"Adam is dead," Miriam said.

"I just found out you weren't with him. You couldn't have called? You couldn't have let anyone know it wasn't you?"

"I didn't know! I get home. I find some man in my house poking around. He tells me my husband got fucking crushed to death!"

"Who told you? The police?"

"Weaver. A private detective."

"Him," Duncomb said.

"Lucy hired him! Why does she have some private eye searching my house?"

"Miriam, listen to me. *Everyone* thought you were dead. *I* thought you were dead. You and Adam."

"The son of a bitch. I think he was with Georgina. They thought Georgina was me."

"It just got confirmed. I'm at Peter's. The police are here. He just found out. He's devastated." He paused. "A little more so than you are."

"I'll grieve in my own way, on my own time, Clive. I've got too much else to think about right now, like who was in my house this morning when Lucy came over here."

"Weaver told you."

"Yeah. Was it you? Was it you who broke into the house? And got into the room downstairs? Someone took the discs. Please, God, tell me it was you."

"It was me," Duncomb said.

"Oh, thank God!"

"Soon as I realized Adam—and you, I thought—had been killed at the drive-in, I knew I had to get in there and get those discs. Adam had given me a key long ago,

315

and the code, when you guys took that trip to Switzerland and wanted me to check in on the place. I knew that sooner or later, Lucy, or someone else going through the house, would discover that room and find the discs. I couldn't let that happen."

"I guess, given the circumstances, it was a smart thing to do."

"I called Peter right away, told him we had a problem. He'd been sitting by the phone, waiting for Georgina to call. God, what a turn of events. I didn't even know she and Adam were seeing each other outside of . . . you know."

"The sex?" Miriam said.

"Yeah, outside of the sex. I'd been worried about Georgina. She's been acting funny lately, having second thoughts. I even thought at one point that she'd gotten in and taken the discs."

"I think what was going on," Miriam said, "was that she wanted Adam to herself and didn't want the rest of us to know."

"Maybe. Maybe that was it."

"What have you done with the discs?" Miriam asked. "Tell me you've destroyed them."

"Not yet. Peter and I have been watching them."

"I don't believe you two. You think Adam and I are dead and you're sitting around getting off on what we did together?"

"No!" Duncomb said. "Listen to me. I needed to go through them, make sure we had them all."

Miriam went quiet.

"You there?"

"I'm here," she said.

"There's at least one missing."

"What are you saying?"

"One of the sessions where we brought in those other girls, put the roofies in their wine. Lorraine, and—"

"I remember. Just get to it."

"I can't find the one where we had the Fisher girl. The one who was killed in the park and—"

"Mr. Duncomb!"

Clive Duncomb spun around. Barry Duckworth was standing on the front step of Blackmore's house.

"Get off the phone," Duckworth said. "You're needed in here. Your friend's going to pieces."

FORTY-THREE

"I want that Harwood bastard," Ed Noble said, examining himself in the bathroom mirror. Garnet and Yolanda Worthington had rented a room for him at the Walcott. He tentatively touched the bandages on his nose. "I knew it was him soon as I saw him. Recognized him from the pictures I took. He was the one who was slippin' it to Sam in the kitchen."

"Whore," Yolanda said to no one in particular as she sat on the bed.

"Ed," Garnet Worthington said gently, standing in the doorway to the bathroom. "I understand how you feel, but you're in enough trouble as it is without going after that guy."

"All thanks to you," he said, turning and looking at Garnet and his wife. "I need to see a doctor. I need to go to a hospital."

"Brilliant idea," said Yolanda, who had gone to a Rite Aid to pick up some first-aid supplies after Ed showed up at the rendezvous point.

Without Carl.

They knew the police would be called, that everyone would be looking for Ed's pickup truck, checking the local hospital to see if he'd shown up in the ER. Out of the dozens of people who'd seen what had happened out

318

front of the school, someone must have taken down the license plate. And even if not, by now Samantha would have told the police about Garnet and Yolanda coming to see her at her work, about Ed's visit in the morning. Once she gave them Ed's name, all the police would have to do was tap a few keys on a computer to find the truck registered to him.

"What a clusterfuck," Yolanda said.

Garnet knew the police would likely be looking for him and his wife, too. Samantha would have told them she believed her former in-laws had put Ed Noble up to trying to grab Carl. "They'll be looking for all three of us," Garnet told Yolanda.

The best option seemed to be to lie low. Hide out in Promise Falls for a while until things cooled down. Maybe, in the interim, find a way to reach out to Samantha, tell her they were sorry, that it was all a terrible misunderstanding. They couldn't make another run at the kid, not now. It was too risky. All they could do now was hope to avoid arrest.

Once Ed's truck had been left in a Walmart lot, Garnet got them a room at the Walcott, a Holiday Inn–like hotel on the road that came into Promise Falls. He went to the counter, ready with his story, which was that he had lost his wallet and had no credit cards or ID, but fortunately did have cash. The young man wasn't crazy about the idea, but Garnet Worthington, in his nice suit and tie, looked like a respectable individual.

He needed a fake name for the registration, and his mind went to people he admired, most notably Donald Trump, whom Garnet believed was just the man who should be running the country. But that was a rather obvious alias, so he wrote down "Daniel Trump," and in the place where he was asked for type of car and license plate, he glanced out the door of the lobby for inspiration, saw a Buick Regal, wrote that in, and copied down the plate. Had any hotel clerk in history confirmed vehicle information on a hotel registration?

Once they had the room, they ushered Ed in through a side door, and Yolanda went to work tending his broken nose. She shoveled some Tylenols down his throat while Garnet went for ice to make into a compress, although it was a little late to try to bring down the swelling.

"I'll kill him," Ed kept saying. "I will."

"Just shut up," Yolanda said.

"We all need to calm down and think about how we're going to handle this," Garnet said. "The simplest way out is money."

"Money?" Yolanda said.

"Yeah," Ed agreed. "I deserve more. I got *hurt*."

Garnet sighed. "Money for Samantha. And Carl."

"Not a chance," Yolanda said. "Not a dime for that slut."

Garnet perched his butt on the dresser, glared at his wife. "The situation has changed."

"We can spend money on Carl when he's with us. We'll get him anything he wants."

"You need to listen to me," her husband said. "Today was a mistake. It's going to take a lot to make it right. To save our own necks."

"*He* made the mistake," she said, leaning her head toward Ed.

"Yes," Garnet acknowledged. "He botched it. And now the police are looking for all of us. I'll call the lawyers, have them contact Samantha with an offer. A good enough one that persuades her to tell the police it was a

320

misunderstanding. That, in fact, she'd intended for us to take Carl back to Boston to spend some time with us, that she'd given Ed the okay to pick him up at school, that the whole reason this became an incident is that Harwood misinterpreted everything."

"How will you get her to agree to that?" Ed asked.

Before Garnet could answer, Yolanda asked, "Can't the police go ahead with charges anyway, even if Samantha says not to?"

Garnet shook his head. "What would be the point? They'd know that once it got to court, it would all be dismissed. We'd make sure that Samantha wouldn't testify. Carl, too."

"How much money you think it'll take to buy that kind of silence?"

Garnet thought. "A hundred."

Yolanda screamed as though someone had stabbed her in the heart. "Thousand?"

Ed was equally outraged. "You only gave me five hundred bucks."

"And we overpaid," Garnet said.

"A hundred thousand is out of the question," Yolanda said. "You disappoint me, Garnet."

Her husband sighed. "Yolanda, you and I will go to jail. The only upside to that is they'll put us in different prisons."

"Then why the hell did we try to grab him in the first place?" she shouted.

The slap was enough to send her sprawling across the bed. She put her hand to her left cheek, where Garnet had struck her.

"Because," he said, "you wouldn't fucking let up. That's why. I tried to please you. I've tried to do what you wanted. But this is the road you've led us down. You've put us in this position, Yolanda, and you're going to have to suck it up and listen to me. We're going to pay her off. I'm not even sure a hundred thousand is enough. We may have to go higher. And believe me, given the lies we've already told her, she'll want to see that money in her bank account before she agrees to let this go."

Yolanda had propped herself up on one elbow. She still had a palm pressed to her cheek, and she was struggling to hold back tears.

"We could make him love us," she said. "Once Carl was with us, he wouldn't want to go back. And when his father got out, he'd be so happy."

Garnet shook his head. "How could Carl love you more than his own mother?" He paused. "How could anyone love you at all, Yolanda?"

Ed Noble, watching all this, said, "Maybe there's a way."

"A way what?" Garnet asked.

"A way to get Carl, a way to save your hundred grand, and a way to get Sam to stop being a pain in the ass for you guys."

"Save it, Ed," Garnet said.

"What I was going to say was, if Sam's no longer in the picture, you don't have to worry about her saying anything against you, taking your money, or standing in the way of you raising the little bastard."

"For God's sake, don't talk that way," Garnet said.

"No, wait, hang on," Yolanda said. "Let's hear what the man has to say."

FORTY-FOUR

"Shit," Clive Duncomb whispered into the phone to Miriam. "The cop wants me. Peter's losing it. I'll call you back."

Duncomb put away the phone, turned, and nodded to Duckworth on his way back into Blackmore's house. The professor was where he'd left him, on the couch in the living room, shaking his head, wiping away tears.

Detective Duckworth said to Duncomb, "You need to keep an eye on him. He needs to make some calls, get in touch with family, and in the morning, he needs to come in and make a positive ID, as best he can, of his wife's remains."

"Of course," Duncomb said.

"He came to you, didn't he?"

"What do you mean?"

"He came to you when his wife went missing."

"Peter's my friend. Of course he did."

"And once again, you took matters into your own hands, just like you did with the Mason Helt business. You could have brought us in from the beginning. Told Professor Blackmore to make a formal report with us."

Duncomb bristled. "And what difference would that have made? Would that have kept that movie screen from falling down on her? What was done was done. You're a small man in a small pond, Duckworth."

Duckworth put his face up close to Duncomb's. "What happened in Boston?"

"Excuse me?"

"Why does a cop walk away from a good job like that? Kiss his pension good-bye? Come to a place like Promise Falls? Because he couldn't take the heat? Or maybe because his bosses had something on him and quitting was his only way out? I'm from here. I grew up around here. But you're the one who came here, who *chose* the small pond because you couldn't handle the rough water anymore."

Before Duncomb could come back with anything, the detective was out the door.

"Asshole," he said to the professor.

Blackmore whimpered.

"Come on, get a grip," Duncomb said.

The man's head shot up. "Get a grip?"

"Okay, okay, I get it. This has been a terrible shock for you. I get that. Look, you go do what you have to do about Georgina. Start making arrangements. I can scan through the rest of the discs. I gotta find her. And not just her. Any of the other girls we brought in."

"I don't care."

"Yeah, well, you *better* care. You ever want to be in the position of having to explain that we just happened to be having that kind of fun with that girl a few weeks before she was murdered?"

"I didn't kill that girl."

Duncomb put his face up close to the professor's. "Do you really think that matters?"

"She wasn't even drugged," Blackmore said. "Not like the others. Not like Lorraine. If anyone ever saw it, they'd see that Olivia knew what she was doing. She consented. She did."

"It amazes me someone can rise to the level you have, teaching at a place like Thackeray, and be so astonishingly stupid," Duncomb said. "All that girl ever had to do was threaten to tell anyone what we'd been doing, and we'd have all been finished. If all we did was lose our jobs, we'd have been lucky. We *should* have made sure she was drugged. She'd have forgotten the whole thing. The truth is, we got lucky when someone killed her. We've never had to worry she'd talk about that night."

Blackmore eyed Duncomb fearfully.

"I've always wondered if it was actually you," Blackmore said. "That you made it look like the work of some random maniac. I don't think there's much you're not capable of."

"You don't know anything," Duncomb said.

"I know getting mixed up in all of this . . . that it was a mistake. The fucking *lifestyle*, it was enough for Georgina and me, for Adam and Miriam. But for you and Liz, it wasn't. You had to up the ante. Bring in some young stuff. College girls. Invite them to dinner with some famous cult writer, slip a little something in their drink, make them part of the show. We should have fought you on it, but at the time . . . I won't lie. I liked it. It made me feel . . . omnipotent. That we were capable of anything, that rules didn't apply to us. That other people existed for our pleasure. That's what you and Liz did to us. That's the kind of people you made us. You made us depraved."

"Oh, please."

"Maybe that's why that screen came down on Adam and Georgina. Some kind of divine retribution. They got what was coming to them, and we're next."

"You're losing it, Peter."

"I'm seeing clearly for the first time in years," he countered. "I see what you and Liz have done to us. You've poisoned us. You connecting with Liz, what are the odds two people that twisted would end up together?"

Duncomb gripped Blackmore by the shoulders. "Peter," he said firmly, "you need to stop talking about this. Especially to anyone else. Because I swear, I'll put a bullet in your head just as fast as I did to Mason Helt."

Blackmore blinked several times. He swallowed, hard. "I need a drink."

"Sure, get yourself one. I have to call Miriam back."

"Miriam," Blackmore said under his breath. "She didn't keep Adam interested enough. If she had, he wouldn't have been with Georgina. It's her fault."

"Jesus, just get a drink." Duncomb got out his phone while Blackmore slunk off to the kitchen. He tapped the screen, put the phone to his ear.

"Christ," Miriam said. "I've been waiting."

"The cop left, and then I had to calm Peter down."

"I was trying to tell you, before you cut me off."

"Trying to tell me what?"

"The disc isn't missing," she said.

"What?"

"The Fisher one, and any of the others with special guests. Adam got rid of them."

Duncomb felt an almost euphoric wave building up inside him. "He did?"

"He hated parting with them, but he knew it was a risk to keep them. He destroyed them months ago."

"God, Miriam, that's the first bit of good news in some time."

"So me being alive, that's not?"

"We've been going out of our minds here looking for that one disc and—"

"All right, fine. I hear you."

"I'm sorry about Adam, Miriam. It's horrible."

"Enough," Miriam said. "I have . . . I have things to do."

She ended the call.

Duncomb slipped the phone into his pocket, made two fists, looked up at the ceiling, and said, "Yes!"

When Duncomb went into the kitchen to share the good news, Peter Blackmore was gone.

Miriam, sitting on the edge of the bed in the playroom, set down her phone on the satin sheet. She pulled herself up onto the mattress, drew the slippery covers around herself, making them into an icy cocoon. She brought her knees up to her chest and gave herself permission to cry.

Except the tears would not come.

She knew she should feel something. Anger? Sorrow? Outrage? Grief? And yet she wasn't sure that she felt any of these things. The only emotion she could identify at that moment was relief.

It seemed so strange to her, of all the things she could feel.

But that was what she felt. Relief. And maybe . . . freedom? Was that it? She was free of Adam and all his bullshit. Free of that ex-wife of his who could never keep her nose out of their affairs. Who was always e-mailing or calling Adam on the phone. She'd never really let go, that one.

Free also of Lucy, and her disapproval. Miriam knew Adam's daughter had never liked her. And she'd be free of that weird kid of hers. Crystal. All the time drawing her little comic books. But Adam liked—God, even *loved*—his granddaughter, so what could Miriam do? Let the little kid come over whenever Lucy needed a babysitter, that's what. Adam would always make sure the sliding bookcase was locked into position before Crystal came over. She was already a strange kid—imagine how much weirder she'd have been if she'd found her way into the playroom.

With her husband dead, Miriam could sever all ties to Lucy and Crystal. She'd sell this house, sort out Adam's estate, move the hell out of Promise Falls. Someplace warmer. The winters here were a bitch. Four feet of snow last year. Who needed that? She was thinking she'd relocate to San Diego or Los Angeles with whatever money the estate left her.

Miriam hoped there was enough to help her start over. Adam had been overly concerned about financial matters in recent months, but secretive about how close to the wire things were. He'd been desperate to get a new book contract.

Suddenly, she did begin to cry. Perhaps it was the uncertainty of her inheritance that tipped her over the edge.

She made huge racking sobs. She buried her head into a pillow and moaned as if she were a wounded animal.

It wasn't just grief. It was relief. The chance to start over. It had overwhelmed her.

After several minutes, the sobs ebbed. Exhaustion was moving in. For a while, perhaps as long as half an hour, she drifted off.

She woke with a start, took a second to realize where she was. While this was a bed she was on, it was not, typically, one she'd ever *slept* in.

It was time to go upstairs, go to sleep in their—her—bedroom. She could start sorting things out tomorrow.

The truth was, she did not like this room, this play-room. There had been some amusements here, to be sure, but she'd had enough.

Miriam threw back the covers, slipped her legs over the edge of the bed, touched her toes to the shag carpeting.

Someone was standing in the doorway.

"Jesus!" Miriam said. "You scared the hell out of me!"

"I rang the bell."

"I didn't hear it."

"I let myself in. Found you down here. I was watching you."

"Get out. I'm sick to death of you. What the hell do you want?"

"What do you think? I'm guessing you know."

"Just get out."

"He said if something ever happened to him, I was to come here. That he'd leave something for me. He told me where to look."

"What? In here? Some gold-plated dildo?"

"Not in here. I think you know. I think you have it."

"Get out."

"I'm not leaving until you give it to me."

"I said get out!"

Miriam charged out of the room, pushed the intruder out of her path. As she started up the stairs, she felt hands try to grab her around the ankles.

"I want what's mine!"

"Get the fuck out of here!" Miriam screamed.

Her pursuer tried to overtake her on the stairs, came up alongside her, grabbed at Miriam's hair to slow her down.

Miriam's head jerked up briefly, and she lost her balance. She made a grab for the railing, but missed it.

Her body pitched backward, seemed almost suspended in midair for a second before she hit the stairs.

A sound of something snapping.

Miriam's head rested on the bottom step, the rest of her body splayed awkwardly on the stairs.

"No! God, no! You're not dead! You're not dead!"

Miriam, in not replying, seemed to be suggesting otherwise.

FORTY-FIVE

Cal

A fireman named Darrell let me go up to my apartment to grab a few things. I didn't notice any actual damage, but an acrid smell overwhelmed the place. The gas had been turned off, so I wouldn't have been able to cook anything—not that I ever did, anyway—and the power had been turned off to the building as well. I tossed a change of clothes into a small travel bag. From the kitchen, I got a small freezer bag, which I stuffed with my toothbrush and toothpaste and half a dozen other things from the bathroom. I found an extra pair of socks and underwear and tossed it all into a backpack.

Took about three minutes.

Before heading up, I had told the police everything I could about what I'd seen, which was not a lot. I'm usually good with cars, but telling a Ford pickup from a Chevy pickup, from the side, when it's moving fast, was not among my skills. All I knew with any certainty was that the truck was black and there was some rust around the rear wheel wells. An older model, judging by how loud and rough the engine sounded. The person who threw the Molotov cocktail was male, white, blondish hair, probably early twenties.

And I remembered what he'd said: "Fucking terrorist!"

I felt sick for Naman. The flames had spread from one

stack of books to another, and were licking at the ceiling by the time the trucks arrived. But they had water on the fire before it had done any significant structural damage. The place, as bad as it looked, was not going to fall down. Naman, disbelieving, surveyed his burned and water-damaged stock.

"I'm finished," he said to me when I reappeared with my stuffed backpack.

"No, you're not," I said. "You'll get this all cleaned up. You'll be open again in no time."

"The water seeped through the floor. Hundreds of books in the basement, ruined. I should never have called it Naman's Books. I should have had a sign that said 'Used Books,' that's all."

I didn't know what to say. All I could come up with was "It was a couple of assholes, Naman. The whole town isn't like that."

He turned his head slowly to look at me. "Is that what you think? That the man who did this, that he's an anomaly? That that kind of racism is rare? You have no idea."

"I'm sorry."

"Not a day goes by that I don't sense it, that I don't feel it. Maybe I've never been firebombed before, but you think I don't hear whispers behind my back? You know how long I have lived here, in America? More than forty years. I am an American." He waved his hand toward the street. "I have taught these people's children. I have worked with these kids, encouraged them, shaped them, cried with them, helped make them good, decent citizens. I have always paid my taxes. I have sent boxes and boxes of free books to troops in Iraq and Afghanistan. And this is my thanks. I am a terrorist. How would you feel about this town if you knew you'd given your whole life to it, and this is how it pays you back?"

He was looking me hard in the eye, and I held his gaze. I said, "You have my cell. If there's anything you need, call me. Okay?"

Naman said nothing. He turned around, bent over, picked up the now singed and waterlogged copy of *The Blue Hammer* that he'd been reading earlier.

I decided it made the most sense to stay with my sister, Celeste, at least for tonight. I didn't know how many days it would be before I'd be able to get back into my apartment, and I might need to rent a motel room. But Celeste had already offered to let me stay with her, even if her husband, Dwayne, was not crazy about the idea. I'd insist she take some money from me. What with the town cutting back on the work it contracted Dwayne's paving company to do, there wasn't much money coming in.

I parked out front, grabbed my backpack, and trudged up the two steps to the front door. I was about to knock when I caught sight of Celeste and Dwayne sitting on the couch together. She had her arm around him, and at first I thought they were making out. Kind of sweet, I thought, for a couple married as long as they had been.

Then I realized I was seeing something very different.

Dwayne's shoulders were hunched over, his head down and propped up on his palms.

The man was crying.

Celeste must have noticed my shadow at the window. She looked my way and caught my eye. She whispered something to her husband, got up, and came to the door. She opened it and slipped outside.

"I'm sorry," I said. "I was about to knock and saw—"

"It's okay," my sister said. "What's with the bag?"

"Never mind, don't worry about it."

"You want to stay here tonight?"

"There was a fire. At the bookstore. Some yahoos tossed a Molotov cocktail through the window."

"What?"

I explained the likely motivations of the idiots in the pickup truck.

"Of course you can stay here," she said.

"No, I don't think so. Looks like you're dealing with something."

She moved me toward the far end of the porch, away from the door. "He's falling apart."

"I figured."

"I mean, I'm worried, too, you know. About how much longer we're going to be able to pay the bills. But we'll manage somehow, right? Maybe it's just as well we never had kids. Think how much worse this would be if we had mouths to feed. But it's just us—we'll get through. But no matter how much I tell Dwayne that, he's just not hearing me. The stress of it's killing him. It goes right to the heart of who he is, being able to look after me. Hey, I can get more hours if I have to, but it's been wearing him down for a long time."

"I have money," I said.

She put a hand on my arm. "Cal."

"No, really. I have some. Enough to get you through a couple of weeks, anyway."

She went up on her tiptoes and kissed my cheek. "You're a good brother. You really are."

"If there's anything I can—"

The front door opened. Dwayne said, "What's going on here?"

"Cal just dropped by."

Dwayne looked at the backpack I'd left on the porch. "What the hell is this? You're bunking in with us?"

"No," I said. He'd wiped his eyes, but I could see where tears had been running down his cheeks.

"I don't have enough problems? I gotta take people in?"

"Dwayne, Jesus," Celeste said. "It's okay."

"You know, Cal," Dwayne said, "you had some awful shit happen to you. I get that. Your wife and your kid, what happened to them, that's a tough break. But we got problems, too, you know? You can't be coming around here all the time bringing us down."

"Shut your mouth," Celeste said. "God, just stop it."

"It's okay," I said. I walked toward the door, grabbed my bag, and went back down the walk to my car.

"Good plan," Dwayne said. "Good plan."

I remembered there was a motel on the road to Albany, but when I got there, I found the place all boarded up. "OUT OF BIZNESS" had been spray-painted across the plywood sheets that had been nailed over the windows.

So then I tried the Walcott, parked under the front apron, and went inside. To my surprise, the place was fully booked. Normally, they'd have had more rooms, but one wing was undergoing renovations.

"Rented my last place to some guy who lost all his credit cards," said the guy at the front desk. "But he had a good roll of cash."

Well, shit.

I supposed I could drive closer to Albany. But I'd be spending the better part of an hour on the road before

335

I had a chance to start looking for anything.

I had a thought.

I called Lucy Brighton's cell phone. She picked up before the second ring.

"Yes?"

"Got a favor to ask. There was a fire and—"

"What?"

I explained. She said, "Can you give me half an hour? To get the guest room ready?"

"Sure," I said. "I really appreciate it."

I was going to hit a diner. A couple of crackers and cheese earlier had not quite done the trick.

Lucy had been watching for me, and opened the door before I reached it. I thought she might be in pajamas or a nightgown, but she was dressed, and in something a little nicer than what I'd seen her in earlier in the evening. A black, low-cut top that showed a hint of cleavage and a pair of tight jeans.

"This is really kind of you," I said. "Sorry to have kept you from going to bed."

She had questions, and I told her more about what had happened. She offered to make some coffee, but I told her no. It had been a long day.

"I've got you all set up in the spare room," Lucy said, her voice just above a whisper. Crystal, I figured, had gone to bed some time ago.

"She left me a surprise in my car," I told Lucy.

"What are you talking about?"

"Her graphic novel. She left it for me to read. I haven't gotten to it yet, but I will."

"That little scamp." Lucy almost looked as though she

336

might cry. "Do you know how rare it is that she'd do something like that?"

I didn't.

"Crystal likes you. She senses that you're a good man. That's why she wants to share her artwork with you. She isolates herself so much, but every once in a while, she reaches out. That's what she's doing with you."

We went upstairs, where she showed me my bedroom. The top of the dresser was stacked three deep in white cardboard business boxes full of files. There were more on the floor, but Lucy had created a path around the bed so I wouldn't stumble if and when I got up in the middle of the night to hit the bathroom down the hall.

"I'm sorry about this," she said, indicating the boxes. "This room almost never gets used, so it becomes a kind of dumping ground." We were standing close together by the foot of the bed, where there was barely enough room for two people to get by.

"Don't worry about it," I said.

"The bathroom's right there, but it's the only one up here, so if it's occupied, you can use the little one, the powder room, on the first floor, and there's another bathroom in the basement, but the one up here is the only one with a shower. God, I'm rambling."

"This is all good," I said, setting my bag on top of the double bed. "I appreciate it."

"That's a small bag. If you've forgotten anything, you can probably find what you need in the bathroom. Every time we go to the dentist, they give us new toothbrushes and I must have a dozen of them that have never been opened. So if you need—"

"I'm good," I said.

"But I don't have shaving cream. I mean, I've got

337

ladies' shaving cream, you know, and it's probably the same stuff—it just comes in a pink can."

I turned to face her and put my hands on her shoulders. "It's okay."

Her lips were twitching. "I know, to many people, he wasn't a good man, my father," Lucy said. "But I loved him."

I waited.

"I did. He was my father. I know there was a kind of . . . hollowness about him. I believe he loved me, and I believe he loved Crystal. At least, as much as he was able to. He could certainly pretend to love. Does that make sense?"

"I think so."

She took two steps toward the door, closed it. "I don't want to wake her up."

"Sure," I said.

"But he taught me well, you know. From the time I was a little girl, he taught me to stand up for myself. I'm a survivor. I'm a single mother. When my marriage wasn't working out, I could have tried to stick it out, but I thought, I can't live like this. Not even for Crystal's sake. Because what would that teach her? That you stay in an unhappy situation, that you surrender your life that way?"

"Your father seemed to be someone who went after what he wanted."

"You mean that room?"

"I guess I mean that he didn't let the conventions the rest of us tend to live by keep him from living the life he wanted. I'm not judging. I'm just saying, that's what I see."

Lucy thought about that. "I wondered sometimes if he was a borderline psychopath, but not in a malicious kind of way. I read somewhere that many successful CEOs are psychopaths. They don't let the feelings of others get in their way because they're not even aware of them, but they're good at acting like they are. Sort of like politicians."

Lightly, Lucy rested the tips of her fingers on my chest.

"You feel things," Lucy said. "I can tell."

I hadn't slept with a woman since Donna and I made love the night before she died.

Three years.

"Lucy, I—"

"Don't say anything. Just hold me."

I did. She trembled slightly, as though my fingers were made of ice.

She turned her mouth up toward me, but she would have had to stand on her tiptoes to put her lips on mine, and even then, she might not have reached, so the ball, as they say, was in my court.

I knew what I wanted to do, and felt guilty about it. A little afraid, too.

The last two decades I'd slept with only one woman, never straying, even when opportunities had presented themselves. Over that kind of time, Donna and I had come to know each other's needs and rhythms. Things were unspoken. I guess you could say we knew the routine, but that was not to suggest that it *was* routine. It had been good for almost all that time, except the last couple of months, when we'd grown distant in our grief over Scott. If we could have seen the future—

No, I couldn't go over all that again.

I feared intimacy with someone whose needs and rhythms I did not know. Who didn't know mine.

Maybe I had to live up to the words I'd spoken to Celeste. I had to move forward.

"I see it in your eyes," Lucy said. "What you feel. So much pain."

I put my mouth on hers and closed the gap between us. Pulled her into me so hard, it was like I was trying to bring her through the other side of me. I eased off, thinking I might hurt her.

How fast did one move in such matters? Did we do this for a while, then move on to something else? Or would one of us break it off, say this was a big mistake, that we were caught up in the moment, that we were both, in our own ways, dealing with loss, and that this was not the way to handle it? And then Lucy would slip quietly out of the room and close the door and that would be the end of that?

Lucy started undoing my belt.

We sat on the edge of the bed, fumbled with clothes, kicked off shoes, went through those awkward preliminaries before ending up under the covers. Twice she whispered that we had to be quiet.

We didn't want to wake Crystal.

Later, for appearance's sake, Lucy returned to her own room so she'd be there when Crystal got up.

I slept like the dead.

FORTY-SIX

It was three minutes after one in the morning when Dwayne Rogers stepped out of Knight's, one of Promise Falls' seedier downtown bars that had been down on Proctor Street since God was in short pants, into the cool night air. He dug into his pocket for a pack of cigarettes. He hadn't smoked in years, but the last couple of weeks, he'd found himself falling back into the habit. Calmed him, at least briefly. The whole ritual of it. Unwrapping the cellophane on the package, tapping the pack against his fist to eject the cigarette, putting it between his lips, opening the matchbook and striking a match, watching it flare briefly, putting it to the end of the cigarette, watching the warm glow as the tobacco ignited.

He'd been drinking more lately, too. You did what you had to do in tough times. Told Celeste he needed to get some air. He'd felt ashamed, crying like that in front of Celeste. Then her brother-in-law shows up, peeking through the window, seeing him that way. Dwayne confronting him and acting like a real asshole.

Celeste gave him proper shit after Cal left. Dwayne didn't realize, until after Cal was gone, that he'd been burned out of his home. Dwayne thought maybe he could have handled that a little better.

He said he needed to go out to think about things.

What he didn't tell Celeste was that he'd already been planning to go out.

He had somewhere he had to be at a certain time.

He'd been at the bar only about five minutes—he hadn't even ordered a beer yet—when he went back outside. Before he left, he said hello to a couple of people he recognized, gave the bartender a friendly wave. Said to him, "Have you seen Harry around?"

"Don't think so," the bartender said.

"Well, if you see him, tell him Dwayne was here," he said.

"Sure thing."

Once he was back on the street, he lit up his cigarette and waited. He wasn't the only one out there. A young couple was leaned up against a lamppost, making out. Three men were huddled together debating which was better: NASCAR or horse racing. Occasionally, someone went into or came out of Knight's.

Proctor Street ran downhill from north to south. When Dwayne was younger, he used to skateboard down the length of it late at night or early Sunday morning, when there was hardly any traffic.

As he looked to the north, he saw something coming, but it was not a kid on a skateboard.

It was a bus. A Promise Falls Transit bus, with a big baylike window at the front.

The buses didn't typically run this late, at least not anymore. They once crisscrossed town until the bars closed, but since the town managers went hacking away at the budget, you couldn't get a bus after eleven.

This didn't look like a bus anyone would want to board, anyway.

It was on fire.

The inside of the bus was aglow with flames. They were flickering out the windows on both sides.

Rolling down the center of Proctor, with increasing speed, the bus looked like a comet. Proctor ran dead straight, but the bus looked like it was coming down on a slight angle, and pretty soon was going to crash into cars parked along the curb.

Dwayne stood, rooted to the sidewalk, mesmerized by the spectacle, as the bus got closer.

The men debating the merits of fast cars versus fast horses spun around and stared, mouths agape, as the fireball approached.

"Son of a bitch!" one yelled.

"Fucking hell!" said another.

As the bus flew past Knight's, it became obvious to everyone that there was no one behind the wheel. Nor were there any passengers.

As the rocket of flame continued to barrel on down the street, the back end of the bus was illuminated every few seconds as it passed below streetlamps.

The number 23, in numerals three feet high, adorned the back of the bus below the window.

"Look!" said the young man who'd been making out with his girlfriend. "It's him!"

"Who?" the girl asked.

"The guy the cops were talking about! Mr. Twenty-three!"

"What?" she said.

The bus sideswiped several parked cars on the other side of the street, setting off multiple alarms and flashing taillights, but the collisions did little to slow the vehicle down.

Proctor T-boned with Richmond about a hundred yards on. The flaming bus raced through the intersection, smashed through two cars parked on the street, and barreled into the front window of a florist shop.

"Wow," Dwayne said.

The sound of the crash brought others out of the bar. "What the hell happened?" someone asked.

"That bus!" Dwayne said. "Went flying past, all on fire! Jesus!"

A growing crowd spilled out into the street. The bar emptied. Across Proctor, customers poured out of an all-night diner to see what was going on.

The man who'd read something into the number on the back of the bus started shouting: "It might have a bomb in it! It's the guy who blew up the drive-in!" He grabbed his girlfriend by the arm and started running up Proctor the other way.

The others on the street exchanged looks, as though pondering what they should do. They seemed torn between moving in for a closer look at what happened—the flower shop's burglar alarm was whooping loudly and the blaze was spreading from the bus to the building—and running for their lives.

Several of them started to run.

Dwayne heard heavy footsteps coming from the north and turned. It was a male jogger in his mid- to late twenties. He came to a stop next to Dwayne.

"What the hell happened?" asked the jogger, his shirt soaked with sweat.

"Beats me," said Dwayne. "Thing just flew past here like a space shuttle on reentry." He gave the jogger a closer look. "You look familiar. Do I know you?"

"Don't think so."

"You were in the bar the other night, kinda mouthing off at everyone."

344

"Yeah, that mighta been me. Had a bit too much. Sorry if I said anything to you—what's your name?"

"Dwayne."

"Well, sorry, Dwayne. I'm Victor, by the way."

"Hey."

Victor Rooney gazed down the street at the fire with something approaching awe and wonder. "Not the sort of thing you see every day, is it?"

FORTY-SEVEN

Derek Cutter had set the alarm on his phone for six, but his eyes were open five minutes before it went off. Early-morning sunlight was filtering through the blinds into his bedroom. He could have lain in another five minutes, even a few more after six, but he wanted to get going.

He was excited.

And surprised. Surprised that he was excited.

Marla Pickens had invited him to come over first thing this morning to have breakfast with Matthew and her. Matthew was her ten-month-old child. Matthew was also, as it turned out, Derek's ten-month-old child.

Derek was stunned to learn that he was a father, but Marla was also somewhat stunned to learn she was a mother.

More than a year ago, he'd known he was going to become a dad, and he was certainly not excited about the news at the time. Scared shitless was more like it. He and Marla, a woman he'd met at the Thackeray pub, had gone out a couple of times, slept together, and even though that was the kind of activity that he was aware could lead to babies, he was dumbstruck when Marla told him she was pregnant.

He didn't want a kid, and he didn't know what the hell to do with one when it arrived. He didn't know whether

Marla even wanted him involved. All he knew was that she intended to have the baby.

Derek was a wreck for months.

Then he got the news.

The baby had died at birth.

He couldn't believe how it hit him. Months earlier, he would have been secretly relieved to hear Marla had lost the baby. Off the hook. Problem solved. Case dismissed. But he was devastated.

My kid died.

Except, of course, as everyone now knew, that wasn't what had happened. Marla's mother and her doctor had tricked her into thinking her baby had not survived. Ten months later, Marla was reunited with her child.

Not that everyone lived happily ever after. Marla's mother and the doctor were dead. Marla remained pretty screwed up. She'd refused to believe, for several days, that her mother had actually killed herself by jumping off Promise Falls. She and Matthew were living with her father, and being checked on regularly by the local child welfare authorities.

But everyone thought it was a good sign that she wanted to bring Derek into the loop.

Even Derek's mother and father.

This was the really good part.

He'd figured his parents, Jim and Ellen, would be all over him about this. Still in school, got a girl pregnant, didn't have a job, why couldn't he keep it in his pants?—that kind of thing.

It hadn't been like that at all.

They hadn't really judged. His dad just made it clear that he had to step up to the plate, do the right thing, accept his responsibility, fill in whichever cliché you want here. The really weird thing was, Derek having a kid seemed to be bringing Jim and Ellen, who had split up a few years ago, back together.

They were grandparents. And they appeared to want to enjoy the experience together.

They'd met a few times for dinner. They'd gone to the Pickens house twice to see the baby. They'd bought stuff. Diapers, clothes, board books.

Jim had asked his son if he wanted to come back to work with him this summer at the landscaping business.

Derek said yes.

So he felt pretty good this morning. The events of two nights ago at the drive-in were still fresh in his memory, but he wasn't going to let that drag him down too much. He jumped into the shower, got dressed, and was out front of his place by seven. He didn't have a car, but Gill Pickens, Marla's dad, had offered to come over and pick him up.

Gill was there.

They didn't have much to say to each other. Derek figured that whenever Gill looked at him, he was probably thinking, *You're the dickwad who knocked up my little girl.* Then again, you couldn't blame the guy for being quiet. His wife had just died, and he had a whole lot on his plate right now.

Marla was at the door, holding Matthew in her arms, when they pulled into the driveway.

"You're just in time," Marla said. "He's really hungry."

Derek followed Marla and his son into the kitchen. "You hold on to him while I get his breakfast ready."

"You sure?" he said.

She handed Matthew over to him. Derek took him under the arms, settled him up against his chest, put his right hand on the child's back.

"I can feel his heart beating."

"Yeah, well, that's a good thing," Marla said.

Matthew made soft gurgling noises. Derek said, "He looks bigger than he did two weeks ago."

"He's growing—that's for sure. You guys look good together."

A cell phone started to ring.

"Who's that?" Marla asked.

Derek could feel the buzzing on his upper thigh. "It's me," he said. "I don't know who'd be calling me this early. Can you take him?"

He handed Matthew off to Marla, then took the phone from the pocket of his jeans. He saw the name on the screen and said, "What?"

"Who is it?"

"Lydecker," Derek said. "As in George Lydecker." The phone continued to ring in his hand. "Except it's his home phone, not his cell. He never uses his home phone."

"Who's George Lydecker?"

"He's this idiot. The other night, before the screen came down? He was shooting at stop signs and stuff." The phone kept ringing. Derek sighed, accepted the call. "Hello?"

It wasn't George on the other end. It was a woman, and she was speaking loud enough that Marla could hear every word.

"Hello?"

"Is this Derek?" the woman asked. "Derek Cutter?"

"Yup."

"It's Hillary Lydecker. George's mother. Is George with you?"

"What? No." Why the hell would George be with

him this early in the morning? Wait, maybe that wasn't so implausible. George had been known to drink too much and pass out at a friend's place, then head home the next morning.

"I've been calling everyone he knows. I found your number on his cell phone bill. I think I've called just about everyone!" The woman sounded frantic. "You sure he's not with you?"

"I'd kinda know. I haven't seen him since night before last."

"We're all set to go. We were supposed to leave for the airport a couple of hours ago. We thought maybe he was out partying or something and maybe he passed out and didn't wake up in time to get home for the taxi. We've missed our flight. We're going to have to rebook everything."

"When did you last see him?" Derek asked.

"Last night, we had an early dinner. Then he said he was going out, and I said to him, 'Be back early, because we're flying out in the morning.' All of us, we're going to Vancouver to see my husband's family, and we told George the taxi is coming really early, at five, and he promised he'd be home in good time, but I've tried his cell and I can't get him and—"

"I'm sure he'll turn up," Derek said. "You know what George is like. I'm sure he's okay. It's probably like you say. He went to a party and had a bit too much and fell asleep on somebody's couch. Too bad about your flight, though. That's really a drag."

Hillary Lydecker said, "I just hope he hasn't done something really stupid."

FORTY-EIGHT

It wasn't as though Barry Duckworth was expecting a plate covered with four scrambled eggs, half a dozen strips of bacon, and a heap of home fries. He rarely got something like that at home. If he wanted a breakfast like that, he hit one of Promise Falls' greasy, wonderful diners.

But a grapefruit and a slice of toast? Seriously?

"Maureen," he said, "we need to talk."

She was drinking her coffee across the table from him, having a quick look at the news on her tablet before heading off to work.

"What's the problem?" she said. "I cut the grapefruit in half, and even took a knife to the little wedges so you won't get any grapefruit juice in your eye and blind yourself. Also, I sprinkled some Splenda on it so it's not so bitter. I couldn't sprinkle sugar all over it. That kind of defeats the purpose, don't you think?"

"What kind of toast is this? It doesn't look like my regular toast."

"That's multigrain," she said, not moving her eyes from the tablet. "There's something pretty amazing on here you're going to want to see."

"It looks like birdseed stuck to the crust."

"It'll make you a better warbler," Maureen said. She

looked at him. "Oh my God, you're not actually picking those seeds off, are you?"

"I don't like them."

"I buttered the bread for you. Not a lot, but that's actual butter on the bread. I would never expect you to eat dry toast. My God, the way you're carrying on, you'd think you were being waterboarded."

"I like my usual toast," he said.

"I'm sure you do," Maureen said. "Really, you're going to want to see this, unless you've already heard about it."

"Heard about what?"

"The bus? That was on fire? It made the Albany station. Someone got video on their phone."

Duckworth beckoned with his hand. Maureen turned the iPad around on its stand, pushed it his way.

"You just press the little play arrow there," she said.

"I know how to do it," he said.

He tapped the screen. Watched the flaming bus roll down the street, crash into some cars, destroy a flower shop.

"Jesus," he said. "I've bought flowers for you there."

"Not lately," Maureen said.

"Hang on," he said. "How do I make it go again?"

"Press the little arrow that's like a circle that—"

"I got it. Hang on. I want to pause it right . . . here."

The image froze. Duckworth had paused the video at the point where the bus had driven past whoever was filming it.

Where you could see the back end of the bus.

With the number 23 three feet high and three feet across.

"Look at that," he said, turning the tablet around.

"Yeah, I see it."

"You see the number on the back?"

"I do." She shook her head. "He's at it again."

Duckworth stared at the screen again. "He's sending a message. I just don't know what the hell it is." He shook his head despairingly. "I feel like we're leading up to something."

"Like?"

"I don't know. But—"

His cell phone started to ring.

"Duckworth," he said.

"Detective, this is Officer Gilchrist."

Gilchrist. *Ted* Gilchrist. Duckworth had last seen him at the Gaynor house, trying to sort things out between David Harwood, his cousin Marla Pickens, and Bill Gaynor, shortly after Rosemary Gaynor's body had been discovered. A good cop, Duckworth thought.

"This about the bus? I just found out about it."

"No, sir. Something else. Figured I'd call you directly, since it's probably going to be you who gets the call."

"Okay."

"I was just doing a regular patrol, going past a house, noticed the front door was left ajar. Decided I should have a look. Went up to the door, rang the bell, no one came, figured maybe someone hurried off to work and didn't pull the door shut all the way, but when I had a look inside, I realized it was something else."

"What?"

"There's a dead lady on the stairs. Her neck's busted."

Duckworth felt like a tire with only a couple of pounds of pressure left in it. *There was too much shit going on in this town.*

"Address?" he asked Gilchrist.

★

Barry Duckworth, hovering over the body of Miriam Chalmers, one police-issue bootie on one step, one police-issue bootie on the other, couldn't help but kick himself mentally.

He should have come out here. He should have come out here last night and interviewed this woman.

At the time, however, it seemed far more urgent to seek out Peter Blackmore, husband of Georgina, the woman who had really died in the Jag with Adam Chalmers. The bad news had to be delivered.

There was bad news for Miriam Chalmers, too, but someone had already told her that her husband was dead, as evidenced by her call to her brother seconds before Duckworth nearly showed him Georgina Blackmore's body.

So there'd been no pressing need for Duckworth to pay Miriam Chalmers a visit. And besides, he was so goddamned tired all he could think about was going home to bed.

Excuses.

If he'd come by here last night, maybe he could have kept this from happening. Maybe he'd have arrived at just the right time. Or maybe he would have learned something that led him to believe this woman was in danger.

All too late for that now.

"Any sign of forced entry?" Duckworth asked Gilchrist, who was standing at the top of the stairs that led to the basement.

"I've been all around the house, checked windows, doors, and I don't see anything," he said.

Duckworth studied the angle of the body, trying to determine how she'd landed this way, head at the bottom step, feet five steps above.

"Tripped?" Gilchrist asked.

"I don't think so," he said. "If she tripped going up the stairs, her head would be that way. If she'd tripped going the other way, she'd be facedown. I'd say she was on the way up, and got pushed, or pulled."

"Yeah," Gilchrist said. "I see what you mean."

Standing on the basement floor, Duckworth noticed a room behind him with a light on. It didn't have a proper doorway, but appeared to be accessed by the bookshelves that had been slid to one side.

Duckworth peered into the room.

"Officer Gilchrist!" he said.

"Yes, Detective?"

"Have you been down here and seen this?"

"Yes, sir, I have."

"And you hadn't thought to mention it?"

"I was going to, then thought I'd let you discover it on your own. So it would have the same impact on you as it did on me. And honestly, I didn't know if there was any way I could really describe it for you. It's one of those things you just have to see. I'm going to take another look around up here."

Duckworth took in the framed photos on the wall. The oversized bed, the retro shag carpeting, the satiny bedcover, which had been disturbed. As though someone had wrapped himself—or herself—in it, without getting underneath it.

The room's theme immediately made the detective wonder whether Miriam Chalmers had been sexually assaulted. He took another look at her, from a good ten feet away. Her clothes appeared undisturbed.

The coroner would tell him more.

Duckworth looked up to the top of the stairs, where

Gilchrist had been a moment earlier.

"You called Wanda, right?" he shouted upstairs.

Gilchrist, from somewhere, said, "Yup." And, "Found something."

Duckworth didn't move. He didn't want to navigate his way around the body again. He waited.

Gilchrist reappeared, holding up something small and white, about the size of a business card.

It was, in fact, a business card.

"This rings a bell," Gilchrist said. "Didn't a Cal Weaver used to work for the force?"

FORTY-NINE

Cal

When Crystal Brighton, still in her pajamas, came into the kitchen, I glanced in her mother's direction. I was sitting at the table, having a cup of coffee, and suddenly realized how this had to look. A strange man—well, not totally strange, given that Crystal and I had already met—here for breakfast?

But Crystal didn't look at me, her mother, or anything else but the clipboard she held in her left hand. She had a pencil in her right and was doodling even as she walked.

Crystal nudged a chair out and took a seat.

Lucy said, "Crystal, you remember Mr. Weaver."

She looked up from her drawing for half a second, took me in, and went back to her work as her mother set a glass of orange juice in front of her. "Yes," she said.

"There was a fire last night where he lives and the fire department wouldn't let him stay the night, so I offered to let him stay in the guest room."

That caught her interest. She looked at me. "How big a fire?"

"My apartment wasn't destroyed," I said, "but the smoke smell is everywhere."

"Was anybody killed?" she asked.

I shook my head. "No."

Lucy came around to Crystal's side of the table and

357

put a bowl of Cheerios in front of her.

"What are you drawing on?" she asked.

"Paper," Crystal said.

Lucy took the clipboard from her, removed the top sheet, flipped it over, and winced. "For God's sake, Crystal, it's the electric bill."

"Only on one side," she said. "The other side is blank."

"How many times have I—" Lucy cut herself off. Maybe she didn't want to tear a strip off her daughter in front of me. "Please don't do that."

Crystal turned to look at me and said, "Did the graphic novel I gave you get burned up in the fire?"

"No," I said. "It's okay. It's still in the car."

"Did you read it?"

"Not yet," I said. "But I'm going to. When I do, I'll let you know what I think."

She turned her attention to her cereal, shoved a spoonful into her mouth and chewed.

"Better get a move on," her mother said. "You slept in."

"I woke up in the night," she said, "and couldn't get back to sleep."

"Well, that's too bad."

I felt it was time to go. I took one last gulp of coffee and stood. "I should be on my way. Going to see just how bad the damage is. Thanks for everything. Nice to see you, Crystal."

"Don't go just yet," Lucy said. "Let me get Crystal off to school."

I shouldn't have been surprised she wanted to talk to me privately, given that we had slept together only a few hours earlier. I was wondering whether that had been such a good idea. I liked Lucy. I liked her a lot, in fact. The time she had spent in the guest room with me, while tentative at first, had turned passionate, even aggressive, quickly. Lucy had assumed a leadership role I was more than happy to concede to her. I wondered whether, after all she had endured in the last couple of days, she needed to feel she had control over at least this part of her life.

"Sure," I said, nodding my understanding. "I can hang in for a few minutes."

But I hadn't been making an excuse when I'd said I had to go back and check my apartment. Odds were I'd have to find another place to live, if not permanently, at least for a few weeks. If the building was deemed unsafe, I'd need permission just to get my stuff out of there.

What little of it there was.

I thought of Celeste and Dwayne. No way was I bunking in with them while I apartment-hunted. I'd find a motel outside Promise Falls. And I certainly wasn't moving in with Lucy. I was open to the idea of seeing more of her, but it was a little early to start sharing quarters. And it wasn't fair to Crystal, having some man she didn't really know living under the same roof with her.

"Come on, sweetheart," her mother said. "You'll be late."

Crystal shoved one last spoonful of Cheerios into her mouth, then ran back upstairs, clipboard in hand.

"I like her," I said.

Lucy gave me a dubious smile, as though she didn't know whether to believe me. She followed Crystal up to the second floor. I could hear muted conversation—mostly from Lucy's side—about the brushing of teeth, the collecting of homework, the remembering of lunch. That, I guessed, was the brown bag on the kitchen counter. Several minutes later, Crystal returned, snatched the bag off the counter, pivoted, and ran for the front door.

"Read my thing," she said as she passed me.

"You bet," I said as Lucy returned to the kitchen.

At the door, we heard Crystal say, "My shoelace is undone!"

"Then fix it!" Lucy said.

We heard some sighing and shuffling, and then the slam of a door.

"And she's gone," Lucy said. She filled a mug with coffee, leaned up against the counter, and took a sip. "I think maybe I could use something stronger."

I smiled but said nothing. I was thinking how much I missed the chaos of a youngster in the house.

"I liked last night," she said, then grimaced. "I mean, I'm sorry you got burned out and all. But aside from that."

"Me, too," I said, standing. I closed the distance between us, slipped my arms around her waist, and pulled her toward me.

Lucy set her mug down, put her arms around my neck and her mouth on mine.

Things went like that for a while. This time, when she went to unbuckle my belt, she was better at it. She slipped a hand down there.

"I don't have to go in today," she whispered. "I'm on a bereavement leave. But I can do my bereaving later."

And I could put off possible apartment-hunting for a while, too.

My cell phone rang.

"Let it go," she said, her lips on my neck.

"*You* let it go," I said. "I should get this."

I put some space between us, reached into my jacket for my phone, and held up my pants with my other hand.

"Hello?" I said.

"Cal, Barry Duckworth. Where are you?"

FIFTY

David Harwood was still half-asleep. He'd heard his cell ring, grabbed it off the bedside table, put it to his ear, and said, "Yeah?"

Randall Finley said, "Let's do it."

"What?" David asked. "Do what? What the hell time is it?"

"It's uh . . . almost five thirty. This is the day. I'm going to announce. I'm ready. I told you I was ready to move. Things are coming together."

David threw back the covers, got his feet onto the floor. He switched the phone to his other ear. "Randy, listen to me. We're *not* ready. You can't just go out there half-cocked. We don't have a final platform drafted. We don't even have a slogan. You need to be more organized before you begin."

"I'm fully cocked," the former mayor said. "I've got an issue, something to run on, to kick-start things. We can put something out there, stir up some shit, and work on the rest of the stuff over the next few days."

"What issue?"

"You'll see."

"Randy, listen, you can't keep me in the dark. If you want me to run things, you have to let me run them."

"You are—don't you worry—but we're moving ahead.

Call whoever it is you call. TV, Albany papers, fucking CNN, I don't care. Just get people out here. I'm counting on you to use your connections. You worked in the media—you know how it works. Let's make it for noon. We'll do it in the park by the falls. Nice background there, with the water coming down."

"If you expect people to come out," David said, "I've got to promise them something good. You deciding to run is not enough."

A pause at the other end of the line. "Okay, you can tell them this. Tell them to expect a bombshell about how things are currently run in this town. Something big. And that's why I'm running. To straighten things out here."

"I need something more," David insisted. "Something specific."

"I don't want to give it all away," Finley said. "It's like taking some hot chick on a date and you come in your pants while you're still at dinner."

David closed his eyes for a moment, kneaded his forehead with his fingers. "I would prefer not to put it to them that way."

"Okay, tell them it's about incompetence in the police department. And whether this force has the tools it needs to catch this twenty-three dude."

"Twenty-three what?"

"Christ, David, do you watch the news?"

"I had some stuff going on yesterday."

Finley told him about Barry Duckworth's news conference.

"That's crazy," David said. "That's absolutely crazy."

"I know," Finley said, unable to keep the enthusiasm out of his voice. "This plays right into what I'm going to talk about."

"What's the thing you're holding back?" *Or made up,* David thought.

"You'll find out when everyone else does. But the good thing is, you can take it to the bank. It's solid."

David sighed in defeat. "Let me start making some calls," he said. "Oh, another thing."

"What's that?"

"I'd like to talk to Mrs. Finley. Jane, is it?"

"Why do you want to do that?"

"Spouses always figure into a campaign. I want to talk to her about her role."

"She's my closest adviser," Finley said. "That's her role. You don't need to talk to her."

He hung up.

David put the phone on the bedside table, held his head in his hands for a moment, elbows on his knees.

"Something bad?" Samantha said.

David turned, looked at her head on the pillow next to his. "Sorry if that woke you."

"It's okay," she said. "I was already awake. I was thinking I got to pick up Carl. Get him back here, get him ready for school."

Carl was having a sleepover with Ethan at David's house. David's sleepover—although there'd been a limited amount of actual sleeping—had been at Sam's.

The night before, they had decided to have that dinner—drinks, actually, with some bar snacks, since the two of them had already eaten—right away. The moment Sam had said yes, she'd be happy to go out with him sometime, David had asked, "How about now?"

Sam didn't feel as though she could say no. The man had, after all, just saved her son from an abduction. When David went back inside and asked Arlene if she could watch the boys for a while, she'd said sure, no problem, they were already getting along just fine, up in Ethan's room.

Around eleven, David had glanced at his watch and said, "Oh, shit."

"God, I haven't been up this late in years," Sam had said. "Get me back to your place. I'll grab Carl and get home."

But something had happened on the way to the car. When he'd opened the passenger door for her, Sam had turned, her face brushing up close to David's, and he'd kissed her. Hungrily. Sam responded. It was the same kind of instantaneous passion they'd felt in her kitchen weeks earlier.

Her back pressed up against the car, she'd said, "My place."

On the way, David had phoned his mother. "Where are you?" Arlene had asked, her voice just above a whisper. "It's past Ethan's bedtime, but it's kind of hard to put him to bed when Carl is still here."

David had said, "Have Carl sleep over." He'd glanced at Sam, who'd nodded.

"Sleep over?" Arlene had said. "He hasn't brought pajamas or a toothbrush or a change of clothes for tomorrow or—"

"*Mom*, make it work."

Silence, for a moment, from his mother. "I'll see what I can do. Will I see you in the morning, or are you going to Mexico?"

"Thanks, Mom," he'd said.

And five minutes later they were in Samantha Worthington's bed. The first time was rushed, frantic. The second, an hour later, was slower, more tender. Sometime around two, they both fell asleep.

So Randall Finley's phone call, only three and a half hours later, was as rude a wake-up call as one could get.

David quickly explained. "Finley. I'm helping him with his campaign. He wants to be mayor again."

"I never heard of him," Sam said, pushing herself up, leaning against the headboard, making no effort to cover her naked breasts with a sheet.

"He was mayor before you moved here. Had a rather spectacular flameout that involved, among other things, an underage hooker. Now he's trying for a comeback."

"Can you come back from something like that?"

David thought. "If anyone can, Finley's the one. Look, I've got a ton of calls to make. Mind if I jump in the shower?"

Samantha smiled. "I'll join you."

Forty minutes later—nearly half of that in the shower—they came out the front door of Samantha's house, David walking down to the curb to his car while Sam, her hair still wet, locked her front door. She had a small bag with her with a change of clothes, and a lunch, for her son.

"You know what might be fun?" Sam asked.

"More fun than we just had?"

"I was thinking—no, forget it."

"No, what?"

"I'm moving too fast. It'll sound pushy."

"It's okay," David said. "Just tell me."

"It's just, the boys seem to be getting along okay after a bumpy start, and maybe sometime we could do something with them. The four of us."

"Yeah, sure. I'd like that. What'd you have in mind?"

"I don't know. A movie, or maybe even—you ever been camping?"

"Camping? Like, in a tent?"

She grinned. "Yes, in a tent. With sleeping bags and burnt marshmallows and mosquitoes. The whole deal."

"I've never been camping. You take Carl camping?"

"A couple of times we've gone up to Lake Luzerne. A place called Camp Sunrise."

As she said it, the sun started making an appearance.

"Let's talk about that," David said. "It could be fun."

As David held open the passenger door, she asked, "How are we going to explain this, exactly, to the boys?"

"We don't have to explain," he said. "We're adults."

"You telling me Ethan won't have questions? Carl sure will."

David smiled resignedly. "My mom, too."

Sam grinned at him. "Should I be seeing a man who still lives with his parents?"

"I don't live with my parents—they live with *me*. And not for much longer, I hope."

David closed the door, walked around to the driver's side, and got in behind the wheel. Sam leaned across, kissed his cheek, and said, "This was good. I like you. But I'm not one of those girls who's going to be waiting for you to call. You call, great. You don't, I'll get the message. I can handle it. You don't have to worry about me."

David turned in his seat and looked at her. "I'll be calling."

Sam's face had appeared ready to crack into a thousand pieces. Now it didn't have to. "Okay," she said.

"Let's get our boys ready for school," he said, and turned the key.

The car pulled away from the curb. Half a block back, Ed

366

Noble sat in Garnet and Yolanda Worthington's Cadillac and watched them leave.

The two of them together, he thought. The fucker who kicked his face in, and Carl's slutty mom.

He could take care of everything at once. Kill two birds with one stone. Literally. Make Garnet and Yolanda's troubles go away, and get even with that Harwood guy. Yolanda could give him the money Garnet was seriously thinking of giving to Samantha to shut her up. What a stupid idea that was. Okay, Ed probably wouldn't get as much as Samantha might have, but it'd be a nice chunk of change.

The kid would end up back with the grandparents, and everything would be fuckin' hunky-dory. Except for maybe the fact that Ed was going to have to hide out for the next several years. But with that cash to keep him going, that wouldn't be a problem. It wasn't like Ed had close family he'd miss. His parents were dead, and he had just the one sister, who, last he heard, was living on the street in Pittsburgh.

Once he came into some money, the last thing he'd want to do was have her find out. She'd want to upgrade her Frigidaire shipping container to a cardboard Miele box.

It had been quite a scene in the hotel room the night before when Yolanda urged her husband to consider Ed's idea of taking Samantha out of the picture altogether. The guy just about blew a gasket. Saying they were in enough trouble as it was. Yolanda arguing that they were already in up to their necks—they might as well go for broke.

Garnet's face had gone deep red. Ed was pretty sure he was going to grab Yolanda by the throat and strangle her.

So Ed spoke up, said, "Okay, okay, forget it." Gave Yolanda a wink, then said maybe it was time for him to move on. If Yolanda could give him a lift to the bus station, or get him to Albany, where he could catch a train, he'd get out of their hair once and for all.

Yolanda piped up, "That sounds good to me."

Garnet said, "Get him the hell out of my sight."

Once Yolanda and Ed were in the parking lot, she handed him the keys to the Caddy. "Do what you got to do. Once it's done, Garnet will come around. I'll pay you well—don't you worry about that. All I got to do now is sit in the coffee shop long enough for him to think I actually drove you to the bus station."

Ed took the keys and was heading for the driver's door when Yolanda said, "Hold up a sec."

She was reaching into her purse for something, handed it over.

Ed got in the car and went hunting for Samantha. She showed up at her house around midnight, with the Harwood guy. When he didn't come back out after half an hour, Ed knew the guy was getting his knob polished, and probably wouldn't be coming out till morning. So he parked on the street and set his phone to wake him up at six. When he opened his eyes, Harwood's car was still there. Half an hour later, the two lovebirds came out.

He'd follow them, see where things led. Wait for an opportunity. He knew this much: He wasn't going to try to run them off the road. Garnet would be some pissed if he put a scratch on his Caddy. He had options, what with Yolanda giving him that little something before he got in the car. Ed reached over to the passenger seat, made sure it was still there.

A pistol. A Ruger LCP. A perfect gun for a woman,

light, easy to carry in a reasonably sized purse. Ed didn't mind that it was a bit girlie if it did the job.

Yolanda had said, "I carry it around a lot. You never know when you are going to run into bad people."

FIFTY-ONE

Cal

"What is it?" Lucy Brighton asked as I returned the phone to my jacket.

"An old friend, a detective with the Promise Falls police," I said. "He needs to see me."

"What about?"

"Don't know," I said, doing up my pants, and feeling a little silly about it.

"You have to go right now?"

I nodded. I gave her a quick kiss. "Okay if I call you later?"

Lucy nodded. "Sure, yeah. I was thinking I'd have to do the rest of the funeral arrangements today, but that sort of falls to Miriam, don't you think?"

"Have you talked to her? Since finding out she wasn't in the car with your father?"

Lucy shook her head. "I hardly know what to say to her."

"She hasn't called you?"

Another head shake. She set her lips firmly together. "I'll call her. After you leave. Tell her what I've done so far where my father's concerned."

"Okay," I said. "Talk to you later."

We walked to the front door. "Oh, for God's sake," Lucy said.

I saw that she was looking at Crystal's bagged lunch. She must have set it down when she retied her shoe, then forgot to take it with her.

"I swear," Lucy said. "And with all I have to do today, I—"

"Let me," I said. "I'll drop it off for her by her lunchtime."

"I can't let—"

"It's no trouble, really."

Lucy told me which school, and when Crystal's lunch was, and, grinning, said she would call ahead to let the staff know some really strange man was coming by with something for her.

I went out to my car. Duckworth had asked to meet me at Kelly's, a downtown diner. I found him in a booth, a cup of coffee in front of him, and a plate, judging by the red smears on it, that had once had cherry pie on it.

We shook hands as I slid in opposite him. "How's things, Barry?"

"Good, good," he said, then pointed to the plate and grimaced. "Didn't really have time for breakfast this morning."

"The pie's always been good here," I said. "And you can never go wrong with pie for breakfast."

"Maureen might be a bit skeptical about that," Barry said.

"How is she?"

"Good."

"And Trevor?"

Barry Duckworth smiled. "You're good, remembering that. He's okay."

"You brought him in to work the odd time, showed him around. But that was a long time ago. I'm guessing he's about four feet taller now."

"He is, he is. And how about you? You settling in back here?"

"I suppose. Although I may be looking for new digs. I'm living over that bookshop that got hit with a Molotov cocktail last night."

Barry blinked. "I don't even know about that. I know about the bus."

"What bus?" I asked.

We filled each other in. He mentioned the number on the back of the bus, and I told him I'd heard about his news conference, about the strange series of events that seemed to be linked.

"Let me ask you this," Barry said. "Is it possible what happened at your place is in any way connected to these other things?"

I thought about that. "No appearance of your infamous twenty-three that I noticed. It was pretty straightforward. Couple of yahoos blaming Naman for the drive-in thing because supposedly he has a terrorist's name."

"Assholes," Duckworth said. "Anyway, the reason I asked you here . . ."

Barry reached into his pocket for something and laid one of my business cards on the table.

"I already have one of those," I said.

"Guess where I found this," he said.

It wasn't as though I'd handed out a thousand of them since I'd returned to Promise Falls. But I had handed out a few. Most recently, to Adam Chalmers's ex-wife Felicia. And I'd handed one to Miriam the night before when she found me in her house.

"Tell me," I said. "It'll save us some time."

"At the Chalmers house. Adam and Miriam Chalmers. You know them?"

"I never met Adam," I admitted. "Miriam, yes."

"Many times?"

"Just once."

"When was that?"

"For God's sake, Barry, just tell me what's going on."

Barry Duckworth took a sip of his coffee. "She died last night. Looks like someone pushed her down the stairs. Broke her neck."

You try to be cool, acting all the time as though nothing surprises you. But my jaw dropped. "What?"

He told me again.

I let that sink in for a moment. "And you found my card there."

"That's right."

I thought about Lucy, and whether she'd yet tried to get in touch with Miriam about funeral arrangements. I hoped she wasn't planning to drop in on her in person. But if the house was a crime scene, she wasn't going to be able to get close to it. Still, a heads-up was in order. She'd be as stunned as I'd just been.

"Someone needs to know this," I told Barry. "Right away." I got out my phone and dialed Lucy's house.

"Cal?"

"Something's happened," I told her.

"What?"

"Have you tried to call Miriam?"

"I'm kind of working up to it."

"Don't. Miriam's dead."

A stunned silence.

"You there?" I'd managed, so far, to avoid saying Lucy's name in front of Duckworth.

"But wait," she said. "You mean she *was* killed at the drive-in? They were right the first time? But you saw her.

You told me you *saw* her. You *talked* to her."

"I did. It happened later."

"God, no."

Barry ran a finger along his plate, gathered up a few crust crumbs and some leftover cherry pie filling, and licked it.

"Cal, how . . . ? Was she killed?"

"Yes. I'm going to have to tell the police why I was at the house."

"You'll have to tell them . . . about that room?"

"My guess is if they haven't found it yet, they will."

"Tell them whatever you have to tell them," Lucy said.

"I'll call you later," I said. "I'll know more then."

My coffee arrived as I was putting my phone away.

Barry was tapping my business card. A slow, steady beat.

"I gave her my card," I said.

"When?"

I hesitated. Even though I had Lucy's blessing to tell Barry everything, it was in my nature to want to hold things back.

Barry said, "You know I could take you in. You were clearly in that house, maybe the last person to see her alive, and that could make you a person of interest." He smiled. "But I like ya. So talk to me. When did you give her the card?"

"Last night," I said. I gave him the time. Barry took out his notebook and scribbled something down.

"Why'd you go out to see her?"

"I didn't."

Barry cocked his head. "You weren't going out there to see her husband, were you?"

"No," I said. "I knew he was dead. The drive-in thing. I thought she was dead, too."

374

Barry said, "So you dropped by to leave your card in case one of them came back to life?"

I explained that I was already in the house. That I had been hired by Adam's daughter, Lucy Brighton. Told him why.

"You found the room?" I asked.

Barry, stone-faced, said, "We found *a* room."

"They called it the playroom," I said. "Adam and Miriam were part of the lifestyle."

"The lifestyle."

Now it was my chance to lord it over someone who didn't know. "Sex with other couples. Looks as though someone busted in, got into the room, and took some DVDs. Home movies, it looks like. Right after the screen came down. Lucy asked me to get them back."

Barry nodded slowly. "Did you?"

"No," I said.

"I thought you were good at this," the police detective said.

I forced a smile. "The client, wisely, I think, decided there wasn't much point in investing a fortune in their pursuit. I have an idea where the DVDs ended up and don't believe they pose a risk. My guess is they'll be destroyed."

"Destroyed by someone else who was on them," he said.

"That's my thinking," I said.

"You know who?"

I shrugged, drank some coffee. "I've got my suspicions. But I wasn't sure that it mattered in the overall scheme of things."

"It might now," Barry said.

"It might," I said.

"You going to tell me?"

"I'm thinking about it."

"I'll pay for your coffee if you tell me," he said. "You know what I make, and what a grand gesture that is."

"I think maybe the guy who runs security for Thackeray might have an interest."

"Duncomb?" Barry asked.

"You know him?"

"We've crossed paths." He appeared deep in thought for a moment, then studied me. I had a feeling he was debating whether to trust me. We had a history—a good one, for the most part, going back to when we worked together—so I figured he'd eventually decide I wasn't his number one suspect.

"Let me ask you something," he said. "Your opinion."

"Okay."

"If your wife was missing, and you didn't know where she was, and you were hanging out with a friend of yours hoping she'd turn up, would you be sitting around watching movies? Because I think that's what they were doing when I showed up last night."

I took another sip of coffee.

"I think it's unlikely," I said. "Which one has the missing wife?" I asked.

"The professor. Peter Blackmore."

"What's the wife's name?"

"Georgina," Barry Duckworth said.

"She was killed in the car with Adam," I said.

"Yup."

"Did they know that when they were sitting around watching movies?"

"I don't think so," Barry said. "I broke the news."

"You thinking maybe they weren't watching a Bruce Willis festival?"

"I don't think so. Blackmore hid the discs so I wouldn't see them. So why, at a time when you have to be wondering what's happened to your wife, do you sit around watching homemade porno?"

I thought about that. "This is going to cost you more than a coffee."

"You want a piece of pie? I'm thinking I might have another."

"Okay," I said.

Barry waved the waitress over. "I'll have a piece of the cherry," I said. "Can you put some whipped cream on it?"

"Jesus, like I'm made of money," Barry said.

"Sure thing," the waitress said. "How about you?" she asked Barry.

"You got blueberry?"

"Yup."

"I'll have a slice of that." As she walked away, Barry said, "Maureen says I need to eat more fruit."

"So what was the question?" I asked.

"Why do you sit around watching homemade porn when you should be worried about your missing wife?"

I gave that a second. "Because there's something on the DVD that worries you even more."

"Yeah."

While Barry was thinking about that, I had something on my mind that I hadn't decided to put on the table yet.

I was thinking about Felicia Chalmers sitting in her car down the block from Adam and Miriam's house before I got there last night. Before Miriam showed up. Before Miriam was murdered.

I'd seen Felicia drive away in my rearview mirror.

Now I was wondering if she might have gone back.

FIFTY-TWO

Clive Duncomb found Peter Blackmore in the professor's office around ten.

"Where the hell have you been?" Duncomb asked him.

Blackmore was in the same clothes he'd been wearing the night before. He was seated in the computer chair behind his desk, staring absently into the room. Looking in Duncomb's direction, but not seeing him.

"I'm talking to you," Duncomb said. "I went into the kitchen after talking to Miriam—with some very good news, by the way—and you were gone. Where the fuck did you go?"

Blackmore mumbled something.

"What?"

"Driving," he said. "I went for a drive."

"For the rest of the whole fucking night?"

"I guess. I drove around. Isn't this a free country?"

"You were supposed to go identify Georgina. Did you do that? Did you identify her?"

Blackmore eyed Duncomb as though he were speaking in a foreign language. "Did I what?"

"Identify her! For Christ's sake, snap out of it."

"No," he said quietly. "I didn't get around to it."

"There's things you have to do," the security chief said.

"You've got to go to the cops, identify her. Then they send her to the funeral home. What about her family? Have you called anyone in her family to let them know?"

"I told you," he said. "I was driving."

"Where did you go?"

Blackmore blinked a few times. "I don't remember, exactly."

"What are you even doing here at work? You shouldn't be here."

"Have a class," he said, shuffling some papers on his desk without really looking at them. "I think."

"Go home," Duncomb said, coming around the desk. "You're a mess." As he got closer, he said, "Jesus, you reek. Have you been drinking?"

"Maybe a little," he admitted.

"You can't drive home. I'll call you a taxi."

"I don't want to go home. I don't like it there. Keep thinking Georgina will walk in."

Duncomb grabbed Blackmore under the shoulders, hauled him up on his feet. As he did, he got a look at the professor's hands.

"What's that?"

"Huh?"

"On your hands. What's that?"

Blackmore examined his palms as though he'd never seen them before. "I think that's blood."

"What happened?"

"I fell," he said absently. "I pulled over at one point. Thought I was going to be sick. And I was." He smiled, as though proud of his ability to predict the near future. "I went down on my hands and knees. Think I cut my hand on the gravel."

"Jesus, we have to get you out of here."

"What good news?"

"Huh?"

"You said you had good news you wanted to tell me."

"I can tell you later when you're sober enough to remember it."

"No, tell me now. I could use some cheering up." He leaned in toward Duncomb, as though confiding a secret to him. "I've had a lot of tragedy in my life lately."

"The discs," Duncomb said. "The one we were looking for in particular, that we worried we couldn't find?"

"The one with Olivia?" Blackmore said, his voice going up.

"Keep your damn voice down!" he whispered. "Yes, the one with Olivia."

"What about it?"

"Adam had already disposed of it. It's gone. It's been gone for months."

Blackmore's eyes did another round of furious blinking, as though he were coming out of a deep sleep. "Wait, what? What did you say?"

"There's no video with Olivia Fisher. Or any of the other girls. Adam got rid of them. He only kept the ones with us. Bad enough if anyone had ever seen them, but at least they wouldn't have run the chance of seeing us dragged in for questioning."

"So Miriam didn't have them?" the professor asked.

"No. They're gone."

"Oh."

"Come on, Peter. It's one less thing for us to worry about."

Blackmore dropped back into his chair. "I suppose," he said.

"Suppose? Come on. We're fine. Everything's good now."

Blackmore swiveled in the chair and looked up at Duncomb. "No, Clive, it's not. We . . . did bad things . . ."

"Water under the bridge, my friend."

"How do you live with her?" Blackmore asked.

"What? What are you talking about?"

"Liz. How do you do it?"

"Peter, don't go there."

"How many men do you figure she's been with? I mean, she was a whore, right? You told me that's what she was."

"I never called her that. She ran a business, she—"

"Yeah, a *whore*house. How do you . . . how do you live with someone that unclean?"

"You need to stop talking, Peter."

"Don't you feel that way? I know I feel that way. Unclean. The things I did with her. The things we all did with each other. Sometimes, at night, in bed, it's like I can feel insects crawling around under my skin."

Blackmore was as easy a target as Duncomb had ever encountered. Sitting there, right in front of him. Duncomb drove a fist straight into the man's face. It knocked him, and the chair, over. Blackmore's arm caught his keyboard on the way down. It landed on his head.

Duncomb pulled the chair out of the way and hovered over Blackmore.

"Don't you ever talk that way about Liz again," he said.

Blackmore put his fingers to his lip, pulled them away, looked at the blood, then looked back up at Duncomb.

"Did you do it?"

"Do what?"

"Did you kill Olivia?"

"Jesus, Peter, I swear, you keep talking like this—" Duncomb raised his fist again.

"Go ahead," the professor said. "Hit me again. Go on. I won't try to stop you. But harder this time."

"You're drunk."

"I've never seen things more clearly. Hit me again!"

"Keep your voice down!"

"Go ahead! Beat the living shit out of me! I want to *feel* something! Come on!"

Duncomb crossed to the other side of the office, closed the door to reduce the likelihood anyone would hear what was going on. Blackmore was struggling to his feet, his head appearing above the desk. Once he could see his onetime friend, he smiled.

"I'm not afraid of you anymore."

Duncomb stared.

"You know why? Because I'm a man with nothing left to lose. A man with nothing left to lose has no reason to be afraid."

Duncomb kept his eyes trained on Blackmore for another five seconds, then said, "You need to get your shit together, Peter. See to Georgina. Take care of things. We have nothing to be worried about. We're going to get through all this."

"Just because those discs are gone doesn't mean those things never happened."

Duncomb chose his words carefully.

"You think you're beyond being afraid. Trust me when I tell you, you're not."

He left the office, not bothering to close the door.

Blackmore shouted after him, "I'm not your puppet anymore! You hear that, Clive? No more!"

Duncomb kept walking.

FIFTY-THREE

Ed Noble first followed David Harwood and Samantha Worthington back to what, he concluded, must be Harwood's house. Parked at the curb was the woman's car, the one Ed had slashed the tires on the previous afternoon.

Harwood pulled into the driveway and he and the woman got out. The woman was carrying a simple plastic bag.

Ed parked five houses back. He had to wait the better part of half an hour before there was any more action. Finally, however, Harwood and the woman came out with two boys. Of course, Ed recognized Carl—the little shit—but the other kid wasn't familiar to him. Ed figured that was the Harwood guy's brat.

The boys were decked out with backpacks. Carl stood next to his mother's car; the other boy positioned himself by Harwood's. But before either parent got into his or her vehicle, they conferred, face-to-face, almost head-to-head.

Ed tried to figure out what they might be saying. His best guess was that they were deciding they didn't need to take the boys to school separately. One of them could drop both of them off.

As if on cue, Sam said something to the kids and they

both jumped into the backseat of her car. But she was slow to follow. She and her fuck buddy—as if there were any doubt, Ed thought—were still talking.

Then they moved in for a quick hug, an equally fast kiss. Couldn't exactly get down and dirty with the boys there, could they?

They each got into their own car.

At which point, Ed was presented with a choice. Follow the woman, or follow the man?

Of course, if Yolanda were here right now, there'd be no question. It was his job to follow Samantha. Ed knew that was where the money was. Yolanda wasn't going to pay him a dime to off Harwood. She didn't give a shit one way or another about him.

But it was a different story for Ed. He really wanted to take the guy out of the picture. As long as the two of them had been together, he'd thought he had a shot—no pun intended—at that. Now it was a lost opportunity.

He could wait until the next time they were together. Judging by how lovey-dovey they were, it would probably be later today. But Ed didn't feel he had that long to get the job done. The police had to be looking for him, as well as Garnet and Yolanda. He had to get on with things.

So that meant following the woman.

Harwood's car headed off in one direction, Sam's in another. Harwood was headed toward Noble, so he scrunched down in the seat, trying to make himself invisible. It must have worked, because when he glanced in his mirror, he saw Harwood's Mazda receding into the distance.

He sat up straight, started the engine. He kept a good hundred yards behind Sam. There was a chance, Ed figured, that she knew what kind of car her former in-laws drove, so he didn't want to get close enough to spook her.

Just as he'd expected, Sam was heading for Clinton Public School. The last thing he wanted to do was get caught in that traffic clusterfuck of moms and vans, just in case someone recognized him in the car, so he held way back.

He could pretty much figure out where Sam was going to go next, anyway. It made some sense to get there before her.

So he drove to the Laundromat, parked down the street.

Sure enough, five minutes later, Sam showed up, drove to the lot behind the business, where he'd found the car the day before. She'd probably come in the back way. In another five minutes or so, the place would be open for business.

Ed figured, walk in and one pop to the head would do it.

The way he saw it, and for sure the way Yolanda saw it, if the police couldn't prove she'd ordered it, what choice would the authorities have but to give the kid to her and Garnet? And when Brandon got out of jail, so long as he behaved himself, he'd probably get custody.

A boy should be with his father, Ed reasoned.

A boy needed a man to teach him the ways of the world. A mother, even a good one, just couldn't do that. Ideally, a child needed two parents, one of each sex—none of this same-sex shit everyone was going on about—but if a boy could have only one, a father was the way to go, he reasoned. Ed supposed the opposite was true with a girl. If she had to be raised by one parent, better that it be the mother.

Ed Noble was something of a traditionalist in these matters.

Carl, years later, would probably look back at what was going to happen today as a good thing. A real turning point in his life.

Now that Ed knew Samantha was at work, he decided to park around back, too. When he came in, it would be through the back door. Walking in through the front, that hadn't been a very good strategy last time. Sam had seen him out there on the sidewalk before he'd even come through the door. Gave her too much time to think. Or run. Plus, there was the chance there'd be people in there doing their laundry.

Like that dipshit who threw soap in his face.

Yeah, back door was the way to go.

He reached over for the gun on the seat next to him. Time to get this done.

FIFTY-FOUR

Cal

Once my pie arrived, I couldn't think of any good reason not to tell Barry Duckworth about Adam's former wife Felicia being parked down the street from the Chalmers house.

"Son of a bitch," he said. "You talked to her?"

I told him of our short conversation. "If she had plans to kill Miriam, she didn't get around to mentioning it," I said.

"But when you saw her, she wouldn't even have known Miriam was still alive."

I nodded slowly. "That's right. She said she'd been talking to a lawyer, about whether she might have any claims on Adam's estate, what with Miriam being dead." I paused. "She seems to think she has a claim, although what it might be, I don't know. If she came back, she might have seen Miriam pull into the driveway. Just before Miriam came into the house and found me."

"That would have been quite a shock," Barry said.

"Far be it from me to tell you how to do your job," I said, "but you might want to have a word with her." I gave him her address.

He smiled. "You shouldn't have quit." A reference, I figured, to my leaving the Promise Falls police, moving to Griffon, north of Buffalo near the Canadian border, and going private. "You were a decent cop."

I hadn't had much choice. I'd nearly beaten to death a man who'd fled a fatal hit-and-run. It had all been caught on my dash cam. The chief at the time made the video disappear in return for my resignation.

Now, when I thought back to that lapse in judgment, I realized just how catastrophic it had been. If I hadn't assaulted that driver, I wouldn't have lost my job, we wouldn't have moved to Griffon, and I wouldn't have been drawn into an ugly mess that took the lives of my wife, Donna, and son, Scott.

I lose my cool for five seconds and everything changes.

"I was a lousy cop," I said. "I was a stupid cop."

"Not so stupid that I won't bounce something off you. Something totally unrelated to all this other shit."

"What?"

"This business with the number twenty-three."

"Yeah?" I said.

"Any ideas? Other than it being the age when you thought you'd finally lose your virginity."

I shook my head. "The Twenty-third Psalm."

"Jesus, that's all anyone thinks of. And maybe that's it, but even if it is, what the hell is the message this guy's sending by referring to it?"

I finished my pie. "And that is why you get the big bucks. Thanks for the pie, Barry. I gotta go see if I still have a place to live."

There was yellow tape strung across the burned-out front of Naman's Books that also blocked the door to the stairs that led up to my apartment. I stood a moment on the sidewalk, surveying the damage. Naman was there with some kind of handyman, putting up sheets of plywood where the windows once had been.

"Naman," I said.

He turned, saw me. No hint of a smile, but you could hardly blame him for that.

"Cal," he said. He waved his arm toward the mess. "Look at this. Just look at it."

"I'm so sorry."

"It's all over for me."

"Maybe not."

"We'll see. The insurance lady comes today. She already told me, all my books, because they are secondhand, because they are old, that they are probably worth nothing. I had thousands of dollars' worth of books, Cal. Thousands. And they say they will give me nothing? What did I have insurance for? And hardly any of my books caught on fire. Most of them are soaked. All ruined by the stupid firemen."

"They had to put out the fire," I said. "If the books hadn't gotten wet, they'd all have eventually burned anyway. The building is still standing. It can be fixed. And, Naman, I know this is maybe hard to appreciate, but you're okay. You weren't hurt. Those idiots who did this, they could have killed you."

Me, too.

He gave me a look that felt like a knife going in. "You are no better than any of the rest of them. '*Be thankful. It could have been worse. Don't make waves. Don't rock the boat.*'"

"That's not what I said. I'm just glad you're okay. I'll help you. What can I do?"

"I don't need your help," Naman snapped. "Go find somewhere else to live. That's what you're going to do, right?"

389

I glanced over at the door to my apartment. There was a sticker on it, posted by the fire department, saying I could not enter the premises without being escorted by a member of the department.

"I'll talk to you later," I told Naman, walked over to the door, ripped off the sticker, and went upstairs to my place.

There was no visible damage, but the place stank. Naman was right. I couldn't live here. Not for some time probably, if ever. It could be weeks, or months, before the building was repaired, the power turned back on.

So I started packing.

I dragged two suitcases from the closet, and filled them not with clothes but with files, bills, a laptop, a handful of books.

The framed pictures on my dresser of Donna and Scott. Perhaps the only items of any real value here.

The thing was, it was amazing how little stuff I had. When I'd emptied out the house in Griffon, and brought it to Promise Falls, most of it—all the furniture—went into a storage unit. I'd thought when I moved back here, I might someday get a house, but I quickly realized how unlikely that was. What did I need a house for? Even this small apartment was more space than I really needed. So I sold the furniture to a wholesaler about a year later and got rid of the storage unit.

The prospect of ever sharing space with another person, or persons, had seemed so remote I saw no reason to hang on to it.

Which made me, now, think of Lucy and her daughter, Crystal.

I was a long way from considering anything serious with Lucy. And yet, she was the first woman, since I'd lost

Donna, I could even imagine settling down with. Perhaps that was the intoxicating quality of sex. I hadn't been sure, for the longest time, whether I could allow myself that pleasure again. It had seemed wrong, somehow. Disloyal. So the previous night had been something of a milestone. It had, somehow, allowed me to consider a future that was not just about grieving.

I liked Lucy. I knew I wanted to see her again.

But first things first.

I opened a dresser drawer, took out some underwear and socks, brought them up to my nose. The smoke smell wasn't just coming from the room around me. It was in the clothes. If it had permeated into the dresser, I was sure all the items I had hanging in the closet—including a couple of suits— would be even worse.

There was a box of garbage bags in the cabinet under the kitchen sink. I grabbed three and began stuffing clothes into them. The suits and dress shirts I'd drop off at the dry cleaner's. Everything else I could deal with at the Laundromat.

There wasn't anything to be saved from the fridge. Given that the power had been off since the night before, nothing was still cold. I poured milk and cream down the sink. Filled a garbage bag with just about everything else. Packaged items in the cupboard—cereal, sugar, peanut butter—struck me as too much to bother with for now, so I left them there.

It took four trips to get everything I was taking with me down to the car. The stuff I'd be taking to a new home I put in the trunk; the bags of clothes went into the backseat.

I went back to the apartment for one last thing.

I kept my gun in a locked box in the top of the closet.

I brought it down, opened it.

I didn't like the idea of leaving a firearm in the car, even in a locked box. Someone could steal it, bust it open later.

So I took the gun out of the box, put it into a holster that fixed to my belt at my side. I had a carry permit, and my sport jacket obscured most views of it.

Time to go.

I parked illegally out front of the dry cleaner's first, left the flashers going. I took in my suits and dress shirts, grabbed a ticket, then got back into the car and drove the rest of the way to the Laundromat. I found a spot on the street and lugged the three bags in, in one trip.

"Hey," said Sam, who was going from washer to washer, unlocking the coin box, dumping quarters into her small canvas bag with the leather drawstring.

"How are you?" I asked. I apologized to her again for not being able to get to the school in time the day before to help her. "But that other guy, David. He came through."

Sam smiled. "He did, didn't he?"

"Still, if you're ever in a jam again, and want to give me another try, feel free to call," I told her. "Although I hope you never need anyone's help like that again."

"Appreciate that."

"Did they get the guy?"

She set the bag of coins on a washer lid. They landed with a heavy thunk. "They're looking. And not just for him, but for my ex-husband's parents, too, who most likely put him up to it."

"I think I can see why you wanted out of that family," I said.

"He—Garnet, my former father-in-law—is almost

a decent human being. *Almost*. But Yolanda, his wife, I swear, there's something wrong with her. Things aren't wired right in her head. She really thinks she can just grab Carl and raise him herself, that there aren't going to be repercussions for that. It's like normal rules of society don't apply to her. She's a dangerous woman."

"Are you concerned for your safety today?"

Sam hesitated. "I don't think so. And I got Carl to school okay, and everyone there knows that he doesn't go anywhere with anyone except me. I'm going to pick him up today and every day for a while, until they find Ed. I mean, they'd have to be totally insane to try anything today after what happened yesterday."

"Let's hope so," I said.

She scanned my bags of laundry. "No matter how much shit happens in the world, we still have to stop and clean our clothes, right?"

I nodded. "Good thing there's no one else here. I may use up every machine in the place."

"Why so much stuff?"

I told her about the fire.

"Jesus," Sam said, hoisting the bag of coins, looping the drawstring around her wrist. "Is this town going to hell or what?"

I'd made no attempt to sort the clothes by color before jamming them into the garbage bags, and now found myself trying to organize things.

Sam said, "Nothing even looks dirty." She picked up a T-shirt at random, put it to her nose, made a face. "I can smell the smoke."

"Yeah," I said, shaking my head.

She loosened the drawstring, reached into the bag, and put at least a dozen quarters in my hand. "On the house."

"That's okay," I said.

Sam rolled her eyes. "You were there for me yesterday. This is the *least* I can do." She drew the string tight, looped it around her wrist.

"Thanks," I said.

Sam continued to empty money out of the other machines while I stuffed clothes into half a dozen of them, poured in soap, loaded the quarters, then drove them home. I was going to sit down, open up a browser on my phone, start looking for apartments for rent in Promise Falls, when I realized I hadn't locked my car.

"Nuts," I said.

"What?" Sam asked.

"Left the car unlocked."

I went out to the curb, intending to lock the car from a distance with the remote, but noticed the front passenger window was down halfway. I walked over to the car, dropped my butt into the driver's seat, one foot still on the pavement, and slid in the key far enough for auxiliary power to raise the window.

That was when I noticed Crystal's comic book adventures on the seat next to me. Sorry, *graphic novel*.

And her lunch.

"Shit," I said to myself. I looked at my watch. There was still time to get my laundry done before Crystal would be expecting her lunch. Maybe, by then, I'd also have had a chance to look at her book and let her know what I thought of it.

I grabbed the stapled pages, locked up the car, and went back into the Laundromat. Sam wasn't around. The door to the office at the back was closed. In there, I guessed.

I dropped my butt into a molded plastic chair, shifting

the holstered gun at my side slightly so it wasn't digging into me, and set Crystal's book in my lap.

The title page, adorned with bold, two-inch-high letters, read: "Noises in the Night by Crystal Brighton."

With a black marker, she'd covered over the entire page, just leaving the letters in white.

I flipped over to page one, careful not to rip the cover from the single staple in the upper left corner. The drawing featured a small girl in her bedroom, late at night, moonlight filtering through the curtained window, covers pulled up to her nose. The girl's eyes were open, and she looked frightened.

The artwork was especially good. The kid, odd though she might be, had real talent.

I flipped over to the second page. Glancing through the coming pages, I saw that Crystal had used all kinds of paper indiscriminately. There were plenty of standard sheets of printer paper, but I guessed when she'd run short, she went to whatever was at hand. The back side of a pale green flyer for Cutter Landscaping, a pink sheet for a maid service. No doubt to her mother's chagrin, she'd drawn all over the back side of a page that detailed school board enrollment projections.

I wondered how long Lucy might have been looking for that.

But it was clearly Crystal's work that was more engaging. As I read on, the little girl, whose name, not surprisingly, was Crystal, slipped out from under the covers and went to the window. "Who is it?" she was saying. "Who's out there? What do you want?"

A word bubble emerged from the darkness. "We are waiting for you."

"Who?" the cartoon Crystal asked. "Who is it? What do

you want?" The girl ran down the stairs and out the front door. "Is it you, Grandpa?" she asked. "Is it you?"

"Come into the woods," the voice said. "Come into the woods and find out who it is."

I glanced up for a second, noticed that the light had gone off on one of my washers. Still holding the book, I got out of my seat and went to investigate.

I opened the lid, saw my clothes sitting there in still water. I hit the start button again, but nothing happened. Maybe, I thought, the lid had to be closed for the machine to kick in again, so I dropped it down, hit the start button again.

Nothing.

"Sam?" I called out, glancing in the direction of the closed office door. "I think I got a bum washer here!"

I waited for the door to open, or for her to shout back from inside the office, but neither happened.

"Sam!" I shouted again, then thought maybe she was on the phone.

Decided to go check.

FIFTY-FIVE

The Chalmers-Duncomb-Blackmore triangle was starting to gel in Barry Duckworth's mind. The three couples
had been friends. Georgina Blackmore had been in Adam
Chalmers's car when the screen came down. The six of
them were in some kind of group-sex *lifestyle* thing.

There was that *room*.

And, according to Cal Weaver, there were sex videos,
which someone had spirited out of that house in a hurry
after word spread that Adam and Miriam had been killed
in an accident.

Except Miriam hadn't been killed.

Not then.

But she'd been murdered since her return home. And
it happened after Duckworth had delivered the news that
she was still alive to Duncomb and Blackmore—who
were busy having a DVD viewing fest when he'd arrived.

You didn't have to be Sherlock Holmes to think all
those things were connected.

Duncomb, Duckworth concluded, was one tough son
of a bitch. But the professor wasn't. He was the weak link.
Duckworth figured if he could get that man alone in a
room, he'd talk. If he didn't confess to Miriam Chalmers's murder himself, he'd point Duckworth in the right
direction.

Plus, there was the ex-wife, Felicia Chalmers. Cal had seen her parked down the street from the Chalmers home shortly before Miriam showed up.

Duckworth wondered what one called a group of suspects. It was a gaggle for geese. Herd for cows. Pack for wolves.

Too bad the collective for crows was a *murder*. It would be so appropriate here for suspects. A *murder* of suspects. But since that was taken, maybe a *guilt* of suspects. A *suspicion* of suspects.

Maybe he had more important things to think about.

When he got to Felicia Chalmers's building, he buzzed her apartment from the lobby. When there was no answer, he hit the button for the superintendent. A short, dark-haired man in a checked shirt with rolled-up sleeves finally showed up. Once Duckworth had shown his ID, the man answered his questions.

"I think she works today," he told Duckworth. "This is Tuesday, right? She gets Sunday, Monday off. If you think she's done something wrong, I don't think so. She's good people. She never causes me any trouble."

"You know where she works?"

"Nissan."

"What?"

"Nissan dealer," he said. "She sells cars."

Duckworth headed for Promise Falls Nissan. He parked in the visitors' area and entered the showroom, where new cars sparkled under the artificial light. He was barely three steps into the showroom when he was pounced upon by a young, eager-looking man in a blue suit.

"How can I help you today?" he said, flashing teeth with a game-show smile.

"I'm looking for Felicia Chalmers," he said.

"Are you sure? Because if you're looking to get into something new, I can certainly help you."

"No, it's Ms. Chalmers I want to see."

The man's face fell. He turned to a woman sitting behind the reception desk and said, "Can you help this guy find Felicia?" Dejected, he wandered off. The woman picked up her phone and instantly her voice could be heard throughout the building. "Felicia? Come to reception."

Seconds later, Felicia Chalmers approached. She'd learned to smile at the same place as the other salesperson.

"You were looking for me?" she said, extending a hand.

"Barry Duckworth," he said. "I wonder if I could talk to you."

"Of course! Follow me to my office."

It was actually a desk surrounded on three sides by gray-fabric-covered partitions. Felicia slipped in behind the desk and motioned to Duckworth to take a chair.

"So you're looking to get a new car?" she asked.

"I'm afraid not," he said.

"Oh. Well, if you're looking for something previously owned, I could have you talk to Gary, but lease payments are so reasonable, it's not hard to get into something new and not have to worry about—"

"I'm with the Promise Falls police." He flashed his ID for the second time in less than an hour. "I'm a detective."

"Oh! I see. If this is about the car that went missing, you should really be talking to the manager."

"A missing car?"

"It was weeks ago. Someone took an Xterra out for a test-drive and never came back. He showed us a driver's license, but it turned out to be bogus."

"That's not why I'm here."

"Oh. Okay."

"I want to ask why you were parked out front of your ex-husband's house last night."

She couldn't have looked any more stunned if he'd stood up and dropped his pants in front of her.

"I'm sorry, what?"

"Last night. You were seen parked in your car near the home of Adam and Miriam Chalmers. I'd like to ask you about that."

"Uh, I was just . . . sitting there is all."

"Why?"

"Well . . . you know he died, right?"

"Yes, I do."

"And I guess I was feeling—I don't know—a little sad. Thinking about our life together. I was out driving and I went by the house where I once had a life with him. Is there a law against that? This has been kind of an upsetting time for me."

"And yet here you are at work, only a couple of days later."

"What am I supposed to do? Sit around at home and mope? Look, Adam was an okay guy, and I feel sick about what happened, but you have to move on, you know?"

Duckworth asked, "What time did you get there? Last night."

She shook her head. "I don't even know. Maybe eight or nine? Maybe a little after that?"

"Did you get out of your car? Did you go up to the house? Knock on the door?"

"No."

"What time did you leave?"

Felicia thought. "This man came by—he's a detective?

400

He'd been out to see me yesterday morning. Weaver? He came by and saw me, and that was when I left." A light-bulb went off. "Hang on, is he the one who told you I was there?"

"You didn't go back?"

"What's this about?" she asked. "So what if I went out there?" When Duckworth didn't answer right away, she said, "Look, I'll level with you."

He sat up in his chair. "Okay."

"I've been telling my lawyer I should be entitled to something as Adam's only surviving ex, to some kind of claim on the estate. He says it'll go to the daughter, but there has to be a loophole somewhere, right? I mean, we were still in touch. I gave him emotional support. Right? So I was kind of checking out the neighborhood, seeing if there were houses for sale. Then I was going to look them up online, see what they were going for. I mean, I don't know what Adam might have left. In terms of an estate, you know? He kind of went through money. But just in case, I wanted to—"

Duckworth leaned forward. "You didn't see Miriam Chalmers arrive home last night? You'd left by then?"

Felicia's mouth opened, but it took a few seconds for her to find the words she wanted to say. Turned out to be only one: "What?"

"Last night, did you witness Miriam Chalmers return home?"

"What—what are you talking about? Miriam's dead. She died in the accident with Adam."

"Miriam wasn't killed in the drive-in bombing."

"Oh no," Felicia said.

"Oh no?"

She tried to recover. "I mean, wow. I had no idea she

401

was alive. But wasn't someone killed in the car with Adam? They said someone was with him."

"Someone was. But it wasn't Miriam."

"Who?"

"Do you know someone named Georgina Blackmore?"

Felicia shook her head. "Georgina? I think Adam might have mentioned her, but . . . holy shit. This changes everything. I'm going to have to call my lawyer, tell him . . . I can't believe this." She cleared her throat, shuffled some car brochures on her desk, raised her head, an actress getting ready to shift roles. "Well, then, my heart goes out to Miriam. What a terrible tragedy for her. But at least she's okay. So, maybe I'm not Adam's only surviving ex-wife. And that's fine. I probably wasn't entitled to anything anyway. Not that this is about me."

She went to reach for the desk phone, then pulled her hand back. "I don't understand why you're here. What difference does it make where I was parked or what I was doing last night?"

"Did you see anyone else, other than Mr. Weaver, last night, around the Chalmers home?"

"No. No one. What is going on?"

"You're still Adam's only surviving ex-wife," Duckworth told her. "I wouldn't call off your lawyer just yet. There may still be a silver lining in this for you."

FIFTY-SIX

David Harwood was bordering on being proud of himself.

There were two TV news trucks out of Albany, each with its own camera operator and an on-air talking head, and reporters from the *Times Union* newspaper and WGY, the news-talk station. The vehicles were lined up along the street next to Promise Falls Park, the cascading water making the perfect backdrop for the news conference.

Okay, so maybe CNN wasn't here. Matt Lauer hadn't made the trek up from Rockefeller Center to do a live feed back to New York. But this wasn't bad, David felt. He'd made some hurried calls to people he knew at the two TV stations, the newspaper, and WGY. He'd called some other news outlets, too, and they'd passed. But this wasn't bad. Getting two TV stations here was definitely a plus.

David was chatting with the assembled press, telling them that the onetime mayor on the comeback trail had a couple of announcements to make. One, that he'd be running once again for mayor of Promise Falls, and two . . . well, they'd have to wait for that one. But they'd be glad they showed up.

"Mr. Finley will be here shortly," David said, then excused himself to run over to see Finley, who was hunkered down behind the wheel of his car. David got in on the passenger side.

"We're good to go," he said.

"That's all you could get here?" Finley asked.

"Are you kidding? This is better than I could have hoped for. Especially on such short notice. It's only been a few hours since you decided this *had* to be done today."

"Did you call Anderson Cooper?"

"Seriously?"

"I'm a good human interest story, David," Finley said. "Everyone loves a comeback story."

"If you were Richard Nixon coming back from the grave, that *might* get Anderson Cooper here," David told him. "But you're not. This is a good crowd. Not one, but two Albany TV stations. I didn't think that would happen. This is good, Randy. Trust me."

"I guess," he said.

"But there's something I want to tell you. Before you go out there, I want to make something clear between us."

"What?"

"Don't ever pull that kind of shit you tried with me yesterday."

Finley's face was a mask of innocence. "What are you talking about?"

"Talking about my wife, about how much my son knows about her. Hinting that maybe you could be the one to fill him in."

"I was just making conversation."

"I told him last night. In fact, there wasn't that much to tell. He'd already found out everything about her online. There aren't any secrets anymore. So I'm telling you, don't think you can hold that over me. You won't

404

ever blackmail me into working for you. You get that?"

Finley nodded slowly. "I believe I do. But, David, you've totally misjudged me here. I—"

"Save it for them." David tipped his head in the direction of the gathered media. "We gonna do this thing?"

"We are," Finley said, and pulled on the door handle.

They walked over together, David letting Finley lead the way. Finley smiled as he approached the small press pack, and at that moment David realized the huge mistake he had made.

The former mayor was going before the cameras alone.

Where were the supporters? Where were members of Randall Finley's immediate and extended family? Where were the regular, everyday Promise Falls folk who wanted to see their town on the rebound? Why hadn't David rounded up some people who'd lost their jobs because of the Five Mountains closing? How hard would it have been to find a few former coworkers who'd lost their jobs when the *Standard* went under?

Shit shit shit.

No, but wait. There was still time for all that. This was not Finley's first and *last* news conference. There'd be plenty more. And the point of bringing out the media today was Finley's bombshell. No sense confusing the message.

Whatever, exactly, that message was.

David hadn't been able to get specifics out of Finley. He'd wanted to write his remarks for him, but Finley said he was going to do it off the cuff. He didn't need a prepared speech. He didn't need notes. A real politician, he told David, talks from his heart, not from a fucking teleprompter.

David knew that approach was risky, but decided to be

optimistic. Maybe this would go just fine.

"Thank you all for coming," Finley said, positioning himself so the falls were behind him, but not so close that they would drown out what he had to say. "Everybody ready to go?"

The two men carrying video cameras moved in closer. The guys from the *Times Union* and the radio station were holding out microphones.

"You people know me," he began. "I'm Randall Finley, and today I'd like to talk to you from the heart about something that means the world to me. This town—the town of Promise Falls—and its people."

Should have brought a crowd, David thought. *I'm an amateur at this.*

"Look at what's happened in this town since I was mayor. An amusement park that was supposed to bring us jobs has packed up. The corporation behind a private-enterprise prison that was going to set up here changed its mind. Businesses small and large have left. The town is cutting back on basic maintenance and infrastructure upgrades."

Finley paused for dramatic effect. "If only our problems were just economic, maybe we could find a way out. But the problems here go much deeper, my friends. This is a town that's living in fear. This is a town where people are afraid to leave their doors unlocked even when they're home, in the middle of the day. There is, and I think some of you may snicker when I say this, but there's an evil in this town. Something's very wrong.

"Just the other week, I witnessed a ritualistic slaughter of animals. Threatening messages were scrawled onto mannequins on the Five Mountains Ferris wheel. Last night, a bus in flames barreled down one of this town's main streets. And clearly worst of all, a madman bombed the drive-in screen outside town, killing four people. That was an act of terrorism that shocked not only this town but the entire country. And now we know that those incidents are all strangely linked. The police admitted as much yesterday, but do they have anyone in custody? Do they even have any leads? If they do, they're sure not telling us. They'd rather keep us in a permanent state of unease."

David heard a car pulling up at the curb. He craned his neck around, saw someone watching from behind the wheel. It was that detective. Barry Duckworth.

"Unbelievable," Finley continued. "How could these kinds of things happen here? What happened at the Constellation, that has every indication of being a terrorist act. And what's being done? Someone blows up a drive-in theater today, and gets away with it, what will they do tomorrow? I repeat, what will they do tomorrow?"

Duckworth had gotten out of his car and was slowly walking across the park, listening.

"But this evil that has infected our town didn't just happen in the last couple of weeks. It has been festering for three years. For three years at least. It began right here, right where we're standing." Another pause. Duckworth had taken a position behind the cameras, arms folded, watching.

"This is the spot where a young woman named Olivia Fisher was brutally murdered. You all remember that night, I know you do. It was a monstrous crime, and three years have gone by without an arrest.

"Perhaps you think that case has been closed. Maybe you're thinking about that recent case, the murder of Rosemary Gaynor. The police would have you believe her doctor killed her to cover up an illegal adoption. But what the police haven't told you is how astonishingly similar the murders of Rosemary Gaynor and Olivia Fisher were, and how unlikely it is the doctor could have committed both. Which means there's a killer out there. A sick, sadistic killer waiting to strike again. And he may very well be the same person who's embarked on a campaign of terror against this town. Mr. Twenty-three, they're calling him."

Duckworth unfolded his arms.

"But it gets worse," Finley said, his voice rising. "The Promise Falls police were slow in recognizing the connection between these two crimes. They lost valuable time putting the pieces together. And the blame for that can be laid right at the door of the chief of police."

Duckworth spotted David, closed in on him, grabbed his arm, and said, "What the hell is going on here?"

"He's running for mayor," he whispered.

"What's this bullshit about Olivia Fisher and Rosemary Gaynor? Where's he getting this?"

David pulled his arm away. "He's got his sources."

Finley continued. "That's right. I'm talking about Rhonda Finderman. Who was the primary investigator on the Olivia Fisher case. But she's so wrapped up with bureaucratic nonsense, caught up with the perks and power of her position, that she took her eye off the ball. She didn't know that the Gaynor case was a carbon copy of the Fisher murder, and who knows how much that put back the investigation?"

Duckworth grabbed for David again. "He can't say this."

David shrugged. "It's already out there now."

"Has he asked the chief about this before blabbing it in front of the cameras?"

David shook his head. "I'm guessing she'll be hearing about it, though."

"And where's our current mayor, Amanda Croydon, through all this?" Finley was saying. "Where's the oversight? Does anyone know what's going on? Does our current mayor have even the slightest notion? I'd like to think maybe she's not paying attention to how the police department is being run because she's so busy bringing new jobs to Promise Falls." He grinned. "If only."

Finley waited a beat, took a breath.

"That's why I'm coming back. That's why, today, I am declaring that I am a candidate for mayor of Promise Falls. I want to run this town again and return it to its former glory. I want to save Promise Falls."

He paused again, as though expecting applause, perhaps forgetting that members of the media did not typically clap their hands for politicians.

He offered up an awkward grin and said, "I'm guessing there must be a few questions."

A woman from one of the TV stations asked, "How do you come back from what happened when you were mayor?"

"I'm here today to answer questions about the current state of Promise Falls and why I want to be its mayor again," Finley said. "Voters won't find anyone more qualified. I know this town from top to bottom. I know every inch of its infrastructure. I know Promise Falls like the back of my hand." He held up his right palm, actually studied the back of his hand.

No no no, David thought.

Finley continued. "I'd be happy to take a question along those lines."

The woman pressed on. "When you were mayor

before, during your campaign for a higher office, you admitted having sex with an underage prostitute. A young girl. Do you really expect voters to go for someone with that kind of character? Do you think the citizens of Promise Falls have forgotten about that?"

"I thought she was older," Finley blurted.

David briefly put a hand over his eyes.

"Would that have made it okay?" asked the *Times Union* reporter.

"Look," said Finley, "nobody cares about that anymore. That's water under the bridge. It was years ago. What people are concerned about are the issues, not some minor indiscretions I may or may not have made in the past."

"Do you know what happened to that girl?" the same TV reporter asked.

"I always said I hoped she got the support she needed to turn her life around."

"She died," the woman said. "Didn't you know that? That she had died?"

Finley's face was starting to flush. "I believe I did hear that, but it was totally unrelated to—"

"But it wasn't. She died from a life of living on the street. She—"

"The question you need to be asking," Finley said, "is how the chief of police could let something like this fall between the cracks. The connection between two grisly murders. And why nothing's being done about a possible serial killer in this town. And what connection may exist between those events and the other things that have been happening here."

"Were there other underage prostitutes?" asked the reporter from the radio station.

Drops of sweat were sprouting up on Finley's forehead.

"This is turning into the *Hindenburg*," David Harwood said to himself, but Duckworth heard it.

"Oh, the humanity," Detective Duckworth said.

"You don't see it as exploitative, to hold your announcement here where Olivia Fisher was murdered?" the *Times Union* reporter said.

"That's the whole point!" Finley said. "Don't you get it? How fucking stupid are you people?"

"Jesus," David said.

"I don't think even he could help you now," Duckworth said.

"I think that's all for today," Finley said. "My campaign manager, Mr. Harwood, is available for any further questions."

He broke through the small gathering and started heading for his car, but the reporters were moving with him.

"How old did you think she was?" someone shouted.

"What does your wife think about you running again?" asked another.

"For fuck's sake!" Finley said, moving forward, head down. "It's all ancient history!"

David was in pursuit, as was Duckworth, who managed to come up alongside the former mayor and say, "Where'd you get that, you son of a bitch?"

Finley glanced at him and, in the midst of the disaster his announcement had turned into, managed a smile.

"Best to your boy," he said, reaching his car. He hit the unlock button on his remote and scrambled into the front seat, locking the doors immediately.

David banged on the passenger window. "Hey!" he shouted. "Let me in!"

But Finley threw the car into drive and took off down

the street, leaving the reporters, and David, standing there.

Duckworth needed a few seconds to catch his breath, then asked David, "How's the new gig working out?"

FIFTY-SEVEN

Ed Noble parked the car close to the back of the Laundromat so he could make a quick getaway once he'd put a bullet in Samantha Worthington's head. He left the car unlocked. What he would've really liked to do was leave the keys in, with the engine running. Pull the trigger, run out the back door, hop in the car, and away he'd go.

But that'd be just stupid. There was always the possibility someone—a kid, more than likely—might stroll by and be unable to resist the temptation to take the car for a joyride.

Ed Noble wasn't sure this was a nice enough neighborhood to take the chance. Didn't matter where you were—you just couldn't trust people. He was no fool.

So he got out of the car, pocketed his keys, untucked his shirt so it hung over the small gun he had tucked into the waistband of his pants. It occurred to him, just then, that this gun Yolanda had given him didn't have a silencer on it. It was going to make a big bang when it went off. All the more reason to have the car close. By the time anyone came to check out what the noise was, he'd be gone.

He was feeling a little bit jazzed about all this. And, if he was honest with himself, scared, too.

Ed had never actually killed anyone before. Hurt, sure. There was that one time he and Brandon—before

Brandon held up that bank and got sent up—one night in the North End they beat up this guy good who'd looked at Ed's girlfriend—well, former girlfriend—the wrong way. Dragged him out the back door when the guy went to take a piss, punched him in the head until he'd lost consciousness, then tried this thing they'd seen in a movie, where they laid the guy out on the street, put his open mouth on the edge of the curb, like he was trying to take a bite out of it, then stomped on the back of his head.

Fuck, the noise. Like you were snapping a two-by-four over your knee.

That was probably the worst thing Ed had ever done. Until he'd tried to kidnap that kid yesterday. But even that was pretty much nothing compared to what he was about to do now. It was like adding to your résumé. When people found out what you could do, you'd get better and better jobs. He knew this would all get back to Brandon, and the guys he knew on the inside. There might be things they'd need done out in the real world, things Ed could help them with.

Word of mouth was everything.

Noble didn't head straight for the back door. He moved quickly for the wall. Then he inched along it, heading for the door, touching the gun beneath his shirt, making sure it was there, even though he could feel it digging into his side. There was a grimy, dust-covered window between him and the door. He leaned into it, putting one eye on the inside of the Laundromat.

The window looked in on the office at the back. It afforded a view of a desk jammed into one corner, cleaning supplies, a worktable with a coin-sorting machine sitting on it, mini-boxes of soap and other supplies, a calendar on the wall from a local appliance firm that probably serviced the machines. There was a door on the opposite wall that led into the main area. It was open, and Noble could see a sliver of what was going on in there.

He could see the woman, talking to someone. The door wasn't open wide enough to make out who.

That wasn't good.

He was hoping there'd be no one there, but of course she was running a business, and there was always the possibility there'd be customers. But if Noble could get Sam when she was in the office, and the door was closed, if someone heard a gunshot, he figured he'd have time to get away without being spotted.

He moved quickly to the other side of the window, gripped the doorknob, and slowly turned it. He pulled the door open half an inch per second until it was just wide enough to allow him to slip inside. Once he was in, he shut the door noiselessly behind him.

He could hear Sam and some man talking. About a fire, about clothes that smelled all smoky.

Noble thought the voice sounded familiar.

Can't be, he thought.

He could swear the guy she was talking to was the same one who'd been there the morning before, who'd thrown soap in his eyes. If Noble ended up having to shoot a witness, was there a better witness to shoot?

Noble stepped quietly to the other side of the room, positioned himself by the door.

Waited.

He heard the man say something about leaving his car unlocked. Noble's heart was pounding as he took the gun into his right hand.

Footsteps headed this way.

Just in case there was someone else out there washing

clothes, he wanted the door shut and locked before he pulled the trigger.

Needed to buy himself those extra few seconds.

She came into the room, right past him.

He rushed her from behind, using his gun hand to reach around her, his left to cover her mouth. She managed a millisecond of scream.

"Not a fucking sound," he whispered into her ear.

She squirmed in his arms, fought hard until he brought up the gun so she could see it.

Sam went still.

"That's smart," he said. "Don't do anything stupid and you'll be just fine."

Yeah, right.

"We're just going to move together over to the door."

He pulled her backward, one hand still over her mouth, his other hand now pressing the gun to her temple. Once they were close enough to the door, Noble shut it with his foot.

There was a dead bolt.

"Don't you make a sound now," he said, taking his hand off her mouth long enough to throw the bolt.

He was pleased she hadn't screamed. The gun, clearly, had scared her into keeping her mouth shut. He felt he could release his grip on her. She turned around, her eyes wide, her face full of fear.

It was kind of a turn-on, seeing how scared she looked.

"What now?" she asked. "What the hell do you want?"

"Who was that you were talking to?" he asked.

"What?"

"Out there. Is that the same asshole from yesterday?"

She had her eyes on the gun. "Just tell me what you want, Ed."

416

"It's what Yolanda wants," he told her.

Just do it. Don't stall. Don't draw it out.

"Carl's not here," she said. "He's at school. And they're not letting him out of their sight. You can't pull the kind of stunt you pulled yesterday."

"That's not what Yolanda wants," he told her. "I mean, yeah, she still wants Carl, but she's thought of another way to go about it."

Sam's chin trembled as the realization set in. "Come on, Ed. You gotta be kidding me. Not even Yolanda would do that."

Ed Noble grinned nervously. "She's something else, you gotta admit." He raised the gun. "It's nothing personal. I mean, with me."

From beyond the door, someone shouted: "Sam!"

417

FIFTY-EIGHT

Best to your boy.

Randall Finley's words were ringing in Barry Duckworth's ears.

Best to your boy.

Trevor had been at the house, Barry recalled. He'd dropped by to pick up some CDs and then wandered into the kitchen just after Barry had been telling Maureen his concerns about the chief.

The last thing Duckworth could have wanted was for his thoughts about Finderman to become public. Okay, so maybe she should have been keeping a closer eye on the Gaynor murder. She'd have seen how similar it was to the Fisher woman's slaying. It would have steered his investigation in another direction from the get-go. But he was never going to point a finger. Wouldn't the chief have been within her rights to throw it back in his lap? Why hadn't he reviewed earlier crimes himself to look for common elements? Why hadn't he brought himself up to speed on cases that had happened while he was away?

He'd been venting when he told all this to Maureen. Seeking to place blame elsewhere. Not wanting to have to carry all the weight himself. Maybe he wasn't being fair, putting any of this on the chief. But now it was out there. If she hadn't already heard about Randall Finley's charges, she would any minute now.

Sitting in his car, he wondered whether he should call her. Get ahead of this. Tell her what Finley had said, and where Duckworth believed he'd gotten his information. Fess up. Fall on his sword.

Except Duckworth didn't know for sure.

So before he called his boss, he had to call his son.

He got out his cell, called up Trevor's number from his list of contacts, and tapped on it with his thumb.

Three rings later, a pickup.

"Hello?"

"Where are you?" Duckworth asked.

"Dad?"

"Where are you, right now?"

"I'm at work," Trevor said.

"You're at Finley Springs? Or you're on the road, doing a delivery?"

"On the road."

"Where?"

"Greenwich," Trevor said. A small town east of Promise Falls. "I'm just coming into Greenwich. Got about five drop-offs to do here."

"I'll meet you there."

"I'm not going to be here all that—"

"There's a gas station and a Cumberland Farms on Main Street. You know where—"

"That's one of the places where I have to make a stop," his son said.

"I'll meet you. Twenty minutes."

"Dad, what's going on? Has something happened to Mom? Is she—"

"Be there." Duckworth ended the call.

★

Ignoring all speed limits, and turning on the flashing red lights set in the front grille, Duckworth made the trip to Greenwich in fifteen. A quarter of a mile away he spotted the Finley Springs van parked in the Cumberland Farms lot, close to the road.

Trevor had been watching for him, and was getting out of the van as the unmarked cruiser pulled into the lot and screeched to a halt. He was standing by Duckworth's door as he got out of the car.

"What is it?" he asked. "You're going to make me late for the rest of my run."

Duckworth got up close to his son, jabbed a finger at his chest.

"You'll never guess what I heard Randy say today."

"Huh?"

"At a press conference. Just now. He had all this stuff to say about my boss. How she missed a connection between two homicides. I'm scratching my head, wondering how he could have come up with something like that."

Trevor swallowed hard. "Why are you asking me about this?"

"I just wondered if you had any idea where he came up with that."

Trevor averted his eyes. "Who the hell knows how he comes up with anything? He's kind of a nutcase. Everyone knows he's full of shit."

"You heard me talking to your mother."

Trevor said nothing.

"You heard me talking about this with your mother. You were standing outside the kitchen and heard it."

"You're always talking about work stuff. How am I supposed to know what's private and what isn't?"

Duckworth placed both palms on his son's chest and

gave him a shove. Trevor stumbled backward, caught himself before tripping onto the asphalt.

"Goddamn it, you really did do it," Duckworth said, his cheeks flushed. "I was hoping I was wrong. I was hoping maybe he got it from somebody else. What the fuck were you thinking?"

"I don't know!" Trevor shouted.

"Do you realize what you've done? That asshole's going to turn this into a campaign issue. He's going after my boss. You think this isn't going to come back to me? You think it's not going to bite me in the ass? What am I going to tell her when I get hauled into her office? What?"

"I'm sorry!" he blurted, starting to tear up.

"You fucked me over! Way to go! My own son! Is this payback? Is that what it is? Some lifelong grievance you decided to settle by putting my job at risk? You think it's just me you're hurting? You think this won't hurt your mother? Jesus Christ, what were you thinking, blabbing to him about that?"

"I said I'm sorry! You just don't know what he's like."

"I know what he's like more than anyone. What are you talking about?"

Trevor turned away, head down.

"Trev," Duckworth said. "Talk to me."

"I owed him," his son said, back still turned.

"Owed him what?"

Trevor turned slowly. "It was about Trish."

Duckworth lowered his voice. "What about her?"

"There was—something happened between us. An accident. A misunderstanding."

Duckworth reached out, gently gripped his son's arm, slowly turned him around. "What kind of accident? When was this?"

421

"Just before we broke up. She was going to slap me and I went to stop her and I . . . I kind of ended up hitting her."

"You *hit* her?"

"And Mr. Finley, he found out all about it because he's close with Trish's family, and he talked to her about whether to go to the police, whether she should have me charged, and he kind of made it sound like he talked her out of it, but that could change, depending on whether I could help him out or not. You know, like if I ever heard anything interesting that might help him, like, politically. And when I heard you talking to Mom about those murders, I thought that was something he could use, so I told him. I didn't want to. But I wanted us to be square, you know, so I wouldn't owe him anymore."

"What'd he say?"

Trevor dropped his head. "He said it was a start."

"He's a fucking blackmailer," Duckworth said. "I'll kill him."

"He was keeping me out of trouble. I didn't want to get in trouble. I did a stupid thing. I never meant to hit Trish. I really didn't. I was just swinging my arm around to deflect her, you know? But my hand, it got her right on the cheek and . . ."

Trevor began to cry. "I really fucked up. I fucked up huge. I hate this job. I hate working for that asshole. I just. I didn't—"

"Come here," Duckworth said. He pulled his son into his arms, patted his back softly.

"I'm so sorry. I'm so sorry," Trevor said, his face pressed into his father's shoulder. "You're in deep shit. You're in trouble."

"We'll work it out," Duckworth said. "We'll work it out."

422

FIFTY-NINE

"I thought I'd find you here," Victor Rooney said.

Walden Fisher, on one knee before the gravestones of his wife and daughter, turned and looked at the man standing on the cemetery lawn behind him.

"Huh? Victor?" Walden said.

"You come up here most every day. I went by the house, and when I couldn't find you there, I thought I'd take a run up here."

Walden put both hands on his bent knee, pushed himself up. His left pant leg was damp from the grass.

"Victor," he said. "You wanted to see me about something?"

Victor stood there in frayed jeans and a faded Buffalo Sabres T-shirt. Hands stuffed in his pockets.

"I came by to say good-bye."

"Good-bye?"

Victor shrugged. "Things aren't working out for me here. I've been trying to get work, but I'm banging my head up against the wall. Can't find anything. This town's got nothing to offer."

"Things are kind of tough everywhere," Walden said. "Not just here."

"Maybe. But I think things are just going to get worse here."

"What do you mean?"

Victor shrugged. "Just a feeling."

"Where do you think you'll go?"

Another shrug. "I haven't worked that out yet. That's what I'll put my mind to over the next few days, while I finish up a few things."

"What things?"

"You know, just stuff. Say good-bye to a few friends, things like that. Do some research online, see where a good place to go might be. Albany maybe. That's close. But I might go far away, too. Maybe Seattle. I got some friends I went to school with out there. Maybe they got some leads on things."

"Good to have options."

"I know you blame me," Victor said.

"Come again?"

"For what happened to Olivia. That you think it was my fault."

"I don't know what you're talking about, Victor. I've never accused you of killing Olivia."

"Did you send that detective to talk to me? Duckworth? He came by my place, asking me how I was dealing with what happened to Olivia. Why would he do that?"

Walden shrugged. "I didn't send him. I mean, he came by to see me, asking a few more questions. I guess they haven't totally given up trying to find Olivia's killer. I guess the conversation got around to you, but—"

"So it was you."

"I'm sorry, Victor. I never meant to cause you any kind of trouble."

"You blame me because I was supposed to meet her. In the park. And I was late. I know you hold me responsible."

"I've never said that," Walden told him.

"You don't have to. I can tell. I blame myself, too. I just . . . I lost track of time. If I'd been there five minutes earlier, we'd have been in the bar, having a drink, getting a bite to eat."

"Plenty of blame to go around," Walden said.

"So, it's not like I've decided to forgive myself or anything, but I've decided I have to move on. I have to try and get my shit together. Maybe I can do that somewhere else, by starting over."

"Just don't rush into anything, Victor. Think on it through the Memorial Day weekend, at least."

Victor glanced at the headstones, then looked back at Walden Fisher. "Maybe you should, too."

"What's that?"

"Move on. I mean, coming up here, every day. Talking to Olivia and your wife, like they can hear you. Maybe that's not that healthy a thing to do. Maybe it's holding you back from getting on with your life."

"This *is* my life. Paying my respects to them."

Victor nodded thoughtfully. "Okay, then. I guess I said my piece." He half turned, as if getting ready to leave, then stopped. "You hear about that thing last night?"

"What thing would that be?"

"The bus."

Walden shook his head. "What bus?"

"A Promise Falls bus. Like, a regular city bus. I was jogging, and coming down the street, there's this, like, fireball. It's a bus, totally empty, the whole thing on fire. Someone would've had to steal a bus from the compound, splash some gasoline around inside, toss in a match, put it in neutral, and let it roll. It crashed right into the flower shop, caught the building on fire."

"That's horrible. Was anyone killed? Hurt?"

Victor shook his head. "Don't think so. Wasn't anybody on the bus. Had a big number twenty-three on the back. You been hearing about that?"

"I have," Walden said.

"All the stuff that's been happening—the drive-in and a bunch of other things—is all connected somehow."

"That's what they say." Walden shook his head in bafflement. "Why would someone be doing something like that?"

Victor smiled. "That's the question, isn't it?"

SIXTY

Cal

"Sam!" I said, still looking at that closed office door only a few feet away from me.

Even over the low-level rumble of the washing machines I had just started, I thought I heard a lock being turned.

Something about that seemed wrong.

Not taking my eye off the door, I set Crystal's graphic novel on the top of the washer. But I'd set it on the edge and it fell, open to some inside page, on the floor.

I left it there and moved toward the door.

"Hey, Sam!" I said. "I think one of the washers is on the blink!"

No response.

I got up close to the door, put my ear to it. Someone was whispering on the other side. I was pretty sure it was Sam's voice.

"Sam, everything okay in there?" I said, my mouth right up to the door.

A pause. Then, "Yes. Everything is fine."

Her stilted reply didn't sound fine to me.

"One of the washers seems to be broken," I said through the door.

Another pause. "I'll take . . . a look at it in a minute."

I unholstered my gun, held it in my right hand,

pointed toward the floor.

I said, "What's the plan, Ed?"

A long pause this time. If Samantha had been in there alone, she would have said, almost immediately, "What?" Or maybe, "Ed?"

The fact that she said nothing right away told me he was in there with her. When I called out his name, it threw him. He needed a few seconds to think of something to tell Sam to say to me.

Finally, it came.

"There's no Ed here," Sam said, her voice sounding close to breaking.

I said, "Ed, you need to open this door and send Sam out. You hurt, Sam?"

"Not so far," she said.

"That's good," I said, keeping my voice even. "That's good, Ed. You let Sam out, and I think there's a pretty good chance no one's going to get hurt. Whaddya say to that?"

Two seconds. Then, "Fuck you!"

Ed's presence confirmed.

"He's got a gun!" Sam screamed.

"Shut up!" Ed shouted.

I moved, took up a position to the side of the door.

"Ed, this is the kind of situation that could get out of hand very quickly. Whatever you came here planning to do, it's not going to work. It's not something you're going to be able to get away with. Best thing you can do now is walk away. You came in through the back, right? So just go. Walk out the door and go. I won't come after you. Just leave Sam where she is and take off. You hearing me?"

"I hear ya," Ed Noble said.

"That sound like a plan to you?"

"I guess. Sure. No harm done, right?"

"That's right. Just get out of here."

"You're right," he said, almost cheerfully. "I don't know what I was thinking. There are better ways to resolve things, right?"

I heard the dead bolt slide back into the door.

"I mean, people have their differences, but the best thing to do is sit down and work them out reasonably."

The doorknob turned slowly.

"That's right, Ed. I like your attitude," I said, bringing up my gun. "I'm glad we could work things out without anyone getting hurt. You still okay, Sam?"

Nothing.

"Sam?"

And she screamed: *"Look ou—"*

The door burst open. Ed Noble, his nose heavily bandaged, came out like a sprinter out of the blocks at the sound of the starter's pistol. He was crouched low, gun in hand, head turning my way as he launched out of the room. He rolled his body a quarter turn, heading deliberately for the floor on his right shoulder, gun up, pointed my way.

It looked like a stunt he'd probably seen in a movie. Maybe Liam Neeson or Kiefer Sutherland could pull off a midflight shot and hit the target, but when Noble fired, the bullet went wide, somewhere off to the left, and into a dryer.

The round glass window shattered.

Just because Noble wasn't the world's best shot didn't mean he wasn't dangerous. Which was why, the second he started coming out the door, I headed for the floor as well. But even though I was armed, I wasn't going to shoot wildly.

If I was going to shoot, I was going to make it count.

Noble wasn't happy with just one shot. Once he'd skidded to a stop, he took another, this one a little closer to home. It hit another dryer on the wall behind me, this time only a couple of feet up from the floor.

"Shit!" he said.

Lying on my side, one arm tight against the floor, I extended my arms, both hands on the gun, and prepared to fire.

But Noble scurried, crablike, toward the broad table near the back of the Laundromat where customers folded their clothes.

This was dangerously close to the office door, where, I now noticed, Sam was standing, wide-eyed, one hand over her mouth, watching.

"Get back!" I shouted.

I was getting to my feet, gun in my right hand, thinking back to the days when I was still a cop and wore Kevlar while on duty. I didn't have any such protection now. Hunched over, I ran to the other side of the room where I'd have a clearer shot at Noble, who was flat on his back now, aiming my way.

Another shot, this one going into the ceiling.

I fired, aiming for body mass. But in the millisecond before I squeezed the trigger, he rolled toward the office. The bullet hit the floor and ricocheted, pinging off an appliance. Any more shots that way might find their way into the adjoining room and hit Sam.

Not even ten seconds had gone by since this had all started.

I was getting to my feet just as Noble was scrambling to his. "Don't fucking move!" I shouted.

He glanced my way, rose and fired again. I leapt to the

right, noticed movement in the open office door.

It all happened very fast.

While Noble was looking in my direction, Sam stepped into the main room, right arm outstretched, like she was getting ready to throw out the first pitch.

But it wasn't a baseball in her hand. It was the leather satchel full of quarters, the drawstring wound tightly around her wrist.

She swung it with everything she had.

Noble saw it just before it connected, but not in time to do anything about it. The sack of metal caught him squarely on that broken nose, and the yelp of pain was louder than any of the shots that had been fired. He stumbled back two steps.

"Fucking Jesus!" he screamed, putting his free hand over his face. He still had the gun in his right hand, but he'd blinded himself with his left.

I could have shot him—and God knows I wanted to—but instead I ran toward him, flat out, tackling him around the waist, bringing him down onto the floor so hard it knocked the wind out of him.

I went for the gun first, putting both hands on his right wrist and slamming it to the floor once, twice, until the gun slipped from his fingers.

Sam didn't waste a second in grabbing it.

Noble was struggling for air, bringing up his knees, collapsing in on himself, blood streaming out from below the bandages that spanned his nose.

"Yo . . . lan . . . da!" he said between gasps. "She . . . ordered . . . it! It's . . . all her . . . fault!"

Sam had Noble's gun pointed straight at his head. "You motherfucker," she said.

"Don't," I cautioned her. "Don't shoot him, Sam. Not

now. Not for you, and not for Carl."

She didn't lower the gun. "I've had it. I've just had it. I can't take any more of this."

"I know, I know. But he's going down for this. Yolanda, too. Give me the gun, Sam."

It took about ten seconds for her to hand it over. I tucked it into my jacket pocket.

She raised the bloodied bag of coins. "Could I hit him one more time with this?"

I sighed.

"What the hell?" I said. "Go ahead."

SIXTY-ONE

As much as Barry Duckworth wanted to go in search of Randall Finley before he did anything else, he had other priorities. When he'd spotted the mayor's news conference under way in the park, he'd been on the hunt for the professor, Peter Blackmore.

He'd gone to the man's house, but no one had answered the doorbell. A peek through some windows suggested it wasn't a case of him refusing to come to the door. Duckworth wondered whether Blackmore, even in the midst of personal tragedy, had decided to head out to the campus. Not to teach, but to confer with his good buddy Clive Duncomb.

He'd have been at the college more than an hour ago if he hadn't made that impromptu trip to Greenwich to see Trevor.

By now, Blackmore might be back home. Rather than search for the man in person, Duckworth made some calls. To the man's house, first, where there was no answer, then to the college's English department. He reached a secretary and asked whether the professor was there.

"I saw him around," the woman said. "He's very distraught. I don't know if you know, but he just lost his wife. I've no idea why he came in here today. I think he doesn't know what to do with himself. He might be in his office right now. Would you like me to put you through?"

Duckworth said the last thing he wanted to do, given the circumstances, was trouble the man.

He pushed his foot down a little harder on the accelerator.

As he was driving onto the Thackeray grounds, he saw a car going the other way with Peter Blackmore behind the wheel. Duckworth hit the brakes, did a fast three-point turn, and sped after the car. He put on the flashing red lights in the grille, whooped the siren for a couple of seconds. Blackmore glanced in his mirror, put on his blinker like a model driver, and pulled over to the shoulder.

Blackmore was powering down his window and craning his neck around as Duckworth came up alongside the car.

"Officer, I'm sure I wasn't speeding or—"

When he saw that he hadn't been pulled over by a traffic cop, he said, "Oh."

"Professor," Duckworth said, leaning over, resting his arms on the driver's windowsill. The detective was immediately alarmed by Blackmore's appearance. His face was bruised and bloody. His knuckles, too. "Professor, what happened to you?"

"Oh," he said, tentatively touching his face, as though he needed to remind himself that he'd been hurt. "Just a misunderstanding."

"Who did this to you?"

He shook his head. "It doesn't matter."

Duckworth stepped back. "Would you please get out of the car, sir?"

"Really, I'm fine."

"Step out of the car, Professor."

Blackmore nodded, turned off the ignition, got out,

closed the door. "I haven't been drinking or anything, if that's what you're worried about. I mean, not in the last couple of hours, anyway."

"I want to see how you are. You've been in some kind of altercation, Professor. Your hands are bloodied, you've got a black eye, and your cheek's all puffed out. Suppose you tell me about that."

"I'm fine, really."

"What have you been doing since I saw you last night?"

"Just . . . you know. Thinking about Georgina. What happened."

"You haven't come in and made an official identification."

"I . . . I've just been too upset. I'll come in today."

"Why did you go to your office?"

"I didn't know what else to do. I was driving around all night, thinking . . ."

"Driving around where?"

"Just around."

"Did you drive over to the Chalmers house?"

The professor looked puzzled. "What?"

"Did you drive over to the Chalmerses'?"

"Why would I do that?"

"To see Miriam," Duckworth suggested. "You were shocked to find out she wasn't killed in the accident, that it was Georgina in that car with Adam. Maybe you had to prove it to yourself, that Miriam was really alive, before you could face going to identify your wife's body."

"I . . . I can see why you might think that. But the truth is, I couldn't bear to find out, for sure. I couldn't face having it confirmed. I didn't want to see Miriam, and I didn't want to go identify Georgina. I know . . .

435

I know I have to face this. I just haven't been ready."

"Maybe," Duckworth said, "it would help if we went out now, together, to see Miriam. Maybe that would be a helpful first step before the identification."

The professor looked at Duckworth, his eyes narrowing. "I don't think that would be a good idea."

"Why's that?"

He shook his head slowly. "She'll . . . she'll blame me, won't she? My wife, with her husband? Maybe she'll wonder whether I knew about it. Why I didn't stop Georgina from seeing him."

"Couldn't it work just as easily the other way around? Don't you have reason to be angry with her? Your wife would be alive if she hadn't been with Adam. If Miriam hadn't taken off for a couple of days, it could have been her in that car at the drive-in instead of Georgina."

Blackmore looked confused. "I just don't know. I don't know what to think of any of this." He looked down at the pavement.

"Maybe you were angry with Miriam about that. Maybe you've been troubled about this whole arrangement you've had with the Chalmerses." Duckworth waited a beat. "And Clive Duncomb and his wife."

Blackmore lifted his head to look the detective in the eye. "I'm sorry?"

"Is 'arrangement' the right word? I'm not quite up to speed on how all this works. Trading spouses. That kind of thing."

The professor appeared to wither before Duckworth's eyes. "I . . . I don't know what you're asking, exactly."

"Wasn't it at the Chalmers house where it all took place? In that special room in the basement? If it was me, and I had a spare room downstairs that size, I think I'd put

436

in a pool table. But then again, look at me. I need to lose eighty pounds. There aren't a lot of women in our social circle who want to have a roll in the hay with a fat bastard like me. I'm not what they call a hunk. Although, I have to say, and don't take this the wrong way, because you're good-looking enough, but you're not exactly Ryan Gosling, either. Clive, he's got that air of authority, the chiseled jaw, so I can see the women going for him, and I'm guessing Adam Chalmers was quite the ladies' man, too. Tell me how it worked. When you swapped partners, did you have sex with Clive's wife one night, and then Adam's wife another? Or both in the same night? Or did everyone just jump in and go at it together? Or, and forgive me if this is too personal, but would the wives also have sex with the wives and the husbands with the husbands? Are you okay, Professor Blackmore? You don't look okay."

"I think I'm going to be sick."

"Maybe you should walk around to the back of the car here." Duckworth put a hand gently on the man's shoulder, moved him back to the trunk. "Just in case you get sick, there's a good spot. Now, I want to be clear. I'm not asking all these questions out of some prurient nature. It just struck me that if these were the kinds of activities you all were engaged in, there might be things on those tapes you made that you'd be worried might fall into the wrong hands. Well, not tapes, exactly. DVDs. Discs."

Blackmore's lower lip trembled. "How do you know—"

"It just seemed odd to me, last night, at a time when you might be expected to be looking for your wife, you and Mr. Duncomb appeared to be having a movie fest. I thought, what could be more important than looking for your wife? Why would those videos be your priority at

437

such a time? Then, when I found that little playroom in the Chalmers house, it started to come together for me. Especially when I saw the video equipment under the bed. You were making movies. Filming your sessions. You were going through the discs and—"

Blackmore threw up.

He took a step toward the curb, leaned over, and vomited. "Oh God," he said. "Oh God."

Duckworth pressed on.

"Like I was saying, you were going through those discs, looking for something that worried you. Something that worried you so much, it was more important than looking for Georgina. And then, you found out Miriam was actually still alive. That changed things somehow, didn't it? That's the part I'm having some trouble with, where I'm wondering if you can help me out."

Blackmore wiped his mouth on the back of his sport jacket sleeve, came back to a standing position. "No . . . it wasn't like that."

"I figure there's blackmail involved in here somewhere, but who was blackmailing who?"

"Not like that."

"Was Miriam holding something over you and Duncomb?" Duckworth asked. He stepped in close to the professor, ignoring the disgusting smells coming off him. "Is that why you went over to her house last night and killed her?"

Blackmore put a hand out, braced himself against the trunk of his car. "What?"

"You heard me."

"Miriam is dead?"

"You act surprised. But look at you. You're a mess. There's blood on your hands. You were in a fight. Did

Miriam do that to you before you pushed her down the stairs?"

"No, no! This—" He pointed to the wounds on his face. "This was Clive! Clive did this to me!"

"Why? Why would Duncomb do this, Professor?"

"Because . . . because he doesn't want me to say anything."

"Say anything about what? About killing Miriam?"

"No! I didn't do that! I didn't know she was dead! When did that happen? Clive was talking to her on the phone! Last night! When you were there!"

"The same time you realized your wife was the one who'd died in the car at the drive-in."

"Yes!" He nodded furiously. "How could Miriam be dead?"

"Why did Clive Duncomb do this to you?"

Blackmore was trembling, his eyes darting, as though searching for an escape. "He thinks I'll talk. But not about Miriam."

"About what, then?"

The professor kept shaking his head.

"Tell me!" Duckworth shouted. "What's he worried about? What's on those videos?"

Blackmore mumbled something.

"What?"

"—via," he said.

"What did you say?"

"Olivia," the professor said.

Now it was Barry Duckworth's turn to be stunned into silence. At least for a couple of seconds.

"Olivia?"

"That's right."

"Olivia who?"

439

"Olivia Fisher," the professor said. "She was the one who—"

"I know who she was. What the hell does Olivia Fisher have to do with the rest of this?"

"Sometimes, Clive . . . Clive invited Thackeray girls out to Adam and Miriam's. There'd be something in their wine—you know, what do you call them—"

"Roofies," Duckworth said. "Rohypnol. The date rape drug."

Peter Blackmore nodded. "That's right. And then they'd join in . . . with the fun. Except Olivia. She got into it. She didn't have to be drugged. But that also meant she'd remember everything that happened."

"Everyone went along with this?"

Blackmore nodded ashamedly. "But it was Clive, and his wife, Liz, who wanted to bring in the girls. We went along." He shook his head. "All of us."

"Georgina, too."

He nodded. "She was torn. She didn't feel right about what we were doing, but at the same time, I think she was infatuated with Adam. I don't know if the drive-in was the first time she'd been out alone with him. Maybe she thought something like that, that it was innocent enough, especially considering she'd already had sex with him."

Duckworth wasn't interested in that part of the story, at least not right now. "When did you involve Olivia Fisher in your games?"

"It was a few years ago. I mean, obviously before she was murdered. Maybe a month or so before."

"You were trying to find the discs featuring her?"

He nodded. "When we—when Clive—heard that Adam and Miriam had been killed at the drive-in, he knew someone would be through the house, find those discs. But it turned out we didn't have to worry. When it turned out Miriam was alive, and Clive was talking to her, he told her we had the discs, that we were trying to find the one with Olivia, and she said it had already been destroyed. Adam got rid of it. He got rid of any of the videos with Thackeray girls. Olivia, Lorraine—"

"Lorraine?"

"I don't remember her last name. It was a huge relief, because Clive was so worried that if someone else had found the discs, eventually, they'd see us, with Olivia, and they'd think . . ."

"You killed her."

"We knew how bad it would look, her being in the videos. That it would link us to her, that someone might think we had something to do with her murder."

"Did you?"

"I didn't. I swear."

"What about Clive?"

Blackmore met Duckworth's look. "I don't know."

"You said he threatened you, if you started to talk. Did he kill Olivia because he was afraid she would?"

Blackmore put his hands on top of his head, as if trying to keep his skull from exploding. "I don't know. I don't know what's going on in that man's head. Maybe that's what he's doing. He's getting rid of everyone who's a possible threat. He blew that kid's head off, you know."

"Mason Helt," Duckworth said.

"Yeah! Him! I get why he did it, but . . . I think he *enjoyed* it. You know what I'm saying? He *liked* shooting that kid. He *liked* that he was able to do that and get away with it."

"Professor Blackmore, I'm gonna need you to come in with me and make a formal statement."

"No, I can't do that."

"You need to. You need to do it for yourself. You need to make a clean breast of this. You'll feel better. It's the right thing to do."

"Clive . . . he'll go nuts."

"We can take care of Mr. Duncomb. Don't worry about that."

"He'll kill me."

"We'll make sure that doesn't happen."

The professor appeared unconvinced. "I have to deal with this," he said.

"You are. By coming in and making a statement."

"No," he said. "Some other way."

"And what way would that—"

Blackmore lunged at him. Hit Duckworth in the chest with both palms, hard, knocking the detective off his feet. Duckworth stumbled backward, landed on the road inches away from Blackmore's vomit, and hit the back of his head on the edge of the curb.

Briefly saw stars.

Blackmore jumped into his car, turned the ignition.

"Stop!" Duckworth said, rising to a sitting position. "Goddamn it, stop!"

The professor threw the car into drive and took off.

SIXTY-TWO

Cal

The first thing Sam did was call the school and tell the office to get Carl out of class, keep him in the office, and not let him out of their sight for one second.

A pair of uniformed cops arrived before anyone else. Turned out they were already on their way even before I'd made a call. People passing by the Laundromat had heard shots and someone had dialed 911.

When I called in, I made clear that the gunfire was over, but I also knew that when the police arrived, they'd be on high alert, so I made sure neither Sam nor I was waving a gun around when they came through the front door. But we were both standing over Ed Noble, ready to pounce on him if he tried to get away.

Once the cops had a look at Noble, sprawled on the floor, whimpering as blood streamed from his nose, they put in a call for the paramedics. Before they arrived, a detective by the name of Angus Carlson arrived.

I explained, as quickly as I could, what had gone down, although a survey of the Laundromat offered more than a few clues. Bullet holes in the ceiling and a washer, a shattered dryer window, blood on the floor. I still had several washers chugging away, dealing with my smoky clothes.

I managed to work in, during my initial chat with Carlson, that I was a former Promise Falls cop, and that if he needed to check me out, he could call Barry Duck-worth.

"That's my partner," Carlson said. "Or my supervisor. Kind of."

"He says he was put up to it," I told Carlson, pulling him to one side. "Ms. Worthington's former in-laws want custody of her son. Sounds like the mother of her ex-husband—he's in jail right now—figured the best way to achieve that was to kill Ms. Worthington."

"Some mothers are just pure evil," Carlson said.

"Yeah," I said. "I think she's still in town somewhere."

The paramedics arrived, but Carlson held up a hand to them. He wanted a few words with Noble before they took him to the hospital.

"Mr. Noble," he said.

"That fucking bitch broke my nose!" he wept. "That's the second time in two days."

"Yeah," said Sam. "I wish I'd done it *both* times."

Carlson turned around, raised a finger to her.

"I'll be quiet," she said.

"Mr. Noble, you're being placed under arrest. You have—"

"I can give you somebody!" he said. "I can give you who put me up to this!"

"The mother of this woman's ex?"

"Yeah! Yolanda. It's all her, man. I'll testify against her. I will. You cut me a deal, and I'll tell you everything."

"Like where she is right now?"

"Yeah."

"Which is where?"

"The Walcott."

Ed Noble clearly hadn't figured out that you try to get your deal before you divulge information.

Carlson stood back up, conferred with the uniforms. I could hear him telling them to get to the Walcott and grab Yolanda and her husband. Then he assigned another officer to ride with Noble to the hospital, keep him under guard.

"We're not losing this guy," he said.

Once Noble had been moved out, he proceeded to take statements, separately, from Sam and me. As absurd as it sounded, I asked Carlson whether I, while he was interviewing Sam, could continue doing my laundry. Fortunately, a bullet had not pierced any of the machines I'd engaged.

Carlson said no, I wasn't to touch a thing. This Laundromat was, after all, a crime scene, and everything within it was potential evidence.

Nuts.

I noticed Crystal's graphic novel was still on the floor in front of the machine I could not get going, and I made an executive decision that it would not be covered by Carlson's edict on evidence. I was pleased it hadn't been damaged in any way. No blood, no broken glass, no water from a bullet-riddled washer.

It had fallen open somewhere in the middle. The cartoon Crystal had evidently, at some point, left her bedroom and wandered into an alley of some dark, dangerous Gotham-like city, lured in by the voice of her grandfather. Clutched in her arm was a teddy bear with one missing arm.

The bubble above the girl's head said: "I'll find you! I'll find you!"

But it was something else, something other than what Crystal had drawn, that caught my eye as I leaned over to pick up the book.

The back of the preceding page was a handwritten letter.

The handwriting was small, meticulous, easily decipherable, and filled most of the page. There was no date at the top.

It began *Dear Lucy*.

It concluded with *All my love, your father*.

I set the letter on top of the washer and read it from beginning to end.

And then I said, "Holy shit."

SIXTY-THREE

Duckworth struggled to his feet, watched as Peter Blackmore's car disappeared up the street.

"Goddamn it," he said, rubbing the back of his head where it had hit the curb. Felt blood. He looked at his hand, reached into his pocket with his other hand for a tissue to wipe it off.

He got out his phone.

"Yeah, it's Duckworth. I need to put out an APB."

He gave the dispatcher complete details about Blackmore's car, including the plate number. Duckworth also provided a description of the driver.

"Officers should approach with caution, but I do not believe this man to be armed. But he is wanted for questioning in more than one homicide. I also need someone to go to Thackeray, find the head of security, a guy named Clive Duncomb—yeah, that's right, the one who shot that kid—and stick with him until they hear from me. Where's Carlson?"

The dispatcher said the new detective was taking statements about a shooting in a Laundromat.

"Jesus," Duckworth said, and hung up.

The phone was back in his pocket for only five seconds when it started to ring.

"Yeah?" he said, expecting more questions from the dispatcher.

"Barry?"

A woman's voice.

Rhonda Finderman.

"Yeah, Chief, hi."

"Have you heard what that son of a bitch Finley is saying about me?"

"This isn't a good time," he said.

"I'll just bet it isn't," she said. "Where would he get something like that? That I'd taken my eye off the ball, that I'm at fault for not seeing a connection between the Fisher and Gaynor homicides? Far as I know, you're the only person who's come to me suggesting there *is* a connection. So where the hell else might he get an idea like that?"

"Chief, I'll tell you—"

"You already told me Finley was sniffing around. Trying to dig up dirt on me, to use it against me for his comeback. If he didn't get this from you, who'd he get it from? Carlson? Was it Angus Carlson? If it is, I swear, I'll have him writing parking tickets for the rest of his natural life. I knew I'd made a mistake, moving him up to detective."

"Not Carlson," Duckworth said.

"Jesus, Barry, you gotta be kidding—"

"Chief—Rhonda—I'm in pursuit of a suspect. I have to—"

"No, hang on. You told that bastard—"

Duckworth ended the call, put the phone back into his pocket. He got into his car and took off after Blackmore.

★

Professor Peter Blackmore struggled to get out his own phone as he drove randomly through the streets of Promise Falls. Glancing back and forth between the road and his phone, he called up a number and entered it.

He had the phone to his ear. One ring, two rings. Then:

"What is it, Peter?"

"Clive, she's dead!"

"What?" Duncomb said.

"Miriam's dead!"

"You're out of your mind," the security chief said. "Peter, you need to accept what happened. Georgina was killed at the drive-in. Miriam wasn't. I spoke to her. You were there. I spoke to her and she's fine."

"After!" he shouted into the phone. "She was killed after!"

"What the hell are you saying? Where are you?"

"Someone went to the house after you talked to her. That's when it happened."

"Where are you getting this from? Who told you this?"

"Duckworth! I just saw him!"

Duncomb was quiet on the other end of the line.

"Clive?"

"I'm here."

"It was you, wasn't it?" Peter said.

"What?"

"You killed her."

"Why the hell would I kill Miriam?"

"Maybe she had something on you. Something more than a video with Olivia Fisher on it. Something about you and Liz, that'd be my bet. Maybe something from when you were in Boston. Was it something like that?"

"You've lost it, Peter. You want to lay this on me, but

449

you're the one who was out all night. The one who shows up this morning with blood on him. What was *your* reason? Why'd *you* kill her? Because it wasn't her in that car with Adam? Because she was the one who should have died anyway, and not Georgina?"

"No! That's not what happened!"

"What did you tell him?" Clive asked.

"What?"

"What'd you tell Duckworth?"

Blackmore didn't speak for several seconds. Finally, "Nothing."

"Bullshit," Duncomb said. "What did you tell him?"

"Nothing. I didn't tell him a thing," the professor lied, struggling to compose himself. "But he had questions about you."

"Like what?"

"This isn't something I should talk about on the phone."

"Jesus, you accuse me of killing Miriam, but suddenly you can't discuss stuff on the phone."

"It's complicated," Blackmore said. "Where are you?"

"I went to the bank. I'm downtown, on Claymore. I can meet you."

"Just stay there. Be out front. I'll pick you up."

"Where are you?"

"I'm five minutes away, if that. I'll tell you everything when I see you." Blackmore ended the call, tossed the phone onto the seat next to him, cranked the wheel hard, and pulled a U-turn, nearly cutting off a Finley Springs truck.

*

When he was getting back on his feet, and touching his hand to the back of his head, Duckworth had noticed Blackmore's car making a right turn before it had disappeared from view.

Once he'd hung up on Rhonda Finderman—a move Duckworth predicted would see him, instead of Carlson, writing parking tickets until the end of time—and dropped in behind the wheel, he took off in the same direction, but there was no sign of Blackmore on the street he'd turned down.

Duckworth's foot was heavy on the accelerator. At each cross street, he glanced quickly in both directions. He hoped, now that all Promise Falls cruisers had been alerted, someone would spot the professor's car.

Where would the man go? Duckworth wondered. Home? Back to the college? Those would be the first two places the police would look for him.

Based on the last comments the man had made, Duckworth had a feeling he was looking for Clive Duncomb. Which meant he was most likely going to the college. Duckworth grabbed his phone again, called dispatch.

"Put me through to Thackeray's security department," he said.

It took about fifteen seconds. A man answered.

Duckworth identified himself. "This is an emergency. I need to speak to your boss. Right now."

"Not here," the man said. "He went into town."

"Where?"

"He said he was going to the bank."

"Which bank? Where?"

The man said he thought it was on Claymore. Before he could say anything else, Duckworth hit the brakes, turned the car around, and went tearing off in the opposite direction.

Red lights flashing, siren on.

Within a minute, he got lucky.

Ahead, he saw Blackmore's car, coming from the other direction, turning onto Claymore. Duckworth had three cars in front of him, but with the siren wailing, they started shifting over to the right, out of his path. He turned hard onto Claymore, the car's two right tires nearly losing grip on the pavement.

About a hundred yards ahead, the professor had his right blinker on, was slowing, easing the car toward the curb.

And there was Duncomb, out front of the bank, stepping off the curb, taking three steps out into the street.

It all happened very fast.

Once Blackmore was about ten yards away from Duncomb, he cranked the wheel hard to the right and floored it. Duncomb had no time to react. The car struck him midthigh, tossing his body onto the hood.

"No!" Duckworth shouted, his hands locked on the steering wheel.

Duncomb's head came through the windshield as Blackmore's car jumped the curb and crashed into the stone wall of the bank.

The driver's air bag deployed like a bomb going off.

Duckworth screeched to a halt, threw open his door, and ran toward the scene. By the time he'd reached Blackmore's car, the air bag had deflated, putting the professor nearly face-to-face with Clive Duncomb.

At least, what was left of Duncomb's bloodied and shredded face.

Duckworth, breathless, opened the driver's door of Blackmore's car.

Blackmore turned his head slowly toward the detective and smiled. "I got him," he said. "I got him good."

SIXTY-FOUR

David Harwood caught up with Randall Finley at his water-bottling plant.

"What the hell was that?" Finley shouted as David entered his office. "That was the fucking 9/11 of press conferences! A disaster! You're an idiot! That's what you are! An idiot! Why did I ever think you could do this?"

David walked right up to the man's desk, leaned over it, and pointed his finger angrily.

"I'll tell you who the fucking idiot is," he fired back. "It's a guy who won't listen. I tried to tell you that this needed to be better planned. It needed to be thought out. We needed to work out a strategy. But no, you wake up this morning, and you go, 'This is the day! Today we do it! I want a press conference in three hours! Make it happen!' Well, that's the way a fucking idiot does it."

Finley kicked his chair across the room. "They didn't even care! About the stuff I had on the chief! They didn't give a shit!"

"They might," Harwood said. "They probably will. But come on, you really thought they weren't going to bring up the very thing that made you leave politics? And you honestly had no idea that this underage hooker was dead?"

"I might have," Finley said. "It slipped my mind."

"You used to be mayor of this town. There were, I'm sure, some people who actually liked you. They voted you in. But somewhere along the line, you lost all your political smarts. Because you've had your head up your ass, that's why. You think I'm an idiot? Fine. I quit. Find someone else. But here's a tip. Do the job interviews at the zoo. Find yourself a trained monkey. That's what you need. Someone who'll just do what you want, who'll never tell you when you're making a mistake, someone who hasn't got an original thought in his head. Someone who'll tell you you're doing a great job when you're actually making a horse's ass of yourself."

David turned and walked out the door.

"Good-bye and good riddance!" the former mayor said, looking for something else to kick or throw. He went over, grabbed the chair he'd already tossed to one side of the room, and threw it to the other.

He stood there, steaming, breathing in and out through his nose, sweat bubbling up on his forehead. He did that for the better part of twenty seconds.

Then said, "Shit!"

Finley came around the desk, ran out of the office, heading for the parking lot. He found David getting into his Mazda.

"Hey!" Finley shouted. "Hold up!"

David, one hand on the top of the door, said, "You can't fire me, you dumb shit. I quit. Weren't you paying attention?"

"I don't want to fire you," he said, catching his breath. "And I don't want you to quit."

"What?"

"I said I don't want you to quit. That's what I'm saying."

"Forget it," David said, dropping into the seat. He started to pull the door shut, but Finley gripped the top of it with both hands.

"No, listen," he said. "Just listen to me for a second."

David waited.

"Okay, you're right." He grinned. "I shot my wad too soon."

David didn't laugh.

"Jesus, what do you want from me? I'm telling you, you were right. I should have taken your advice. I should have known what was coming, that they'd bring up the stuff about the hooker. I was dumb to think they wouldn't. I'll listen to you from now on. I will."

David slowly shook his head.

"I'll give you another two hundred a week," Finley said. "Truth is, I don't know who the hell else I could find. I mean, who's as smart as you? Who'd work with me."

David turned his head away, looked at the dashboard.

"I don't think so," he said.

That was when Finley knew he had him. "You want me to say I'm sorry? I'm sorry. I'm sorry for not listening to you, and I'm sorry for calling you a fucking idiot."

David looked at him. "I should have had some supporters there."

"Hm?"

"I should have rounded up some people, put some *Finley for Mayor* signs in their hands. Something for the cameras. Even if it was just friends and family. Half a dozen people. Even that would have helped. But I didn't think of it. You didn't give me enough time."

"Yeah, I get that. Totally."

"We have to sit down and figure everything out. Stake

456

out your position on all sorts of issues. Work out your responses to the embarrassing questions. Because they're always going to come out. You know that stuff is coming, so you have to get in front of it, turn it into a positive instead of a negative. You admit it: You're a man with flaws—you've done things you're not proud of—but that doesn't mean you don't care about this town, that you don't want to do right by the people who live here."

"I like that," Finley said. "Will you remember this, or should you be writing this down?"

"You should be able to remember it yourself. You're a fucking politician. You know everything there is to know about the art of persuasion. You just have to remember to use it."

"I couldn't agree more."

David sighed. "Four hundred," he said.

"What?"

"I'll stay on, but on two conditions. You take my advice, and you give me another four hundred a week. What's that, a couple hundred flats of spring water?"

Finley made a hissing noise through his teeth. "I don't know about four. I was thinking—"

David turned the ignition.

"Okay, four hundred. That's fine. I can live with that."

David turned off the ignition.

"There's one other thing," David said. "What we talked about just before the press conference."

"That stuff about your kid," Finley said, nodding.

"Don't ever try to blackmail me again."

Finley raised his hands defensively. "Never." He smiled. "So you're back?"

It took David Harwood several seconds to admit it. "Yeah, I'm back."

"That's good, that's good, because I've been thinking."

David closed his eyes wearily.

"No, listen, I'm just spitballin' here, but what I was thinking was, to make up for the disaster that was today, we need to do something big. Something that will show this town how invaluable I am to them. That even though I can be a bit of an asshole—"

"Oh, stop," David said.

"Even though I can be a bit of an asshole, I love this town, that I'm there for the people of Promise Falls when they need me."

"You mean, like when you went up to the drive-in to have your picture taken helping people? Because that did not play well. It was opportunistic. It was insincere. It's a good thing Duckworth booted us out of there before you made a total fool of yourself."

Finley looked hurt. "I did care. I felt terrible for those people. Those little girls, who were so scared when that screen came down? You may not believe it, but my heart went out to them."

"Sure, it did."

"But what I'm saying is, something like that, if it was to happen again, I need to get in there, roll my sleeves up, get my hands dirty, show the people I'm right there with them."

"What are you saying? We keep our fingers crossed for a flood, or a tornado?"

"Well, of course not," Finley said. "But if something like that does happen, I wanna be in there like a dirty shirt."

458

SIXTY-FIVE

Cal

I wanted to talk to Crystal. I wanted to talk to her without her mother present.

Not a problem. I still had her lunch to deliver. Lucy had said her lunch hour began at twelve thirty. If I could get Angus Carlson's permission to leave the scene, I'd get it to her in time.

I went up to him, asked if there was anything else he needed. He said I'd have to come in and make a more formal statement, which I said I would be happy to do. Once he had my contact info, he allowed me to leave.

Sam also wanted a moment before I took off.

"Thank you," she said.

"Just making up for yesterday," I said.

She smiled. "I called the school, talked to Carl, said I'd be over for him as soon as possible. And the detective, he tells me they just picked up my ex-in-laws. I hear Yolanda passed out or something when the police showed up."

I smiled, gave her hand a squeeze.

"Maybe they'll finally get what's coming to them," she said.

"I'd like to say all bad people do, eventually. Let's hope in this case it really happens."

"So many bad people, they just get away with things," she said. "And other people, they let them."

459

"Yeah," I said. "I know."

I had to leave my laundry behind in the machines. Sam promised me that if Carlson would allow normal operations to resume, she'd look after it for me. I went out to the car, Crystal's work in hand. I reached behind the passenger seat, where her bagged lunch was sitting. I arrived at the school at twenty minutes after twelve, making one stop along the way at a big-box office supply store.

Lucy, as she'd promised she would, had told the school I'd be dropping by. An office secretary greeted me, and apologized for having to ask me for some identification. I showed her my driver's license, which more than satisfied her. I thought showing her my private investigator's license might unnecessarily alarm her. She said Crystal had already been told to come straight to the office when class was dismissed.

She wandered into the office at twelve thirty-two. I was sitting in one of half a dozen chairs, waiting for her, her lunch, a plastic shopping bag, and her graphic novel all resting in my lap.

"Hi, Crystal. I brought your lunch."

"Oh yeah," she said. "I forgot it."

I handed her the bag. "You having a good day?"

She shrugged.

I held up the stapled pages. "I wanted to tell you how much I enjoyed your book. Your graphic novel."

"Okay," she said.

"Also, I got you something."

I peeled back the bag to show her a package of expensive markers, and a package of five hundred sheets of white printer paper.

"You always seem to be running out," I said, "so I

thought you could use a big package of paper like this."

"Yes," she said, taking it from me. It was a lot heavier in her arms than it had been in mine. "Mom gets mad at me when I'm taking her papers."

"I hope the markers are the right kind. There's a lot of different colors there."

She yawned. I wondered whether I was boring her. But then she examined them and said, "Yes, these are good." A pause, then, "Thank you."

"Can you sit with me for a second?"

"Okay."

She hopped up onto the chair to my right. I slid her book over slightly so that it was straddling her knee and mine.

I flipped the title page back so we were looking at the first page. "This drawing here, of the little girl in bed, that just blew me away. You're a very talented artist."

Crystal nodded without saying anything.

"I noticed the girl is called Crystal. So this is you?"

She shrugged. "I guess. It's my adventure that happens in my head." Another big yawn.

"You're a very tired girl today."

"I didn't sleep good."

I flipped ahead a few pages, found the one where the girl is walking down the alley late at night. "That's a really good drawing, too. Do you get scared when you're doing creepy scenes like this?"

She shook her head.

"Have you ever taken art lessons?"

"No. I mean, I've had art in school, but mostly I learned to draw from looking in comic books."

I had turned over the page that had the letter on the back side.

"Crystal," I said, pointing to it, "where did you find this sheet of paper?"

She glanced at it. She studied it for a moment and said, "My grandpa's. My grandpa's and Miriam's house."

"You liked to draw when you'd go to their house?"

Crystal nodded. "Grandpa liked my drawings. I'm sad about my grandpa."

"I'll bet."

"Miriam didn't die."

"In the accident, you mean," I said.

The girl nodded. She hadn't heard about Miriam's latest reversal of fortune, and I didn't think it was my place to tell her.

"I probably won't see her anymore. I won't go over if Grandpa is dead."

"Maybe not," I said. "But when you did go over there, did you have a good time?"

A nod.

"Did your grandfather like your drawings?"

"Yes."

"Did he give you lots of paper?"

"He told me to take it from his printer."

Another big yawn.

"In his study," I said. "In his office."

Crystal nodded.

"But this page must not have come out of the printer. It's got writing all over it."

"When the printer got empty, I would look for paper in other places," she said in her flat voice.

"Sure. So, then, where did you find this sheet?"

"Grandpa's desk."

"Oh. So it was sitting in one of the drawers."

"Not exactly. It was in an envelope with tape on it."

462

"Tape."

"Duct tape. I reached into the drawer and I felt something rubbing the back of my hand. It was tape. It was sticking something to the bottom of the drawer on top of it. That seemed dumb to me."

"Yeah," I said. "That is kind of weird."

"It was an envelope and that piece of paper was inside. It only had writing on one side, so I was able to use the other."

"Did you read this?" I asked her.

Crystal shook her head.

"Why not?"

"I wasn't interested," she said. "I'm only interested in blank pages so I can use them."

"All you cared about was that one side was untouched."

"Yup," she said.

"I was going to give this back to you, but I wonder, would you let me take this one page out? So I could keep this letter?"

"That'll ruin the book," she said. "Maybe they'd let you copy it."

She hopped off the chair, taking the book with her, and called over to the secretary, "Mrs. Simms, I need you to copy something for me. It's just one page."

Mrs. Simms came over to the counter. "Darling, for you, anything."

"This page here," she said, pointing.

Mrs. Simms, without even looking at the letter, put it on the office printer, closed the lid, and hit the button. She returned with the book, and the single sheet, which Crystal handed to me.

"Can I go to lunch now?" she asked me, gathering the package of paper and markers in her arms.

"You sure can," I said.

She stifled yet another yawn.

"You're going to need a big nap when you get home," I said.

"I hope Mom doesn't wake me up again tonight," she said.

"Why did she wake you up? Were you having a bad dream?" Given the nature of her drawings, she seemed a natural for nightmares.

Crystal shook her head. "No. I heard her leave, and the car starting. I stood at the window and watched until she came back home. And then I heard you come, too. And then I heard you and Mommy in the guest room. So I had a bad sleep."

If I hadn't already been rendered speechless, what happened next would have done it.

Crystal, almost eye level with me, since I was still seated, gave me a hug.

"I like you," she said, then left the office with her bag of paper and markers.

SIXTY-SIX

"Professor Blackmore has indicated to me he wishes to waive all his rights and is willing to answer any of your questions," Nate Fletcher said. "As the professor's attorney, I have strongly advised him against this, but I'm afraid I'm not able to change his mind. Just the same, I'm going to remain here to look after his interests, as best I can."

"Sure," Barry Duckworth said.

"I've got nothing to hide," Peter Blackmore said calmly.

The three of them were sitting in an interrogation room at the Promise Falls police headquarters. Duckworth was recording the interview. Audio and video.

Once the formalities were over—a statement of when and where the interview was being conducted and the names of everyone in attendance—the detective kicked things off.

"Mr. Blackmore, did you arrange to meet Mr. Duncomb today out front of his bank on Claymore Street?"

"I did."

"Did you call him?"

"I did. I said I wanted to meet with him, and he told me where he was."

"What did you say to him?"

"I told him I was going to come by, that he should stand out front."

"That's what you asked him to do? To stand out front?"

"That's correct," Blackmore said.

"Why did you ask him to do that?"

"Because I wanted to run him down."

"You'd already decided that."

"Hang on," said Nate Fletcher.

"It's okay," the professor said. "Yes, I had already decided that. I had decided to kill Clive if I had the opportunity. He's a more powerful man than I am. Stronger than I am. I figured I'd be more successful using my car."

"Why did you kill Mr. Duncomb?" Duckworth asked.

"He was a bad person."

"Had he threatened you?"

"Yes. He said if I told anyone about our activities, that he would kill me."

"What activities are you referring to?"

He paused. "The sex."

"You're talking about that room in the basement of the Chalmers home, the multipartner sex parties."

"That's right. Georgina and myself, Clive and Liz, and Adam and Miriam."

"And sometimes, others."

Blackmore nodded. "That's right. Sometimes Thackeray students. Girls excited about meeting an author. Clive would set it up. They'd come out for dinner. Have a little wine—"

"The drinks were spiked. With the roofies."

"Sometimes. Sometimes not."

"So you're saying you ran Clive Duncomb down with your car out of fears for your own safety?"

"Only partly. I've stopped being concerned for myself. You could take your gun out now and shoot me in the head and I wouldn't try to stop you."

"I'm not going to do anything like that," Duckworth said.

"I know. I'm just saying there's a part of me that would welcome it. My wife is dead. I'm overwhelmed with shame. I know you'll have people watching me, but I will probably try to kill myself at the earliest opportunity. But I'm happy to answer your questions first. I killed Clive because he was an evil man."

"Did he kill Miriam Chalmers?"

"It wouldn't surprise me," Blackmore said. "He said he didn't, but . . ." He shrugged.

"What did he say exactly?"

"He just said he hadn't. He tried to turn it around. He accused me of killing her."

"Did you?"

He shook his head wearily.

"When I found you this morning, you had blood on you," Duckworth said.

The professor nodded. "That's mine. I stumbled last night, and then Clive hit me. I have no reason to lie. You've arrested me for killing Clive. I was of totally sound mind when I—"

Nate Fletcher held a hand up. "Peter, hang on, we don't know that. We need a psychiatric assessment to determine—"

"Stop," he said. "I was of sound mind when I ran Clive down with my car. It's the most sane thing I've ever done. I know I'll go to jail for that. So if I'd killed Miriam, I'd have no problem admitting it."

"So you think Clive did."

Another shrug. "I just don't know. But if he did it, I think maybe it's okay. Almost all the people that *should* die *have* died, one way or another. Clive, Adam and Miriam, and Georgina. The only ones left are me and Liz."

"Mr. Duncomb's wife."

Blackmore nodded. "She might be the worst of all of us." He leaned toward Duckworth and whispered, "She's a snake."

"We'll be talking to her."

"Liz isn't beautiful, but she makes up for it. She knows every trick in the book. Georgina and I, we'd been having troubles. Our . . . our sex life wasn't what it once was. Clive had hinted around that he and Liz were into something a bit different, and finally he invited us to be part of the group. It changed things for Georgina and me. It made her feel more alive, at first anyway. She was very taken with Adam."

"She saw him outside the group," Duckworth said. "Wasn't that against the rules?"

He nodded. "Yes. I don't know if she saw him many times before they were killed at the drive-in. But Adam . . . I don't know how to explain Adam. I think he was a true psychopath. He could be anything you wanted him to be. He could lie to you so convincingly. He could pretend to care about you while betraying you. He wanted you to love him in the moment, but didn't care what you thought of him later. Even his own daughter, and granddaughter. Lucy, and Crystal. He loved them, and he wanted them to love him, but I bet he couldn't have cared what they'd have thought of him once he was gone. Georgina was caught up in his spell."

"Maybe you were, too."

"Maybe. Adam and Clive, they were . . . they were men's men, if you know what I mean. One a former biker, the other a former cop. Both sides of the law. Just being in their company, it made me feel like more of a man. And Georgina felt like more of a woman with Miriam and Liz. They were both very sensual. It was like we finally got to hang out with the cool kids. We became so enmeshed in the dynamic that by the time Clive and Adam suggested spicing it up with our . . . our guests, we just went along."

"Like Olivia Fisher."

"That's right."

"How long was this before she was murdered?"

"Not long. A few weeks."

"How did you feel when you heard about her death?"

"Shocked, of course. Stunned. We all talked about it. We all viewed it—I swear—as a terrible tragedy, because she was such a free spirit, a lovely young woman."

"That you raped."

"Detective," said Nate Fletcher.

"Not . . . in her case," Blackmore said. "She was getting married soon. I'm not so sure she wanted to go through with it."

"What did she say?" Duckworth said.

"Just that she'd been going with some guy so long it just seemed to be inevitable."

Duckworth let that float around in his head for a few seconds before asking, "Did you believe her murder was connected to what had gone on with all of you?"

Blackmore was slow to answer. "It crossed my mind."

"Why?"

"Because of the kind of person Clive was."

"You thought Clive killed her."

"I just thought, of any of us, he'd have been the one most capable. He asked Adam once about the disc that had her on it, and all he would say was Clive shouldn't give it a thought. So he tried not to worry about it. But

469

then when he thought Adam and Miriam were dead, and there was a chance it, and the other discs, might be found, he had to get into the house and find them. But then last night, when he found out Miriam was alive, she told him Adam got rid of them long ago."

"Tell me about Rosemary Gaynor," Duckworth said.

"Who?"

"Rosemary Gaynor. Or Bill Gaynor."

"I've never heard of either of them in my life. Who are they?"

Duckworth gave him a brief recap. "It was all over the news."

"It was exam time," Blackmore explained. "I had a lot of grading. I wasn't really following current events."

"Why are you asking about the Gaynor case?" Fletcher asked Duckworth.

The detective waved the question away and asked Blackmore, "You never heard Adam or Clive mention them? Is it possible the Gaynors were earlier swapping partners with the Chalmerses? Or the Duncombs?"

"I'm telling you, I've never heard of them."

Duckworth strummed his fingers on the tabletop. Clive Duncomb might have had a real reason to kill Olivia Fisher, but there was no apparent connection to Rosemary Gaynor. Dr. Jack Sturgess might have had a real reason to kill Gaynor, but there was no apparent connection to Fisher.

And Bill Gaynor was still off in the wings.

There was a rapping at the interrogation room door. Duckworth shifted around in his chair, saw the stern face of Chief Rhonda Finderman in the small rectangular window.

Just when he thought his day couldn't get any worse.

★

Once Peter Blackmore had been returned to a cell, Nate Fletcher had gone home, and Rhonda had been given ten minutes to carve him a new one, Duckworth sat at his desk.

He was the only cop in the entire room. There was someone down at reception, but up here, where the detectives worked, there wasn't a soul.

Duckworth rested his head in his hands. *Even my hair's exhausted,* he thought. So much had happened in the last couple of days—God, the last couple of weeks—that his world was feeling off-kilter, as though the horizon were on an angle, and nothing lined up true.

It was time to go home. Maureen would probably be in bed. He couldn't wait to crawl in next to her. He'd be asleep in seconds.

His cell phone rang.

He dug into his pocket for it, saw a Boston area code on the display. He accepted the call and put the phone to his ear.

"Duckworth."

"Hello, this is the detective?"

"Yes."

"It's Sandra Bottsford."

"Oh!" He sat upright in his chair.

"I'm so sorry not to have called you back sooner. I only just found out you'd called the hotel. Is this about Mr. Gaynor again?"

"Right, yes, it is. I know when we last talked, you'd said Mr. Gaynor's car had never left the hotel garage, that he'd been seen occasionally around the hotel, but I need to take another look at that."

"You're still wondering if he could have driven to Promise Falls and back to Boston during the night?"

"Pretty much."

"Well, as I've told you, the car never left, and it's not as if there's a high-speed train running back and forth between the two places in the dead of night."

"I know, but—"

"Unless he's the one who stole the car."

Duckworth shifted the phone to his other ear. "Say again?"

"It had slipped my mind before, but now, maybe it's important."

"What stolen car?"

"We had an incident," she said. "I didn't even find out about it for a week. Our concierge didn't let me know. I might add, our *former* concierge."

"Ms. Bottsford, what happened?"

"Someone checked into the hotel late that evening and handed over his keys—to *someone*. But later, when the front desk was trying to track the car down, no one had seen it."

"Go on."

"They were all in a panic, wondering how they'd lost a car, and they kept putting off calling the police, thinking maybe it had been misplaced in the garage, hoping it might turn up before the guest who owned the vehicle wanted it brought up the next morning. And they got lucky."

"The car came back."

"As the sun was coming up, they found it on the street, half a block away."

"So how many hours was that? Between the time the car disappeared and when they found it on the street?"

"At least six hours," Sandra Bottsford said.

"Whaddya know?" Duckworth said.

"I'm sorry I wasn't able to tell you this the first time. I didn't know."

"It's okay. Thank you for this. I'll be following this up."

He ended the call, let the phone drop onto the desk.

Gaynor could have done it.

He could have stolen a car, driven home, murdered his wife, and returned to Boston.

It was possible.

But was it likely?

Duckworth still liked Duncomb for Olivia Fisher's murder. Maybe there was something that connected the security chief to Rosemary Gaynor, something he hadn't yet found, something that would make it possible to consider him a suspect in both murders.

He'd get back to it tomorrow. Right now, he had absolutely nothing left. He started to get out of his chair when his desk phone rang.

"God, just let me go home," he said under his breath, grabbed the receiver, and snapped, "What?"

"Detective Duckworth? Barry Duckworth?"

It was a man's voice, but it was garbled and raspy, as though coming through an old, badly wired speaker.

In some ways, after only four words, it reminded the detective of Darth Vader.

"Yeah, this is Duckworth. Who's this?"

"I just wanted you to know I'm proud of you."

"Proud of me?"

"I wasn't sure anyone would put it together. See the links. I was afraid I was making it too hard."

"Who is this?" A demand this time, not a request. "Tell me who the hell this is!"

But there was no one to talk to. The line had gone dead.

SIXTY-SEVEN

Cal

I spent a couple of hours thinking. Just thinking. Finally, I phoned Lucy.

"Did you get Crystal's lunch to her?" she asked.

"I did."

"No problems with the office?"

"None."

"Thank you for that. I really appreciate it. I was on the phone for ages today with an estate lawyer and the funeral home and it's just been more than I can take."

"I need to see you. Can I come by?"

"Of course." She paused. "I can open a bottle of wine."

"Maybe just coffee."

"Right," she said. "I'll do that."

It wasn't like the last time when I arrived at her house. This time, instead of inviting me in and offering me a seat in the living room, Lucy slipped her arms around my neck, pulled my body into hers, and kissed me.

I had some involuntary responses, and I was sure she noticed. Which was why, when I gently pulled her arms from around me, she looked surprised.

"What's wrong?" she asked. "Is something wrong?"

"No, it's okay," I said. "It's just been . . . it's been quite a morning."

"There was something on the news, about shots being fired at a Laundromat. And then I thought about what you said, that all your clothes were damaged in the fire, and there aren't that many Laundromats in Promise Falls, and—"

"I was there."

"Oh my God."

I told her, as briefly as I could, what had happened.

"You need something stronger than coffee," she said, leading me into the kitchen.

"No, coffee is perfect," I said.

She had already made a pot, filled two mugs and set them on the kitchen table. We both sat.

"Do you want to talk about it?" she said imploringly. "Sometimes, when you've been through something like that, it helps to talk it out. To ease the stress."

"That's not why I'm here," I said.

Concern washed over her face. "What is it, Cal?"

"Tell me about the letter," I said.

"I'm sorry, what?" she said.

"There's something you've been holding back from me from the beginning. About what you thought had been taken from your father's house."

"I have no idea what you're talking about," Lucy said slowly.

"I think the discovery of the room downstairs was a genuine surprise. And I think when you heard someone running from the house, it was the person who'd taken those discs. But I don't think you've ever really been worried about those DVDs. It was something else. A letter."

"How do you know this?" she asked.

"So I'm right."

She nodded slowly. "Maybe you are. But it was very personal."

"Your father told you that if something were to ever happen to you, that he'd left something for you. Something from his earlier days. Money. That he wanted you to have. For you, and for Crystal."

"I don't understand how you can know this."

"Level with me, Lucy. Tell me about the letter, what you're expecting it to say if and when you find it."

Her eyes glistened. She wrapped both hands around her mug, as though using it to stay warm.

"Dad always said he would look out for me. I mean, he said it all the time, that he'd be there for me, and he'd do just enough so that he wasn't actually lying. But one day, he said, he'd make everything up to me. He said there was money . . . a lot of money. Several hundred thousand. All cash. It dated back to those days when he was still with the bikers, before he got out. Dad . . . did bad things back then. He ripped off his own people. Left them for dead. The money was . . . well, it was dirty. It wasn't the kind of thing he could put in the bank, at least not in an account. A safe-deposit box, maybe. He had it tucked away. Didn't even tell Miriam about it. At least, that was what he'd said. For years, since he'd written those books, he'd lived this aboveboard life. Well, not counting the sex stuff. But I mean, he left that biker life behind. All the time, though, there was that money. And he wanted me to have it."

"Go on."

"He said if anything ever happened to him, to look in his desk. That there was a letter. Taped to the bottom of one of the drawers. That it would tell me how to get the money."

"You went to the house, after you learned your father

had died in the accident, to get that envelope. You heard someone leaving out the back door, and when you didn't find the envelope, you thought it was that person who'd taken it."

Lucy nodded.

"I thought my father must have confided in someone else. Told someone about the letter. I'm sorry I didn't tell you. I just needed to know who'd broken into the house. Once I knew that, I'd approach them on my own. In fact, I did try to reach this Mr. Duncomb you found out about. I called his home last night, and got his wife, and she was very unpleasant. I was going to try again today, but now that you know about it, maybe you could do it for me?" She forced a smile, but it seemed no more genuine than a politician's handshake.

"Why didn't you tell me all this at the outset?"

"Before I got to know you, for all I knew, you'd want to find the money and keep it for yourself. And then there's the whole moral issue of where the money came from in the first place. But I don't care. I'm a single mother. I have a daughter who needs help. I'm going to do what's right for her and I don't care about anything else."

A tear ran down her cheek.

"Where do you think the money is?" I asked her.

She bit her lip. "I don't know. Like I said, maybe a safe-deposit box somewhere. Or maybe it's like in that movie *The Shawshank Redemption*. It's hidden under a rock in a field someplace. Wherever it is, I want to find it. But I have to get my hands on the letter first."

I reached into my pocket for the page that had been photocopied from Crystal's book.

Lucy's entire body went rigid. She sat up straight in her chair. One trembling hand went to her mouth.

"What is that?" she asked.

"This is the letter," I told her.

"Where did you get it?"

"Crystal had it," I said. "She's had it for some time. Once, when she was at your father's house, she went into his desk looking for paper when she'd used up everything in the printer tray. It was one of the pages in her graphic novel."

"Crystal?" she said.

I nodded.

"So she . . . she could have had it for weeks?"

I nodded again.

Lucy pushed back her chair, stood, turned, and took three steps over to the counter, braced herself against it, her back to me.

"Oh God," she whispered. "I never . . . I can't believe . . ."

"Lucy," I said.

"I should have thought . . . it should have occurred to me it could have been her, but . . . I didn't think my father would let Crystal into his office."

"Evidently he did."

Still with her back to me. "But he had hidden it. He said he taped it—"

"Crystal felt the tape on the back of her hand when she reached into the drawer for paper."

She turned, her eyes red. "You talked to her."

"Yes. When I found it, and read it, I needed to know where she'd gotten it. She remembered, although she claims she never even read the letter. She didn't care. All she cared about was that I not tear the page out of her book, so what I'm holding here isn't the original, but a photocopy."

Lucy looked at the folded piece of paper in my hand with equal measures of curiosity and fear.

"Things started to make sense," I said. "Like when we were looking through your father's house, and you asked me whether I could get fingerprints off his desk, off the drawers. All along, it was about finding this. For a while, you must have thought it was taken by whoever you heard running out the back door when you came in. But that person was only after the DVDs."

Her eyes were locked on the letter.

"I know," she said. "That's why I thought it had to be someone else who'd found it . . . Someone else."

I had an idea who she was talking about.

"Do you want to see it?" I asked.

She took a step toward the table and held out her hand. I placed it on her palm.

It had been folded in thirds. Her fingers shook as she opened it up and began to read.

I had read it several times. It said this:

Dear Lucy:

I guess if you are reading this, then something has happened. I'm gone. You've found this in my desk drawer, where I told you it would be. I can only imagine my fate. I've always felt that the least likely way I would go is natural causes. I'm not one to grow old and fade away. Was it someone from my past? Someone who'd come to even up the score? A spurned lover? A jealous husband? God knows, maybe Miriam has taken one of the knives from the kitchen and put it into my heart. I've been pretty lucky to have lived as long as I have.

There's much about my past I've never told you. The broad strokes, of course, you know. I ran with bad people. I did bad things. When I broke away, I left with my pockets full, and covered my tracks well. Some of the secrets I left behind are, literally, buried. I think you are better off not knowing more.

The thing I want you to know is that I have loved you and Crystal with all my heart. I know life for the two of you has not been easy. Crystal, I adore, and I hope one day she finds her way. She is a tremendously gifted child. Often, those with great gifts are tortured for them when they are young. The day will come when her talents will be appreciated. I think she will be a famous artist one day.

So I very much wanted, once I was gone, to be able to leave the two of you, as they say, well-fixed.

And I am so sorry to tell you that things have not turned out the way I had planned.

I could tell when Lucy had reached this point. Her face fell as though it had been dropped out of a plane.

There was a time when I thought I would be able to leave you a great deal. But my financial needs in recent years have exceeded my expectations. My books did not bring in the kinds of advances I had hoped for. I began many projects that I did not finish. Ultimately, I believe I had nothing left to say. So my legitimate income stream came to an end. But I still had to support myself, and Miriam had come to deserve a certain lifestyle. I did not want to disappoint her.

It became necessary to return to the well—the well

being a safe-deposit box in a bank in Albany—more often than I had anticipated.

I wish there were something left to give you.

I know I should have discussed this with you in person, but there never seemed to be a right time. But maybe what has transpired, in the end, is a good thing. We must all assume responsibility for our own lives. We can't be waiting around for that proverbial ship to come in. Perhaps this new reality will force you to reassess your priorities. There are bumps in the road of life. Good God, did I actually write that? Is it any wonder that I am no longer published?

I know it's not much, but I have, in my will, stipulated that you receive my Jaguar. It's a rare set of wheels, and you should be able to get some decent money for it.

All my love,
Your father

I watched as she read it to the end, then allowed the page to slip through her fingers and flutter to the floor.

"The bastard," she whispered. "The miserable, self-consumed, lying son of a bitch. He told me ... He promised me ..."

"Adam Chalmers looked after himself first," I said. "Everyone else came second."

"But how could he ... it would be enough, doing this to me. But to Crystal? To his granddaughter?"

I didn't know what to say.

"How could he do this to me? How?"

I shook my head slowly.

Her eyes rolled toward the ceiling. She tented her hands over her mouth. "Oh no, no, no, this is not happening."

481

I had another question.

"Where did you go last night, Lucy?"

"What?"

"Before I came over, and spent the night. After you'd put Crystal to bed. You went out."

"No," she said quietly. "No, I didn't. How do you know . . . why do you think . . . ?"

"Crystal heard you leave. She watched you drive away, waited for you to come back."

"No, that's not possible."

"You weren't wearing the same clothes when I came over last night."

"I . . . I wanted to look nice for you."

I said nothing.

"Oh, God, oh no, oh no . . . what have I done?"

I said, "What *have* you done, Lucy?"

"I thought it must have been her . . ."

"Miriam. You thought Miriam must have found the letter. That's what you're saying."

She nodded without looking at me, as though my voice were disembodied, coming to her through a speaker.

"If Miriam had found the letter, she'd be able to get her hands on the money that was to be left to you," I said. "That's why you went to see her, when you found out she was actually alive."

Now she turned her head to look at me. "She said she didn't have it, that she didn't know what I was talking about . . . I didn't believe her."

I watched as the realization took hold.

"Miriam was telling the truth," Lucy said. "She didn't know anything about it. Because Crystal had it."

"What happened when you got there?" I asked. "Did Miriam attack you? Is that what happened? Was it self-defense?"

"I . . . she fell . . . running up the stairs. I just wanted to talk to her . . . I grabbed her arm, and . . . she went backwards. Oh my God, it was an accident . . . I never went over there to . . . I just wanted to get the letter from her."

"She never had it," I said.

Now she looked at me. "Do they know? The police, do they know?"

I stood up. "I don't know. It's early yet in the investigation."

"I . . . I was going to call an ambulance, but I could tell . . . she wasn't breathing. When she fell . . . there was this horrible, horrible noise." Lucy reached up and touched her own neck. "It made a noise. I . . . I decided there was no point in calling. I got out of there. It was dark. I'm pretty sure no one saw me arrive or leave . . . I'd parked up next to the house, where you can't really see from the street . . . I didn't have any blood on my clothes, but I thought . . . maybe there was something of her . . . something on me . . . I showered. I got cleaned up. I put my clothes in the wash."

She looked at me pleadingly. "I think I'm okay. I mean, even if they find my fingerprints in the house, that means nothing, right? I was there often. You can tell them I was with you. You're a witness. You were with me all night. You can back me up on that. Cal, please?"

I hadn't said anything.

"I can't . . . I can't go to jail. I have Crystal. I *can't* go. Her father . . . he's not up to it. I don't want him to raise her. It has to be me. She could end up in a foster home or someplace like that. That *can't* happen. They can't take a mother away from her child. It would be inhu*mane*."

"I don't know," I said.

"Do you think I'm okay?" she asked. "You know all

483

about these things. You used to be with the police. Do you think I'm in the clear? If no one saw me? If there's no blood?"

"I have no idea what the police have," I told her, moving around the table, standing within two feet of her. "But I think there's something you've overlooked."

Lucy studied me, not understanding.

"What?" she asked. "Was there a camera? My father didn't have surveillance cameras."

"No," I said gently. "That's not what I mean."

She figured it out. "I don't believe it," she said. "You wouldn't tell. You wouldn't do that to me. You wouldn't do that to Crystal. You wouldn't take a mother from her child."

She stepped closer, placed her palms on my chest. "We have something," Lucy said. "Last night. I felt it. It wasn't just a one-night thing. I felt a connection. Are you telling me you didn't?"

"I felt something, too," I admitted, circling her wrists with my hands and pulling her away. "But now I'm not sure you felt anything at all. Having me come back, that was a lucky break for you. I could be your alibi."

"Cal, no. I'm falling in love with you. Crystal, too. I can tell. We . . . we need you. I need you. Please. *Please.* I'm not some kind of monster. It was an *accident*."

"I . . . should go," I said.

"What are you going to do?" she asked, grabbing my arm. "Are you going to the police?"

I pulled away, moving for the front door.

"Please, Cal, don't do this to me. You have to understand. I didn't mean for it to happen. I was thinking of Crystal. I want a better life for her. I want a better life for both of us. I thought that was what my father was going to give us. I couldn't let Miriam stand in the way of that. I—I went insane for a minute. One minute of insanity can't be held against me. Not after what I've been through. Cal—"

"I need to go, Lucy."

I had the front door open. Crystal was walking up the driveway. More like trudging. Her backpack seemed to be weighing her down like a soldier's gear.

"Oh God," Lucy said under her breath, and began frantically wiping tears from her face, wiping her hands on her blouse. "Hey, sweetheart!" she said. "How was school?"

As she reached the door, she swung the backpack off her shoulders and it hit the ground with a thunk.

"This is so heavy," Crystal said.

"What've you got in there?" her mother asked.

She unzipped it, brought out the package of paper I'd given her, and then the new markers.

"Mr. Weaver gave me these," she said.

"Wasn't that nice of him?" Lucy said, her voice breaking. "Did you thank him?"

"Yes," she said.

"She did," I said.

"I need a snack," Crystal said, moving past both of us on her way to the kitchen.

Lucy Brighton, her eyes swimming, touched my arm.

"What are you going to do?" she asked one last time.

"I don't know," I said, and headed for my car.

SIXTY-EIGHT

It was after midnight, but this was when Lorraine Plummer got most of her work done. Plenty of Thackeray students were like that. Lorraine's parents said they were all "night owls." They slept through the day, never getting up before noon, sometimes staying in bed until three or four in the afternoon. But it didn't mean they were lazy, or unproductive. They were just on a different clock from everyone else.

Lorraine often read and studied and wrote essays until three or four in the morning. Sometimes, she'd work straight through, head down for breakfast in the college cafeteria, and, once full of scrambled eggs, greasy bacon, and a bruised banana, head back up to her dormitory room, collapse on top of the bed, and fall asleep before she could get under the covers.

Of course, if you had an early-morning lecture, that could be a bit of a problem. When she had one of those, she'd force herself to go to bed no later than one, and set the alarm on her phone to make sure she got up in time. But often, she'd toss and turn and stare at the ceiling and lie awake until five, finally drifting off into a deep sleep a few minutes before her phone went off.

Her first class the next day wasn't until one in the afternoon, so she planned to work until she could no longer keep her eyes open. She was writing an essay for Professor Blackmore's English and psychology class that was due the end of the following week. Blackmore was pretty open to letting students stray from the curriculum if they had a good idea for an assignment, and he had liked her proposal to explore the themes of cyberbullying and intimidation in modern young adult fiction designed for a female audience.

Blackmore had said, "Go for it."

He could be pretty cool like that, although, boy, something was very wrong with him at the lecture the other day, when he left the hall only a couple of minutes after everyone had come in. And he hadn't been around for the tutorial he was supposed to have led that afternoon.

Lorraine had long thought that one day she would like to write a novel, but so many people said she should write about what she knew, and she believed her own life was too boring to write about. Who cared about some girl who grew up in a normal house with normal parents and led a perfectly normal life? And not everyone wrote about what they knew. What about Stephen King? She was betting he didn't actually know any evil clowns living in the sewer.

That was more the kind of thing Lorraine wanted to write. She wanted to know what real honest-to-God writers thought about this issue, so she'd been totally thrilled when Clive Duncomb, the head of security at Thackeray, whom she had met one day when he was talking to Professor Blackmore, arranged for her to meet Adam Chalmers. Duncomb said he'd written a whole bunch of books.

She was a dinner guest at the house once. Chalmers's wife, Miriam, who was absolutely beautiful, was there, as well as Blackmore and his wife, Georgina, who was sort of pretty but in a mousy kind of way. Also there was Duncomb, who, Lorraine learned, used to be a Boston cop and got to know Chalmers when the writer was looking for inside info on the life of a police detective. Duncomb's wife, Elizabeth, or Liz, was this thin woman in her forties with skin that had seen way too much sun. Almost leathery. It added to a hardness about her, Lorraine remembered.

Although, she had to admit, there was a lot about that night she didn't remember at all. She was so excited to meet a real, live writer that she got ridiculously nervous. Everyone was so nice, telling her to have some more wine to calm herself down, even though, technically speaking, Lorraine, being twenty years old, was not of legal drinking age in the state of New York. Not that she hadn't had a drink or two—thousand—but these were *grown-ups* offering her booze.

Lorraine had made a joke about this, how they were all going to get into trouble.

It was Duncomb who pointed out that while the law did forbid anyone under twenty-one from purchasing alcohol, it did allow parents or legal guardians to offer someone under that age a drink in their home.

Lorraine laughed. "You guys aren't my parents."

Duncomb smiled. "Well, for the purposes of dinner, let's say we are your legal guardians."

That was good enough for her.

Trouble was, the wine went straight to her head. Big-time. Next thing she remembered, the Duncombs were driving her home.

"Please, please tell the Chalmerses I am so sorry," she said. "I feel like such an idiot."

"Don't you worry about it," Liz Duncomb said. "He

488

thought you were lovely. We all did. Didn't we, Clive?"

"You bet," Clive Duncomb said.

The weird thing was, the next morning, she didn't just feel stupid. She felt *sore*. Like that time after her high school grad dance, with Bobby Bratner, in his mom's minivan, parked behind a church. But nothing like that could have happened at the Chalmerses' place. They were all, like, *good* people. She couldn't figure it out.

But what really blew her mind now was that Adam and Miriam Chalmers were dead. Crushed under that drive-in movie screen. That was *so crazy*. There seemed to be no end of shit going on around here.

First, there was that whole business of getting attacked by that guy in the hoodie with "23" on the front. Which was totally nuts. Why does some guy drag you into the bushes, and then tell you he isn't actually going to do anything to you?

Not that she was sorry that nothing worse happened. But still, it was weird.

And then the guy turns out to be Mason Helt, whom she didn't really know, but had seen around campus. Gets his head blown off by Duncomb.

What a place Thackeray was.

Despite all that, she felt safe in this cocoon of a room, which was about the size of a walk-in closet in some of her friends' houses. There was a desk built into the wall, but she did most of her work on the bed, sitting on it sideways, her back propped against the wall, a pillow tucked in to provide comfort.

She had the laptop resting on her thighs, a couple of paperback novels, spines cracked, open and facedown on the covers next to her. Just within reach on the shelf above her pillow, a cup of tea.

Lorraine figured she had at least two more hours in her before she wouldn't be able to keep her eyes open, but found, only minutes later, that she was nodding off. She had her fingers poised over the keyboard, was staring at the screen, when she felt her eyelids growing heavy.

Her phone trilled. A text.

She reached for it. It was from someone else in her English class with Blackmore. A girl named Cleo. She wrote: *Did u hear about Bmore?*

Lorraine texted back: *What?*

Cleo wrote: *He got arrested. Ran down someone with his car*

To which Lorraine wrote back: *Holy shit*

Cleo said: *Yeah*

Lorraine wrote: *Hate to think of this first but what about essay*

Cleo wrote: *Yeah I know*

The knock on the door was like a thunderclap.

Lorraine texted: *GTG someone here*

She tossed the phone onto the bed and called out, "Who is it?"

From behind the door, a man's voice: "Lorraine? Sorry to trouble you so late. But I need to talk to you."

Lorraine slid the laptop off her thighs and padded in her bare feet to the door. All Thackeray dorm rooms had peepholes in the doors. She went up on her tiptoes to get a look at whoever needed to see her at such a crazy hour.

"Oh!" she said. "It's you!"

"Do you have a second?"

"I'm—God, I'm just in my sweats. I look like a horror show!"

"I'm really, really sorry. I wouldn't be coming by if it wasn't important."

"Okay, okay," she said.

She turned back the dead bolt and swung open the door.

"Hey," she said. "What's going on?"

"May I come in? Just for a second?"

Lorraine shrugged. "Sure, but excuse the mess."

Her visitor just needed her to turn around, have her back to him for a second. It was always easier that way.

She obliged when she turned to walk back to her bed. He was able to do it the way he had with Olivia Fisher and Rosemary Gaynor.

They struggled, but it went quickly. Surrender was almost instant once the blade went in, and across.

Like a smile.

SIXTY-NINE

Water, water everywhere and not a drop to drink.
  It's time.

ACKNOWLEDGMENTS

As always, I had help. Thanks go to Sam Eades, Eva Kolcze, Heather Connor, Loren Jaggers, John Aitchison, Paige Barclay, Danielle Perez, Bill Massey, Carol Fitzgerald, David Shelley, Helen Heller, Brad Martin, Kara Welsh, Ashley Dunn, Amy Black, Kristin Cochrane, Spencer Barclay, Louisa Macpherson, and Juliet Ewers.

And, once again, booksellers.

Don't miss the next Linwood Barclay thriller
set in Promise Falls,

THE
TWENTY-THREE

Patricia Henderson, forty-one, divorced, employed at the Weston Street Branch of the Promise Falls Public Library System as a computer librarian, was, on that Saturday morning of the long holiday weekend in May, among the first to die.

She was scheduled to work that day. Patricia was annoyed the library board chose to keep all of the town's libraries open. They were slated to close on the Sunday, and on the Monday, Memorial Day. So, if you're going to close Sunday and Monday, why not close for the Saturday, too, and give everyone at the library the weekend off?

But no.

Not that Patricia had anywhere in particular to go.

But still. It seemed ridiculous to her. She knew, given that it was a long weekend, there'd be very few people coming into the library. Wasn't this town supposed to be in the midst of a financial crisis? Why keep the place open? Sure, there was a bit of a rush on Friday as some customers, particularly those who had cottages or other weekend places, took out books to keep them occupied through to Tuesday. The rest of the weekend was guaranteed to be quiet.

Patricia was to be at the library for nine, when it opened, but that really meant she needed to be there for eight forty-five a.m. That would give her time to boot up all the computers, which were shut down every night at closing to save on electricity, even though the amount of power the branch's thirty computers drew overnight was negligible. The library board, however, was on a "green" kick, which meant not only conserving electricity, but making sure recycling stations were set up throughout the library, and signs pinned to the bulletin boards to discourage the use of bottled water. One of the library board members saw the bottled water industry, and the bins of plastic bottles it created, as one of the great evils of the modern world, and didn't want them in any of the Promise Falls branches. Provide paper cups that can be filled at the facility's water fountains, she said. Which now meant that the recycling stations were overflowing with paper cups instead of water bottles.

And guess who was pissed about that? What's-his-name, that Finley guy who used to be mayor and now ran a water-bottling company. Patricia had met him the first—and, she hoped, last—time just the other evening at the Constellation Drive-in. She'd taken her niece Kaylie and her little friend Alicia for the drive-in's final night. God, what a mistake that turned out to be. Not only did the screen come crashing down, scaring the little girls half to death, but then Finley showed up, trying to get his picture taken giving comfort to the wounded.

Politics, Patricia thought. How she hated politics and everything about it.

And thinking of politics, Patricia had found herself staring at the ceiling at four in the morning, worried about next week's public meeting on "Internet filtering." The debate had been going on for years and never seemed settled. Should the library put filters on computers used by patrons that would restrict access to certain Web sites?

The idea was to keep youngsters from accessing pornography, but it was a continuing quagmire. The filters were often ineffective, blocking material that was not adult oriented, and allowing material that was. And aside from that, there were freedom of speech and freedom to read issues.

Patricia knew the meeting would, as these kinds of meetings always did, devolve into a shouting match between ultraconservatives who saw gay subtext in the Teletubbies and didn't want computers in the library to begin with, and ultra left-wingers who believed if a kindergartner wanted to read *Portnoy's Complaint*, so be it.

At ten minutes after five, when she knew she wasn't going to get back to sleep, she threw back the covers and decided to move forward with her day.

She walked into the bathroom, flicked on the light, and studied her face in the mirror.

"Ick," she said, rubbing her cheeks with the tips of her fingers. "A. B. H."

That was the mantra from Charlene, her personal trainer. Always Be Hydrating. Which meant drinking at least seven full glasses of water a day.

Patricia reached for the glass next to the sink, turned on the tap to let the water run until it was cold, filled the glass and drank it down in one long gulp. She reached into the shower, turned on the taps, held her hand under the spray until it was hot enough, pulled the long white T-shirt she slept in over her head, and stepped in.

She stayed in there until she could sense the hot water starting to run out. Shampooed and lathered up first, then stood under the water, feeling it rain across her face.

Dried off.

Dressed.

Did her hair and makeup.

By the time she was in her apartment kitchen, it was six thirty. Still plenty of time to kill before driving to the library, a ten-minute commute. Or, if she decided to ride her bike, about twenty-five minutes.

Patricia opened the cupboard, took out a small metal tray with more than a dozen bottles of pills and multivitamins. She opened the lids on four, tapped out a calcium tablet, a low-dose aspirin, a vitamin D, and a multivitamin that, while containing vitamin D, did not, she believed, have enough.

She tossed them all into her mouth at once and washed them down with a small glass of water from the kitchen tap.

Patricia opened the refrigerator and stared. Did she want an egg? Hard-boiled? Fried? It seemed like a lot of work. She closed the door and went back to the cupboard and brought down a box of Special K.

"Whoa," she said.

It was like a wave washing over. Light-headedness. Like she'd been standing outside in a high wind and nearly got blown over.

She put both hands on the edge of the counter to steady herself. *Let it pass,* she told herself. *It's probably nothing. Up too early.*

There, she seemed to be okay. She brought down a small bowl, started to pour some cereal into it.

Blinked.

Blinked again.

She could see the "K" on the cereal box clearly enough, but "Special" was fuzzy around the edges. Which was pretty strange, because it was not exactly a tiny font. This was not newspaper type. The letters in "Special" were a good inch tall.

Patricia squinted.

"Special," she said.

She closed her eyes, shook her head, thinking that would set things straight. But when she opened her eyes, she was dizzy.

"What the hell?" she said.

I need to sit down.

She left the cereal where it was and made her way to the table, pulled out the chair. Was the room spinning? Just a little?

She hadn't had the "whirlies" in a very long time. She'd gotten drunk more than a few times over the years with her ex, Stanley. But even then, she'd never had enough to drink that the room spun. She had to go back to her days as a student at Thackeray for a memory like that.

But Patricia hadn't been drinking. And what she was feeling now wasn't the same as what she'd felt back then.

For one thing, her heart was starting to race.

She placed a hand on her chest, just about the swell of her breasts, to see if she could feel what she already knew she was feeling.

Tha-thump. Tha-thump. Tha-tha-thump.

Her heart wasn't just picking up the pace. It was doing so in an irregular fashion.

Patricia moved her hand from her chest to her forehead. Her skin was cold and clammy.

She wondered whether she could be having a heart attack. But she wasn't old enough for one of those, was she? And she was in good shape. She worked out. She often rode her bike to work. She had a personal trainer, for God's sake.

The pills.

Patricia figured she must have taken the wrong pills.

But was there anything in that pill container that could do something like this to her?

No.

She stood, felt the floor move beneath her as though Promise Falls were undergoing an earthquake, which was not the sort of thing that happened often in upstate New York.

Maybe, she thought, *I should just get my ass to Promise Falls General.*

Gill Pickens, already in the kitchen, standing at the island, reading the *New York Times* on his laptop while he sipped on his third cup of coffee, was not overly surprised when his daughter, Marla, with his ten-month-old grandson, Matthew, in her arms, appeared.

"He wouldn't stop fussing," Marla said. "So I decided to get up and give him something to eat. Oh, thank God, you've already made coffee."

Gill winced. "I just killed off the first pot. I'll make some more."

"That's okay. I can—"

"No, let me. You take care of Matthew."

"You're up early," she said to her father as she got Matthew strapped into his high chair.

"Couldn't sleep," he said.

"Still?"

Gill Pickens shrugged. "Jesus, Marla, it's only been a little over two weeks. I didn't sleep all that well before, anyway. You telling me you've been sleeping okay?"

"Sometimes," Marla said. "They gave me something."

Right. She'd been on a few things to help ease the shock of her mother's death earlier that month, and

504

learning that the baby she'd thought she'd lost at birth was actually alive.

Matthew.

But even if her prescriptions had allowed her to sleep better some nights than her father, there was still a cloud hanging over the house that showed no signs of moving off soon. Gill had not returned to work, in part because he simply wasn't up to it, but also because child welfare authorities had only allowed Marla to take care of Matthew so long as she was living under the same roof as her father.

Gill had felt a need to be present, although he wondered how much longer that would be necessary. All the evidence suggested Marla was a wonderful, loving mother. And the other good news was her acceptance of reality. In the days immediately following Agnes's jump off Promise Falls, Marla maintained the belief that her mother was actually alive, and would be returning to help her with her child.

Marla now understood that that was not going to happen.

She filled a pot with hot water from the tap, set it on the counter instead of the stove, then took a bottle of formula she'd made up the day before from the refrigerator and placed it in the pot.

Matthew had twisted himself around in the chair to see what was going on. His eyes landed on the bottle and he pointed.

"Nah," he said.

"It's coming," Marla said. "I'm just letting it warm up some. But I have something else for you in the meantime."

She turned a kitchen chair around so she could sit

immediately opposite Matthew. She twisted the lid off a tiny jar of pureed apricots and, with a very small plastic spoon, aimed some at the baby's mouth.

"You like this, don't you?" she said, glancing in her father's direction as he scanned his eyes over the laptop screen. He appeared to be squinting.

"Need glasses, Dad?"

He looked up. Gill suddenly looked very pale to her. "What?"

"You looked like you were having trouble looking at the screen."

"Why are you doing that?" he asked her.

Matthew swatted at the spoon, knocked some apricots onto his chair.

"Why am I doing what?" Marla asked.

"Moving around like that."

"I'm just sitting here," she said, getting more apricot onto the spoon. "You want to bring that bottle over?"

The pot with the bottle in it was sitting immediately to the right of the laptop, but Gill appeared unable to focus on it.

"Is it funny in here?" he asked, setting down his mug of coffee too close to the edge of the island. It tipped, hit the floor and shattered, but Gill did not look down.

"Dad?"

Marla got out of the chair and moved quickly to her father's side. "Are you okay?"

"Need to get Matthew to the hospital," he said.

"Matthew? Why would Matthew have to go to the hospital?"

Gill looked into his daughter's face. "Is something wrong with Matthew? Do you think he has what I have?"

"Dad?" Marla struggled to keep the panic out of her voice. "What's going on with you? You're breathing really fast. Why are you doing that?"

He put a hand on his chest, felt his heart beating through his robe.

"I think I'm going to throw up," he said.

But he did not. Instead, he dropped to the floor.

Ali Brunson said, "Hang in there, Audrey. You're going to be fine. You just have to hang in a little bit longer."

Of course, Ali had said that many times in his career as a paramedic, and there were many of those times when he hadn't believed it for a second. This looked as though it was turning into one of those times.

Audrey McMichael, fifty-three, 173 pounds, black, an insurance adjuster, resident of 21 Forsythe Avenue for the last twenty-two years, where she had lived with her husband, Clifford, was giving every indication of giving up the fight.

Ali called up to Tammy Fairweather, who was behind the wheel of the ambulance, and booting it to Promise Falls General. The good news was, it was early Saturday morning and there was hardly anyone on the road. The bad news was, it probably wasn't going to matter. Audrey's blood pressure was plummeting like an elevator with snapped cables. Barely 60 over 40.

When Ali and Tammy had arrived at the McMichael home, Audrey had been vomiting. For the better part of an hour, according to her husband, she had been complaining of nausea, dizziness, a headache. Her breathing had been growing increasingly rapid and shallow. There had been moments when she'd said she could not see.

Her condition continued to deteriorate after they loaded her into the ambulance.

"How we doing back there?" Tammy called.

"Don't worry about me. Just get us to church on time," Ali told her, keeping his voice even.

"I know people," Tammy said over the wail of the siren, trying to lighten the mood. "You need a ticket fixed, I'm the girl to know."

The radio crackled. Their dispatcher.

"Let me know the second you clear PFG," the male voice on the radio said.

"Not even there yet," Tammy radioed back. "Will advise."

"Need you at another location ASAP."

"What's the deal?" Tammy asked. "All the other units book off sick? They go fishing for the weekend?"

"Negative. All engaged."

"What?"

"It's like an instant flu outbreak all over town," the dispatcher said. "Let me know the second you're available." The connection ended.

"What'd he say?" Ali asked.

Tammy swung the wheel hard. She could see the blue H atop Promise Falls General in the distance. No more than a mile away.

"Something going around," Tammy said. "Not the kind of Saturday morning I was expecting."

Whenever Tammy and Ali got the weekend morning shifts, they usually started them with coffee at Dunkin's, chilling out until their first call.

There'd been no coffee today. Audrey McMichael, it turned out, was their second call of the day. The first had been to the home of Orrin Gruber, an eighty-two-year-old retired airline pilot who'd called 911 after experiencing dizziness and chest pains.

He never made it alive to Emerg.

Hypotension, Ali thought. Low blood pressure.

And here they were again, with another patient experiencing, among other things, dangerously low blood pressure.

Ali raised his head far enough to see out the front window, just as Tammy slammed on the brakes and screamed, "Jesus!"

There was a man standing in the path of the ambulance, halfway into their lane. Standing was not quite accurate. More like stooping, with one hand on his chest, the other raised, palm up, asking the ambulance to stop. Then the man doubled over, and vomited onto the street.

"Goddamn it!" Tammy said. She grabbed her radio. "I need help!"

"Drive around him!" Ali said. "We don't have time to help some geezer cross the road."

"I can't just—he's on his knees, Ali. Jesus fucking Christ!"

Tammy threw the shift lever into PARK, said, "Be right back!" and jumped out of the ambulance.

The dispatcher said, "What's happening?"

Ali couldn't leave Audrey McMichael to tell him.

"Sir!" Tammy said, striding briskly toward the man, who looked to be in his late fifties, early sixties. "What's wrong, sir?"

"Help me," he whispered.

"What's your name, sir?"

The man mumbled something.

"What's that?"

"Fisher," he said. "Walden Fisher. I don't feel . . ."

509

something's . . . not right. My stomach . . . just threw up."

Tammy put a hand on his shoulder. "Talk to me, Mr. Fisher. What other symptoms have you been experiencing?" The man's breaths were rapid and shallow, just as they were for Audrey McMichael and Orrin Gruber.

This is one serious clusterfuck. That's what this is, Tammy thought.

"Dizzy. Sick to my stomach. Something's not right." He looked fearfully into the the paramedic's face. "My heart. I think there's something wrong with my heart."

"Come with me, sir," she said, leading him to the back of the ambulance. She'd put him in there with Audrey.

The more the merrier, she thought, shaking her head, wondering, *What next?*

Which was when she heard the explosion.

When Emily Townsend had her first sip of coffee, she thought it tasted just a tiny bit off.

So she poured out the entire pot—six cups' worth—as well as the filter filled with coffee grounds, and started over.

Ran the water for thirty seconds from the tap to make sure it was fresh before adding it to the machine. Put in a new filter and six scoops of coffee from the tin.

Hit the button.

Waited.

When the machine beeped, she poured herself a cup—a clean one; she'd already put the first one into the dishwasher—added one sugar and just a titch of cream, and gave it a stir.

Brought the warm mug to her lips and tentatively sipped.

Must have been her imagination. This tasted just fine.

Maybe it was her toothpaste. Made that first cup taste funny.

Before Patricia Henderson decided to try to get herself to the hospital, she dialed 911.

She figured, when you called 911, someone answered right away. First ring. But 911 did not respond on the first ring, nor did it respond on the second.

Or the third.

By four rings, Patricia was thinking maybe this was not the way to go.

But then, an answer.

"Please hold!" someone said hurriedly, and then nothing.

Patricia's symptoms—and there were more than a few—were not subsiding, and she did not believe, even in her increasingly confused state, that she could wait around for some 911 dispatcher to get back to her.

She let go of the receiver, not bothering to place it back in the cradle, and looked for her purse. Was that it, over there, *waaaay* over there, on the small table by the front door?

Patricia squinted, and determined that it was.

She stumbled toward it, reached into the bag for her car keys. After ten seconds of digging around without success, she turned the bag over and dumped the contents onto the table, most of them spilling onto the floor.

She blinked several times, tried to focus. It was as though she'd just stepped out of the shower, was trying to get the water out of her eyes so she could see. She bent over at the waist to grab what appeared to be her keys, but was snatching at air, some three inches above where her keys lay.

"Come on, stop that," Patricia told the keys. "Don't be that way."

She leaned over slightly more, grabbed hold of the keys, but tumbled forward into the hallway. As she struggled to get to her knees, nausea overwhelmed her and she vomited onto the floor.

"Hospital," she whispered.

She struggled to her feet, opened the door, made no effort to lock it or even close it behind her, and went down the hallway to the elevators, one hand feeling the wall along the way to steady herself. She was only on the third floor, but she still possessed enough smarts to know she could not handle two flights of stairs.

Patricia blinked several times to make sure she hit the DOWN instead of the UP button. Ten seconds later, although to Patricia it might as well have been an hour and a half, the doors opened. She stumbled into the elevator, looked for G, hit the button. She leaned forward, rested her head where the doors met, which meant that, when they opened on the ground floor a few seconds later, she fell into the lobby.

No one was there to see it. But that didn't mean there was nobody in the lobby. There was a body.

In her semidelirious state, Patricia thought she recognized Mrs. Gwynn from 3B facedown in a puddle of her own vomit.

Patricia managed to cross the lobby and get outside. She had one of the best parking spots. First one past those designated for the handicapped.

I deserve one of those today, Patricia thought.

She pointed her key in the direction of her Hyundai, pressed a button. The trunk swung open. Pressed another button as she reached the driver's side, got in, fumbled about, getting the key into the ignition. Once she had the engine running, she took a moment to steel herself. Rested her head momentarily on the top of the steering wheel.

And asked herself, *Where am I going?*

The hospital. Yes! The hospital. What a perfectly splendid idea.

She turned around to see her way out of the spot, but her view was blocked by the upraised trunk lid. Not a problem. She hit the gas, driving the back end of her car into a Volvo owned by Mr. Lewis, a retired Social Security employee who happened to live three doors down from her.

A headlight shattered, but Patricia did not hear it.

She put the car into drive and sped out of the apartment building parking lot, the Hyundai veering sharply left and right as she oversteered in the manner of someone who'd had far too much to drink or was texting.

The car was quickly doing sixty miles per hour in a thirty zone, and what Patricia was unaware of was that she was heading not in the direction of the hospital, which, ironically, was only half a mile from her home, but toward the Weston Street Branch of the Promise Falls Library System.

The last thing she was thinking about, before her mind went blank and her heart stopped working, was that when they had that meeting about Internet filtering, she was going to tell those narrow-minded, puritanical assholes who wanted what anyone saw on a library computer closely monitored to go fuck themselves.

But she wouldn't get that chance, because her Hyundai had cut across three lanes, bounced over the curb at the Exxon station, and driven straight into a self-serve pump at more than sixty miles per hour.

The explosion was heard up to two miles away.

Those sirens woke Victor Rooney.

It was a few minutes past eight when he opened his eyes. Looked at the clock radio next to his bed, the half-empty bottle of beer positioned next to it. He'd slept well, considering everything, and didn't feel all that bad now, even though he hadn't fallen into bed until almost two in the morning. But once his head hit the pillow, he was out.

He reached out from under the covers to turn on the radio, maybe catch the news. But the Albany station had finished with the eight o'clock newscast and was now onto music. Springsteen. "Streets of Philadelphia." That seemed kind of appropriate for a Memorial Day Saturday. On a weekend that celebrated the men and women who had died fighting for their country, a song about the city where the Declaration of Independence had been signed.

Fitting.

Victor had always liked Springsteen, but hearing the song saddened him. He and Olivia had talked once about going to one of his concerts.

Olivia had loved music.

She hadn't been quite as crazy about Bruce as he was, but she did have her favorites, especially those from the sixties and the seventies. Simon and Garfunkel. Creedence Clearwater Revival. The Beatles, it went without saying. One time, she'd started singing "Happy Together" and he'd asked her who the hell'd done that. The Turtles, she'd told him.

"You're shittin' me," he'd said. "There was actually a band called Turtles?"

"*The* Turtles," she'd corrected him. "Like *The* Beatles. No one says just Beatles. And if you could name a band after what sounded like bugs, why not turtles?"

"So happy together," he said, pulling her into him as they walked through the grounds of Thackeray College. This was back when she was still a student there.

The better part of a year before it happened.

Three years ago this week.

The sirens wailed.

Victor lay there, very still, listening. One of them sounded like it was coming from the east side of the city, the other from the north. Police cars, or ambulances, most likely. Didn't sound like a fire truck. They had those deeper, throatier sirens. Lots of bass.

If they were ambulances, they were probably headed to PFG.

Busy morning out there on the streets of Promise Falls.

What, oh, what could be happening?

He wasn't hungover, which was so often the case. A relatively clear head this morning. He hadn't been out drinking the night before, but he had felt like rewarding himself with a beer when he got home.

Quietly, he'd opened the fridge and taken out a bottle of Bud. He hadn't wanted to wake his landlady, Emily Townsend. She'd hung on to this house after her husband's death, and rented a room upstairs to him. He'd taken the bottle with him, downed half of it going up the stairs. He'd fallen asleep too quickly to finish it off.

And now it would be warm.

Victor reached for it anyway and took a swig, made a face, put the bottle back on the bedside table but too close to the edge. It hit the floor, spilling beer onto Victor's socks and the throw rug.

"Oh, shit," he said, grabbing the bottle before it emptied completely.

He swung his feet out from under the covers and, careful not to step in the beer, stood up alongside the bed. He was dressed in a pair of blue boxers. He opened the bedroom door, walked five steps down the hall to the bathroom, which was unoccupied, and grabbed a towel off one of the racks.

Victor Rooney paused at the top of the stairs.

There was the smell of freshly brewed coffee, but the house was unusually quiet. Emily was an early riser, and she put the coffee on first thing. She drank at least twenty cups a day, had a pot going almost all the time.

Victor did not hear her stirring in the kitchen or anywhere else in the house.

"Emily?" he called out.

When no one called back, he returned to his room, dropped the bath towel on the floor where the beer had spilled, and tamped it down with his bare foot. Put all his weight on it at one point. When he'd blotted up all the beer he believed was possible, he took the damp towel and placed it in a hamper at the bottom of the hallway linen closet.

Back in his room, he pulled on his jeans and took a fresh pair of socks and a T-shirt from his dresser.

He descended the stairs in his sock feet.

Emily Townsend was not in the kitchen.

Victor noticed that there was an inch of coffee in the bottom of the pot, but he decided against coffee today. He went to the refrigerator and pondered whether eight fifteen was too early for a Bud.

Perhaps.

Sirens continued to wail.

He took out a container of Minute Maid orange juice and poured himself a glass. Drank it down in one gulp.

Pondered breakfast.

Most days he had cereal. But if Emily was making bacon and eggs or pancakes or French toast—anything that required more effort—he was always quick to get in on that. But it did not appear that his landlady was going to any extra trouble today.

"Emily?" he called out again.

There was a door off the kitchen that led to the back-yard. Two, if one counted the screen door. The inner door was ajar, which led Victor to think perhaps Emily had gone outside.

Victor refilled his glass with orange juice, then swung the door farther open, took a look at the small backyard through the screen door.

Well, there was Emily.

Face-planted on the driveway, about ten feet away from her cute little blue Toyota, car keys in one hand. She'd probably been carrying her purse with the other, but it was at the edge of the drive, where, presumably, she had dropped it. Her wallet and the small case in which she carried her reading glasses had tumbled out.

She was not moving. From where Victor stood, he couldn't even see her back going up and down ever so gently, an indication that she might still be alive.

He put his juice glass on the counter and decided maybe it would be a good idea to go outside and take a closer look.